WINDFALL

WINDFALL

Managing Unexpected Money
So It Doesn't Manage You

MARLA BRILL

ALPHA

A Pearson Education Company

To my husband Rob and my daughters Rachael and Lauren—my greatest windfalls.

International Standard Book Number: 0-02-864205-8
Library of Congress Catalog Card Number: 2001093557

04 03 02   8 7 6 5 4 3 2 1

Interpretation of the printing code: The rightmost number of the first series of numbers is the year of the book's printing; the rightmost number of the second series of numbers is the number of the book's printing. For example, a printing code of 02-1 shows that the first printing occurred in 2002.

Printed in the United States of America

Contents

Introduction

"What would you do if you had a million dollars?"

"I dunno. What would you do?"

"Well, first I'd buy a great car, maybe a Lexus or even a Ferrari. Then I'd take a trip around the world. And maybe I'd give a little to charity."

This conversation takes place every day in one form or another, among children and adults, around the world. Chances are, you've probably had a couple of them yourself. Then, suddenly one day, the question of what to do when a big pile of money comes your way is no longer hypothetical. It's very, very real. And it's your life that's deliriously and with dizzying suddenness in the middle of it all.

Perhaps you are one of the increasing number of people facing the question of how to handle a financial windfall, on both a financial and an emotional level. It may not be a million dollars at stake—it might be substantially more or substantially less. However, it's a sum that, in your eyes, has the power to change your life.

You're Not Alone

These days, thanks to some strong demographic and economic trends, more and more people are finding themselves on the receiving end of a financial windfall. Consider these typical scenarios and how you would react to them:

❖ You are 45 years old, earn $125,000 a year, and have a successful and satisfying career. Your mother passes away unexpectedly and you inherit $500,000. Should you use the money for retirement, loan money to a friend who's facing tough times, or buy that 40-foot yacht you have dreamt about all your life? With the added backup of the inheritance, you wonder if early retirement is now a viable option. In the back of your mind, you also wonder why you have such mixed feelings about having this money in the first place.

❖ At age 32, you have recently exercised your stock options from a company plan and received $130,000 worth of stock. How should you sell the stock in a way that makes the most sense from a tax standpoint? You wonder whether you should use the money to pay down $16,000 in credit card debt, as a down payment on a house, or to start a college fund for your newborn daughter.

- After working at the same company for 12 years, you leave at age 56 with a balance of approximately $650,000 in your 401(k) plan, about half of which is in company stock that you could not sell as an employee. Now that you've left the company and have full control over the money, should you sell all or some of that stock to diversify your portfolio? Even though it sounds like a lot of money, you heard on a radio talk show that it may not be enough to retire on. Could that possibly be true?

- When your father passes away, he leaves an estate valued at approximately $3 million. Your understanding, though it was never spoken of or discussed among family members, was that most of the money would go to you and your three siblings. At the reading of the will, you find out that your father left about half of his estate to a woman you have never met who lives 1,500 miles away.

These hypothetical situations reflect a trend in which the challenges posed by sudden wealth are impacting more people than ever. Not long ago, the road to riches was paved by a gradual process of making a good living, saving carefully, and investing wisely. While that formula still defines what many consider the American work ethic, monetary windfalls are a powerful trend already affecting millions of people across a broad spectrum of ages and classes.

Several major forces are already converging that underscore the quiet explosion of the windfall phenomenon.

Inheritances

For many years, most American children could expect to inherit a few mementos, some furniture, and perhaps a small bank account from their parents. Today, economic growth and the extraordinary performance of financial markets have created an unprecedented creation and distribution of wealth, even among the middle class. The baby boom generation stands to collect enormous sums from their parents that they, in turn, will pass along to their children.

According to one study, Americans stand to inherit between $11.6 trillion and $17.5 trillion, reflecting mainly estates passed to children by the World War II generation. Between 2018 and 2052—years covering the estates of those children—estates will total between $29 trillion and $119 trillion. Between rising housing prices and a buoyant stock market, inheriting an estate of several hundred thousand dollars, or even several million, is no longer unusual.

Stock Options and Other Stock Plans

Once granted only to corner office big shots, stock options have found their way into the cubicles of middle managers and entry-level workers as well. According to the National Center for Employee Ownership, between 7 and 10 million employees now receive stock options in the United States, up from about 1 million 10 years ago. The Bureau of Labor Statistics reports that almost 13 percent of employees making over $75,000 a year received stock options in 1999. Stock options are most popular at publicly held companies, where 27 percent of employees making more than $75,000 a year receive them.

From Internet start-ups to the likes of Bristol-Meyers Squibb and Microsoft, stock options have become a popular way to attract and retain employees. Throughout most of the 1990s, a buoyant stock market fueled the trend. Job applicants willingly exchanged lower compensation for a shot at participating in the upside of a growing company and were handsomely rewarded. This cornucopia of wealth helped fuel sales in everything from real estate to Porches. While the slowdown in the stock market will no doubt affect the number of individuals reaping wealth from stock options, at least in the short term, incentivizing through employee ownership is a trend that is unlikely to fade.

401(k) Plans

These employer-sponsored savings plans, which are rapidly replacing the traditional pension plan, have changed the way people plan for retirement and make wise decision making more critical than ever. Currently there are about 228,000 401(k) plans in force, representing some 30 million participants. With a booming stock market over the last decade, many people who have been saving for years, even those with relatively modest salaries, have amassed account balances of several hundred thousand dollars or more.

While a 401(k) plan isn't strictly a windfall—after all, as it has been accumulating for years, it's not exactly a surprise when you receive it at retirement—it still brings many of the same issues that other sudden wealth events do. During the contribution and saving years, investment options are often limited to a few mutual funds and company stocks. Since the money is locked in (with the exceptions of loans or distributions), there is no decision making required about how to handle it from a tax standpoint.

When you leave a company, however, a new range of choices present themselves. Recipients must cope with minimizing taxes when they take a distribution, investing the amount received, deciding how much to spend on luxuries, making their money last through retirement, and finding the most efficient ways to pass these amounts on to children.

Other Events

In addition to those three common sources of windfalls, a number of other sudden money events involve many individuals. These include insurance settlements, disbursements from trust funds, winning a lottery or other contest, a divorce settlement, or an insurance settlement.

Will My Life Change?

That's probably the most common question windfall recipients ask themselves. The answer is "Of course!"—but probably not in ways you've imagined.

If you have received a windfall, or are expecting to receive one in the future, your life will be pretty much the same as it always has been. If you woke up on the right side of the bed, relished picking up bargains at yard sales, and took your coffee black in the morning before you got rich, chances are you'll do the same after.

Your friends may be surprised to learn that some things never change, even among rich folks. A few years ago, I was having lunch with a very wealthy, self-made venture capitalist who came from a middle-class family. He parked his Lexus several blocks from the restaurant where we were dining. When I asked him why he didn't take advantage of the garage that was right next door to the restaurant, he responded that he wanted to save the $10 parking fee!

In other ways, however, things will be more different than you can imagine. People, even those closest to you, may view you in a different light. You'll have to examine your own core philosophy and zero in on what really matters to you in order to arrive at a comfortable definition of what money means in your life. You'll need to come to terms with things you haven't considered before, such as how your money can make a difference to those closest to you as well as to less fortunate people you will never meet.

Handled properly from an emotional and financial standpoint, a windfall can usher in a new era of personal realization, fulfillment, security, and enjoyment. Handled poorly, a windfall can destroy relationships and create unhappiness and strife among family members. The outcome depends, to a large extent, on how well you prepare yourself for the challenges that sudden wealth brings.

Think of a financial windfall as magic money. Like magic, it can be a powerful, positive force that creates something lasting and wonderful, such as a philanthropic charity or newfound freedom for its recipient. Or it can cast a negative spell that splits up families and alienates friends. A windfall appears suddenly, transforming its recipients in fundamental, profound ways while prompting them to examine their guiding philosophies and goals.

The Road to Success

The key to success lies in avoiding the common mistakes that often derail dreams and taking the steps you need to make your money work for you. This book is designed to help you reach two main goals:

1. On an emotional level: Coming to terms with what money means to you and those around you, and making decisions that create harmony rather than discord.

2. On a financial level: Taking steps to avoid common financial pitfalls such as overspending, paying too much in taxes, trusting the wrong advisors, or making poor investment decisions.

Several of the chapters include stories about people who have come into windfalls through a variety of ways. Most of them are hypothetical examples drawn from typical experiences or from interviews in which individuals requested that only their first names be used. The two exceptions are Brian Murray, a mutual fund marketing consultant who made his fortune through stock options, and Barbara Stanny, an inheritor of a trust fund, who graciously agreed to share their stories.

Throughout the book and in the appendix, you'll find some common questions people ask about windfalls and investing with answers from financial planners. These questions originally appeared at Brill's Mutual Funds Interactive (www.fundsinteractive.com), a Web site founded by my husband Rob and myself in 1995. The financial planners answering the questions have been on the site's advisory panel and include Frank Armstrong, CFP, Investor Solutions, Inc., Miami, Florida; Richard Ferri, CFA, Portfolio Solutions, LLC, Troy, Michigan; Greg Hilton, JD, CPA, CFP, Chicago, Illinois; Paul Pignone, CFP, CLU, ChFC, Salem, New Hampshire; Lou Stanasolovich, CFP, Legend Financial Advisors, Pittsburgh, Pennsylvania; Sidney Blum, CFP, CPA/PFS, ChFC, and Richard Chiozzi, CFP, both of Successful Financial Solutions in suburban Chicago.

Finally, throughout the book I have incorporated information pertaining to the tax law President Bush signed in May 2001, including the new income tax rates, the new provisions regarding estate taxes, and expanded opportunities for retirement and education savings. As of this writing, the provisions of the law are slated to disappear in 2011 unless Congress takes action to keep them in place.

Acknowledgments

Although writing is a solitary occupation, it has brought me into contact with some of the most knowledgeable professionals in the business, some of whom had a direct role in making this book possible. These individuals include John Woods, my agent, who kept my book idea circulating until it finally struck a chord; Renee Wilmeth, senior acquisitions editor at Pearson who moved the project forward with enthusiasm and energy; and Joan Paterson, my copy editor, who lent her keen eye and cogent comments to the review process.

Over the course of my 20-year career in financial journalism, I have had the pleasure of picking the brains of financial planning professionals who have generously shared their knowledge with my readers. Special thanks go to Frank Armstrong, CFP, and Cathy Pareto, both of Investor Solutions, Inc., in Miami, for their prolific and continuous contributions to Brill's Mutual Funds Interactive (fundsinteractive.com), and to Greg Hilton, JD, CPA, who reviewed the chapters in this book on estate planning.

Although they have not had a direct hand in this book, the editors and journalists I have come to know and respect over the years also deserve mention. They include Steven Kaye of *Mutual Funds Magazine;* Evan Simonoff of *Financial Advisor Magazine;* Bruce Brumberg of mystockoptions.com; Ted Miller, former editor of *Kiplinger's Personal Finance Magazine;* Alan Lavine and Gail Liberman, the husband-and-wife author team of numerous personal finance books and articles; and Angie Hollis Finch of *Investment Advisor Magazine.*

As I sit working at my computer, I often think about the thousands of people I'll never meet who will read my work and perhaps use it in their daily lives. I would like to thank those individuals for entrusting me with that wonderful responsibility.

CHAPTER 1

Will Money Make You Happy?

Everyone wonders about the relationship between money and happiness from time to time, but receiving a windfall brings the issue to the forefront with a new immediacy and urgency. It forces us to reexamine the often contradictory lessons we have learned throughout our lives about money and how it should make us feel.

Money and Happiness

Do you remember that feeling you got as a kid when you saw a birthday card in the mail from a friend or relative who could be counted on to faithfully send you a check every year? Like many kids, you probably tore open the envelope, fumbled for the check, and, if you remembered, read the card.

How did you feel about getting the money? Were you happy because you knew you could finally buy that whatchamacallit you'd been eyeing for weeks? Maybe you felt indifferent because you really didn't need anything. Perhaps you felt a little guilty because you didn't like the giver all that much or hadn't kept in touch as regularly as you should have.

What did you do with the check? Did you save any of it or spend it all? If you spent it, did you feel more satisfied after the initial euphoria wore off than before you made your purchases? Did you use the money to buy anything for siblings or friends? Did they feel jealous about the amount of money you had unexpectedly received?

Although the windfalls you receive as an adult are much bigger than birthday checks, many of the same questions and quandaries arise. You'll probably face questions like how much to spend, how much to save, and how much to give to others. You may also have to deal with your own mixed feelings about the money, particularly if was associated with a negative event such as the death of a loved one or an insurance settlement.

If this sounds familiar, you're not alone. Quite often, people in your seemingly enviable shoes aren't in a state of euphoria when they receive a windfall; in fact, many people experience a confusing rush of both positive and negative emotions.

A windfall can be a double-edged sword. Certainly it opens up new opportunities that weren't there before. Dreams such as early retirement, financial independence, or the ability to pursue a lower-paying but more rewarding job (or not work at all) can suddenly become a reality. However, you may also experience uneasiness, or even anxiety, about how you and those around you react to your new wealth.

Part of this mixed bag of emotions comes from the jumble of messages we receive about money throughout our lives. On the one hand, literature, the Bible, social research, and many moms caution that money doesn't make us happy. At its worst, money can be an evil tool that exposes greed in ourselves and others. At the same time, television commercials peddling an enticing display of high-end automobiles, hot tubs, computers, and cruise trips shout the message that the road to satisfaction and fulfillment is paved with stuff—and lots of it. From the mansions of glamorous movie stars to our neighbor's new lawnmower, when someone else has something we don't have, we think we'd be happier if only we could have it, too.

Somehow happiness seems as if it should be an entitlement of the wealthy. Many of us react with surprise—with perhaps a touch of smug satisfaction—when we learn that a rich and famous person is an alcoholic, or has a crumbling marriage, or endured a difficult childhood. After all, we believe having money should take a lot of the sting out of such tragedies or eliminate them altogether. Yet money and misfortune don't always go hand-in-hand, either. While there are no doubt many unhappy people with vast wealth, there is likely an equal number of poor individuals in the same frame of mind. It's no wonder people are confused about their feelings concerning money. Consider these reactions from respondents to a recent survey from the AARP's *Modern Maturity* magazine when asked if they would like to become wealthy:

- ❖ Thirty-three percent would prefer not to be wealthy.
- ❖ Eighty percent fear wealth would make them greedy.
- ❖ Forty percent of women and twenty-seven percent of men do not want to be wealthy.

As these statistics show, many people find money to be a mixed blessing. For one third of the respondents, the prospect is so frightening that they would rather avoid wealth altogether.

The Sudden Wealth Syndrome

When you consider the mixed messages about money and happiness and the increasing number of newly wealthy who are trying to adjust to their improved financial status, it's no surprise that sociologists and therapists have come up with the twenty-first century's term *du jour:* the sudden wealth syndrome. Loosely defined, the sudden wealth syndrome is the realization that money is not an unmitigated blessing.

Receiving a windfall has long been an American dream. A sudden and unexpected influx of cash opens up new options and provides a freedom that most people can only dream about. But wealth also brings new concerns. Many people who come into a windfall report that they begin to receive phone calls from friends and family members whom they haven't spoken to in years. Other people find themselves questioning why they, out of all the people they know, deserve the nod of good monetary fortune.

And then there is the problem of reverse snobbism. Neighbors, friends, and some family members might develop mixed feelings toward you when you are suddenly able to afford what they can only fantasize about. Revenge may take the form of ostracism or coolness, suspicion, and outright hostility. Let's face it: Sympathy for your plight will be hard to come by when you have a fat balance in your bank account.

Consider this paragraph from the Web site of an organization called More Than Money (morethanmoney.org), a forum for individuals seeking to come to terms with the emotional aspects of handling new wealth:

> People with wealth supposedly have it all. Targets of envy and resentment, we rarely have a safe forum for addressing the unique challenges and opportunities that come with having surplus while deeply caring about others who have too little.

I've heard it said that the only thing more frightening than not having money is having it. No doubt, a growing number of windfall recipients—perhaps you, too—hear a ring of truth in those words.

Affluenza

The increasing number of suddenly rich individuals has fostered a growing offshoot of the psychological profession that specializes in helping wealthy individuals cope with their emotional issues surrounding money. One Milwaukee therapist, Jessie O'Neill, uses the term "affluenza" to describe a malady characterized by "a dysfunctional relationship with money and wealth, or the pursuit of it." She has even devoted a Web site, affluenza.com, to addressing the issue. According to Ms. O'Neill:

> Many people are coming to the realization that, far from guaranteeing happiness, money quite often destroys it. At the very least, it exacerbates existing problems. The malaise that currently grips our country comes not from the fact that we don't have enough wealth, but from a terrifying knowledge that has begun to enter our consciousness that we have based our entire lives, our entire culture, and way of being on the wrong premise. The golden ghetto is inhabited by people from all walks of life who are bound together by a common illusion: the myth of the American dream.

People who come into large amounts of sudden money often suffer an identity crisis when there is no longer a monetary need to work, particularly if they have defined themselves in terms of their career. If they are parents, they may wonder how to balance their desire to provide children with the material possessions they didn't have as youngsters with the fear of creating an atmosphere that gives their children little reason to develop a strong work ethic.

The Power of Positive Transformation

A windfall can, of course, bring happiness and open up opportunities to recipients. Freed from the day-to-day concerns of having to make a living, people can focus on activities they find fulfilling, both for themselves and others. Some windfall recipients discover that having a financial cushion gives them the courage to pursue a low-paying career they might not otherwise consider or to start their own business.

Twice a Millionaire

Brian Murray, a 44-year-old entrepreneur, experienced sudden wealth twice. The first time, when he left his position as manager of western U.S. mutual fund supermarket operations for a major discount brokerage firm in 1990, he had a high six-figure nest egg from stock options and an employee stock ownership plan.

"The human resources department handled things really well," he recalls. "They talked to me about some of the emotional issues of sudden wealth as well as financial planning issues and tax considerations. It was a very sobering discussion that made me realize that while I had a nice chunk of change, it wasn't going to be enough to live on for the rest of my life."

Even so, the money gave Murray the financial cushion he needed to start his consulting business, where he specialized in advising mutual funds about distribution and marketing issues. Aside from being able to weather the income fluctuation that often comes with consulting, his nest egg had little effect on his lifestyle.

"Sure, it gave me a lot more confidence about not having a regular income. I had the freedom to turn down jobs and pick and choose among the clients I wanted to work with. But I am old enough to remember what a recession looks like, and I'm very conservative financially, so I didn't go out and buy a fancy car or a bigger house. My major indulgence, I think, was that I started eating at better restaurants."

In 1998 Murray left his consulting practice to join a new online brokerage firm as head of mutual fund operations. Part of his compensation package was stock options.

"Back then, no one could imagine how lucrative those options would be," he says. "In fact, I wasn't as impressed with getting them as having the opportunity to help build the mutual fund side of the business."

That changed, however, after six months or so.

"At that point I started disliking my job and the people I worked with. But it was also when the stock market started going crazy. So I stayed on for another two years, purely to be able to get vested and exercise my options."

After a total of two and a half years, and with slightly over $5 million in stock options, he left the brokerage firm. That amount of money was enough for a fiscally conservative, recession-savvy baby boomer like Murray to change his outlook and his life.

"I'd describe the feeling immediately afterward as quietly ecstatic," he says. "It wasn't the thought about how rich I was or how much I'd be able to buy. It was knowing that I had the ultimate control over my future."

Murray bought a nicer, though not extravagant, home and paid cash so he did not have to worry about a mortgage. And for the first time in his life, he bought a brand-new car.

"My father had always told me that it's better to get the last five years out of a great car that the first five out of a mediocre one," he says. "So I had always purchased used Mercedes or BMWs." With a seven-figure stash, he felt confident enough to purchase a new Beemer and to buy a sports bar with his brother.

Murray also felt more comfortable about giving a larger amount of money to charities than he had previously.

"Most of my activity before had to do with the time I spent volunteering. Now I can write checks to charities for thousands of dollars rather than for a few hundred. I used to be one of the people at a homeless shelter who worked on the food line. Now, I also buy the food."

Today, Murray helps run a sports bar that he bought with his brother soon after he left the brokerage firm. He also invests in up-and-coming companies as a venture capitalist. "My goal has been to create a sustainable lifestyle with relatively little need for additional income," he says. "I think I've finally achieved that."

New Options, New Choices

We've all heard stories about people who have won the lottery or a huge game show prize and then show up for work the next day. Why do billionaires like Bill Gates or Warren Buffet, who could have retired decades ago, choose not to retire? Why do people who clearly have enough money continue to work?

For some, the reason is simply that they love what they do. Oprah Winfrey has stated many times on her television show that she would be doing what she does even if she weren't paid just because she loves it. For others, it's the notion that paid work is essential to self-esteem and provides a motivation for getting up in the morning.

Eric was 32 years old when he received a $3.4 million inheritance. Two weeks after the estate was settled, he quit his job as copywriter for an advertising agency to become a full-time volunteer for several animal rights and environmental organizations.

At first, Eric felt fortunate to be able to spend his time this way. After about a year, however, he started to yearn for the sense of self-worth that comes with a paycheck. He was also troubled by the notion that some of his associates perceived him as a person of privilege who didn't have to work for a living. And even though he hated to admit it, he began feeling less motivated to put a 100 percent effort into his volunteer work because it was unpaid. Eric then decided to continue volunteering but to pursue paid career options as well.

If they can afford it, some windfall recipients devote themselves to full-time philanthropic work or to pursuing lifetime passions that they could previously only squeeze into weekends. Freed from the burden of having to make as much money as possible to achieve a desired lifestyle, others take jobs that offer relatively low pay but provide greater enjoyment, satisfaction, and less stress than positions that pay more. They may even decide to start their own businesses.

After inheriting a substantial sum at age 23, Christopher Mogil founded More Than Money, a firm that publishes books and magazines dealing with the emotional and financial issues faced by the wealthy. Part of his motivation, he says, came from his surprise at the stream of people close to him who popped up asking for gifts and loans. "These were people I respected, which made it even more disturbing to hear their requests," he says. "I realized that there were many resources for people to deal with the practical aspects of inheriting money but not with the emotional or human issues."

Even though people who receive more modest windfalls may not have the freedom to quit work, take a lower-paying job, or start a business, they will still find new doors opening to them with new choices to make. Someone who wins $50,000 in a state lottery may be tempted to quit his or her job or buy a new BMW. But a better move would be to pay down any credit card debt or start a child's college fund.

Take a Time Out

When you get a windfall, take some time to let things cool down. Don't make any snap decisions about what do with your windfall. Instead, park the money in a safe place like a money market fund or Treasury bill and give yourself some time to think. If you really feel as if you need to splurge right away, allocate a small amount of mad money—no more than 10 percent of your windfall—to satisfy that urge.

Don't—I repeat don't—go on a spending spree. Before you run out and buy that sport utility vehicle or travel around the world, consider whether the money might be better spent addressing immediate concerns—paying down credit card bills, for example, or as a stepping stone to long-term goals such as a college education for your children or early retirement for yourself.

In the end, the path you ultimately choose, whether your windfall is $15,000 or $15 million, will depend on the inner voice that you had long before you ever came into money. Never forget: Your inner voice must be guided by practical considerations to make the dreams you see for yourself a reality.

The Do's and Don'ts of Getting a Windfall

Do stay cool. Spending sleepless nights worrying about something that should be a positive influence in your life is wasted energy. Eventually, you will grow into your newfound wealth and feel comfortable with it.

Don't make any sudden decisions. If the money isn't tied up, put it in a safe investment like a money market fund or certificate of deposit for a couple of months. If it's invested, let it stay put for a while until you decide what changes you're going to make, if any. Give yourself time to develop a solid course of action and to seek out the right professional help.

Don't equate money with happiness. While a windfall might give you more freedom to pursue goals or to obtain luxuries, it isn't a panacea.

Do develop a plan of action. Once things have settled down—anywhere from a couple of days to a couple of months—develop a plan that will turn your windfall into lasting wealth.

CHAPTER 2

Heir Apparent

*Money is one of our last discussion taboos. We can talk about sex
or even the probability of our own death. But when it comes to
money, anything other than general references are considered off
limits—particularly when the subject of an inheritance comes up
and even more so when children broach the topic.*

*If you think you may inherit money from a parent or someone
close to you who is avoiding the subject, it isn't necessarily crass
to try to get the discussion ball rolling. It's the responsible thing
to do. When everyone involved is fully informed about the details
of an estate plan, everyone will be better equipped to cope with
the financial and emotional aspects of inherited wealth. Keep in
mind that you need to approach the issue delicately and diplo-
matically.*

Opening Up a Discussion

One reason I felt that it was important to write this book resulted from
my own experiences when my mother passed away in 1996, leaving my
brother and I an estate that, while certainly not a vast fortune, was more
sizable than her modest lifestyle as a long-time widow had suggested.
Mother rarely traveled, never invested in the stock market, and had lived
in the same house for over 30 years.

Although she was frugal and never spent money frivolously, she
always gave generous gifts and never asked either of us for anything.
Naturally we suspected she was "comfortable." But we never, ever dared

ask her how much money she actually had. As was her way, she never ventured such information herself. On both sides, it seemed that the subject was too ghoulish to approach—an uncomfortable acknowledgment of mortality. The closest we got to that kind of discussion was learning where she kept her will (written some 20 years before her death and never updated) and where her safe deposit box keys were stored.

My experience is the rule rather than the exception. A long-held cultural taboo keeps the subject of inheritances shrouded in mystery, particularly for children. According to a survey by U.S. Trust, an investment and trust management firm, 89 percent of affluent individuals have discussed their estate plan with a spouse. While 75 percent of those surveyed also said, "It is a good idea to talk with children about inheritances," only 34 percent had actually held that conversation. As you might expect, there are exceptions. Frequently, a widowed mother who had allowed her husband to manage all financial affairs will turn to a child to advise her on how to handle an inheritance. In most cases, however, children remain in the dark when it comes to their parents' finances.

Next to sex, death and money are the most volatile yet shrouded topics of conversation in most families. Long accustomed to keeping money matters away from the prying eyes and loose lips of young children, parents often fear shedding the cloak of secrecy when their children become adults. At the same time, confronting the prospect of death is uncomfortable for everyone in the family. Unfortunately, a lack of dialogue can produce devastating results that, at its worst, can tear families apart when the will is read.

One frequent bone of contention occurs when parents treat children unequally in a will, which happens more often than you might think. While 84 percent of affluent parents participating in the U.S. Trust survey intended to divide assets equally, a significant number—16 percent—said that certain circumstances, such as a child's mental or physical health, might cause them to differentiate among their children in determining the amount of an inheritance.

The prevalence of divorce, blended marriages, and stepchildren complicates the picture. If children from a current marriage suddenly learn they are being treated in a manner they consider less fair than those from a previous union, or vice versa, the chasm created between families may never close.

Estate Planning or Root Canal?

Given a choice between estate planning and a root canal, many people would choose the latter option. Chances are the words "estate planning" either scare or bore you. There are probably few personal financial tasks as widely avoided as estate planning—even talking about it is put off for another time. Yet a good estate plan is critical if you want to …

- ❖ Avoid family squabbles by letting heirs know exactly what someone's wishes are and who should carry them out.
- ❖ Minimize estate taxes and preserve assets for a surviving spouse or children.
- ❖ Provide enough liquidity to pay for taxes and other expenses, including the funeral.
- ❖ Appoint a guardian for minor children under age 18 (instead of allowing the state to do the honors).
- ❖ Keep the decision-making process about an estate from getting bogged down in probate court.
- ❖ Eliminate the element of financial surprise, helping to alleviate the burden on family members at a difficult, emotionally exhausting time of crisis.

Don't assume that parents or others who are responsible in most aspects of their lives have covered their bases effectively. Even alluding to one's mortality is so difficult for some people that they either avoid addressing their estate plans entirely or do so in a superficial manner. Warren Burger, former Chief Justice of the Supreme Court, left only a 176-word handwritten will bequeathing his entire estate to his two children. But he didn't grant any power to his executors and failed to make provisions for estate taxes—mistakes that cost his children thousands of dollars.

The next few chapters will address financial topics that people who expect to inherit money might wish to discuss with family members. We will also touch on some of the emotional issues of receiving an inheritance—an aspect many people are less prepared for than the financial issues. While this book is by no means a substitute for sound advice from an attorney or estate planning expert, it will provide some insight on the most important financial bases to cover as well as how to cope with what can be one of the most trying personal experiences of life.

Although I've written the early chapters from the viewpoint of children who expect to inherit money from a parent, many of the same principles and guidelines apply to spouses, grandchildren, domestic partners, or anyone who may inherit money. You can also use this part as a guideline for planning your own estate—something you may want to bone up on, especially if you've received a windfall of your own.

Getting the Conversation Ball Rolling

The question of how to bring up the delicate subject of estate planning with a parent or family member is not easy to address. The ways that families communicate with each other are firmly rooted in patterns established long before estate planning comes into play. If uncomfortable topics of conversation have been avoided for years, you can't expect barriers to suddenly crumble in deference to your earnest intentions.

Aside from helping prepare the family emotionally, making conversation inroads can sometimes mean thousands of dollars in tax savings. A frank discussion between you and your parents can help both generations coordinate estate planning efforts. For example, if a couple in their 50s has substantial assets of their own, it may make better financial sense for their parents to bequeath an inheritance to their grandchildren through a trust, rather than passing it on to their middle-aged offspring. Unless someone brings the subject up, however, the opportunity to take advantage of potential tax savings from intergenerational transfers will fall through the cracks.

Even in families whose communication skills are rough around the edges—and that's probably most families—the following conversation starters may serve as icebreakers:

"I'd like you to take a look at my will. What do you think?" One of the best ways to get someone to open up about personal matters is for you to do it first. If you've drawn up your own will (and there is no reason why you shouldn't, whether you are wealthy or not), show it to your parents and talk about your assets, liabilities, guardianship of your children, and other personal information. Tell them you know it's a difficult subject, but that it makes you feel better knowing someone close is aware of your wishes. Sometimes, being the first to bare your soul gets the conversational ball rolling.

"Hey, did you see this on the Internet? It's pretty interesting stuff." Wills on the Web (www.ca-probate.com/wills), contains wills of the rich and famous including Princess Diana and John Kennedy Jr. Not only does this Web site make for interesting reading, it may also provide a launching pad for personal discussion. Another Web site, fidelity.com, has a section called Legacy with interactive worksheets and calculators as well as pointers on the basics of estate planning.

Okay, these Internet gambits may seem a little obvious. Then again, they may be worth a try if they open the door to family discussions of a personal nature.

Whatever you do, don't bring up the subject in an accusatory fashion ("It's my right to know!"). Instead, broach it at a quiet, calm time in a setting that's conducive to private discussion, for example, at a family member's home. If possible, let siblings know about the discussion and invite them to take part. That way, they won't think you're trying to gain any advantage behind their backs.

Topics to Address

Before delving into nuts-and-bolts estate planning techniques (setting up a trust or using life insurance to minimize estate taxes, which we'll discuss in the next chapter), it's important to cover some basic issues.

The Will

A will is an extremely important document and serves as the foundation for any estate plan by outlining who will receive property after your death. If someone dies without a will—called dying intestate—the state will decide how to divide property. In many cases, those decisions will conflict with the wishes of the individual who died as well as with the wishes of family members.

In many states, for example, statutes divide property equally between children. That would happen even if one child were disabled and incapable of earning a living and the other had a seven-figure bank account and a successful business. Often, the provisions of state-imposed wills are not in sync with what the family members really need or what the deceased individual would have wanted. Nor are they always the best arrangement from a tax standpoint.

Dying without a will may also be expensive and time-consuming. If someone dies without leaving instructions about how to distribute an estate, a probate court supervises the process. The court may need to appoint an attorney to handle administration matters such as paying debts and distributing assets. That costs time and money.

Some people think that making wishes known orally is an acceptable substitute for a written will. Usually it isn't. In fact, oral wills are recognized in only a few states and only under unusual circumstances, such as when a soldier dies in wartime.

Other people, wishing to save money in legal fees, draw up their own wills without the help of an attorney. The quality of these documents may take the form of anything from a handwritten document—sometimes called a holographic will—to a more sophisticated typed document from a $50 software program. While these might prove adequate, there is also a good chance that they will be declared invalid if executed improperly. To prevent that from happening, hire an attorney to do the job. If you don't have one, you can use the guidelines at the end of this chapter to interview prospective candidates.

Updating the Will

Even when a will exists, it may need to be updated. Usually this becomes necessary under the following circumstances:

- ❖ Assets have appreciated in value, creating the potential for taxes when none existed previously. The generally upward direction of real estate and stock values over the last decade makes it likely that a will that made sense 10 or even 5 years ago is no longer the optimal solution now.

- ❖ A significant life event, such as marriage, divorce, adoption, or the death of a spouse, takes place. With the excitement and confusion that often surround these events, many people forget to change the beneficiaries they named in their wills, as well as in IRAs and other retirement accounts, years ago. All too often, people end up leaving significant assets to someone they have come to dislike or to whom they haven't spoken in years.

- ❖ Someone moves to a different state where the laws governing community property are different.

There have been recent changes in federal or state laws that could affect an estate. A tax bill passed by Congress in May 2001 could make obsolete many estate plans put in place prior to that date. The provisions affecting estates are outlined in the next two chapters. Consult your attorney to see if you're affected.

Don't avoid updating a will because you think it may be too complicated or expensive. Often, minor changes to an existing will can be made quickly and inexpensively with a short amendment called a "codicil." This document will affect only the terms of the will it addresses, not its other provisions.

Where Is the Will?

Although most people leave their original will in a safe deposit box, some states, such as New York, seal contents of safe deposit boxes upon the death of the renter. When that happens, family members may find it extraordinarily difficult to obtain the will and other important documents at a critical time. To avoid this headache, leave the original will with the attorney who drafted it and keep copies in an easy-to-access, secure place such as a home safe.

The Estate's Cast of Characters

All too often, parents assign children or others close to them important roles in administering the estate but fail to mention their decision to them. When a death occurs, those charged with making key decisions may be unprepared or even unwilling to take on the role. It's important to ask about what, if any, role you or others may have in your parents' wills.

The primary responsibility for administering an estate plan rests with three parties: the executor, the trustees of any trusts in a trust agreement or will, and the guardians who will be responsible for caring for minor or disabled children.

Executor

The executor, also called a personal representative, may choose to consult with an attorney to verify what the duties are. The executor is responsible for the following:

- ❖ Collecting assets, paying creditors, and distributing the remaining assets to heirs and other beneficiaries.
- ❖ Collecting unpaid receivables such as insurance and employee benefits.
- ❖ Preparing federal, state, or local income tax returns for any year of the decedent's life in which no return has been filed, including the year of death.
- ❖ Filing for death benefits such as Social Security or veteran's benefits.
- ❖ Paying expenses of the estate.
- ❖ If the gross estate is subject to taxes, filing any income tax return and the estate tax return when it is due.

* Deciding how to handle investments, including whether or not to sell them either to raise cash to pay expenses such as accountants and appraisers, or to protect the estate from declines in market value of securities, real estate, and other property.

* Arranging property appraisals. This is important as it helps determine the value of the estate.

* Submitting life insurance claims.

The role of the executor can range from a simple one to a complex nightmare, depending on the estate. Duties may be relatively limited in simple situations as, for example, when a husband who passes away has owned most property jointly with his wife and leaves everything to her. In that case, the executor may only need to file a copy of the will with the state. At other times, the role can be much more complex, particularly when the estate must go through probate. (For more information on probate, see Chapter 4, "Moving Forward: Handling the Legacy.") Depending on the complexity of the estate and the laws of a particular state, the probate process can last anywhere from a few months to a few years.

An executor can be an attorney, bank, or trust department, or it can be an individual. In many cases, an individual working with the appropriate professionals such as accountants or attorneys can get the job done. Although an executor need not be someone with specialized knowledge of taxes or estate law, it should be an individual who isn't afraid to admit what he or she doesn't know, who will seek outside help if necessary, and who will coordinate the efforts of the professionals involved.

Trustee

If the estate plan includes a trust, it will also require a trustee. This individual, bank, or other financial institution is charged with the difficult task of making ongoing distributions to one or more beneficiaries in a manner specified by the terms of a trust. Typically, a trust will outline the terms under which a trustee may make distributions; for example, for education purposes, health care requirements, or purchasing a home.

The trustee's role can be much more encompassing and long-lasting than the executor's. An executor's duties might typically last for several months, perhaps for a year. A trustee's responsibilities can literally extend through someone's lifetime.

Trustees fulfill a particularly difficult role because they have enormous discretion in deciding how to distribute money to beneficiaries, who may or may not agree with their decisions. In worst-case scenarios, the two sides end up "going to war" with each other, particularly if the trustee and the beneficiary are both family members.

To avoid this kind of familial discord, some people appoint a trust company to act as trustee. Be aware, however, that trust companies are paid fees of 1 to 1.5 percent of assets under management, so they have a vested interest in distributing funds as gradually as possible. Still, trust companies can be a good solution if no one in the family is willing or able to take on a difficult job that could last for many years, or if beneficiaries are likely to make inordinate demands to support expensive lifestyles.

An individual named as trustee should be someone who is not afraid to make appropriate judgments about when to dole out money from the trust. Don't choose a pushover who will write checks from the trust whenever the beneficiaries make a request just to keep peace in the family. On the other hand, some trustees have been known to go to the other extreme by using their authority to gain control over family members and being stingier than circumstances warrant.

Naming more than one trustee might be a solution for someone who wants to take a "checks-and-balances" approach. A common arrangement is to name an institution, such as a trust company, and an individual, often a family member, to act as co-trustees. To avoid potential conflicts, it's important to make sure any parties named as co-trustees understand your wishes and can work together to carry them out.

Guardianship

Guardians oversee care and custody issues for minor children or disabled individuals and administer their assets. Since most children do not own assets outright, issues surrounding guardianship revolve around where the child will live, medical care, education, and other care-centered matters.

The person you charge with handling such responsibilities should be a reliable individual with a stable family situation whose views on lifestyle issues such as religion and education are compatible with your own.

If you find out that you have been named as an executor, trustee, or guardian for an estate, make sure you understand the responsibilities that come with those roles and are willing to accept them. If others are named, each person should receive a copy of the will.

Power of Attorney

If someone becomes disabled and is unable to make financial or property-related decisions, family members may need to step in to handle that individual's affairs. If property is owned jointly—a bank account in the names of both husband and wife—the healthy co-owner can often step in and assume control fairly quickly.

However, individually owned property is another story. When the property owner becomes disabled, family members may be unable to access funds to perform important functions like paying taxes or bills unless the court appoints a conservator or guardian, which can be an expensive and time-consuming process. An easy and relatively simple solution is a *durable power of attorney*.

A durable power of attorney is a short, inexpensive document prepared by a lawyer in which one person (the principal) authorizes one or more individuals (the attorney[s]-in-fact) to handle financial affairs in the event of a disability. The document may also grant the attorney-in-fact discretion over health care issues as well. Usually, a durable power of attorney becomes effective immediately so that it can be activated as soon as necessary. To prevent those powers from premature implementation by overzealous relatives or others, some states recognize a document called a springing power of attorney, which goes into effect only when the principal becomes disabled.

This mechanism is not recognized in some states. Even where it is recognized, implementation may be difficult because of the proof required to establish the existence of a disability. If a court must make that determination, the process can be time consuming, potentially eliminating any advantage that a power of attorney has over the appointment of a guardian.

In some cases, the power of attorney may stipulate the requirement for determining a disability, such as a notarized statement by a physician. Complications can arise, however, when physicians hesitate to make that determination because of liability concerns or when third parties do not recognize the document as valid.

Principals who want to avoid premature implementation of a power of attorney but wish to circumvent some of the potential complications of a springing power of attorney might instead simply store the document with an attorney or trusted advisor. The attorney-in-fact cannot take any action without having this document, making the professional with whom it is stored something of an overseer regarding its use.

Be careful about naming an attorney-in-fact since that individual will have broad discretionary power to write checks, sell assets, and perform other functions necessary to manage financial affairs. One attorney related a story to me about a woman put in such a position of power who gained financial control over her bachelor brother's assets when he was stricken with cancer. She performed the necessary duties such as paying bills during the few months of his illness. After the funeral, she kept the substantial amount of the money that remained as repayment for her efforts. Without a will, it was difficult for the other siblings to claim a portion of those assets.

Living Wills

Another important document to have in the event of a disability is a living will. This document ...

* Specifies the conditions under which you would refuse medical treatment to prolong life.

❖ Details the physical conditions intended to trigger the will's provisions.

❖ Lists the kinds of treatments an individual wishes to avoid.

As a backup to a living will, some people also have a legal instrument similar to a durable power of attorney called a durable health care power of attorney. The individual named in this document is charged with making decisions about health care matters that may not be specifically addressed in the living will.

In an Emergency

No matter how carefully you have planned your future with a living will or health care power of attorney, you won't want to tote those documents around in a wallet or pocketbook. If you are unable to communicate because of an accident or other emergency, a small card in your wallet with the name and phone number of the individuals who have those documents can help the attending health care professionals determine your wishes regarding life-sustaining measures.

Nursing Home Care

Many people don't consider nursing home care in discussions about wills or estates. That's not surprising since it is one of the few subjects that may be even more unpleasant that estate planning. But as too many potential inheritors have learned, few things can drain a sizable estate more quickly than nursing home care. Currently, it costs between $40,000 and $50,000 to stay in a nursing home for one year, a figure that the United Seniors Health Cooperative in Washington, D.C., expects to double over the next 10 years. As more people survive once fatal illnesses such as heart disease, strokes, and cancer, the number of people who enter nursing homes will almost certainly increase.

John provides his widowed mother with financial guidance. Recently, he voiced this concern:

> My mother will be retiring in about five years. After doing some math, I've determined that she will be able to maintain the standard of living she has now with the money she has saved. The fly in the ointment is the long-term-care problem. If she enters a nursing home, she'll probably exhaust the portfolio in a few years. I'm not sure what to do.

Many individuals are in the same boat as John and his mother. The problem is that unless you have very little in private assets, Medicaid will not pay for an extended nursing home stay. To qualify for the program, you must have $2,000 or less in savings and other assets. A few assets, such as a home or a burial fund, may be excluded. Many nursing home patients foot the full bill for their care when they are admitted, then qualify for Medicaid once they have depleted their assets.

Years ago, people found creative ways to give away their assets. The goal was to qualify for Medicaid yet maintain the ability to leave assets to children or other beneficiaries rather than spend the money on nursing home care. But Congress has done away with many of those loopholes and imposed penalties for improper transfer of assets.

One increasingly popular solution is long-term-care insurance, which is designed to cover extended nursing home stays. However, annual premiums are expensive, ranging from $900 to over $8,000, depending on age. Someone in his 50s in good health would pay an average annual premium of less than $1,000. But the price spikes up quickly, with a 75-year-old paying over $4,000 a year. And roughly one fourth of those who apply do not qualify because of preexisting health problems such as multiple sclerosis, Alzheimer's disease, or Parkinson's disease.

Still, the cost may be worth it compared to the exorbitant expense of a nursing home stay. As a guideline, The United Seniors Health Cooperative suggests that no more than 7 percent of income go toward the cost of this coverage. If children can afford it, they might offer to chip in for all or part of the premiums.

For more information, The American Association of Retired Persons offers a free booklet called *Before You Buy: A Guide to Long-Term Care Insurance* (Publication D12893). To get it, write to AARP Fulfillment, 601 E. Street, NW, Washington, DC 20059.

Finding an Attorney

Using an attorney to draft or update a will can cost as little as $100 or as much as a few thousand dollars, depending on the complexity of the situation. It's money well spent to avoid complications down the road and avoid potential costly tax consequences.

Friends and family members are often a good source of estate attorney referrals, as are other professionals you may use, such as accountants or financial advisors. You can also check local chapters of well-known national agencies and groups such as the Alzheimer's Association or the Older Women's League.

A few resources on the Internet can help you find an attorney or check out credentials. Lawyers.com (www.lawyers.com) is part of Martindale-Hubbell, a major publisher of legal directories. The site has biographies and other background information on over 400,000 attorneys in its database. The National Association of Elder Law Attorneys (www.naela.org) provides referrals to attorneys specializing in a variety of elder law issues, including nursing home funding and placement, estate planning, and long-term-care insurance. The American College of Trust and Estate Counsel (www.actec.org) provides referrals to estate attorneys in your local area. Another good resource is Nolo (www.nolo.com), which has clearly written, detailed articles for laypeople researching legal issues, including those involving estate planning.

Call several lawyers who have been referred by friends or outside sources. It's worth the time, since the individual you choose may be someone with whom you'll be dealing both now and several years down the road. Interview at least three candidates thoroughly by asking the following questions:

1. How long have you been in practice? For a simple will, a relatively new attorney may be a cost-effective choice. However, for a complex estate plan, you are likely to prefer someone with more experience.

2. Do you specialize in estate planning law?

3. Can you provide me with references from trust officers, other attorneys, and clients?

4. Can you give me an idea of how much this will cost? What is your hourly rate? Attorneys who handle wills and estates generally bill an hourly rate, which generally ranges from $100 an hour to $300 an hour or more.

   Don't be seduced by a low hourly rate. An inexperienced attorney who charges less than someone with more expertise and a higher price tag may take more time to handle an estate plan. In many cases, a higher fee is likely to be balanced by not having to pay an attorney to learn on the job. If a paralegal or assistant will be working with the attorney, ask if his or her time is billed at a lower rate.

5. What hours will you be available for meetings? Can the attorney meet after work, make house calls, or visit a nursing home if necessary?

Don't choose an attorney just because you share an interest in common or are impressed by the firm's reputation. Although it is critical that you feel comfortable with an attorney, it is equally important to have confidence in his expertise.

Never choose someone from an unsolicited direct mail flyer. Inexperienced attorneys who use boilerplate will-and-trust planning packages often rely on direct mail to generate business quickly. Others use scare tactics at seminars to frighten audience members into thinking that they must implement expensive trusts or other mechanisms to avoid saddling their heirs with excessive taxes. Later, they try to sell expensive, high-commission products to fund those trusts. While trusts can be a useful planning tool under certain circumstances, they aren't for everyone. They are certainly not for individuals who feel pressured into using setting one up.

How Affluent Americans Leave Their Money

Spouses or children expecting to inherit money, or those who have recently done so, might like to compare themselves with how other families like theirs transfer wealth. Here's what a survey of affluent Americans reveals:

Where Inheritances End Up

Estate Planning Action	Cited By (Percent)
Discussed estate planning with their spouse	89
Named an executor of their estate	86
Consulted an attorney	83
Familiarized themselves with federal estate tax laws	79
Consulted an accountant	73
Familiarized themselves with estate laws in their state	72
Named a guardian for their children	68
Named a trustee for their estate	67
Put some property into trusts	55
Developed an estimate of the amount their taxes are likely to total at their death	55
Consulted an estate planning professional other than an accountant or an attorney	43
Discussed their estate plan with their children	34

Most married affluents surveyed (85 percent) plan to leave the majority of their estates to their spouses. If there is no living spouse at the time the estate is distributed, the children will inherit about two thirds of their wealthy parents' assets.

Kids Don't Get It All

Don't assume that an inheritance will be passed exclusively to children. Almost one third of estates go to friends, relatives, charities, and other sources. Here is a customary breakdown:

Recipient	Cited By (Percent)
Children	64
Grandchildren	10
Other relatives	11
Friends	3
Employees	2
Charity	8
Former spouse	1
Pets	1

Source: U.S. Trust.

Opening up a discussion about estate planning is rarely easy. It involves acknowledging the inevitability of death and revealing personal information many of us would prefer to keep under wraps. Ultimately, however, doing so will benefit both estate owners and heirs by providing an idea of where they stand and what to expect.

CHAPTER 3

Estate Planning: The Next Step

After you have reviewed the basics of estate planning, including the cast of characters who will have a role in planning the estate, the next step is figure out whether or not the estate may be subject to taxes. This chapter will help you determine whether it is, as well as outline ways to minimize the taxes.

Tackling the Nitty-Gritty

Here is where the discussion may get uncomfortable. Even if you've talked about family responsibilities and other general issues outlined in the previous chapter, getting down to the nuts and bolts of the size and content of an estate is another matter. Many parents do not feel comfortable discussing those details with their children. In these instances, children who think that they might be inheriting substantial assets can plant the discussion seeds by making broad suggestions or references, as outlined in the previous chapter. This might prompt parents or loved ones to recognize the need to act in order to minimize estate taxes. On the other hand, you may be viewed as greedy, grabby, or nosy. Only you can decide how to walk this fine line.

Whether your approach to the discussion is direct or indirect, estate taxes are one of the more complex—and frankly, boring—areas of financial planning. The question-and-answer guide that follows will introduce you to some of the more important estate planning rules and techniques in a digestible, easy-to-understand format.

Death of the Estate Tax?

Officially, the 2001 tax cut passed by Congress just before Memorial Day weekend is called the Economic Growth and Tax Relief Reconciliation Act of 2001. Unofficially, one lawyer has described the estate tax provisions in the legislation as the Estate Tax Lawyers' Full Employment Act of 2001. That's probably not far from the truth.

Rather than eliminate the federal estate tax immediately, as some people had hoped would happen, the Act postponed that happy event until 2010. Until then, it provides some relief for wealthier taxpayers by raising the amount that is exempt from federal estate taxes through 2009. But here's the catch: All the provisions of the legislation, including the higher estate tax exemption amounts and eventual elimination of the estate tax, only remain in place until 2011. At that point, the bill expires unless Congress votes to renew it.

Think about the ridiculous possibilities of this scenario. In 2009, the year before the estate tax disappears, heirs to a large fortune delay "pulling the plug" on Grandpa until 12:01 A.M. on January 1, 2010, when the estate tax vanishes. Or how about 2010, when the estate tax disappears, only to rise from the grave in 2011? Maybe we'll see a rash of mysterious deaths among the wealthy with their tax-averse heirs, hoping to squeak in before the 2011 deadline, as prime suspects.

Dark humor aside, the new tax law has made the already complex area of estate planning even more difficult. Even professionals are trying to sort out what to do. What does all this mean to you? Reviewing an estate plan periodically with an attorney has always been a good idea. Now it's an even better one.

How Is the Size of an Estate Determined?

To determine the size of an estate, first add up the value of all property you own or have an interest in, including the following:

❖ Personal property such as cash, automobiles, stocks, and bonds

❖ Bank accounts

- ❖ Real estate
- ❖ Interests in a partnership or sole proprietorship
- ❖ Death benefits from life insurance
- ❖ Retirement plans, including IRAs, 403(b)s, and 401(k)s
- ❖ Stock options
- ❖ Promissory notes or receivables
- ❖ Furs, jewelry, artwork, and other miscellaneous items of value

   (Note: Include only half of any assets you share in joint tenancy with a spouse.)

Next, subtract debts, such as:

- ❖ Home mortgage
- ❖ Charge account(s)
- ❖ Alimony (if you are paying it)
- ❖ Child support
- ❖ Unpaid taxes

Finally, deduct anticipated expenses at death, including:

- ❖ Burial expenditures, including a headstone
- ❖ Administration costs (such as attorney's fees, court costs, and executor's charges)

It's important to know the value of your estate to determine whether or not it may be subject to taxes and to plan accordingly. If you haven't tallied up your assets and liabilities in many years, you may be surprised to learn that they may have appreciated enough to be subject to estate taxes unless you take action.

How Are Jointly Held Assets Included in the Value of the Estate?

Half of assets held by married couples under an arrangement known as joint tenants with right of survivorship (or tenants by the entirety) are included in the estate of whoever passes away first. The unlimited marital deduction, which allows a married couple to postpone paying estate taxes until the death of the second spouse, shields the property transfer from federal estate tax. When the surviving spouse dies, however, the entire amount that remains will be subject to tax. Generally, a spouse must be a U.S. citizen to use the unlimited marital deduction. It can only be used if assets are passed outright to a spouse, with no strings attached.

If joint tenants are unmarried, the entire value of the property is included in the estate of the first individual to die, unless the survivor can prove that he or she paid for all or part of the cost of acquiring the property.

My Dad Owns Everything Jointly with My Mom. Is That a Good Idea?

It depends on how large the estate is. Holding property as joint tenants with right of survivorship is certainly a convenient and common form of ownership. When a husband and wife own property jointly, one half of its value is included in the estate of the first spouse to die. As the property qualifies for the marital deduction, there is no estate tax at that point. Another plus is that jointly held property avoids probate.

Despite its convenience, joint ownership can sometimes create unforeseen problems, particularly for larger estates. After one spouse dies, the surviving partner becomes the sole owner of all the jointly held property. While no taxes are due at that point because of the marital deduction, heirs of the longer-surviving spouse's estate may get stuck with a big tax bill if the remaining estate exceeds the exemption amount, explained in the following section. Using joint ownership liberally for estates in which assets do not exceed the exemption amount is probably okay. But it may not be a good idea for estates larger than that, with the possible exception of a residence and perhaps a checking or savings account. As an alternative to joint ownership, a couple with a large estate may wish to use a bypass trust, described later in this chapter.

Joint ownership may also pose problems when an older individual puts a child's name on an account so that he or she can pay bills and handle a parent's other financial affairs conveniently. Problems often arise in these situations because when the parent dies, the surviving co-owner child may try to keep the funds remaining in the account, regardless of whether that was the intended outcome.

What Is the Exemption Amount and How Does It Affect Estate Taxes?

An estate may be subject to taxes if it exceeds what is called the exemption amount—the amount of assets an individual can transfer free of federal estate taxes. In 2001, Congress increased the exemption amount as follows:

Year	Exemption Amount Under Old Law	Exemption Amount Under New Law
2001	$675,000	$675,000
2001	$700,000	$1,000,000
2001	$700,000	$1,000,000
2004	$850,000	$1,500,000
2005	$950,000	$2,000,000
2006	$1,000,000	$2,000,000
2007	$1,000,000	$2,000,000
2008	$1,000,000	$2,000,000
2009	$1,000,000	$3,500,000

If an estate is larger than the exemption amount, it will be taxed at rates as high as 50 percent in 2002. The maximum estate tax rate will scale down gradually to 45 percent in 2009, providing a modicum of relief for large estates. In 2010, the estate tax is repealed. However, as noted earlier, it will return again in 2011 unless Congress takes action.

What Is the Unified Credit?

The unified credit refers to the tax credit that effectively eliminates taxes on the exemption amount. When a tax preparer files an estate tax return, he or she first calculates the tax based on the net estate value, then applies the credit to reduce or eliminate any taxes due. Based on the exemption amount of $675,000 for 2001, the unified credit is $220,550.

What Happens If an Estate Is Larger Than the Exemption Amount?

Unless you take the right steps, the estate will generate a huge tax bill.

Example: Jim, a widower who never remarried, died in 2001, leaving an estate of $725,000 to his two children. His estate owes no taxes on the first $675,000 of that amount. However, the remaining $50,000 was taxed at a rate of 37 percent, creating a liability of $18,500.

Because estate tax rates are so high—ranging from 37 percent to 55 percent in 2001—an amount that is even a few thousand dollars above the exemption amount can generate a nice-sized tax bill. It's important to review the value of your assets every two to three years to make sure they have not appreciated enough to put you over the exemption equivalent.

Will Using the Unlimited Marital Deduction and the Unified Credit Eliminate Estate Taxes for Heirs?

Not necessarily, because the unlimited marital deduction postpones, rather than eliminates, estate taxes. Even though the surviving spouse pays no taxes, subsequent heirs may get hit.

Example: Judy died in 2001 with an estate worth $1.375 million. She left a total of $675,000 to her children, and $700,000 to her husband Fred. The amount that passed to her husband qualified for the marital deduction and, therefore, was not included in the taxable estate. The taxable estate was then $675,000.

An estate tax return needed to be filed because the gross estate excluding the marital deduction was more than $675,000. However, the marital deduction reduced the taxable estate to $675,000. Because that sum did not exceed the exemption amount, the immediate estate tax was eliminated for surviving family members. However, when Fred dies, his estate may be taxable to his children.

Leaving everything to a spouse may also be a bad move for similar reasons. Assume that George and Isabel, a married couple, have a $1.35 million estate. George dies in April 2001, leaving everything to Isabel, who pays no estate taxes because she uses the unlimited marital deduction. Isabel passes away six months later with the value of the estate remaining unchanged. After the $675,000 exemption, the remaining $675,000 is taxed at a 37 percent rate, producing a big tax bill for their children.

In both these situations, a bypass trust, described in the following section, may provide an effective planning tool.

What Exactly Is a Bypass Trust?

A bypass trust, also called a credit shelter trust, is probably the most widely used type of trust. It is usually used in combination with the unified credit and the marital deduction to help ensure that the heirs of a surviving spouse do not have to face a huge tax bill.

Let's go back to our example of George and Isabel, the couple with a $1.35 million estate. When George passes away, he leaves half the estate to Isabel, which remains untaxed because of the unlimited marital deduction. The rest of the inheritance, $675,000, goes into a bypass trust, a name derived from the fact that the trust property "bypasses" the surviving spouse's taxable estate. During her lifetime, Isabel receives all the earnings from the trust. When she dies, her children receive the principal from the trust. Their inheritance will not be taxed because it is shielded by the unified credit.

By setting up the bypass trust, you essentially disqualify the amounts in it from the unlimited marital deduction because there are now strings attached for the surviving spouse beneficiary. Because the amounts in the trust do not fall under the umbrella of the unlimited marital deduction, they can be shielded by the unified credit at the death of the surviving spouse.

Although some couples hesitate to use a bypass trust because they do not want to tie up the surviving spouse's money, an attorney can tailor provisions to maintain a fair degree of flexibility. Children, grandchildren, and other beneficiaries can also receive income from the trust. In addition, the trust can stipulate that discretionary payments of principal be available to the surviving spouse or other beneficiaries.

What If Someone Does Not Want a Spouse to Control the Disposition of Assets?

The wedding vow phrase "till death do us part" applies to a bypass trust in the sense that when one spouse dies, the surviving spouse retains the right to name the ultimate beneficiary. If all goes as planned, that would probably be the children. If it doesn't, the beneficiary could be a new lover, a dog, or a cult group.

Someone who wants to retain control over who inherits the remaining estate after a surviving spouse's death could use a QTIP trust. Under such an arrangement, the survivor receives a lifetime income and some principal. Using a QTIP trust allows more control over a surviving spouse's access to trust principal because the trust document—not the surviving spouse's will—designates who receives the second estate. This type of trust is often used in family businesses where the surviving spouse is not active in the company. It is also common in second marriages when someone wants to provide lifetime income for a mate, while ensuring that his or her children ultimately inherit the trust's principal.

Is Life Insurance Included in the Estate?

For many people, life insurance can be the factor that catapults an estate into the taxable range. Although the proceeds themselves are generally not taxable as income, they are included in the estate if you own the policy when you die. There are three major ways to exclude life insurance proceeds from the estate.

Transfer Ownership

Transfer ownership of the policy to someone else. As a policy owner, you simply fill out an assignment or transfer form from the insurance company and have the policy amended to reflect this change. The policy transfer must be completed more than three years before the original owner dies. If the transfer occurs in less than three years, the proceeds will come under the umbrella of the estate. You must also give up any control you have over the policy, such as the ability to change beneficiaries, borrow against it, or cancel it.

Transferring ownership from the insured owner to a beneficiary may also result in a gift tax if its present value is more than $10,000. However, that tax may be much less than the estate tax due if the policy remains in the estate, since insurance policies are almost always worth more when someone dies. Ask your insurance company about the current value of a policy to determine if any gift tax would be due on a transfer.

If a policy is paid up and no premiums are due, you simply sign it over to a new owner. However, the new owner will have to make payments on policies with annual premiums. If you do the transfer, the IRS may include the proceeds in your estate. You can still give a tax-free gift of up to $10,000 a year, which the recipient can use to pay the premiums.

Although transferring ownership of a policy may seem relatively simple, it does have a major stumbling block: You can't reverse the decision. Once you give someone else the policy, it's theirs. The person who benefits financially from your death may be a spouse you later divorce or an irresponsible child you cut off contact with a few months after the transfer. What a horrible thought—giving someone who has a reason to celebrate your demise even more reason to celebrate!

Set Up an Irrevocable Life Insurance Trust

Another way to get life insurance proceeds out of an estate is to set up an irrevocable life insurance trust. By transferring ownership of the policy to the trust, you remove the proceeds from the estate (assuming you live three years or more after the transfer). A life insurance trust provides more flexibility than a simple transferal because the policy owner maintains legal control. To qualify for estate tax savings, you must follow these rules:

❖ You can't be the trustee if you owned the policy that went into the trust—someone else has to do that job.

 * The former policy owner must live three or more years after establishing the trust, or the proceeds from the policy go into the taxable estate. This rule was designed to eliminate the possibility of someone who is terminally ill from making last-minute estate tax moves.

 * The trust must be irrevocable. If you reserve the right to discontinue or change it, the proceeds will be included in your estate.

Even though the last provision may seem restrictive, you can include provisions in the trust that make it possible for your wishes to be carried out. Often, the trust document states that the trustee will maintain control over the disbursement of any insurance proceeds payable to children. By using an irrevocable life insurance trust, you allow a beneficiary such as a child to receive life insurance proceeds without ceding full control of the policy to someone you may feel is not responsible enough to handle such a large sum of money.

Example: Sally is a widowed mother of a 23-year-old daughter and believes her daughter has never been responsible with money. Sally has an estate of $600,000, plus a universal life insurance policy that will pay $600,000 when she dies. To ensure that her estate is not subject to estate taxes, she transfers the policy into an irrevocable life insurance trust, naming her brother as trustee. When she dies, her brother will assume the responsibility of distributing the money to her daughter under the terms outlined in the trust document.

You can also write provisions into the trust document such as when beneficiaries receive the proceeds, or who may borrow against the policy.

Choose a Charity

Assign a life insurance policy to your favorite charity if your heirs do not need the money. Your estate will not need to pay taxes on the death benefits, and you'll get a tax deduction for a charitable donation. Plus, you'll feel really good about leaving a legacy that extends outside your family.

Can an Irrevocable Trust Hold Assets Other Than Life Insurance?

Yes. An irrevocable trust can hold a wide range of property, including stocks and bonds, mutual funds, or real estate.

My Mom Would Like to Have More Flexibility Changing the Provisions of a Trust Than an Irrevocable Trust Allows. Is There Any Way to Do That?

A living trust, also called a revocable trust, can be modified, cancelled, or changed at any time. Once you die, the terms of the trust become irrevocable. The added flexibility of a revocable trust comes at a price, though. Because you maintain the right to control the trust, the property in it will be included in the estate for tax purposes.

Many people establish a living trust so that the assets in it pass directly to heirs without going through probate—a court process that validates a will and oversees distribution of assets under its terms. Because probate proceedings are public, estates passing through the court system will be open to outside scrutiny. (For a more detailed explanation of probate, read Chapter 4, "Moving Forward: Handling the Legacy.")

A revocable or living trust is often used in conjunction with a pour-over will, a document that allocates property that for some reason has been left out of a trust, and names a guardian for minor children. The words "pour over" come from the fact that anything not covered by this document is poured over into the living trust.

Aside from the fact that assets in a living trust are included in the estate for tax purposes, they may also carry significant set-up costs, such as attorney's fees. These costs might be high enough to offset any money saved in probate expenses. Moreover, a living trust will not reduce other estate-related expenses such as legal or accounting fees.

Some attorneys use living trust arrangements liberally, while others advocate their use only under certain circumstances, such as the following:

- ❖ Probate is likely to be lengthy and costly. The amount of time it takes for an estate to pass through the probate court depends, to some extent, on the deceased's state of residence. Some states have streamlined probate procedures, while in other states probate remains cumbersome.

- ❖ You want to avoid claims by a surviving spouse. Many states give a surviving spouse the right to claim assets from an estate, regardless of the deceased partner's stated wishes. In some states, assets in a revocable trust are protected from claims by a surviving spouse.

- ❖ You wish to guard your privacy. Unlike wills, which are public documents, trust agreements are private.

While revocable trusts are useful under some circumstances, they are often overpromoted by aggressive salespeople, says the American Association of Retired Persons. In recent years, the association warns, several groups have been aggressively selling living trust kits consisting of boilerplate documents that may or may not fit an individual's planning needs and lack the proper instructions to make them effective.

Additionally, creating a trust may affect Medicaid eligibility for nursing home care. An application for Medicaid may be rejected if a trust naming a spouse as beneficiary was established within five years of the application, since these assets are considered available for paying nursing home costs.

What Is a Trust?

Trusts come in many shapes and sizes and have many purposes. All are arrangements under which a person(s) or institution(s) named as the trustee(s) administers and invests property for the benefit of one or more beneficiaries. An irrevocable trust cannot be changed or revoked once it is established. A revocable trust may be changed or discontinued at any time. An attorney usually charges anywhere from $1,000 to $3,000 to set up a trust.

An Insurance Agent Recently Tried to Sell My Parents Something Called "Second-to-Die" Insurance. What Is That?

Also called *survivorship life insurance*, this type of policy pays off at the second of two deaths—typically, the last to die of a husband and wife. These policies have become increasingly popular since the early 1980s, when the unlimited marital deduction made it possible for a couple's estate to escape taxes until the death of the second spouse. Many people use these policies to pay taxes on the "second estate."

Shopping for these policies can be confusing. Some insurance agents try to sell survivorship life policies based on the premise that they cost much less than two single-life policies. However, that really isn't a fair comparison because they are two different kinds of coverage. With two separate policies, the surviving spouse has the advantage of being able to use the proceeds during his or her lifetime. With survivorship life, it's a sure thing that neither spouse will reap the fruits of their premiums when the policy finally pays out.

Still, second-to-die insurance does provide some benefits. The policies are cheaper and easier to obtain than regular single-life insurance. If the goal is to provide a fixed sum of money at the second spouse's death—for example, to pay taxes or even to provide an estate for children—survivorship life can be a cost-effective alternative. This is particularly true for larger estates where using the marital deduction and bypass trust may not be enough to shield heirs from estate taxes.

Gifting to Family Members

Aside from setting up trusts and titling property wisely, there is another, perhaps more enjoyable, way to reduce estate taxes. If parents have sufficient income and assets, they may want to consider a gifting program. Gifts to family members or charities during your lifetime can reduce assets and potential estate tax liability as well as remove any appreciation and earned income from the estate. As an added benefit, you get to see the people who are getting the gifts use and enjoy them.

If the gifts follow certain guidelines, they are tax-free for both the donor and recipient. Gifts that qualify for this gift tax exclusion include the following:

- ❖ Transfers of up to $10,000 per person, per year (indexed annually for inflation). This amount is called the *annual gift tax exclusion* because it is how much one person can give to any number of recipients every year without incurring a gift tax or eating into the unified credit permitting lifetime tax-free transfers. You generally can give up to $10,000 each year to as many people as you wish. A generous person could give away $100,000 to 10 lucky (and hopefully grateful) relatives. If you are married, you and your spouse can together give up to $20,000 a year to each person without any tax liability if you split the gift (explained in the following section). This means a married couple could give up to $40,000 to a lucky daughter and son-in-law.

- ❖ An unlimited amount of money if it is used to pay tuition or medical expenses. (The opportunities for reducing the size of an estate are substantial, since the amounts that you can gift for tuition and medical expenses are in addition to the $10,000 per person exclusion described in the preceding section.) However, you have to follow these rules:

  Payments must be made directly to the school or medical facility.

  Only tuition payments—not room, board, and living expenses—qualify.

  Medical payments must be for procedures that would qualify for a tax deduction, a requirement that would generally leave out orthodontics or cosmetic surgery. And only the portion of the medical expense not reimbursed by the insurance company qualifies for the exclusion.

- ❖ Unlimited amounts you contribute to qualified charities. As an added benefit, these amounts often qualify for an income tax deduction as well.

- ❖ Unlimited amounts of property to a spouse.

From the Answer Desk

What is the cost basis of a mutual fund gift?

Q. For the past couple of years my parents have given me $10,000, which is tax-free to me. This year, however, they wanted to give me some mutual fund shares instead of cash. They figured that at the day of the gift, the fund was worth $10,000. Now I hear that when I sell the fund, my cost basis will be what they paid for the shares, which is about half their value when they gave them to me. Is that true?

—Duncan

A. The $10,000 is the amount of money your parents can give to an individual without any gift tax liability. Hence, it is called the annual gift tax exclusion. This amount is measured by the fair market value on the date of the gift. One more thing to remember about gifts—you take the same basis (cost) as the person who gave it to you. When you go to sell the gifted property, your gain for tax purposes is calculated from this basis.

First, your parents can only give you $10,000 of the mutual fund, as valued on the date they transfer it to you. Second, if you sold it the same day, you will pay up to 20 percent on the capital gain ($10,000 minus what they paid for it).

If your parents sold the fund and gave you cash, they would pay the capital gain tax and you would have the full $10,000 in your pocket.

—Greg Hilton, JD, CPA, CFP

Gift Splitting

If a married couple makes a gift to someone else, the gift is considered as one that each partner makes half of. This is called gift splitting. You can each take the $10,000 annual exclusion for your part of the gift, allowing you to give up to $20,000 to a person annually without making a taxable gift.

Example: Peter and his wife Gloria agree to split the gifts they made in 2001. They give their nephew, George, $17,000, and their niece Anita $12,000. Although each gift is more than $10,000, gift splitting allows them to make these gifts on a nontaxable basis.

George's gift is treated as one half from Peter and one half from Gloria, splitting it into two $8,500 pieces—well below the $10,000 limit. Anita's gift is split into two $6,000 pieces, again below the $10,000 annual exclusion.

Taxable Gifts

Because of the unified credit, you do not have to pay any tax unless you give away more than $675,000 during your lifetime in 2001. However, because the unified credit applies to both gifts and estates, any part that gets used because of taxable gifts—that is, gifts that do not qualify for the annual exclusion described in the preceding section—is subtracted from the credit available to the estate.

For most people, gifts that qualify for the annual gift tax exclusion are large enough to whittle down the size of an estate to a comfortable level. Individuals with substantial wealth, however, might wish to consider making gifts over and above what these guidelines allow. This can serve to reduce estate taxes by removing any earnings attributable to gifted amounts from the estate.

Note that while Congress repealed the federal estate tax in 2010, it did not do the same for the federal gift tax, which remains in place even after the estate tax repeal.

Keep a Balance

Don't give less than you think you can. A common mistake occurs when donors use the annual exclusion to gift family members, who then use the money to pay medical or educational expenses. By paying the institutions directly, the donor can make unlimited payments for those purposes, in addition to the $10,000 under the annual gift tax exclusion.

Don't give more than you can afford. Some parents or grandparents have enough money to make occasional gifts, some none at all. Even if you have a mid-six-figure nest egg, you may need to keep most of it around to live on, particularly if you are healthy and relatively young. One attorney told me about a couple in their late 50s with about $500,000 in assets who asked him whether they should start a regular gifting program. They scaled back their plans after he showed them how much they will need to live comfortably in retirement. Parents should not feel obligated to make gifts beyond what they feel they can afford, and children or grandchildren should not pressure them to do so.

Shifting Income to Children

Many individuals use the annual $10,000 gift tax exclusion to shift income and assets to minor children for tax reasons, using a UTMA (Uniform Transfer to Minors Act) or an UGMA (Uniform Gift to Minors Act) account. These accounts are fairly easy to open through a bank, brokerage firm, or mutual fund. Shifting income to kids can sometimes make sense, given the huge gap that stands between the highest marginal income tax rate of 38.6 percent in 2002 and the lowest rate of 10 percent, which usually applies to children.

Special rules apply to the tax treatment of children's investment income when they are under 14. Specifically, the first $750 of unearned income—the kind of income that comes from investments like stocks, bonds, or mutual funds, rather than from a job—is currently tax-free, using the standard deduction. The next $750 is taxed at the child's marginal tax rate, which is usually 10 percent for income and for capital gains. Any earnings above $1,500 are taxed at the parent's marginal rate—the so-called *kiddie tax.* As a result, any income over $1,500 may be taxed at rates as high as 38.6 percent. Once a child reaches age 14, all earnings above $750 are taxed at the child's rate.

While shifting investments that produce no more than $1,500 in income each year to young children can make sense, it does have several drawbacks:

❖ The kiddie tax effectively limits the size of the account. A $30,000 UTMA invested in a money market fund could easily churn out as the maximum amount of unearned income that qualifies for lower children's tax rates. Any excess is taxed at the parent's higher rate.

❖ The child typically gains control over the account at age 18 or 21, depending on the state. At that point, the custodian no longer controls the account, and the beneficiary might use the money for a frivolous purpose. It isn't unheard of for money that a parent intended for college tuition to find its way to a sports car or a girlfriend.

❖ The UTMA will be counted more heavily in financial aid formulas than parental assets, making it more difficult to qualify.

From the Answer Desk

Is a UTMA a good idea for a six-year-old?

Q. I am looking for a mutual fund for a six-year old. My objective is to avoid the kiddie tax and defer as much tax to after she reaches age 14. I assume I should look for a fund with little turnover and high tax efficiency. Do you agree? How should I go about researching my goals? Do any specific funds come to mind? Should I use a UTMA for her?

—Steve

A. You are on the right track. Rather than give the funds to the child—in a Uniform Gifts to Minors Act (UGMA) account—I would hold them in my own name until the child is old enough to use them responsibly. This keeps your options open and ensures that the funds are used for their intended purpose.

The use of a tax-efficient mutual fund like the Vanguard Total Market Index Fund will reduce the tax drag on performance to a tolerable minimum while you hold the fund. When the child is of age, you can gift shares to him or her. When the shares are sold, the child will pay the tax on the appreciation at the child's presumed lower capital gains rate (presently 10 percent).

—Frank Armstrong, CFP

Sheltering funds in a trust can prevent a child from misusing funds earmarked for college tuition. Although trusts can be more expensive to set up and maintain than a UTMA or UGMA, they may be worthwhile for larger accounts.

You can set up a 2503c Trust, named for the applicable section of the Internal Revenue Code. You can transfer property such as mutual funds, stocks, or bonds into the trust and maintain control of the income and principal until the child reaches age 21. Once that happens, the trust terminates automatically or the child has the right to withdraw its assets within 60 days. Many trusts stipulate that if the child does not withdraw the trust assets, the trust will continue until a later date.

The trust is a separate tax-paying entity with lower income tax rates than you might pay as an individual.

Gifting Series EE Bonds

From births to bar mitzvahs, Series EE Savings Bonds are a favorite gift for minors because of their convenience, reasonably competitive interest (85 percent of the average return of five-year Treasury securities if held for at least five years), and low minimum purchase. These U.S. government issues are purchased for half of their redemption value of anywhere from $50 to $10,000, and are unique because taxes on earnings can be paid either yearly or when the bonds are redeemed. If the bonds registered in a child's name are redeemed after the child reaches age 14, the accumulated interest is taxed at his or her usually lower rate. You can find out more about Series EE Savings Bonds at www.savingsbonds.gov.

Advance Planning

For most people, the estate planning techniques mentioned in this chapter will minimize estate taxes as much as possible or avoid them altogether. However, those with larger legacies or more complex family situations may consider some other types of trusts as well.

Charitable Remainder Trust

A charitable remainder trust is useful if you want to contribute to a favorite charity but hold on to the property and use the income from it while you're living. Using this technique, you donate stocks, bonds, or other assets to a charity for use in the future and receive a tax deduction in the year of the donation. You also avoid a potentially large capital gains tax bill on the appreciation in the property.

The income beneficiaries can draw income generated by the trust over a specified number of years, over your lifetime, or over the lifetime of yourself and a spouse. The income is subject to income taxes as you receive it. After a specified period, the charity you name receives the donated property. Assuming you are receiving income from the trust, the value of the trust will be included in your estate. However, the offsetting estate tax charitable contribution deduction will effectively remove the property's value from the estate.

A variation on this theme is called a charitable gift annuity. Under this arrangement, you transfer assets to a charity in exchange for payment from an annuity and recognize taxes on the gains as annuity payments come in. Actuarial calculations determine how much you can deduct as a charitable contribution.

Generation-Skipping Trust

A generation-skipping trust allows families to pass an inheritance to grandchildren and other generations. Prior to 1986, families often passed their estates directly to grandchildren or great-grandchildren through trusts or other means to avoid estate taxes. In 1986, however, Congress imposed a generation-skipping transfer tax that curtailed such techniques by imposing a tax of 55 percent whenever a grandchild or other "remote descendant"—generally defined as someone at least two generations removed from the gift-giver—receives a gift or bequest (assuming it does not qualify for the annual or medical/educational exclusion).

However, slightly over $1 million of an individual's assets ($2 million for married couples) is exempt from this surtax. Many people establish a generation-skipping trust for future generations to take advantage of this exemption. Assets in the trust, as well as any earnings they accrue, remain shielded from both estate taxes and the generation-skipping transfer tax. Since assets in the trust might remain there for decades, the tax savings on that appreciation could be substantial.

The generation-skipping transfer tax will disappear with the estate tax repeal in 2010. Until then, the amount exempted from this tax will rise in accordance with the exemption amount for federal estate taxes.

Qualified Personal Residence Trust

In many cases, a home is the largest asset in the estate. For many people, particularly those with substantial home equity, removing it from the estate would yield substantial tax savings.

This is where a qualified personal residence trust comes in. Using this technique, the donor places a personal residence in an irrevocable trust, with ownership passing to the named beneficiaries at the end of a specified period. The property passes to beneficiaries at a lower cost than a bequest or gift, because its value is calculated based on the *remainder interest* in the property that beneficiaries receive at the end of the term. It's a complicated formula, but the bottom line is that the longer the term of the trust, the lower the value of the home will be. However, if the donor dies before the trust's term ends, the home is included in the estate based on its current market value.

Grantor-Retained Annuity Trust

Also known by its acronym, a GRAT is an irrevocable trust that allows the donor to gift property to specified beneficiaries but retain the right to receive annuity payments from the trust for a specified period. After that period, the property goes to the beneficiaries or continues to be held in the trust for them. The value of the property in a GRAT at the time of donation is calculated according to IRS actuarial guidelines that substantially reduce its current value, creating the potential for substantial tax savings.

Although lifetime gifts to trusts that exceed the amounts eligible for the gift tax exclusion may be subject to transfer tax, making these gifts during your lifetime may be more tax-efficient than doing so at death. Once you make a gift, any appreciation and income it generates will not be subject to taxes in your estate.

Plan Ahead

With the repeal of the estate tax in 2010 and the possibility of a world free of estate taxes after that, it may be tempting to put off estate planning altogether. Since no one can predict the future, that would be a big mistake. Under current law, it's possible to eliminate or minimize estate taxes even for large estates, but only if you plan.

CHAPTER 4

Moving Forward:
Handling the Legacy

If you have been called upon to make decisions as executor or any other party responsible for disposition of estate assets, your actions will depend on the arrangements made by the individual who passed away. In addition to a will, some individuals leave detailed instructions about everything from funeral arrangements to who gets which piece of furniture. On the other hand, some individuals don't. In many cases, survivors will need to make some decisions based on what they believe the deceased may have wanted rather than on specific, written instructions.

Even if someone has been ill for many years, his or her death is often a sudden, crushing event. Yet many individuals reeling from the emotional aspects of the death of someone close must try to overcome those feelings, at least temporarily, to make immediate decisions that could have important financial and familial ramifications for years to come.

Making Final Arrangements

Making funeral arrangements and choosing a mortuary is the first responsibility to fall on family members and others close to the deceased. Although the executor usually has primary responsibility for funeral planning, other family members may be involved. The people responsible for making these arrangements will need to consider the following:

* Which mortuary or facility will handle interment or cremation?
* Who will the pallbearers be?
* Details regarding the ceremony, such as where to scatter ashes or whether or not to have an open or closed casket.
* The type of casket.
* Location where remains will be buried, stored, or scattered.
* What will the marker or headstone look like and what will it say?

Burial Costs and Trends

Cremation has become an increasingly popular alternative to burial in the United States. Some 600,000 cremations were performed last year, a five-fold increase from 1975. A basic cremation costs about $1,000, compared to $7,000 or more for the average traditional funeral.

Cremation ceremonies have become more creative as well as more common. For the celestially minded, Houston-based Celestis launches cremated ashes into Earth's orbit for a charge of $5,300. Among the 100 or so people who have taken the ride are *Star Trek* creator Gene Roddenberry and 1960s radical writer and philosopher Timothy Leary. In Des Moines, Canuck's Sportsman's Memorials will place the ashes of duck and pheasant hunting aficionados into shotgun shells, which they later fire into the air in a ceremony for friends and family.

Some people keep a final arrangement document with other important papers that provides detailed specifications about their final wishes. If such a document is not available, you will need to make those decisions yourself, based on conversations you may have had with the person who died or on personal knowledge about the individual.

The mortuary or funeral home will guide you through the process and handle responsibilities such as collecting the body, making burial arrangements with the cemetery, preparing the body for burial, and arranging for transportation. As you discuss various options with the mortuary, you will not be in a frame of mind to bicker about costs. Still, try not to succumb to any pressure you may feel from sympathetic outsiders to spend more than you feel comfortable with.

Navigating the Probate Process

Although the word "probate" (which derives from the Latin verb "to test") strikes fear in many hearts, it is not always the hellish process you may have heard about. Many states have streamlined procedures that make it easier and less expensive than in the past. Some states allow a small amount of property to pass free of probate. Other assets, such as certain trusts, will be allowed to pass to beneficiaries outside of the probate process.

In some instances, however, probate can be a difficult, lengthy procedure that can take a year or more. If you have been named as the executor for an estate, there is a good chance you'll have to deal with it. Although you don't have to hire an attorney, most people do to make sure they comply with applicable state laws. Attorney's fees generally run between 2 and 3 percent of the estate's value.

What Is Probate?

Probate is a proceeding by which a deceased individual's will is declared valid (see the sidebar later in this chapter for the requirements of a valid will) and processed by a court. The goal is to transfer title from the deceased to the intended beneficiaries under the will.

If a will names an executor, that person is charged with carrying out probate-related tasks. If there is no will, or if the will does not name an executor, the court appoints someone to perform them. Usually this appointee, called an administrator, is a close relative or someone who is inheriting most of the estate's assets. Duties of the executor or administrator include presenting the court with a property list and appraised values, debts, and names of beneficiaries. Relatives and creditors must also receive death notification.

Once probate is completed, the beneficiaries can finally receive the property as directed in the will or, if no will exists, under applicable state law. If you have been appointed executor, you may need to make a number of decisions before that happens, such as deciding which property to sell to pay debts. If assets are tied up in the court and family members need money for short-term needs such as paying the deceased's debts or taxes, you will need to receive permission from the court to release the necessary funds.

Be aware that banks or other institutions will sometimes freeze certain jointly held assets such as safe deposit boxes and bank accounts once the death of one of the joint owners is reported. Even though the deceased may have intended that these funds be passed directly to heirs outside of probate, their transfer may be delayed until a court order releases them.

Not all property is subject to probate. Assets that pass outside a will do not have to go through the probate court. According to the legal Web site www.nolo.com, these include the following:

* **Retirement accounts.** Beneficiaries named in an IRA or 401(k) plan can claim assets directly from the account custodian without going through the probate court.

* **Savings bonds.** This applies to savings bonds that are payable to a named beneficiary or co-owned with a survivor.

* **Revocable living trusts.** Because the property in a revocable living trust belongs to the trust, not to the individual who passed away, it does not go through probate. Instead, the assets automatically pass to the beneficiaries specified in the trust document. However, a revocable living trust is included in the estate for estate tax purposes. For further explanation of a revocable living trust, see Chapter 3, "Estate Planning: The Next Step."

* **Transfer-on-death registration of securities.** Transfer-on-death registration works similarly to POD (payable-on-death) accounts at banks, except that it is used for mutual funds, stocks, and bonds. Under the Uniform Transfer-on-Death Securities Registration Act, someone named as a beneficiary in a brokerage

account can claim securities by providing a death certificate and identification to the transfer agent (the business authorized to transfer securities from one individual to another).

* **Jointly owned property.** Property owned jointly automatically goes to the surviving owner. Most joint accounts carry *right of survivorship*, which means that the surviving co-owner automatically becomes the sole account owner. If someone owns a joint account with a spouse, the POD designation takes effect only when the second spouse dies.

* **Community property.** In a community property state, property acquired during a marriage automatically becomes community property. An inheritance that is segregated from other marital assets is not community property unless it has been mixed with other marital assets; for example, if it has been placed in a joint bank account. Some states require community property to pass through the probate court, while others do not. Community property states include the following:

Alaska (if a married couple signs a community property agreement)	Nevada
	New Mexico
Arizona	Texas
California	Washington
Idaho	Wisconsin
Louisiana	

* **Payable-on-death bank accounts.** If you are named as the beneficiary of a payable-on-death (POD) bank account, all you need in order to access the funds are a death certificate and your own identification. Some individuals leave large amounts to heirs in POD accounts, while others set aside a few thousand dollars so that heirs will have quick access to the money to cover burial and other immediate expenses.

* **Small estates.** States have different definitions of "small," with the highest limit, $100,000, in California. If an estate is small enough, it is often possible for it to pass through a simplified probate procedure that usually doesn't require an attorney.

What Makes a Will Valid?

As some people responsible for handling an estate find out too late, some wills are not worth the paper they are written on. You can't just type out a three-paragraph document, sign it in front of your dog, and hope for the best.

The ingredients that make a will valid vary from state to state. At a minimum, a testator (the legal word for someone executing a will) must sign a will in the presence of two or three individuals, who must also sign the will as witnesses. Procedures may vary from state to state. A hand-written will, also called a holographic will, is valid in some states even if there are no witnesses. Such wills are frequently subject to challenge, however, because of questions concerning possible forgery and concerns that they are just fleeting expressions of intent rather than binding documents.

Death and Taxes—No One Escapes

The cost and time involved with the probate process depend on the size and complexity of the estate. Even for the rich and famous, shrinkage—the term used for assets and property lost due to estate settlement costs—can be substantial.

Individual	Estate	Settlement Costs	Percent
F. D. Roosevelt	$1,940,999	$574,867	29%
Rick Nelson	$744,357	$238,194	32%
W. C. Fields	$884,680	$327,331	37%
Marilyn Monroe	$819,176	$450,546	55%
J. D. Rockefeller	$26,905,182	$17,219,316	64%
Elvis Presley	$10,165,434	$7,420,766	73%

Duties of the Executor

As an executor (or executrix, if a woman), you will be responsible for administering estate property, paying debts, and distributing property in accordance with the instructions left by a decedent. Your duties will include the following:

- ❑ Locate important documents:
  - ❑ The will (This could take some time if it is located in a safe deposit box you do not have access to.)
  - ❑ Trust document, if there are any trusts
  - ❑ Power of attorney
  - ❑ Income tax returns for the last several years
  - ❑ Bank, mutual fund, and brokerage firm statements
  - ❑ Life, health, and property insurance policies
  - ❑ Mortgage and loan papers; credit card statements
  - ❑ Prenuptial agreement
  - ❑ Business partnership agreements
- ❑ Obtain at least a dozen copies of the death certificate from the coroner's office or funeral home. Present them to the deceased's employer, bank, life insurance company, and others involved with estate assets.
- ❑ Find an attorney in the deceased's state of residence who is familiar with laws in that state (unless the deceased already had one and you know who it is). Use the question checklist in Chapter 2, "Heir Apparent," to interview the attorney. Assuming you are unfamiliar with what steps to take as executor, a good attorney should help make things a bit easier by walking you through the process.
- ❑ Apply for an employer identification number (EIN) from the IRS for the estate as soon as possible as it will need to be included on returns, statements, and other documents.
- ❑ Set up a checking account for the estate to pay any estate-related debts and expenses. The account will be in the name of the estate, listing you as executor. If you need cash before any life insurance policies begin paying, you may be able to get a cash advance for any life insurance benefits you are entitled to receive. Remember to keep careful records of what you spend, since you will need this for tax returns.

- ❏ Provide banks, insurance companies, and brokers with a death certificate and the EIN. After someone dies, Form 1099 used to report interest and dividends must reflect the identification number of the estate or beneficiary to whom these amounts are payable.
- ❏ Call the deceased's employer to report the death so that any benefits payments can begin.
- ❏ If the deceased was eligible for Medicare, notify Medicare of the death.
- ❏ Prepare a list of the estate's assets. Arrange for valuations of tangible assets such as real estate, automobiles, or collectible items as well as valuations for a business.
- ❏ Determine the amount of any outstanding debts, including mortgages, credit cards, or utilities. These liabilities will reduce the size of the taxable estate. Identify any claims against the estate such as unpaid taxes.
- ❏ Collect unpaid receivables, as well as wages, insurance, and employee benefits.
- ❏ Contact the Social Security Administration to find out about filing for death benefits for survivors, which includes a $250 burial fee. A widow can collect survivor benefits beginning at age 60, or earlier if she is disabled. If you have time, go personally to the local Social Security office to expedite the claim.
- ❏ Oversee distribution of assets to beneficiaries.
- ❏ File tax returns, including:
    - ❏ A final tax return (Form 1040). The executor or other personal representative of the estate is responsible for filing the final tax return of the individual who died by April 15 of the following year. The income includible on the final return is generally determined as if the person were still alive, except that the taxable period is usually shorter because it ends on the date of death. This final return may include income from wages paid prior to death, interest from bonds and other securities, or self-employment income.

❑ An estate tax return (Form 706). This is required only for gross estates over $675,000 in 2001, rising to $3.5 million in 2009.

❑ A return reflecting post-death income from the deceased's assets (Form 1041). All gross income that the person who died would have received if death had not occurred that was not includible on the final tax return is called income in respect of the decedent. These amounts may include uncollected receivables, wages or commissions that had been earned and not paid, and interest accrued on savings certificates that had not been received as of the date of death. (If a beneficiary receives a lump sum distribution from an IRA, all or some of it may be taxable as income in respect of a decedent and will need to be reported by the recipient.)

Example: John Jacobs had a small business with $5,000 of receivables when he died. When the estate was settled, payment had not been made and the estate transferred the right to those payments to his widow. This amount is considered income in respect of the decedent. When she collects the $5,000, she must include the amount on her return, since it was not reported on her husband's final return or on the return of the estate.

State taxes at death operate under different rules than the federal tax system. If the deceased lived in more than one state, you'll need to know which state is the primary state of residence to determine the applicable laws. Usually, someone needs to live in a state more than six months a year to call it a primary residence.

Some states impose a tax on inherited assets. The rate differs from state to state. States with inheritance taxes are Connecticut, Delaware, Indiana, Iowa, Kansas, Kentucky, Louisiana, Maryland, Michigan, Montana, Nebraska, New Hampshire, North Carolina, Pennsylvania, South Dakota, and Tennessee.

When You Inherit an IRA

For many people, qualified retirement plans such as an Individual Retirement Account (IRA) can be one of the estate's largest assets. Yet rules governing how to handle these assets in an estate can be complex and confusing. Distribution rules clarifying the treatment of inherited retirement plan assets were changed in January 2001. Although they were designed to simplify the rules governing such plans before that date, they are so new than many financial planners are still sorting through them.

Usually when you inherit a retirement plan, the rule of thumb is this: Unless you have an immediate and pressing need for the money, it's best to postpone or minimize distributions to the extent allowed by law. This helps reduce taxes, because distributions are subject to income tax in the year you receive them. (You don't have to pay the usual 10 percent penalty on withdrawals before age $59^1/_2$ in the case of an inherited retirement plan.) Stretching out payments also allows the money to continue growing tax deferred in the account as long as possible.

You can't just let the account sit there, though. Depending on their age, relationship to the deceased, and other factors, heirs may have to begin receiving minimum distributions from the retirement plan by the end of the year following the year of death. The amounts of these required minimum distributions will vary and depend largely on a number of factors. These include the following:

* **Ages of the designated beneficiaries.** Generally, the younger they are the longer they can stretch out payments, since the IRS bases required minimum distributions on life expectancy. If a spouse inherits an IRA, for example, minimum distributions will be based on his or her life expectancy. The same applies to children or other nonspousal inheritors.

* **Relationship to the former account owner.** If a spouse inherits an IRA as a sole beneficiary, it can be rolled over into a new IRA in his or her name. The minimum distribution rules for regular IRAs will then apply, allowing the account owner to postpone required minimum distributions until he or she

reaches age 70½. Children and other nonspousal inheritors do not have the rollover option.

❖ **Whether the account is segregated.** If the retirement plan is segregated into different accounts for each beneficiary, the minimum distributions from each respective account are based on the life expectancies of each beneficiary. If the plan is not segregated and there is more than one beneficiary, required minimum distributions are based on the life expectancy of the oldest beneficiary.

If, for example, a retirement plan is to be divided between a spouse and children and the account is not segregated, the children will have to use their surviving parent's life expectancy. This will probably result in higher required minimum distributions for the children than if they had been able to use their own life expectancies for those calculations.

Designated beneficiaries are determined on December 31 of the year following the year of death. This gives the heirs the chance to keep an IRA going as long as possible in order to minimize taxes; it also presents some planning opportunities. A spouse who receives 100 percent of an IRA, for example, could "disclaim" some or all of the assets to children, who could then use their own longer life expectancies to calculate required minimum distributions.

From the Answer Desk

How will an estate's heirs be taxed on the decedent's traditional IRA?

Q. A relative of mine died in 1998. He had no will. He had traditional IRAs. Unfortunately, the beneficiary had passed away years ago. My relative has a taxable estate in which the IRAs are subject to estate tax. Do the beneficiaries of the estate get taxed on the IRA distributions also? If so, wouldn't this be taxed twice?

—Mitch

A. Your relative's IRA will go to his heirs, as determined by state law. The value of the IRA will be included in his estate for estate tax purposes, and the ultimate heir will pay ordinary income tax on the money as received. This tax is on what is known as income in respect of a decedent (IRD) and can be confiscatory. If your relative has a $10,000 IRA and is in a 50 percent estate tax bracket, he will only pass $5,000 on to the heir/beneficiary. If the heir/beneficiary is in a 30 percent income tax bracket, he will end up with $3,500 of the original IRA!

This may seem unfair to you, but think of it this way. Everything your relative owned at death had been subjected to the income tax at one time or another. Everything, that is, but his IRAs, 401(k)s, and similar assets. To make sure the IRA doesn't slip by, the government catches it after death as IRD.

—Greg Hilton, JD, CPA, CFP

Special Rules for Roths

The new Roth IRAs are handled differently from the traditional IRA previously described. First, retirees are not required to take minimum distributions from the plan, allowing the money to grow tax-deferred. And, as a bonus to heirs, qualified distributions from a Roth are not subject to income tax. A distribution made to a beneficiary or to the Roth IRA owner's estate on or after the date of death is considered qualified if it is made after the five-taxable-year period, beginning with the first tax year in which a contribution was made.

Different Assets, Different Rules

From a tax standpoint, some assets are better to inherit than others:

❖ **Life insurance.** Death benefits from life insurance policies are generally not subject to income tax although they may be subject to federal estate tax, depending on who owns the policy and who the beneficiary is.

❖ **Stocks, bonds, and mutual funds.** Heirs receiving stocks, bonds, mutual funds, and other types of assets that qualify for capital gains tax treatment get a nice tax break. When you sell these types of securities, you figure out your capital gains tax based on the difference between your purchase and selling price. In tax talk, the price you paid is called the *cost basis*.

When you inherit securities, their cost basis is not what the deceased owner paid. It's their value on either:

❖ The date of death

Or ...

❖ If the executor or the estate's personal representative elects, up to six months after the date of death.

This adjustment is called the *stepped-up* basis, and it can mean significant tax savings for inheritors.

Example: Two years ago, Jean inherited stock from her father that he had purchased five years before for $10,000. When he died, it was worth $30,000. Jean sold all of the stock 18 months after her father died for $50,000. Instead of paying the 20 percent tax on capital gains on $40,000 (the difference between her father's purchase price and her sale price), which would come to $8,000, she instead pays the tax using the stepped-up cost basis on his date of death, creating a much lower tax bill of $4,000 ($20,000 × 20 percent).

Important note: Beginning in 2010 with the repeal of the estate tax, the use of the "stepped-up" basis for figuring out the tax on inherited property will be repealed. Instead, your basis will be the smaller of the former owner's cost basis, or the date-of-death market value.

Not all securities qualify for the stepped-up cost basis. Some types of bonds accrue interest rather than pay it out on a regular basis. Series E and Series EE savings bonds are among them. Instead of paying out current interest, these bonds accrue interest and increase in value. Although some people report the interest every year on their tax returns—even though they don't actually receive it—most prefer to put off paying taxes until they redeem the bonds.

When you redeem inherited bonds, the tax will be based on the difference between the purchase price of the original owner and the redemption value, unless he or she reported the interest for tax purposes every year (which most owners of savings bonds don't do). Since the increase in value comes from accrued interest, not capital gains, the difference is subject to federal income taxes.

If you're an executor, you'll need to decide whether it is better to value assets at the date of death or up to six months later. Whichever choice you make, it must apply to all estate assets. There are times when the six-month option seems to make sense, such as when a parent dies after a long bull market and you think the market is headed for a downturn. If the stock market reacts as you anticipate, choosing the six-month option could reduce the size of an estate that was heavily invested in the stock market, resulting in potential tax savings.

The trouble is, no one can predict what will happen tomorrow, much less six months from now. The stock market could dash your tax-saving plans if it continued to climb, creating an even larger tax liability. And because the election must apply to all estate assets, other property in the estate, such as bonds, gold coins, or real estate, could appreciate in the interim months even if the stock market went down.

Longer-Term Considerations

After a few months, things will settle down and you can begin thinking about some longer-term considerations and the new changes to your financial picture if you have received an inheritance.

- ❑ Change ownership registration. If you owned property jointly with the deceased, you will need to change ownership registration. Remember to change all jointly held property, including:
  - ❑ Automobiles, boats, and other big-ticket personal items
  - ❑ House
  - ❑ Real estate
  - ❑ Safe deposit boxes
  - ❑ Stocks, bonds, mutual funds, and other investments
  - ❑ Savings and checking accounts

❑ If a spouse has died, contact service providers such as utilities and telephone companies to have his or her name taken off the account. Do the same for lending institutions such as credit card companies and automobile lenders.

❑ Update beneficiary designations. Beneficiary designations on your own life insurance policies, IRAs, retirement plans, and other assets that include the deceased as a beneficiary need to be changed.

❑ Figure out your new net worth. If you have received an inheritance, your net worth may change dramatically. Figure out where you stand so that you can mold your financial plan to conform to your new picture.

❑ Retool your budget. Receiving an inheritance may drastically change the way you live. Then again, it may have little or no impact. You may be perfectly satisfied with your preinheritance lifestyle and make only minor changes, such as taking a more exotic vacation or sending your children to a private school instead of to a public one. Or, with your new wealth, you may finally be able to heed the siren call of early retirement.

Not all changes will be positive ones. Husbands or wives who have received benefits from a spouse's employer, for example, will need to adjust their lifestyles to the new reality of having reduced survivor's benefits from a pension and Social Security.

❑ Pay off credit card debt. One of the most sensible things you can do for yourself after things have settled down is to use your inheritance to pay off any outstanding credit card balances. It's just too expensive to continue forking over interest charges of 18 percent or more when you can now afford to step out of that usurious revolving debt door.

❑ Revise your estate plan, if necessary. If an inheritance has left you with a larger estate than you had before, you may wish to consider speaking with an attorney to revise your estate plan and designate new beneficiaries.

❑ Review your insurance needs. Now that you have more money, you stand to lose more in a lawsuit. Talk to an insurance agent about the possibility of increasing your personal liability insurance coverage.

❑ Consider reducing or paying off your mortgage. Many people who come into an inheritance wonder if they should use it to reduce or pay off a mortgage. Beyond the peace of mind that comes with having a roof over your head, free and clear, are a couple of other considerations:

❖ Your tax bracket. The higher your tax bracket, the more valuable your mortgage interest deduction is to you. If you are in the 38.6 percent tax bracket and write off the entire mortgage payment, the after-tax cost of a 7 percent mortgage is actually around 4.3 percent. In the 27 percent bracket, the after-tax cost is a little over 5 percent.

❖ What alternative investments pay. Compare the after-tax cost of the mortgage to what you could get after taxes if you invested the money somewhere else. If a tax-free bond fund were paying 5 percent, for example, someone in a high tax bracket might prefer to keep the mortgage and invest the money in the bond fund. Someone in a lower tax bracket who doesn't get as much benefit from the mortgage interest deduction might find the investment a better bet. This is a tax question, so you should consult your tax advisor.

Once you've taken care of practical, immediate concerns, such as those above, you can start formulating a plan for saving, spending, and enjoying your money.

Sometimes, what you shouldn't do after you receive an inheritance can be just as important as what you should do.

A Few Don'ts

Don't make any sudden decisions, such as selling a house, for at least six months. Give your head a chance to clear before making those kinds of life-altering decisions.

Don't get taken in by scamsters. It may sound predatory, but it happens. Unscrupulous brokers, insurance salespeople, or home repairmen comb the obituaries to find out about people who may have recently come into money. Hang up on any telephone solicitations you receive from these vultures.

Don't give your money away immediately. Gifting is a great idea to reduce the size of an estate, but don't feel pressured to open your wallet just because children or charities ask you to. Wait until you've had time to sort things out and figure out where you stand financially. You may find, after drawing up a budget, that you need the money yourself.

CHAPTER 5

Coping with Your Reaction

The nuts and bolts of estate planning and financial considerations, as well as the whirl of events after someone passes away, are often difficult to deal with. Perhaps more difficult are the confusing emotions that accompany the death of a loved one.

Many people recognize that when someone close to them dies, feelings of grief and bereavement are often overwhelming. What many people may not recognize or be prepared for are the inextricable, powerful emotions that are linked to inheriting the individual's money. But there are ways to cope.

A Death in the Family

I recall the rush of emotions when my mother passed away. The money she left was a legacy of decades of hard work, regular savings, and frugality. My brother and I both wished that, rather than living a comfortable but modest lifestyle, she had spent more on herself. When the initial shock passed, my thoughts did not immediately turn to how I would invest or spend my share of the inheritance money. Instead I felt burdened with the responsibility of not squandering money that represented what my parents had worked all their lives to achieve. Only after several months did I feel comfortable calling the inheritance my own and making financial and investment decisions. Eventually, I came to view the inheritance as a growth-enabling experience that provided a stepping-stone toward a financially secure future for my family.

Many factors will influence your reaction to receiving an inheritance. Most people would gladly trade the inheritance money for the return of a loved one, and their immediate feelings about receiving the inheritance are decidedly mixed—even negative.

Although I did not recognize it at the time, the range of emotions I experienced—from grief to guilt and indecisiveness to acceptance and action—is not unusual. Dr. Dennis Pearne, a Boston-area psychologist who specializes in counseling individuals on wealth-related issues, says the road to feeling comfortable in your role as inheritor can take several months, sometimes longer. Often the circumstances under which you receive the inheritance, as well as your relationship with the deceased, has a lot to do with the emotions you attach to it.

"When you inherit wealth," he says, "you may, in your mind, associate the money with the person who died, with the dying process, and with the grief that followed."

According to Dr. Pearne, the feelings about an inheritance will shift as you move through the stages of grief: shock and bewilderment; depression, anguish, or detachment; and acceptance and recovery.

Shock and Bewilderment

During the first stage of shock and bewilderment, which may last from a few hours to several weeks, you may cry frequently, lose your appetite, or experience loss of memory or sleep disturbances. You may experience just one of these symptoms or all of them.

In the first few weeks, your top priorities should be practical tasks such as handling day-to-day matters, making funeral arrangements, informing friends and relatives, notifying attorneys, and locating the will and other important papers such as trust documents or prenuptial agreements. These chores will take time and energy that you may feel you do not have. Communicating with loved ones, friends, and family members will help you cope with the immediate shock and feelings of loss.

Depression

The second reaction to death—depression, anguish, or detachment—may reveal itself as hypersensitivity, anger, or detachment from others. You may also continue to feel somewhat disoriented or be unable to sleep through the night. At this stage, you may be angry because you were left with too much money and responsibility or, on the other hand, too little of both. If the person who died took care of money matters or was the family's main source of income, you may feel hurt, abandoned, and confused about what to do next.

Martha was paralyzed regarding all money decisions, large or small, after her mother passed away. She could do nothing constructive with her half-million-dollar inheritance, which was parked in a savings account. Martha was unable to understand why she couldn't do something with it. Furthermore, if she even went out for dinner, easily within her means, she would be plagued afterwards by feelings of self-hate.

Martha's therapist decided to try a basic shame-reduction exercise and asked her the following questions: What rule are you following? Whose rule is it? How was that rule taught? How would that person let you know you were breaking the rule? How did it feel to break the rule? In your most rational grown-up mind, what do you think about the rule?

The answers came painfully. The rule Martha discovered she was following stated: "You don't deserve anything unless you suffer for it." It was Mom's rule and had been explicitly taught as part of her mother's philosophy of life. As a child, if Martha accepted something she had not "deserved"—such as a gift from a friend—she knew it from the terrifying scowl on her mother's face or by banishment to her room. Whenever Martha broke her mother's rule, she felt excitement at first, as if she were getting away with something. But this initial feeling was inevitably followed by the belief that she was evil. When the therapist asked Martha what she thought of the rule in her rational grown-up mind, she burst into tears of rage. That rage began to break the spell caused by Martha's feeling of shame that had for so long inhibited not just her money decisions but also her overall competence and confidence in other areas.

Feelings of guilt may surface. If the money came from a life insurance policy, you may not feel right about enjoying the "death benefits" that you would truly rather share with the person who died. You may regard the inheritance as a symbol of your inability to have saved that person. Some people experience feelings of detachment or apathy that lead them to ignore the money or let someone else control it.

Unresolved conflicts with the person who died may make you wish you could rid yourself of the inheritance or avoid dealing with it altogether. You might feel an emotional obligation to the deceased and take on his or her spending patterns or money values. If an inheritance consists of a portfolio, you may refuse to sell the stocks because you think it is disloyal to the person who died. Sometimes, as in the case of Martha below, the shame that is related to money turns out to be more pervasive.

Acceptance and Recovery

Following shock and depression is the stage when you accept the loss, move on, and reestablish your footing in the world. At some point, the inheritance takes on a new, more positive meaning. You feel more confident and less guilty about investing it yourself. For surviving spouses, fears about running out of money or taking responsibility for it may diminish after they have a better picture of their assets, budget, and cash flow.

Part of your reaction to inheriting money will come from whether or not you knew you were coming into an inheritance. Often, an inheritance is a complete surprise.

As Chapter 2, "Heir Apparent," pointed out, money is one of the biggest discussion taboos in families and inheritors often have little or no idea about how much they will receive from an estate. Usually, the reason is that money matters are simply off limits as a topic of discussion. In rare instances, someone receives a surprise inheritance from an unexpected source, such as a distant or long-lost relative or a family friend who named beneficiaries but never told them.

Individuals who have been surprised by an inheritanc, or by the size of one, will react differently from individuals who are prepared. Some will want to control the money immediately. Others will avoid doing anything with the money because it reminds them of their loss.

Moving On

At some point, the inheritance becomes a growth-enabling experience. Perhaps you contribute a portion of it to a charity or a cause the decedent felt strongly about. You might use it to realize a goal, such as starting a new business or going back to school.

Using part of the inheritance to contribute to my mother's favorite charity helped jump-start the healing process for me. My brother made a generous donation to our local community center, which my mother had frequented several times a week. Because my mother had a beautiful voice and was an amateur opera singer, I contributed some of my inheritance to the Metropolitan Opera in New York. These gestures helped both of us recognize some of the good that can be extracted from a sorrowful event and to move forward.

Avoid making major financial decisions regarding an inheritance at least until a few months have passed and you are more emotionally stable. Unless immediate decisions are necessary, don't make any major changes to investments in the estate. If there is money that needs to be invested, put it into a short-term certificate of deposit, savings account, or money market fund. Then, forget about it until you have dealt with your loss and are able to think more clearly and objectively.

Despite the wisdom of stepping back and letting your head clear, however, it is not always possible to avoid making decisions, financial or otherwise, if you have been charged with responsibilities for handling an estate. Often, you'll need to make these difficult and complex decisions at a time when your mind is perhaps more clouded or confused than it has ever been. Preparing for that time will help make that difficult period a bit easier to get through.

Talking with Ghosts

Dr. Dennis Pearne suggests this exercise for inheritors who want to establish what the deceased had in mind for an inheritance:

As if in a dream, you will converse with the person who has died and left you money. Begin by imagining a likely setting, for example, a room in a house in which you actually had conversations with the person. Imagine enough of the surrounding detail to make the room present for you. Place the individual in a chair facing you.

First, discuss your feelings about each other. Next, discuss your feelings about the deceased's death. Then, talk about your feelings about the inheritance. Discuss options about what to do with the money and to what extent you feel influenced by his or her wishes versus your own. You don't need to reach a resolution. Explore and learn about the forces affecting you.

(*Note:* If this exercise seems frightening to you, do it in the presence of a therapist or someone else you trust.)

A Portrait of Inheritors

Until recently, stories about how people react to inherited wealth were mostly anecdotal. But as more individuals come into inheritances, financial services firms with the goal of capturing their business are trying to find out more about how they think and what they feel.

A recent study in *Financial Advisor Magazine*, May 2001, commissioned by Merrill Lynch and conducted by the consulting firm Prince & Associates sheds an interesting light on inheritors who received at least $1 million in the last three to five years and their reactions to their new wealth. Among the 388 people surveyed, 70.4 percent had portfolios of under $500,000 before the inheritance. The other 29.6 percent already had portfolios exceeding that amount. As for amounts, 56.4 percent received between $1 million and $2.99 million; 32.5 percent inherited $3 million to $5.99 million; the rest, 11.1 percent, inherited over $6 million. Here are some highlights of the study:

* One quarter of the respondents said their lives had "changed dramatically" for the better because of the money they had inherited. Of the group receiving an inheritance of between $1 million and $2.99 million, only 7.3 percent reported a dramatic change, compared to over 95 percent of those receiving $6 million or more.

* One quarter of the respondents said the inheritance caused family conflicts, which increased with the size of the inheritance. Two thirds of those receiving $6 million or more reported such conflicts.

* Most inheritors kept their day jobs. Fewer than 20 percent of those receiving $1 million to $2.99 million gave their boss the boot.

* Only 11.3 percent spent at least half their inheritance on luxury items.

* Of those who had portfolios of $500,000 or more before the inheritance, nearly half had received some kind of financial education from their parents that helped them manage their new wealth. Among those with lesser amounts, only 4.4 percent had received such guidance. This may be because much of their wealth came from money parents did not have while they were alive, such as insurance or lump sum payments from retirement plans.

* Nearly 16 percent of those with over $500,000 in their portfolios before the inheritance changed financial advisors afterward, compared with 71.8 percent for those with smaller portfolios. Apparently, the latter group wanted to work with advisors who specialized in wealth management for high net worth individuals whom they did not have access to before. The others probably had access to such advisors before the inheritance. Only 3.6 percent of the entire group retained their parents' advisors after receiving the inheritance.

Common Issues

The study, which only included inheritances of $1 million or more, clearly indicates that the size of the inheritance influenced the actions people took after they received it. The more someone inherits, the more likely they are to quit a job, experience a dramatic change in their lives, or encounter family conflict.

If you've inherited much less than $1 million—which includes the vast majority of estates—you probably won't be able to quit your job or make the major life changes you'd be able to make if you'd inherited a seven-figure sum. But you will encounter many of the same emotional issues inheritors face regardless of the size of an estate.

As the Merrill Lynch study shows, the range of reactions to receiving an inheritance varies and would certainly fill an entire book. Couples, widows, siblings, and spouses each have their own, unique issues to come to terms with.

Couples

Money styles or the habits people have in the way they spend, hoard, or save money tend to come to the forefront among couples when one or both partners inherit money. Once the inheritance becomes integrated into their lives, these issues tend to die down although it can take some time.

Steve had been an overspender and Katy was a penny-pincher, but in the course of the marriage, each had accommodated to each other's style. When Katy's windfall arrived, however, Steve's reaction was "Great! Now we can get anything we want!" He began to propose to his dismayed wife one purchase after another. Katy responded to her inheritance by becoming more frugal than ever, fearfully protecting her fortune so as not to risk blowing it all. Both were perplexed by the other's reactions. Steve complained, "How can you be so miserly now, when we have so much?" And Katy hurled back, "How can you risk throwing away the best chance we've ever had for ourselves and our children's future!" Katy and Steve had retreated to extreme positions.

Your money style usually traces its roots back to childhood. Couples experiencing difficult transitions after an inheritance should explore the motivations behind their beliefs regarding how to handle their new wealth, either through discussion or with the help of a therapist. On a practical note, someone who is married to an individual who has inherited money should not necessarily assume that all the new assets will be held jointly and shared equally. Some people just won't feel comfortable doing this, at least not in the beginning, and perhaps not ever. To the extent possible, try to share decision-making and arrive at a solution that works for both of you.

Widows

Widows may have a difficult time coping with the emotional and financial responsibility of an inheritance. Sometimes an older widow will transfer financial dependency to a child or close relative. The loss of a spouse is nearly always devastating, but women face special challenges because:

- ❖ On average, women live seven years longer than men. As a result, they are more likely to face the loss of a spouse than their husbands.

- ❖ Women are typically less informed about money matters than their husbands are. Despite the inroads women have made in the workplace, it is often men who control major investment and financial decisions in a household. Once the primary decision-maker is gone, women often have a difficult time feeling comfortable about filling the role themselves. For younger women, these problems may be exacerbated by the responsibilities of caring for young children in the face of overwhelming grief.

- ❖ Whether they are age 30 or 90, women are likely to get all kinds of advice from well-meaning friends and relatives. Children may urge them to sell a house that's suddenly "too large to knock around in by yourself" or to move to a distant location to be closer to grandchildren. Financial planners and insurance sales-man, hearing of their plight, may suddenly appear out of nowhere offering helpful high-priced products and advice.

❖ Another common reaction among widows is concern about out-living their money, even if they have inherited relatively large sums. They may keep all or nearly all of it in certificates of deposit or a money market account because they are concerned about losing even a dime to investment losses.

While preserving principal is important, it's also crucial to invest in ways that help ensure that inflation won't erode the purchasing power of your money. What may sound like a lot of money now may not sound like a lot 20 years from now. For example, say you have a nest egg from which you can comfortably draw an income of $50,000 a year. If inflation aver-ages just 4 percent a year over the next 20 years, it will take over double today's annual income to continue buying the same goods and services that $50,000 buys today.

Investing in a diversified portfolio of stocks, bonds, and money market securities, either through mutual funds or individual securities, is the best way to fight the eroding effects of inflation on purchasing power. Chapters 10 through 13 explore some of the tools and techniques you can use to build a diversified portfolio.

Siblings

Who gets the baseball card collection? Questions like this can dominate as arguments surface among siblings over who gets what. Some of the most heated discussions center not around a large IRA or 401(k) plan but family collectibles, heirlooms, and furniture. If clear instructions have not been left about what do with these items, they're pretty much up for grabs, literally. The law of finder's keepers, rather than fairness, takes hold.

If you have valuable collectibles or antiques and are determined that your heirs do not go through the same sibling squabbles that you may endured, make a list of these assets and who you want them to go to. Do not include this list in a will, however, because the items in it may change over time. Instead, write them on a separate letter that addresses specific allocations of personal possessions and keep this document with other estate-related documents in a safe deposit box or other secure location. Making your wishes known verbally, though not binding, will underscore your intentions regarding family heirlooms.

Unequal treatment among siblings is big area of contention. While parents usually try to divide the estate fairly equally among children, that's not always the case. Sometimes a child who is disabled or just bad at handling money will get a larger share than a brother or sister who is more self-sufficient or who has greater financial resources. And even in the twenty-first century women may still get less of the family business or other assets than men.

Another sticking point is resentment over who is appointed as executor. When a parent appoints one child as executor, siblings may resent his or her authority. The executor may resent the time and effort required to perform necessary duties, especially when siblings do not appreciate the work (and they're usually more focused on the fact that they're not in control to do that). Sometimes, siblings manage to iron out their differences or correct perceived inequities amongst themselves. In other instances, they never speak to each other again. In drawing up your own estate plan, the best way to limit these problems is through open discussion and by promoting a policy of equality among family members.

Divorced Couples

When couples divorce, each former partner may move to different parts of the country, marry different people, and lead different lives. However, their financial lives remain linked if they have had children together. In situations where there are children from a previous marriage, ex-spouses need not have the same wills or leave the same amount of money to their children, but they should co-ordinate their estate plans to make effective decisions and head off family fights down the road. In couples where one or both partners have been previously married with children and now live together, the problems they normally experience may become exacerbated by issues surrounding separation of assets among all the children.

Alice expected George, an inheritor, to pay for college for her two children, ages 16 and 17, from a previous marriage. As she saw it, funding her children's education would barely make a ripple in her husband's assets. But George had mixed feelings. Even though he loved his stepchildren, he couldn't help feeling taken for granted. In addition, he felt that the children, Jennifer and Steve, would benefit from contributing to at least some of the cost of their education. To make matters worse, Jennifer had taken sides with her stepfather while Steve supported his mother.

Family therapy helped the family understand some of the reasons behind their feelings. George described his first wife as a "gold digger" who had chosen to depend on his wealth. She had manipulated him into spending money by equating how much he spent with how much he loved her. He came to realize that he was taking out feelings about his ex-wife on Alice, who had not reacted to his wealth in that manner.

The children described their mother as overprotective, a perception Alice accepted. She agreed to soften her stand that George pay for her children's education. The couple reached a compromise in which George agreed to pay most of his stepchildren's expenses, with Steve and Jennifer contributing a small portion with their own earnings.

When it comes to inheritances, famous people are not immune to family squabbles. One of the most famous ones in recent history centers around the secret double life of Charles Kuralt, the television commentator who died in 1997.

Squabbles of the Rich and Famous

Kuralt, best-known for weaving television tales of Americana in his weekly travel commentary *On the Road*, shared an intimate relationship with a woman named Patricia Shannon for almost 30 years. During that time, he was married to a woman in New York. The dual relationship escaped the public eye until Kuralt died, leaving behind what seemed like conflicting instructions in a will and a hand-written note.

The instructions involved around 110 acres of property he had purchased near Twin Bridges, Montana, as well as a cabin and old schoolhouse located on it. In July 1997, three months before his death due to complications from lupus, Kuralt arranged for Ms. Shannon to purchase 20 acres of the land and the cabin. He deeded the rest of the land and the schoolhouse to his wife in his will.

In the hospital, Kuralt apparently changed his mind about the property. In a handwritten letter to Ms. Shannon, he said, "I'll have a lawyer visit the hospital to be sure you inherit the rest of the place in Montana, if it comes to that." Ms. Shannon said that the letter amounted to a holographic will, the legal term for a handwritten will that is signed without witnesses.

After Kuralt passed away, Shannon contested the part of his will that left the Montana land and schoolhouse to his wife, based on the contents of his letter to her. Initially, the district court allowed the will's provision to stand. But after an appeal, another judge ruled in Shannon's favor, stating that Kuralt's intention to leave the land to her was made clear in the letter.

Trusts: The Living Inheritance

Most people associate inheritances with someone's death. The dictionary defines an inheritance as something of value that is passed from one generation to the next. In well-to-do families, an inheritance may also come in the form of a trust that someone receives, often while the benefactor (usually a parent or grandparent) is still living.

Inheriting a trust when a grantor (the legal term for someone who establishes a trust, usually a parent or other relative) is still living may be less painful emotionally than inheriting a trust as part of an estate.

Trust fund recipients, however, face their own unique challenges. Often they are kept in the dark about the presence of a trust until they reach 21 years of age. When they finally learn about the trust, reactions might range from going on a spending spree to calm acceptance to denying that the money is even there.

Beyond the immediate reaction to receiving a trust fund comes the reality that unless the money is managed properly, it could take only a few years to decimate what may have taken generations to build.

Relationships with Trustees

Trusts are extremely flexible and the grantor can tailor provisions to specific family needs. The individual or institution that manages assets for the trust, called a trustee, is appointed by the grantor. Often, the trust document specifies the age at which the beneficiary receives the funds. Until that time, the beneficiary may be entitled to receive only the income produced by the assets in the trust. Trust documents may also allow for "extraordinary distributions" at the request of the beneficiary. The trustee, however, may or may not grant such a request.

If you have received a windfall in the form of a trust and the assets have not been distributed to you, it's important that you take an active role in understanding how the trust works and how it is being managed. Ask the trustee for a copy of the trust document and read through it to understand its provisions. Talk to the trustee about investment strategies and voice any reservations or suggestions. Although most trust documents do not allow beneficiaries to remove the trustee, you may have other avenues available to do so, such as working through family members who may have that ability.

If the trust's assets have already been distributed to you, you may be perfectly happy with the investments and advisors handling them. Perhaps you may feel some major changes are in order, including the financial advisor who may have been responsible for the trust before. If that's the case, Chapter 9, "Do You Need a Financial Advisor?" will give you some pointers on how to find the kind of financial professional to whom you feel comfortable entrusting your family fortune.

Barbara Stanny: Rich, Broke, and Reborn

Barbara Stanny, 53, says she came into a windfall twice in her life. "The first time was when my father told me at age 21 that I would be inheriting a substantial trust fund," she says. "The second time was when I took charge of my own money." Between the two events lay almost 20 years and an emotional and financial upheaval that would eventually change her life for the better.

As one of the founders of H&R Block, Stanny's father, Richard Block, knew more than most people about money. During the 1960s and 1970s, he and his brother, Henry, had built up the tax preparation giant into one of the best-known brand names in the country. But when it came to Stanny, her mother, and her two sisters, financial affairs were simply never a topic of discussion. "I spent much of my life thinking that Prince Charming would always take care of things," says Stanny. "Unfortunately, he never arrived."

Something else did land unexpectedly at her doorstep at age 21, when she learned she was about to inherit a substantial trust fund. She remembers the day her father told her about it as a day filled with excitement and anticipation. "My dad flew me to Las Vegas in his private jet, where we stayed in a magnificent penthouse overlooking the city," she said. "He began telling me about the trust fund by saying, 'Barbara, you are now a very rich girl.' At the time, I thought it was really cool."

What was always understood, both implicitly and explicitly, was that Barbara would not have a say in managing the trust. That job would be left first to her father, and then, when she married at age 23, to her husband. "I was always told not to worry about the money because someone would be taking care of it," she says. "So I didn't think about it."

After her marriage, Stanny came to realize that her husband was a compulsive gambler who used her money for risky stock market speculation. Still, she did not acknowledge the financial hole he was digging. "I was in a free-fall, and it was easier to close my eyes than to notice what was going on," she says. "I never talked to anyone about what was happening to me, not even my therapist."

By the time the couple divorced after 15 years of marriage, the trust fund had been depleted. Stanny was left with $1 million in tax bills, three young daughters, and an ex-husband who had fled the country. For the first time in her life, deeply in debt and with no resources, she had to face the specter of financial insecurity.

"It really hit me when I went to an ATM to take out $60 and the screen told me there was no money in the account," she says. "I was completely terrorized."

Her fears were compounded by her father's refusal to pay her tax bill. "I thought I died that day. But really, it was the day I finally grew up. I realized that staying stupid was no longer an option." Two things happened to change her life: Her lawyers got the tax bills down to a manageable level, and she started learning how to take charge of her money.

The rebuilding process began when she was hired to write a book about women who were successful with money. "As I interviewed these women, I learned things I needed to know about managing money that I'd never known before. It was really a revelation." Eventually, she started investing in mutual funds and stocks herself.

Today Stanny, who is remarried, lectures around the country about the importance of financial education for women. She has even written a book titled *Prince Charming Isn't Coming—How Women Get Smart About Money* (Penguin Books, 1997).

"What I've noticed is that even when a woman is earning a six-figure salary, she hesitates to take change of her finances. Most women don't really get serious about their finances until they lose a job or a spouse."

Stanny has come to terms with her father's belief that women should not be bothered with money matters. "My father and I were on a radio talk show, and the host asked him why he had never talked about money to the family. His response was simply that he didn't want his wife and daughters to have to worry about it." When she sent her father a copy of her book, he realized how important it is for women to know how to manage money. He then became more open with her mother about their finances. "The experience," she says, "has been a healing process for myself and my parents."

Resources: The Inheritance Project (www.inheritance-project.com) is an organization dedicated to exploring the emotional and social impact of inherited wealth. Offers books and other resources for heirs and their advisors.

Note: Case studies are from the booklet *From Wealth Counseling, A Guide for Therapists and Inheritors,* by Dennis Pearne, with Barbara Blouin and Katherine Gibson (Trio Press, 1991). Reprinted with permission.

CHAPTER 6

Stock Incentive Plans

Would you invest thousands of dollars in the company you work for? Twenty years ago, that kind of question would have drawn laughs, and maybe boos, from employees who wanted the solid guarantee of a steady wage and a predictable pension. "Never mind the upside," was a common response. "I just want the security of a regular check."

Today many people find their futures increasingly tied, in one way or another, to their employer's stock. For some people, that tie comes in the form of stock option plans, stock purchase plans, or other forms of compensation pegged to company stock.

While the downturn in the stock market has taken some of the bloom off the stock-based compensation rose, there's little chance that companies will stop cultivating the garden. Stock-based compensation has become too popular a way to motivate employees. And they seem to make perfect sense: If the company's stock does well, so do you.

The Stock Option Mystique

Here's an image Americans have grown to love and loathe—the barely-out-of-college techno-whiz-kid who becomes a millionaire after his one-year-old company with no revenue goes public in a $500 million offering. To some people, this portrait represents the ingenuity and ambition that makes capitalism tick. To others, it reeks of an arrogant, get-rich-quick mentality made possible by Wall Street greed. Or maybe, it's your face in the mirror that's smiling—if you're that rich, who cares what anyone thinks?

Whatever your interpretation, stock options and other types of stock-based compensation have captured the hearts and minds of workers across the country. And despite widespread stereotypes, not everyone who gets stock or stock options from the company they work for is a young kid or technologically inclined.

Today, it's common practice in corporate America to pay employees not only with wages but with a piece of the pie as well. PepsiCo, Starbucks, and DuPont are among the many companies that provide stock options to most of their employees. Perhaps you're one of the fortunate individuals who, thanks to the long bull market of the 1980s and 1990s, have benefited from the trend.

In the best of times, stock-based incentive plans can make you rich. But there's more to them than just cashing out and enjoying the upside. The fact that stock compensation plans are widespread or popular doesn't mean they are easy to understand; people often make mistakes when they use them. According to a recent survey by Oppenheimer Funds, a mutual fund group, 37 percent of option holders believed they understand Einstein's theory of relativity better than they understand their stock options. Some 11 percent said that they had inadvertently allowed options that they could have exercised at a profit expire and become worthless.

These benefit plans are often governed by complex tax rules and corporate guidelines and require you to make decisions with long-term lasting implications. Just about anyone, whether he or she has already become wealthy from stock-based compensation plans or hopes to in the future, can benefit from boning up on these plans for the following reasons:

❖ If you own stock options that make you look wealthy on paper but you haven't exercised them, you can plan ahead to make the right wealth-maximizing moves and avoid wealth-draining mistakes.

❖ Perhaps you've already exercised your stock options and you're now holding lots of the same stock. The question then is how to decide when, or if, to sell. Should you wait until the stock market picks up? Have you thought about tax considerations?

❖ Perhaps you've exercised your options, sold the stock, and made a fortune. If you're like many people, you paid more in taxes than you should have, or exercised your options at the wrong time. Chances are, you still have some options you haven't exercised. As stock-based incentive rewards are so common in corporate America, you'll probably need to make similar decisions again.

❖ If you've never participated in a stock-based compensation plan, there's a good chance you will at some point in your career.

❖ If you already own a lot of company stock through an Employee Stock Ownership Plan (ESOP), a stock purchase program, or through exercising stock options, you may have too many eggs in one basket. You need to start diversifying.

Financial planners have found that people who have stock options or who own a lot of stock in their companies through other types of plans tend to make the same mistakes, over and over again. Could any of these wealth-withering remarks could come from your mouth:

"I want a new car (or boat or trip around the world). And I want it now."

Example: Alan joined Technobable in June 1998. He received a stock option grant as soon as he started and exercised a portion of it a little over a year later to buy a sailboat he had always dreamed of. The stock rose another 25 percent over the next six months, appreciation Alan didn't get to enjoy with the option he exercised because he was too focused on buying a depreciating asset—his boat.

People with stock options sometimes make large purchases before they've even worked long enough to exercise them. They are convinced their company stock has nowhere to go but up and that the future wealth they anticipate from their options is a sure thing. But when the company stock goes down, all too many find out that paper wealth is very different from cold hard cash in a bank or brokerage account.

"Taxes? What taxes?"

The tax treatment of options varies depending on what type of option you get. But make no mistake about it, when you profit from your options, you will owe taxes at some point. If your company's stock plummets between the time you exercise and the time you need to pay taxes, you could have a tax liability that takes a chunk out of the value of your stock or, in a worst-case scenario, exceeds it. Just ask the thousands of option holders who suffered such a fate in 2000 when the stock market, and technology stocks in particular, sank.

Example: Dave, who works for an Internet consulting firm, exercised his stock options in early 2000 when his company's stock was selling near its peak, making a profit of $60,000. He continued to hold on to the stock. But by the end of the year, after the sector took a nosedive, his shares were only worth $20,000. Because his tax liability was based on the value of the stock when Dave exercised his option, his tax bill wiped out much of his profit. Had the stock fallen even further—not an impossible scenario in a bear market—his tax bill could easily have exceeded the value of his stock.

"I don't need to diversify. I work for a great company."

With equity compensation so popular, many employees find their future financial well-being closely tied to company stock. If that stock goes down, so does their personal fortune. You need to think in terms of your total portfolio, which could well include a 401(k) or other plan that's also packed to the gills with company stock.

"I worked hard. I deserve better."

Stocks don't always go up and, despite the motivational goal of these plans, the reasons may have little or nothing to do with your job performance. Here's the worst-case scenario: Your company's stock languishes or tanks due to circumstances beyond your control, such as a lousy economy or stock market or bad decisions by management. The stock founders for years, making any compensation based on it much less valuable to you, or even worthless. Or, the company goes out of business. Your willingness to sacrifice pay, job security, or personal time has gone unrewarded.

All this doesn't mean that stock options and other stock-based compensation plans aren't valuable. You just have to look at all the people who've gotten wealthy from them to know that they are. As you can see, they're also tricky and difficult to understand. And if you don't know how to handle them, you could end up sitting on some big losses, or falling into some ugly tax traps.

Stock Options: The Basics

Before we talk about specific strategies for exercising stock options and minimizing taxes on profits, it helps to know some basic stock option lingo:

- ❖ **Stock option:** The right to buy shares in the future at a price set when the option is granted.
- ❖ **Grant** (sometimes called an award): Receiving stock options from a company.
- ❖ **Exercise:** Implementing your right to use the option to buy company stock.
- ❖ **Exercise price** (also called the strike price): The price at which you exercise the option.
- ❖ **Spread:** The difference between the exercise price and the current value of the stock. When the current value of the stock exceeds the exercise price, the option is said to be "in the money." When the difference is negative; that is, when the current value of the stock is below the exercise price, the option is "underwater" and will have no value until the stock price recovers.

Example: Sally has an option to buy 100 shares of Mogul Corp. stock at $20 a share. Her exercise price is $20. A year later, when the current value of the stock is $30, she exercises her option to buy the stock at $20 a share. She makes money from the spread—the $10 a share difference between the current value of the stock and the exercise price. If the current value of the stock were below the exercise price of $20 a share, it obviously would make no sense to exercise the option. The option would then be underwater, or out of the money.

- ❖ **Vesting:** The point at which you can exercise the option, usually a year after the option grant. Options usually vest gradually. You may, for example, be allowed to exercise 25 percent of your options after one year, then 25 percent in each of the three years after that. Some smaller startup companies permit immediate vesting of options but require you to hold on to the stock for a specified period of time before you can sell it.

Example: Charlie joins a company that grants him an option to buy 160 shares of its stock. His vesting schedule allows him to exercise 25 percent of the option beginning with the first anniversary of the grant, or up to 40 shares. After the first year, he may exercise the option to buy up 40 shares a year over the next three years. These amounts are cumulative. If Charlie doesn't exercise the first 25 percent after the first year, he can exercise half his options the second year, 75 percent the third year, and up to 100 percent the fourth year.

- ❖ **Expiration:** The point at which you no longer have the right to exercise an option, making it worthless.

How will you pay for the stock? What if you want to exercise a stock option but don't have the money to do it? Many companies allow employees to execute "cashless exercises." Instead of having you pay for the stock in cash, the company arranges with a brokerage firm to sell some or all the stock immediately to cover the exercise price as well as any income tax withholding.

Kinds of Stock Options

Options come in two main flavors: nonqualified stock options, the most commonly used variety, and incentive stock options. If you have received stock options and are unsure which type you have, ask to see your company's option agreement to find out. It's important to know because, from a tax standpoint, the two are handled very differently.

Nonqualified Stock Options

With nonqualified stock options, profits are subject to taxes at two points: when you exercise the option and when you sell the stock. Some of the profit will be taxed at ordinary income rates.

Grant: No tax.

Exercise: The difference between the market value and the strike price is taxed as ordinary income on that year's tax return. You must report this income even if you don't actually sell the stock. (Very rarely, when options trade on a securities market, the tax accrues on the grant date.)

Sale of stock: When you sell the stock, your tax is based on the market price on the day you exercised the option. If you hold the stock for more than one year after the exercise date, your gain will be taxed as a long-term capital gain. If you sell before that time, the gain will be taxed at ordinary income rates.

Example: On June 1, 2000, you exercise an option to buy stock in your company for $30 a share. On that date, the stock's market value is $45. You report the difference of $15 a share as income for that year. Your new cost basis in the stock becomes $45. If you sell your stock more than a year after the original exercise date for $50 a share, the $5 gain is taxed as a long-term capital gain and qualifies for the 20 percent tax rate. If you sell before then, any gain is taxed at higher ordinary income tax rates.

Incentive Stock Options

Profits from incentive stock options receive more favorable tax treatment than those from nonqualified stock options. If an employee meets the holding period requirements described below, all profits will be taxable as long-term capital gains.

Grant: No tax.

Exercise: The difference between the market value at exercise and the strike price is generally not taxable.

Sale of stock: When you sell the stock, your tax is based on the difference between what you paid (the strike price) and what you sold the stock for. This amount is eligible for favorable capital gains tax treatment if you hold the shares for more than a year *and* if the sale occurs more than two years after the option grant date.

Example: On June 1, 2000, you exercise an option to buy stock in your company for $30 a share. On that date, the stock's market value is $45. There is no tax due when you exercise the option. You wait more than a year after the exercise date and more than two years after the option grant date to sell the stock for $50 a share. Your tax on the gain of $20 a share ($50 selling price minus the $30 you paid for each share) is treated as a long-term capital gain and qualifies for the 20 percent tax rate.

If you don't follow both of those rules—that is, if you wait less than a year after the exercise date or less than two years after the option grant date to sell the stock—the IRS will consider the transaction a "disqualifying disposition." This means some or all the gain will be taxed at ordinary income rates.

Although you don't owe regular income taxes on incentive stock options when you exercise them, the difference between what you paid for the stock and what you sold it for is treated as income for alternative minimum tax (AMT) purposes. (For more on the alternative minimum tax, see Chapter 14, "Tackling Taxes.")

Tips from a Pro

John Barringer, a stockbroker specializing in company stock options and a columnist for Mystockoptions.com, knows how easy it is to blow a stock option fortune. "I see too many smart people who have substantial gains in their stock options do dumb things," he says. "But a disciplined stock option exercise strategy can prevent some big mistakes and significantly increase the value of an option grant package." Here are some guidelines he offers:

1. **Don't exercise too soon.** Don't wait too long. Barringer's clients frequently exercise their options soon after they vest because they want the money for a large discretionary purchase like a boat or a car. "The most expensive boat or car I can imagine is the one bought with options. If left unexercised, the options would have greatly appreciated—something a car or boat is not likely to do—and the gains would have remained tax-deferred."

   On the other hand, you don't want to wait too long to exercise. If there is a prolonged downturn in the stock market, your options could expire before the stock recovers.

2. **Recognize that your risk rises with your profit. Don't be greedy.** Short-term rallies in the price of your stock are probably selling opportunities particularly if you think the price of the stock is likely to drop in the near future. If you expect to continue to receive future option grants, exercise your oldest options when these price increases occur. This requires you to spend some time getting to know about and paying attention to the price behavior of your company's stock.

3. **Consider the alternative investment cost.** Your alternative investment cost is determined by how much an alternative investment must appreciate to justify exercising your options and putting the net profits into another investment.

   Let's say you have an option that was granted to you nine years ago at $3.00. Today, the stock is trading at $62. Earlier in the year, its trading range was $50 to $64. Should you exercise or continue to wait?

   The best course of action would be to exercise. Here's why: The stock is trading only 3 percent away from its high, and 22 percent away from its recent low. Since the stock has recently traded at both those prices, it could go back to either of them again. To put it another way, the upside potential is 3 percent, the downside potential is 22 percent.

The alternative investment cost is the 3 percent return you must beat in order to exceed the expected return from holding on to the option. This low figure means the risks of continuing to hold probably outweigh the rewards. At this point, you are likely better off taking the profit and investing the proceeds into a stock or mutual fund whose performance would complement your other holdings.

4. **Use an "average out" strategy.** Exercising options gradually, rather than all at once, reduces the risk of being forced to accept a lower price for all your options if the stock market declines near the expiration date. You can combine this with an "average in" strategy whereby you periodically invest the proceeds from the option exercises in a diversified portfolio of stocks, bonds, or mutual funds.

5. **Know your company's exercise rules and procedures.** Look at your plan documents and the ancillary forms and materials your company provides that explain the rules and procedures governing its options exercise transactions. Failure to follow company procedures can result in a violation of securities law and even a forfeiture of your profit.

6. **When it comes to margin loans, don't let tax issues cloud your judgment.** Tax-averse employees sometimes use borrowed funds from a broker in a margin account to exercise and hold an incentive stock option instead of putting up their own cash. By holding the stock for one year after the exercise, the owner will be able to apply long-term capital gains treatment to the profit.

Sounds good, but here's the hitch. When you buy stock on margin, the broker can loan up to 50 percent of the stock's market price. So if you have, say, 1,000 incentive stock options with a strike price of $10 and the stock is trading at $20 or more, you can borrow the $10,000 you need to exercise the option and hold on to the stock. You'll need to pay interest on the loan until it is repaid (presumably when you sell the stock after the one-year holding period is up).

This works out fine if the stock stays about the same price, or goes up, after the exercise. But if it drops, you'll need to pony up additional funds to bring the margin collateral back up to the 50 percent level. If this happens, you'll either have to send a check or provide other assets to make up the shortfall or allow the broker to sell some of your stock. Selling stock defeats the tax avoidance strategy. And any money you pay to the broker, whether it's interest or money to meet a margin call, is gone, just as if you had sent it to the IRS.

Example: Picture this unhappy scenario of someone caught in a margin call vortex:

Beth uses margin to exercise 1,000 incentive stock options at a price of $15 at a time when the stock has a market value of $30. A few months later, her company announces lower-than-expected earnings, causing the stock to plunge. Beth is forced to liquidate her stock at prices well below her exercise price to bring the collateral level in the margin account back up to 50 percent. Too bad she couldn't hold on to her stock, because it rose to $50 a share a year later. The original purpose of the margin account—to borrow the money needed to exercise the option and hold on to the stock long enough for the profit to qualify for long-term capital gains treatment—backfired in a big way.

7. **Don't forget to exercise.** If you fail to exercise before the option expires, the value of the option is lost. Some companies do not keep option holders apprised of approaching expiration dates. Keep track of important dates. It's surprising how many people let their options expire worthless. Don't be one of them.

8. **Finally, accepting lower pay for stock options isn't always a great idea.** As many employees of Internet companies have learned, stock option wealth is never a sure thing, particularly in a start-up that that may or may not go public or achieve prof-itability.

Aside from the danger of having the stock go down, there's also the possibility that it will just sit there. Taking their cue from the excitement generated by stock option programs at start-ups, many large, mature organizations have begun offering stock option programs. Trouble is, the share prices of these dinosaurs can go nowhere for years. Often, what lured employees in the first place turns out to be a worthless benefit as the stock treads water.

Although the ins and outs of stock options can be difficult to understand, few employers who offer them provide guidance in this area. Mistakes can cost thousands of dollars, or even wipe out option profits. Before you exercise your stock options, be sure to consult an investment or tax professional familiar with how they work, particularly if large amounts are at stake. The Web sites listed at the end of this chapter also provide guidance on how and when to exercise stock options.

Employee Stock Ownership Plans (ESOPs)

Although they've taken a back seat lately to sexier stock options, employee stock ownership plans (ESOPs) are still very popular among companies. According to the National Center for Employee Ownership, there are currently over 10,000 ESOPs in the United States covering over 9 million participants and controlling over $210 billion in company stock. Of these, about 15 percent are publicly traded companies; 85 percent are in closely held private companies.

ESOPs are a kind of employee benefit plan funded exclusively with company stock. In an unleveraged ESOP, the employer contributes shares, or cash to buy shares, to a trust in which participants become vested (accrue ownership of those contributions) over a maximum of five years. Public companies use this framework most often. In a leveraged ESOP, the stock is purchased by the trust with borrowed money. As the trust pays off the loan, the stock, which is pledged as collateral, is assigned to employees.

The main thing to remember about either type of ESOP is that if you stay with a company long enough, there's a good chance that much of your net worth is tied up in company stock. Bruce, who is in that situation, voices this concern:

> I work for a small company that has an ESOP plan. I have no access to the account until I leave the company, which I currently have no plans to do. I am fully vested, in my mid-40s, and the account value is around $500,000. Compared to the ESOP account, the remainder of my assets are insignificant. I'm worried about what will happen if the stock goes down.

With so much of his financial future tied up in the ESOP, Bruce should be concerned. However, there's really nothing he can do with his ESOP money because he can't touch the stock in the account until he retires or leaves the company.

If you have a lot of your net worth tied up in an ESOP, asking a few important questions will help you determine how risky your investment is and how you should include it in your financial planning:

- ❖ **Is the ESOP augmented by another retirement program that holds a more balanced mix of investments?** Many smaller companies use an ESOP as their only retirement plan.

- ❖ **How volatile is the company stock?** If you leave or retire from a company when the stock is on a sharp downswing, your distribution will be correspondingly reduced.

- ❖ **Is the stock publicly traded?** ESOP shares that trade on a stock exchange can be bought and sold just like any other kind of publicly traded stock when you're eligible to cash out. In a private company, or a thinly traded public company, the employer must repurchase shares from departing employees at their fair market value, as determined by an independent appraiser. If a company is tight on cash, you could have trouble getting money for the shares right away. Many private companies have provisions in their plans allowing them to "cash out" employees over a period of several years, and the value of the stock can fluctuate significantly over that time.

ESOPs are designed to incentive employees by tying their financial futures to employer stock. Anyone with large amounts in these plans, however, should take into account the potential pitfalls of having a large chunk of one's net worth hinge on a single entity.

Employee Stock Purchase Plans

Many employees pass up the opportunity to participate in their company's stock purchase plan because they think they already own too much company stock. These plans can be so attractive, however, that they often makes sense even for those with stock options or other forms of equity compensation.

Under what's called a Section 423 Employee Stock Purchase Plan (ESPP), a company gives you the option to purchase company stock, often at a discount, through payroll deduction. The purchase price can be as much as 15 percent below the stock value. To participate, you must sign up by a specified date to permit the company withhold up to 15 percent of your paycheck (to a maximum of $25,000 annually) to purchase the company stock over the stated purchase period, which typically runs for six months.

Here's the interesting part: The maximum discount on the stock price of 15 percent may be much greater because of the look back feature. This feature bases the purchase price discount on the lower of the market price at the beginning of the offering period or the price at the end of the period. For example, if the stock is selling for $10 a share at the beginning of the purchase period and goes up to $20 by the end of it, the purchase price remains just $8.50 a share. So you own stock worth $20 a share but only paid $8.50 for it. That's a stellar 135 percent return in just six months!

And you don't lose even if the price goes down. If a stock sells for $10 a share at the beginning of the purchase period but drops to $5 by the end, you only pay $4.25 a share for it. Typically, ESPPs permit refunds of amounts owing to you up until the final purchase date. If this becomes necessary, the company will refund any amounts you had withheld from your paycheck. Unfortunately, you won't get any interest on that money.

Even at companies that don't offer stock at a discount, you still can't lose regardless of whether the stock goes up or down. If the stock priced at $10 a share at the beginning of the purchase period rises to $20 by the end of it, you still receive a significant discount because you get each share at half-price. If the stock drops during the offering period, you can just instruct the company to refund amounts withheld from your paycheck for the stock purchase.

Tax Treatment of ESPPs

For tax purposes, ESPP purchases are treated as follows:

- ❖ **Payroll deduction:** Amounts deducted from your paycheck that are used to buy stock are included in income. You don't get a tax deduction for them.

- ❖ **Stock purchase:** No taxes are reported when you acquire the stock.

- ❖ **Selling the stock:** If you hold on to the stock for at least one year after the you bought it and two years from the beginning of the purchase period, the amount of the discount (or the gain on the sale, if lower) is taxed at ordinary income rates. The rest is treated as a long-term capital gain. Other tax rules apply if you don't satisfy this holding period. As the rules are fairly complex, it's wise to check with a tax professional before you make any moves.

The fact that you can buy stock at a significant discount and get your money back if you later change your mind, make ESPPs an attractive option for many employees. Be sure not to overlook this benefit.

Keep Good Records

Don't expect your company to remember when you exercised stock options or sold stock. That's something you need to do yourself. If you have stock options, create a spreadsheet that lists the date and number of stock grants, type of grant (e.g., nonqualified or incentive stock options), strike price, expiration date, and vesting schedule. Mystockoptions.com has an options record keeper that you can complete online.

Good records will also come in handy when you sell the stock. People often don't exercise options or buy stock all at once but do it gradually over a period of several months or years. If they don't provide specific instructions when they sell the stock, the IRS assumes they are using FIFO, or first-in, first out. Under this method, the shares sold first are those you bought first. If the shares you bought first were the cheapest, your taxable gain will be larger than if you specified shares you bought later on.

Example: Sam bought 100 shares of Silly Software Solutions stock in 1998 at $10 a share and another 100 shares in 1999 at $20 a share. He sold 100 shares of the stock in 2000 for $30 a share. Because he didn't specify which shares he sold, the IRS assumed he sold the shares he purchased earliest first and based the tax on that cost of $10 a share. Had he instructed his broker to sell the second share lot, his tax would have been lower.

If you specify which share lot you're selling, be sure you get a confirmation spelling out your instructions from the broker.

The Value of Diversifying

Good news is having your efforts rewarded to the point where your company's stock constitutes a large chunk of your net worth. Bad news is putting too many eggs in one basket, whether that basket is company stock, gold bullion, or pork belly futures, your risk level shoots up dramatically. To moderate that risk, you need to diversify into other kinds of investments. If you can't sell the stock because you are still working for a company or have some other type of restriction, emphasize personal investments outside the plan that balance the risks of your stock plan.

For example, someone who has lots of stock in an employer's small growing company might wish to emphasize more conservative investments such as conservative, dividend-paying stocks, or perhaps some bonds, outside the company plan.

If you are in a position to sell some of the stock and diversify into other types of investments, it may be wise to do so. Usually, it's best to exercise options or sell stock gradually to average out your price in a choppy market. The trick is to strike a balance that will allow you to continue participating in your company's upside potential without exposing you to too much risk. Chapter 13, "Putting It All Together: Your Game Plan," covers diversification principals and strategies in more detail.

Resources: Mystockoptions.com has a variety of articles on stock options as well as calculators that help you make option-related decisions, such as the tax consequences of exercising options and deciding when to exercise your options and determine what they are worth.

Tax Guide for Investors (www.fairmark.com), from Chicago area tax attorney Kaye Thomas, has an extensive section on stock options and stock-based compensation plans. Thomas also wrote a book called *Consider Your Options* (Fairmark Press, 2000), which is also worth a look.

The National Center for Employee Ownership (www.nceo.org) provides information and guidance on Employee Stock Ownership Plans (ESOPs). It's geared for employers but also offers helpful guidance to employees.

CHAPTER 7

401(k) Plans

Although many people have large 401(k) balances, these retirement plans don't fit neatly into the definition of a windfall—which occurs when a large chunk of change suddenly falls into your lap. Instead, the assets in a 401(k) accumulate for many years through careful saving and investing. Think of it as an expected rather than an unexpected windfall.

In many ways, however, a 401(k) plan bears the markings of a sudden windfall when you leave a job or retire. Suddenly, the money is under your full control. No longer is your nest egg tucked under the protective wing of your employer. It's yours to do with as you wish, and you need to make some immediate decisions to protect it.

Everyone's Windfall

Over the last 20 years, 401(k) plans have grown from a little-known section in the tax code to the plan that millions of Americans will depend on for retirement security. They represent the largest chunk of money many employees have as well as a critical source of retirement income for the future.

With regular contributions and the help of a long-running bull market during the 1980s and 1990s, it's not unusual for an employee to have several hundred thousand dollars, or more, in a 401(k) plan. Even people with relatively modest salaries who still have decades until retirement have been able to amass substantial sums.

Growth of Assets in 401(k) Plans

Year	($ in Billions)
1990	$385
1991	$440
1992	$553
1993	$616
1994	$675
1995	$864
1996	$1,061
1997	$1,264
1998	$1,459
1999	$1,715
2000	$1,712*

Preliminary data

Figures for 1997 through 2000 are estimates; source: Investment Company Institute, Federal Reserve Board, and Department of Labor

While tax consequences are an immediate concern when you leave a job or retire, you will also have to weigh new investment choices down the road if you move your money out of the company plan. Whereas your company may have only offered its own stock and perhaps six or seven mutual funds, the world of investment options is virtually limitless once your money leaves the company.

Your 401(k) and You

Companies have your money pretty much locked up as long as you're working for them. They generally cannot allow employees with a 401(k) plan to make withdrawals before age $59\frac{1}{2}$, unless the employee can prove extreme financial hardship such as imminent eviction from a home or heavy uninsured medical expenses. Certain education expenses and the expenses of buying a first home also qualify. Many companies allow you to borrow from your 401(k) plan, but you still have to pay it back on a regular schedule. Once you leave your job, however, it's a whole new ball game. The money is yours. For better or worse, you can do whatever you want with it.

The $471,000 401(k) Spending Spree

By the time 36-year-old Sandy decided to leave her job of seven years, she had accumulated $100,000 in her 401(k) plan. Her last two years at the company had been particularly difficult, marked by long hours and an uneasy relationship with new co-workers. As she had committed to making regular contributions to her 401(k), Sandy had led a relatively modest lifestyle, making it all the more difficult to watch some of her peers take exotic vacations and buy expensive cars.

When she left the company, she decided it was finally time to treat herself right. Not wishing to abandon her retirement plan altogether, she decided to put half of it, or $50,000, into a retirement plan called a rollover IRA (we'll talk about these later in this chapter). The other $50,000 would go toward buying a new car, financing her new pool, and paying off some old credit card debt.

Unfortunately, Sandy hadn't factored in the impact that income taxes and the early withdrawal penalty would have on her savings. Before sending Sandy the check with the plan balance, her employer withheld 20 percent, or $20,000, for taxes. That left her with $80,000 in hand. With $50,000 already committed to other things, she had only $30,000 for the rollover IRA.

Sandy's total tax bill and penalty from the distribution was based on the $70,000 she had not put into the rollover IRA and came to $28,000. Because her employer had only withheld $20,000, Sandy needed to come up with the $8,000 difference herself.

Perhaps more disturbing is the fact that she'll have far less for retirement than if she had rolled over the entire amount. Assuming the $100,000 rollover earned an average return of 10 percent a year for 20 years, the account would have grown to $673,000. The $30,000 she actually put into the plan will only grow to $202,000. In long-term dollars, Sandy's between-job spending spree cost her $471,000!

Keep your retirement money for retirement. This may sound like obvious advice, but people often ignore it when they change jobs. Who can blame them? With six figures from a 401(k) plan staring you in the face, it's more fun to think about a new car, outdoor deck, or dream vacation than sequestering the money in a retirement account. But even if you think you'll be able to contribute more to your next 401(k) plan to make up the amount you take out, there's a good chance you won't get around to it.

The urge to splurge retirement plan money is particularly strong for people who are 20 years or more away from retirement. They believe they have plenty of time to replace any money they take out. If you're one of them, try to resist. Money from a retirement plan should be used for what the name implies—retirement. Expenses like college tuition or car payments always seem to come along, foiling even the most sincere plans to beef up retirement savings. Over the long term, you'll drastically reduce the amount you save for retirement.

Preserving Your Windfall

There are several alternatives to spending all or part of your 401(k) balance when you change jobs or retire that will allow your money to keep growing tax-deferred.

Option 1: Leave the Money in Your Former Employer's Plan

If your 401(k) balance is over $5,000, the employer has to let you leave your money in the plan, if you elect to do so, until you reach normal retirement age (usually 65). Here are two reasons you might want to choose this option:

- ❖ **You're not ready to make any changes.** Changing jobs or retiring is a big step. Maybe you're not ready to start thinking about what you want to do with your 401(k) just yet. Staying put may sound lazy, but it's not a bad choice if you know you want to keep your money in a tax-sheltered retirement account but haven't evaluated all your alternative investment options. And it's not an irrevocable decision. You can move your money somewhere else months, or even years, down the road.

❖ **You have made after-tax contributions.** Most people contribute to a 401(k) on a pre-tax basis, thus their contributions are deducted from current income and not subject to income tax until withdrawal. In certain situations—most commonly when a highly compensated employee wants to contribute more than the plan allows on a pre-tax basis—a 401(k) account might contain after-tax contributions. In that case, withdrawing money from the rollover IRA may be a bit more complicated than you may be comfortable with right now. (For more details on this, see the sidebar in this chapter that addresses the question "How do I handle after-tax contributions in a rollover?")

From the Answer Desk

How do I handle after-tax contributions in a rollover?

Q: As a recent retiree, I am considering rolling over my 401(k) into an IRA to expand my investment choices. Approximately 25 percent of the 401(k) consists of after-tax contributions and their earnings. Here are my questions:

Are the after-tax contributions eligible for a rollover?

Are the earnings on the after-tax contributions eligible for a rollover?

If that portion of the 401(k) is ineligible for rollover, can the eligible portion be rolled over? And what happens to the ineligible portion?

—Tom

A: According to Greg Hilton, JD, CPA, CFP, a Chicago-area financial planner, "You can roll over your entire 401(k), including nondeductible contributions, into an IRA."

When you take the money out, says Hilton, all the IRS will care about is the total amount of the nondeductible contributions and the total current value of your IRAs. Any withdrawal you make, regardless of whether it is from an account that was started with deductible or nondeductible contributions, will be taxed the same, based on the fraction of the current value of all your IRAs that was already taxed.

Putting it another way, your pre-tax contributions and all earnings in the account will be subject to income taxes when you take the money out. However, the portion attributable to after-tax contributions will be excluded from income because you've already paid taxes on it. To avoid overpaying, you need to keep track of the portion of your IRA money that's attributable to those after-tax contributions so you don't pay taxes on those amounts twice.

Sound complicated? It is! You need to keep meticulous records. If you're considering a rollover from a 401(k) plan that contains after-tax contributions to an IRA, consult a tax professional.

Let's say you like your former employer's plan. The range of investment choices among 401(k) plans varies widely from company to company. Some offer company stock and two or three mutual funds while others give employees access to just about any investment they could get on their own outside the plan. If you are perfectly happy with your former employer's investment options, there's nothing wrong with just staying put.

Let's say you are age 55 or older and want access to the money. Employer 401(k) plans allow withdrawals from a 401(k) account without the 10 percent early withdrawal penalty for individuals who have separated from service in the year they reach age 55 or older. (Once you open an IRA, you may be subject to a 10 percent early withdrawal penalty on any distributions you take before age 59$\frac{1}{2}$.)

If you leave the money with your old company, your account will remain pretty much the same as before you left. You will still receive account statements from the mutual fund family or other plan administrator, who you can contact to answer any questions or to make any changes. The difference is that you won't be able to add any money to that account.

Option 2: Move Your 401(k) into a Rollover IRA

An IRA rollover is a way to transfer money tax-free from a 401(k), IRA, or other retirement plan into another kind of retirement plan called a rollover IRA. The amount you roll over is not subject to current taxes and continues to accumulate tax-deferred until you take it out of the plan.

If you leave your job and wish to conduct a rollover, there are two ways to do it:

❖ **A regular rollover.** With a regular rollover, you instruct your employer to send you a check for the amount in your 401(k) plan. You'll actually receive 20 percent less than that because companies must withhold 20 percent of your money for income taxes. You must deposit the money into a rollover IRA within 60 days of receiving the check. Otherwise, the IRS will consider it a distribution and the amount will be subject to income taxes and a 10 percent penalty if you're under age 55.

❖ **A trustee-to-trustee transfer.** In what is often called a direct rollover, you do not receive a check from your employer. Instead, the money in your 401(k) plans is wired directly to a brokerage firm, mutual fund, or other trustee. You never get the tempting smell of money on your hands.

Some people prefer a regular rollover because it's similar to a temporary loan that you pay back within 60 days. For example, if you are changing jobs and moving to a new city, you can use the rollover money to pay moving expenses that you know your new employer will reimburse within 60 days.

But here's where things can get complicated. Let's say you are rolling over a $150,000 plan balance into an IRA, using the regular rollover method rather than a direct rollover. You receive a check from your employer for $120,000 ($150,000 less 20 percent for withholding). After a couple of months, you are ready to complete the transaction by depositing the $150,000 from your 401(k) into an IRA.

But wait a minute! Because of the withholding, you only have $120,000. What about the rest? You have to wait until you file your income taxes to get a refund for the $30,000 that your employer withheld.

Bottom line: Unless you can come up with the $30,000 out of your own pocket, you'll only be able to deposit $120,000 into the regular rollover IRA. If you can't, the amount that was not rolled over into the IRA—in this case, $30,000—will be treated as a taxable distribution, which means it will be subject to regular income taxes and a possible 10 percent penalty. You'll still get the $30,000 refund, but with a big chunk removed because of the income tax and penalty.

If you plan to do a regular rollover, just be sure to re-deposit the entire rollover amount, as well as any amounts withheld by your former employer, within 60 days to avoid the tax and penalty. As a precaution, keep documentation for both sides of the transaction to show when the withdrawal and re-deposit were made. If you're depositing the money by mail, leave at least a few days' leeway because the 60-day period ends when the financial institution receives the check, not when it is mailed.

From the Answer Desk

Can I roll over my 401(k) into a Roth IRA?

Q: I am about to change jobs. I have a 401(k) with my current employer and a self-funded Roth IRA. When I change jobs, can I roll over my 401(k) into the Roth IRA even if I have already made the maximum $2,000 annual contribution?

—Fred

A: Under present law, you may roll over your current employer's 401(k) into a rollover IRA and then convert to a Roth IRA. You may not directly convert your 401(k) to a Roth IRA. The contribution limits imposed on traditional and Roth IRAs are coordinated. Thus, the maximum total yearly contribution that can be made by an individual to all IRA's (traditional and Roth) is $2,000 (for 2001), not counting rollovers or conversions.

—Sidney Blum, CPA, CFP

(*Note:* Amounts you can contribute to an IRA and other retirement savings plans increase beginning in 2002. For more details, see Chapter 14, "Tackling Taxes.")

Option 3: Move the Money to Your New Employer's Plan

While most people associate a rollover with IRAs, you can also roll over the balance from your former employer's 401(k) plan to your new employer's 401(k). You will probably decide to do this, for example, if you like the new employer's investment options and if you want to have all your money in one account. Not all companies allow for rollovers from an old plan because of the eligibility waiting period—be sure to check with your new employer first.

Taking Your Lumps

Most people are better off keeping their 401(k) money in a tax-deferred retirement account through one of the three options discussed in the preceding section. Some people, however, might want to take the money in one lump sum, pay income taxes (and, if you are under age $59^1/_2$, any penalties), and use it right away. This generally isn't a good idea, though, because:

- ❖ You get a big tax bite and possible penalty up front.
- ❖ You lose the benefit of tax-deferred compounding.

One bit of solace: If you were born before 1936, you will be eligible for more favorable tax treatment, such as 10-year averaging. Otherwise, the distribution is taxable as ordinary income. You won't have to pay the 10 percent penalty, however, if:

- ❖ You are at least age $59^1/_2$ or are disabled or dead (will you really care at that point?).
- ❖ You have reached age 55 and have retired or left your job.
- ❖ The money goes toward medical bills that exceed 7.5 percent of your adjusted gross income.
- ❖ You take the money gradually in annuity-like payments.

❖ The money is going to an ex-spouse pursuant to a divorce decree.

A Little-Known Payout Option

There is a little-known payout option that allows individuals of any age to take money out of a 401(k) plan without penalty. The catch is, you have to establish a regular withdrawal plan and stick with it for at least five years and until you reach age 59½. Therefore, if you begin taking money out at age 50, you'll need to continue doing so for about another 10 years.

The withdrawal amounts are based on complicated IRS formulas (for more information on these formulas, you can comb through IRS Publication 590, "Individual Retirement Arrangements") that stretch out payments over many years if you are young. This is not something you would choose to do if you need a big chunk of money right away. Furthermore, it's probably not a sensible idea for anyone to raid his or her retirement account for anything other than retirement.

Company Stock: Take the Money and Run

Most of the time, it makes sense to keep your money in a tax-sheltered retirement plan when you retire, either by leaving it with your old employer or by rolling it over into an IRA. One possible exception: company stock.

If the stock has appreciated significantly, you may save on taxes by withdrawing the shares and putting them in a taxable account rather than rolling them into an IRA. If you do that, the gains on the stock after you leave the company will be taxed at favorable capital gains rates rather than ordinary income tax rates when you make withdrawals from a retirement plan.

Here's how it works: Assume you have left your job and have stock worth $50,000. If you take it as a distribution, you'll need to pay income tax. But that tax isn't based on $50,000. It's based on what the stock cost the plan, or the cost basis. If the average cost for the shares is $20,000, that means you will pay income taxes only on that amount. The difference between the market value at the distribution date and the cost of the shares—called net unrealized appreciation—will be eligible for the favorable 20 percent maximum long-term capital gains tax rate. And that $30,000 gain will be postponed until you sell the shares. Further, any appreciation after the distribution will also be eligible for long-term capital gains treatment if the holding period exceeds one year.

By contrast, if you rolled the shares into an IRA, you would not pay any tax immediately. But you would pay presumably higher income tax rates on the value of the stock when you take the money out.

Holding company stock in a taxable account is also better for your heirs. They will receive the stock at its market value at the time they inherit it and pay taxes only on the difference between that price and what they sell it for. The entire gain between the time you left the company until the time they inherit the stock escapes taxation. (*Note:* Beginning in 2010 with the repeal of the estate tax, this "stepped-up" basis for figuring out the tax on inherited property will also be repealed.)

Success the Second Time Around

Congratulations! You've navigated the tax minefield of rolling over a 401(k) plan, made the right choices, and are planted behind the desk of your new job. Even if your previous retirement plan grew by leaps and bounds, whether through the luck of working for a company whose stock has gone up, careful saving, or both, you can't assume that will necessarily happen again.

Despite the popularity of 401(k) plans, evidence suggests that people often invest in ways that frequently leave them coming up short when they are ready to retire. A few guidelines can help you repeat the success you had with your first plan.

Don't Get Too Conservative

Many people pour money in very conservative, low-yielding investments such as guaranteed investment contacts, or GICs. Under a GIC, sometimes called a stable value fund, an insurance company guarantees payment of a set rate of interest over a specified period of time.

According to a recent survey by Buck Consultants, a benefits consulting firm, 62 percent of companies offer some form of stable value fund as an investment option. At these companies, participants have an average of over 28 percent of assets invested there.

Many people make the mistake of equating conservative investing with safe investing. But conservative investments often earn less, so you lose out to inflation over the long run.

Squeezing out just a couple of extra percentage points in return through more aggressive investing can make a big difference over time. Someone who contributes $100 a month to a 401(k) account earning 10 percent, for example, could expect to retire with $227,933 after 30 years. If the account earned 7 percent, the nest egg would grow to $122,709.

Don't Get Wedded to Company Stock

Many public companies match employee contributions with company stock. Individuals who also allocate much of their voluntary contributions to their employer's stock can easily find the lion's share of their 401(k) plan invested in their employer.

With the stock market bull blessing so many companies with good fortune in the 1980s and 1990s, some participants might feel satisfied with the strategy. But as the recent bear market has shown, however, stocks don't always go up. Loading up on employer shares could backfire if your company's stock plunges into a prolonged downturn. Many experts recommend that no more than 10 to 15 percent of your overall savings from all company plans be allocated toward company stock. It's a message worth listening to.

The Downside of Betting the Ranch

Even if you've managed to accumulate a sizable sum in your 401(k) plan, nothing can decimate its value more quickly than having your employer's stock take a prolonged turn for the worse. Despite this, a recent study by the Employee Benefits Research Institute and the Investment Company Institute found that employees who work at companies that match their 401(k) contributions with company stock still allocate nearly 30 percent of their own contributions to that same stock. In total, they have over half their total 401(k) account balances in company stock. At companies where there is no employer stock match, employees still direct about one fifth of their contributions to company stock.

While this kind of dedication might seem like a good idea, it's dangerous to pin so much of your retirement future on one stock. Even if you think your employer has a great new product set to conquer the world or just a good business plan, bear markets have a nasty habit of dragging good companies down with bad ones. The stock may not recover for many years.

That message hit home in early 2001 when media headlines trumpeted the impact that a bear market had on 401(k) retirement accounts. In March, *USA Today* ran an article titled "Sinking Stocks Scramble Nest Eggs: Americans' Retirement Savings Are Shrinking At an Alarming Rate, Exposing the Risks of Do-It-Yourself Investing." The article mentioned one 53-year-old employee who had put 100 percent of his 401(k) assets into his employer's stock. The account had lost 60 percent of its value in the past year.

Consider the *Time* magazine story about 401(k) plans overloaded with company stock titled "Time Bomb." In it, author Daniel Kadlec relays the plight of a Lucent employee whose 401(k) balance, which was invested exclusively in employer stock, plummeted from $500,000 to $130,000 in just one year.

With stock options or an ESOP, you don't have a choice about where to invest. These plans are what their label implies—incentive plans designed to motivate employees to do well—that have at their core company stock. You know what you're getting into.

A 401(k) plan should be viewed differently. It's not a stock incentive plan. It's a retirement savings plan that provides access to company stock and other investment options. Unless you want to bet the ranch on the company you work for, you should take advantage of the other investment options, too.

Diversify

People typically invest in just a couple of mutual fund options, regardless of the number of funds available to them. Rarely do they spread their choices across a broad spectrum of asset classes. The most common choices are a bond fund and a balanced fund or a bond fund and an index fund.

Employees generally ignore investment options that are even a little out of the mainstream. International funds, for example, draw only six percent of 401(k) assets at companies offering that option. Emerging markets funds attract much less than that.

Companies have been criticized for not offering a variety of investment choices. Plan administrators often find it too expensive and cumbersome to offer more exotic options, such as a commodities or emerging markets fund, when few people are likely to choose them.

Remember to Rebalance

Asset allocation is a continual process. As the markets fluctuate, you'll need to rebalance your account at least once a year to bring it into line with your desired asset allocation strategy. While it may be tempting to leave your stock market gains on the table rather than transfer them to the more conservative side of your investment balance sheet, spreading your bets by rebalancing will help cushion the impact of a market downturn.

People who don't want to be bothered with periodic rebalancing, or who want to have their asset allocation decisions made for them, might consider "lifestyle funds," an increasingly popular choice for 401(k) plans. These funds have preset asset allocations related to a particular investor profile, such as conservative, moderate, or aggressive.

The main drawback of lifestyle funds is a "wrap fee," which fund companies charge for assembling and managing the portfolio of funds. This fee generally ranges from 0.5 to 1 percent of assets and is charged in addition to regular mutual fund expenses associated with the component funds.

Balanced funds are another popular option. These funds maintain a fairly consistent 60/40 split of stocks to bonds and don't carry a wrap fee.

Stay Tough When the Going Gets Rough

R. Theodore Benna, president of the 401(k) Association, a consumer group, recalls how 401(k) investors bailed out of the stock funds in droves after the October 1987 stock market crash. Ten years later, after the Asian currency crisis hit, most of them stayed put.

"I think people are getting more knowledgeable about investing and the benefits of hanging in during rough markets," says Benna. "But we haven't tested how people might react with a more prolonged downturn."

Ask About Other Investment Options

Sometimes the mutual fund company acting as plan administrator allows participants to occasionally purchase funds from outside the fund family. They don't always advertise or encourage this service, though, so you need to ask if it's available.

Coordinate Your Investments

Remember that asset allocation recommendations from mutual fund literature or guidebooks are intended to be rough guidelines to use in tailoring your personal situation. Traditional wisdom such as "shift your 401(k) investments into cash as you get closer to retirement," may not always apply, says Dee Lee, a Harvard, Massachusetts, financial planner and author of *The Compete Idiot's Guide to 401(k) Plans* (Alpha Books, 1998). Lee adds:

> Most people tend to diversify within each account, rather than view their assets in the aggregate. If you have lots of money in CDs or a money market fund outside your 401(k) plan, it's okay to remain fairly aggressive, since you may not be tapping the plan for many years. On the other hand, if a

401(k) is likely to be your only source of income, a gradual shift to safer investments may be appropriate.

Once you retire, it's best to use other available sources of income first to allow your retirement plan balance to continue taking advantage of tax-deferred compounding, Lee recommends.

Borrowing from Your 401(k) Plan

One of the fastest ways to put a crimp in your 401(k) fortune is to borrow money from your plan. The move becomes especially dicey if you are changing jobs or retiring because borrowed money that isn't paid back into the plan when you leave will be treated as a distribution and subject to ordinary income tax plus the 10 percent penalty if you're under age 59^1/$_2$. In a worst-case scenario, you could be laid off from a company, have no income, and be faced with the prospect of paying back a substantial loan or facing a hefty tax burden. If you can't pay off the loan or the tax and penalty with outside funds, you'll need to take money from your 401(k) plan to do it. So much for your windfall.

Not that borrowing from a 401(k) isn't tempting. Many employers have loan provisions that allow employees to borrow up to one half of their account balance, to a maximum of $50,000. You can usually take up to five years to pay back the loan unless the funds are used to purchase a principal residence. In that case, payback can take up to 25 years. And there's no lengthy approval process. Usually, getting a loan takes less than two weeks. The interest rate is about what you'd get from a local bank, and the loan is repaid back into your account through money that is taken out of your paycheck. The nice thing is that you're paying back principal and interest to yourself, not the bank.

But beyond the ugliness of an unpaid 401(k) loan when you leave a company, borrowing from your plan probably isn't all that wonderful an idea even while you're working because:

❖ There's a good chance you won't make contributions, or will reduce them, when you're paying back the loan. You may feel as if you're contributing to your retirement plan through regular repayments, but all you're really doing is putting back money that was there before.

❖ The money used for paying back the loan is deducted from your paycheck and subject to taxes. Your original, pre-tax contributions have suddenly become taxable. And interest payments on 401(k) loans are not tax deductible.

Bottom line: Don't borrow from a 401(k) plans unless you really, really have to.

New Minimum Distribution Rules

If you are getting ready to retire, a recent change in the minimum distributions rules for 401(k) plans, IRAs, and other qualified retirement plans may affect your planning decisions. These rules can be implemented immediately and become mandatory starting January 1, 2002, for 401(k) plans. The people affected most are those who have other sources of income at retirement and wish to postpone drawing from retirement plan assets as long as possible so that their money can continue to grow tax-deferred.

The mandatory date at which you must begin taking payments has long been April 1 of the year following the year you reach age 70¹/₂. That doesn't change. Here is what has changed:

❖ **The way minimum payments are calculated.** The new rules make it easier to compute minimum withdrawals, and to stretch them out over a longer period than you could before, by changing the way you determine life expectancy.

Prior to the changes, plan owners had to choose from a number of complex calculation methods. Now they can use just one uniform IRS life expectancy table that applies to most people. Generally, the new method allows you to stretch payments out longer than you could before. If a spousal beneficiary is more than a decade younger than the account owner, minimum withdrawals can be based on the actual joint life expectancies of the couple instead of on the uniform table. This results in even smaller required withdrawals.

❖ **The rules governing changes in beneficiary designations.** Under the old rules, any beneficiary designations you made when required withdrawals began had a permanent effect on minimum distributions. Once you made the election, that was it. Now you can revise beneficiary designations and alter any future minimum payment calculations based on those changes.

Beneficiaries can now alter beneficiary designations after the death of the account holder, which couldn't happen before. This might be helpful, for example, if two siblings are named as beneficiaries of a retirement account, but only one needs the money. Previously, they could not change the designation the account holder had made. Now, if one wishes to disclaim the benefit, they can alter the original beneficiary designation until the end of the calendar year following the account holder's death.

From the Answer Desk

Now that I'm on disability, should I take my 401(k) money and put it into an IRA?

Q: I have a 401(k) with my ex-employer, and I'm currently on disability and not working. My ex-employer is giving me the option to either leave it where it is until I retire or pull it out.

My question is whether I'm better off leaving it as is or pulling it out and putting it into an IRA. Also, will I encounter any type of penalties if I decide to pull it out (again, I'm on disability)?
—John

A: As a general rule, I think you are better off rolling your 401(k) balance into an IRA rather than leaving it with your employer.

The primary reason is that your 401(k) investment options are limited to what is in the plan. This could be as few as four or five mutual funds. An IRA offers the whole universe of investment products. Another reason to roll over is because your 401(k) may be subjected to fees and administrative costs, which your IRA will avoid.

But not so fast. You haven't mentioned how old you are or when you will need the money. Be aware that, with limited exceptions, you will pay a penalty for money taken out of your IRA prior to age $59^1/_2$. If, however, you are 55 or older when you leave your job, withdrawals from your 401(k) are penalty free.

The conclusion seems to be that if you are over age $59^1/_2$, you should switch to an IRA, taking out money later, as needed. If you are between 55 and $59^1/_2$, you could take the cash you are going to need up front and put the rest into an IRA. If you are under age 55, balance your future withdrawal needs against the investment options.

—Greg Hilton, JD, CPA, CFP

Your Estate and You

Many people know that a 401(k) or IRA is included in the assets column when you are trying to figure out the size of an estate. What they often don't remember is how those assets are treated when they pass to heirs.

Attorneys say one of the biggest mistakes people make when planning estates is forgetting that some or all the money in these tax-deferred accounts has never been taxed. While Uncle Sam has generously allowed the earnings to grow tax-deferred and contributions to be made on a pre-tax basis, the party doesn't last forever. The tax bill comes when you take the money out of the plan; or, if you die before that happens, when your heirs take the money out.

In the latter case, the beneficiaries have to pay income taxes. That's bad enough. If there isn't enough money to pay estate taxes, your heirs may have to raid the retirement account to do it, and immediately lose up to three quarters of its value.

Bottom line: If you think your estate may be subject to taxes, make sure you have enough life insurance or liquid assets outside the retirement plan for heirs to pay them.

Moving On, Wisely

All too often, people think of a 401(k) plan as a standby source for a loan, a place to load up on employer stock, or a temporary parking spot for savings they can tap into as soon as they leave a job. With many companies no longer guaranteeing their employees a steady pension, however, 401(k) plans have taken on a critical role in retirement planning and security. Understanding your options when you leave a job or retire will help you preserve what may well be your largest financial asset.

CHAPTER 8

Other Windfall Events

While inheritances, stock plans and stock options, and retirement plans are among the most common windfall sources, windfalls can come from a variety of other channels as well. Among them are divorce, the lottery, or an insurance settlement.

Financial Consequences of Divorce

With legal fees that can send shudders down your spine and your checking account into a tailspin, divorce may look like a quick route to the poorhouse rather than a road-to-riches windfall. While divorces are inarguably costly affairs much of the time, they also can involve receiving a sizable lump sum settlement that carries with it the necessity to make numerous far-reaching financial decisions. More importantly, the process requires spouses to make informed choices about who gets what before they sign on the dotted line so that they don't feel cheated months or years after the divorce is final.

Unfortunately, these choices must be made at a time when both partners are going through what may be the most wrenching experience of their lives. Emotions can range from fear and helplessness to anger and a desire to manipulate. One or both partners may view money as a medium for playing out feelings of anger and revenge. Yet because of taxes and other considerations, making the wrong choices in a divorce can take the wind out of a windfall fairly quickly.

Here are some of the assets often involved in a divorce-related windfall and some common sticking points to consider during negotiations.

Divorce Statistics

Percent of first marriages that fail	Over 50
Percent of second marriages that fail	Over 60

Median Age of Divorce

Men	35.6
Women	33.2
Average length of a divorce proceeding	One year

Home Is Where the Heart Is

Often the most valuable piece of marital property, the house, is the core of a contentious battle. The key consideration here, whether or not you intend to continue living in the house, is how any equity in the home is taxed when it is sold.

If you sell a primary residence that both of you lived in for at least two of the last five years before the sale, you may exclude up to $250,000 if you are single (up to $500,000 if you are married and filing jointly) from capital gains, which are taxed at a maximum rate of 20 percent. If you are still married by the end of the sale year, you and your soon-to-be ex may be able to walk away a maximum of $250,000 each, tax-free.

Things get a bit more complicated when one partner remains in the home after the divorce and the other leaves. When the home is transferred between spouses, it is not taxable because it is treated as a gift. This rule automatically applies between ex-spouses up to one year after the end of the marriage. However, the individual who now owns the home will have to worry about taxes when it is sold.

Example: A husband and wife buy a house for $200,000. The wife gets full ownership of the house when they divorce, at which point it is worth $350,000. There is no tax due at this point. When she sells it, however, she will need to calculate her capital gains tax based on the original purchase price, not on the value at the time of divorce. If she is single when she sells the house and her gain exceeds $250,000, she may be liable for capital gains taxes. For this reason, any divorce settlement involving appreciated property—which can also include stocks, bonds, and other assets—should take into account taxes the owner will need to pay on the gain.

A common mistake, particularly among women, is to give up more than they should to get the house in a divorce. Even though you can't live in stock options or remodel a retirement plan, in the long run they may be more valuable than a home. Furthermore, consider your ability to pay the mortgage if you choose to become the sole owner. With escalating real estate values, it often takes more than one income to keep up mortgage payments.

Stocks, Mutual Funds, and Other Securities

During divorce negotiations, your spouse proposes transferring to you $30,000 worth of XYZ stock, instead of $30,000 in certificates of deposit as originally planned. As the stock seems to be doing well, that sounds fair enough. But before you jump at the proposal, think about what happens when you sell the shares.

There's no problem when the transfer occurs because spouses can transfer investment assets in taxable accounts tax-free while they are still married. This holds true even after the divorce if the transfer is pursuant to a divorce property settlement and is made up to six years after the divorce. But the picture changes later on.

Let's say you decide to take the stock in lieu of the cash and you become the sole owner of the shares, which had been jointly owned before the divorce. You want to celebrate the end of the grueling divorce experience you've been through, so you decide to sell the stock and take a trip around the world. Assuming the stock is still worth $30,000, you'll receive that much from the sale. But you'll also have to pay taxes on any gains.

The original date of purchase determines the cost basis and holding period of the shares for tax purposes. Thanks to a long bull market, the stock, which you originally bought with your spouse 10 years ago for $10,000, has seen a $20,000 gain. This means that when you sell, you will owe taxes on that gain. Assuming the $20,000 is taxed at long-term capital gains rates, a tax bill of $4,000 plus any state or local taxes that may apply will land on your doorstep.

If you had instead received the CDs and sold them, no tax would be due (although you would have to pay income taxes on the interest they produced). Keeping this in mind, you should either …

- Try to get securities that won't leave you with a hefty tax bill when you sell them, such as certificates of deposit.
- Factor taxes into the negotiation process.

In other words …

- Reduce the value of any security by the amount of the tax liability.
- Agree to a reimbursement arrangement when the property is sold or disposed of.

The same principle applies when weighing the merits of various securities against each other. Assume that you and your near-ex jointly own two mutual funds, each worth $20,000. You might think the fair thing would be for each of you to become sole owner of one of the funds.

Not so fast! If you purchased Fund 1 ten years ago and Fund 2 last year, chances are the capital gains tax for Fund 1 will be a lot higher because it has had more time to appreciate. What seems like an equal split would not really be equal after all.

To avoid taxes when transferring property after the divorce, be sure to make it clear that the transfer is incident to divorce. Transfers made up to one year after the breakup automatically qualify for tax-free transfer treatment. So do transfers made up to six years afterward if they are pursuant to a divorce settlement. To make sure the IRS does not consider the transfer a taxable sale, however, the divorce papers should stipulate that the property that is transferred is part of the settlement.

Inheritances and Gifts

Marital property includes all property that each spouse has acquired during the marriage. Separate property consists of …

- Anything that either individual acquired before the marriage.
- An inheritance or gift acquired during the marriage.
- Property acquired after a separation.

Don't automatically assume that any of these items, including inheritances and gifts, are up for grabs in a divorce. Even community property states where earnings and assets acquired during the marriage are assumed to belong to both partners make an exception for inheritances and gifts, regardless of whether or not someone acquired them during the marriage. If you received an inheritance from a family member either before or during the marriage, for example, you may be able to walk away from the marriage with your legacy intact.

Then again, you may not. The trouble with keeping separate assets separate is that people often don't. Once separate property is commingled into the marital pot—for example, if someone receives an inheritance and puts it into a joint account, it becomes increasingly difficult to prove where separate property begins and marital property ends.

Keeping separate property like an inheritance or gift in your name alone may seem a bit cold and calculating in a marriage where both partners are supposed to trust each other and have faith in their union's stability. In the event of a divorce, however, it will create a cleaner line between "mine" and "ours."

Retirement Accounts

Even though you may consider retirement plan assets to be off limits until retirement, that doesn't mean they are off limits in a divorce. In many cases, retirement plans constitute the largest chunk of financial assets a couple has.

Company Plans

If part of your divorce settlement involves a qualified retirement plan, such as a 401(k) or pension, you need to follow some guidelines to avoid tax missteps. The key document here is what's called a qualified domestic relations order, or QDRO. This establishes an ex-spouse's right to receive part of the account balance, or in the case of a pension plan, benefit payments. It may also outline specific terms such as which retirement plans are to be split or the percentage of the plan to be paid out in the settlement.

If you are seeking to obtain assets from a spouse's plan ...

❖ Make sure you have QDRO. Otherwise, the plan administrator at the company may not permit access to the assets.

❖ When you receive the distribution, figure out whether you want to roll it over into an IRA, keep it with the employer, or take it in a lump sum. The last option would trigger income taxes but not the 10 percent penalty that normally applies to distributions if you're under age $59^1/_2$.

❖ Be sure to check with all your spouse's ex-employers to see if he or she was entitled to a "defined benefit pension"—the kind of plan that pays a guaranteed income at retirement versus a self-funded savings plan like a 401(k).

Although these kinds of plans are becoming increasingly rare in the corporate world as they are expensive for companies to maintain, but they still exist. In companies that offer them, it can take as little as three years for someone to vest or qualify to receive a pension. Even though a spouse may not be eligible to receive that pension for many years, you may still have a right to a part of it. Think back and be sure to check with employers where a spouse has worked for three years or more.

❖ If you work for a company with a 401(k) plan or other retirement plan that will be part of a divorce settlement, make sure your plan administrator does not make distributions without a qualified domestic relations order. Otherwise, you could be liable for taxes and penalties on the distribution.

IRAs and SEP-IRAs

If an IRA or SEP-IRA (a kind of IRA for the self-employed) is part of the divorce settlement, your spouse can roll over the money from his or her IRA to one that you have set up for yourself, which will then become yours to invest and manage. Neither of you will be liable for taxes or penalties at that point. You do not need a QDRO to divide IRA accounts, but the transfer needs to be outlined in the divorce settlement.

From then on, the rules that apply to any other IRA apply to you. If you take the money out before age 59½, you will be socked with a 10 percent penalty for early withdrawal plus any income taxes unless you qualify for one of the exceptions to this rule. Since the exceptions to the penalty rule include such nasty occurrences as death and disability, you probably won't want to be part of the club that qualifies. Once you begin taking withdrawals at retirement, you will pay applicable income taxes.

The important thing to remember about retirement plans such as 401(k)s and IRAs is that the pre-tax contributions and any earnings in the account have not been taxed yet. That will happen when the money comes out. If you have received such plans as part of a divorce, you will be the one footing the bill. If you are in the top federal income tax bracket when you make withdrawals, that means nearly 40 percent of those amounts could go to Uncle Sam.

This treatment is very different from money outside of a retirement plan that's held in a taxable account. Because you (or you and your spouse) have already paid taxes on the principal and any interest or gains in the account, there is no tax liability when you take the money out. The only thing you need to worry about is paying future taxes on investment income and capital gains. In addition, the money is easier to get to before retirement.

Bottom line: Weigh your options carefully. With taxes in mind, $100,000 from an account in which contributions and earnings have already been taxed may be more valuable to you than $100,000 from an IRA.

Caution: Be sure that the wording in the divorce papers specifies that the transfer of an IRA or SEP-IRA has been made pursuant to a divorce settlement. Otherwise, your ex could be hit with income taxes and a possible penalty in the year the transfer is made. Sure, that leaves you with a tax-free windfall and your ex with a nasty tax headache. But do you really want to stick someone else with a tax bill (yes, even the person you are divorcing) because of an oversight?

Stock Options: Worth More Than You Think

A few years ago, divorcing couples often paid little attention to stock options. Today, with more companies including stock options in their compensation packages, they can be the focal point of contentious battles. To understand why, consider the sad story of Silicon Valley Sarah and her husband Sam.

> When Sarah and Sam were in the middle of a messy divorce battle, Sarah and her lawyer were too busy worrying about dividing up the couple's assets such as the house and retirement accounts to think about some stock options Sam had with his up-and-coming software company. After all, the company consisted of only a dozen or so people and had not turned a profit yet. How much could the stock options be worth?
>
> As it turns out, plenty. A year or so after the divorce was finalized, Sam's company went public, and he made $2 million by exercising his stock options. Even though he had acquired those options during his marriage to Sarah, when they seemed fairly worthless, they had suddenly become much more valuable than even he could have imagined. Unfortunately for Sarah, she didn't receive a penny of the profits from the exercise that occurred after their marriage.

Although Sarah and Sam are a fictional couple, their situation is being played out more and more across the country as stories of sudden stock option wealth grab the headlines and people recognize the potential value of their own stock options. The question isn't always whether or not a spouse is entitled to stock options in a divorce. In many situations, the answer is yes. But who foots the tax bill and how the options are divided will depend on several factors, including whether ...

* You live in a community property state.
* The company's plan permits the transfer of stock options in a divorce.
* The options are vested at the time of the divorce.
* The spouse received the options before, during, or after the marriage or separation.

The divisibility, tax treatment, and valuation of stock options in a divorce are a tricky and confusing area of divorce law. If you or your spouse own stock options, seek out a divorce attorney who is well versed in how to handle them. To get some basic background on how stock options work and some of the tax issues surrounding them, see the guide in Chapter 6, "Stock Incentive Plans."

Most states recognize vested options as part of a property settlement, and some consider unvested options as well. Don't let a spouse try to convince you that just because the company just missed its earnings estimates or the stock is tanking, your stock options aren't worth anything. Stock markets and companies can turn around and when they do, those "worthless" options can suddenly look golden.

The next section discusses some ways to ease the transition and maximize your divorce windfall.

Find a Good Divorce Lawyer or Mediator

This may sound like obvious advice, but many people turn to the same lawyer they used for an estate plan to handle a divorce. Or, they might ask cousin Vinny who's a real estate lawyer if he can handle a divorce on the cheap. Divorce law is complex and requires the knowledge and experience of a specialist to help prevent you from coming out on the short end of things. If you don't know one, contact the American Academy of Matrimonial Lawyers at www.aaml.org, or call 312-263-6477 for a referral.

If you can sit down with a soon-to-be ex without tearing each other's hair out, divorce mediation offers a less costly option to a divorce attorney. Rather than communicating through your respective attorneys (and running up astronomical fees that can easily end up totaling $20,000 to $30,000 for each of you by the time it's all over), mediation offers the opportunity to arrive at a mutually agreeable settlement for a lot less money. If all goes smoothly, the whole thing can be handled in a few sessions for as little as $1,000.

Although mediation is most often associated with couples who have a relatively small pie to divide, wealthier couples with millions of dollars at stake have also found it useful. In complex divorce situations, you may want to check with a divorce attorney to understand negotiation points before you begin the mediation process (though you'll have to depend on his or her willingness to let a good billing opportunity slide). Even though mediation can be less costly than battling it out with lawyers, it's not always feasible in certain situations; for example, when you and your spouse are spitting bullets at each other or you suspect a spouse is hiding assets that mediation won't uncover. To learn more about the mediation process, contact the Academy of Family Mediators at 781-674-2663, or visit www.mediators.org.

Don't Overestimate the Value of a Lump Sum

Even though the lump sum you receive in a divorce might sound impressive, it may disappear more quickly than you think. Say, for example, you receive $200,000 in a divorce settlement and you put the entire amount in an account earning an 8 percent rate of return after taxes. In the first year, you make modest withdrawals totaling $24,400. Assuming your withdrawals increase by 4 percent a year to account for rising prices, the money will be depleted in 10 years.

Retitle Assets and Change Beneficiaries

Any assets you owned jointly with a spouse need to be changed to sole ownership after the divorce. Remember to change beneficiary designations on any life insurance policies you own as well as on wills and retirement plans. If you have a retirement plan at work, you will not be able to change those designations without your spouse's consent.

Don't Go on a Spending Spree

Some men and women react to the financial challenges of divorce by hunkering down and slashing expenses to the bone. Others, feeling the freedom of leaving a difficult breakup behind them and the energizing power of a large lump sum of money, go on a buying binge. If you feel the need to splurge, that's okay. However, recognize the difference between treating yourself to a well-deserved vacation and putting your financial security at risk with a prolonged spending spree.

The Lottery

Every week or so, I buy a scratch ticket to try my luck at winning the lottery. The most I've ever made at one time from this grand scheme is $20, and I know I've spent many times more on tickets than I've won. But it's hard to beat that thrill of anticipation as I scratch my little dog-eared ticket, hoping that maybe, just maybe, this time will be the charm.

We have all heard that the odds of winning any sizable amount in the lottery are something like a gazillion to one, but that doesn't stop us from dreaming about it and trying our luck. Occasionally, those dreams become reality. If you're one of the fortunate few who have struck it rich in the lottery, you'll need to do some serious planning that starts right after you've heard the good news.

Claiming the Prize

Every so often you hear about a lottery winner who hasn't claimed a multimillion dollar jackpot for several days after winning. Chances are that person knows darn well he or she has won. Most big-prize winners have been playing regularly for years and wouldn't miss an announcement for the world. Their absence can probably be explained by their foresight in assembling an advisory team to make sure no wrong moves that could cost thousands, or even millions, of dollars are made.

Like those mystery winners, you, too, should consult with advisors such as accountants, financial planners, and attorneys *before*, not after, claiming your prize. Although you may be sorely tempted to enter the ranks of the rich and fleetingly famous by rushing in to the state's lottery office and thumping your ticket on the table to collect your winnings, it is not a good idea. In many states, you can wait several months to present your ticket and claim your winnings. You may not want to wait that long, but take at least a week or two to get some solid financial advice. One decision you'll need to make fairly quickly is how to collect the money.

Example: Let's say you've won $2 million in the state lottery and you want to give $100,000 to each of your two minor children. If you collect the winnings and gift the money to them yourself, you will pay the top federal tax rate (38.6 percent in 2002) on your prize. In addition, you will have to file a gift tax return. A better alternative, if your state allows it, is to have the state pay the money to the children directly. It won't count as a gift from you but as their own separate winnings. If the money is taxed at a rate of 30 percent in 2002, that would translates to a saving of $8,600 in taxes for each child.

Generally, lottery winnings are taxable in the year you cash a winning ticket, not the year the announcement is made. Consult a tax professional about the best time to cash in your ticket. Some states allow you to collect your prize anonymously. If you wish to avoid the media circus that often accompanies the announcement of large jackpot winners as well as the barrage of brokers, insurance agents, and long-lost relatives who are likely to come out of the woodwork, consider this option seriously.

Payout Options

Years ago, most lottery winners had to take their payout over 20 or 30 years. Today, many states offer winners the option of either taking the money as a lump sum payment or taking it gradually. For example, if you win $55 million in the lottery, you could take it as one lump sum or in increments of $1.83 million over 30 years. Because those amounts catapult the winner into the highest federal income tax bracket, the take-home winnings are reduced to $33.8 million for the lump sum and $1.12 million a year for the spread-out payments.

A number of considerations factor into the decision of whether to take a lump sum or gradual payments:

* ❖ **How desperately you need the money.** Heavy debts, pressing medical bills, unemployment, or other considerations may make the lump sum payment option a necessity rather than a choice.

* ❖ **Your ability to control your spending.** Some lottery winners spend vast sums on expensive vacations, homes, gifts to friends

and family members, or cars only to find themselves with empty pockets in a year or two. It may seem hard to believe, but even newly minted lottery millionaires need to set up a budget. If you don't live within your means, you could join the ranks of lottery winners you may have heard about in the media who find themselves drowning in debt a few years after they claim their prize.

If you take payments gradually, you can only blow a little at a time. If you take a lump sum, it can be gone in a matter of weeks. If you know you're not the best person when it comes to budgeting, go for the gradual payments.

On the other hand, perhaps you have a knack for investing wisely and spending within your means. If you have that kind of discipline, the lump sum is generally the better option because you have greater control over investment and tax decisions. With the right moves, you could easily make more over the years than the total amount you'd collect under the gradual payment alternative. For better or worse, the vast majority of lottery winners who have the option take their money in a lump sum.

Keep Your Day Job

The amount you win may sound like a heck of a lot of money. After taxes and with the high cost of living, however, you may find that you'll need to keep your day job.

Estate planning is another area you'll want to take care of right away, as estates can be taxed at rates as high as 50 percent (as of 2002). Check on any retirement plans, insurance policies, and other documents that name beneficiaries to make sure they are still the same people you want to inherit your vastly expanded estate. Make sure to update your insurance. Sad to say, when you come into a windfall, especially a highly visible one like a lottery, your chances of being sued increase dramatically.

Ira was elated when he learned that he had won $1 million in his state's lottery. One of his first thoughts was how wonderful it would feel to tell his belligerent boss that he'd have to find another grunt to do his dirty work. After Uncle Sam got his share in taxes, though, Ira was left with about $600,000. After spending $100,000 on an exotic vacation for his family, a new car, and a down payment for a home, he had $500,000 to invest.

To make the money last, he'd have to limit his withdrawals to a modest amount every year. Assuming that money earned an after-tax return of 7 percent, he could only withdraw $33,500 in the first year and increase his annual withdrawals a modest 4 percent before the money would run out in 20 years. Wisely, Ira didn't say anything to his boss about quitting—at least until he finds another job.

Insurance Settlements

The tax implications of an insurance payout or legal settlement depend on several factors including who owned the policy and whether you received the money in a lump sum or as an annuity—a series of payments made over a specified period of time.

Disability Income Payments

If you have become disabled, payments from a disability policy will be subject to income taxes if you obtained the policy through your employer. If you own the policy and pay the premiums yourself, the income will be tax-free. Keep in mind that disability income payments typically stop at age 65 and are usually designed to replace between 60 and 70 percent of income.

Life Insurance

The tax treatment of proceeds from a life insurance policy depends largely on who owned the policy at the time of death. If you or your children owned the policy and your spouse dies, the proceeds will not be subject to income taxes and will not be included in the estate. If the deceased owned the policy and you are a beneficiary, the proceeds will also be income tax free. However, those amounts will become part of the estate and could be subject to estate taxes. For more information on the tax treatment of life insurance proceeds, see Chapter 3, "Estate Planning: The Next Step."

Settlements

Any settlement or award money you receive because of a physical injury, either as a lump sum or a series of payments (also called a structured settlement), is not subject to taxes. However, other types of settlements such as awards for discrimination claims, breaches of contract, or settlements for emotional distress are generally subject to income tax.

The treatment of legal fees in settlements is a somewhat fuzzy area. Lawyers working on a contingency basis, often the arrangement in personal injury cases and other types of lawsuits, usually receive between 30 and 40 percent of the settlement. Most courts have held that when a settlement is subject to taxes, the entire amount, including attorney's fees, is included in gross income. However, much of the tax attributable to those fees is offset by the deduction for the amount you paid to the attorney.

Cash for Future Payments: Just Say No

Windfalls don't always come in one big lump sum. Often people who have been injured as a result of a car crash, medical malpractice, or other legal claim receive their settlement payments gradually over time. This is called a structured settlement.

The reasoning behind structured settlements is basically sound. Allowing all or part of the windfall to be paid out over time, rather than in a lump sum, ensures accident victims and others that their money won't run out in a year or two. Many people entitled to such payments have become physically incapacitated and must rely on these payments to pay living expenses for many years. Other people, such as lottery winners, don't have a choice as most states spread large payments over 20 or more years.

A growing group of companies now offers the structured settlement recipients an alternative: Instead of waiting to receive a windfall over many years, you can sell the value of future payments from a structured settlement to a *factoring company* for an immediate lump sum. Lottery winners who are receiving their payments over time can also sell these payments in a similar manner.

Factoring companies have burgeoned in the last few years. Their ads fill hour upon hour of daytime television. Type the words "structured settlement" on an Internet search engine and up pop hundreds of links to factoring companies around the country.

The idea of receiving a large chunk of money now rather than in bits and pieces over many years holds a lot of appeal. This paragraph from the Web site of one of these firms states the case succinctly:

> Why should you convert future payments into a lump-sum payment? Converting a deferred asset offers you countless ways to control and benefit today from the value of long-term payments. With the certainty of inflation and tax increases, a dollar is worth far more today than it will be in the future. Rather than receiving small annual payments, the fundamental principles of finance demonstrate that a lump sum payment is more valuable. A lump sum payment with proper handling and investing will produce income for you that is far greater in total value than the original asset amount.

Sounds logical. So why are insurance companies and state regulators giving factoring companies such a hard time?

The problem lies with how they figure out how much to pay. The process works like this: Say you've received a structured settlement consisting of $200,000 worth of future payments. The factoring company won't give you a $200,000 lump sum because inflation, the length of the payment schedule, and other factors make the value of those future payments worth less now than in the future. Instead, it uses actuarial formulas that take those factors into account to determine the present value of your future payments—your lump sum.

Once you agree to the lump sum amount, you instruct the insurance company paying your structured settlement to send your checks to the factoring company address. Your name remains on the checks, but the company can cash them by using a power of attorney you have granted. Essentially, you are transferring the income stream to the factoring company in exchange for the lump sum payment. Under another type of arrangement, the company extends a kind of loan that is collateralized by future payments.

Whichever arrangement prevails, critics charge that factoring companies pay lump sums at steep discounts to their actual value and don't disclose the details of the transaction to consumers. In one lawsuit in New York, a man who was injured by a subway train received a settlement that guaranteed a monthly payment of $1,100 and annual cost of living increases of 3 percent. Several years later, he gave up future payments of $198,000 to a factoring company in exchange for $54,000 so that he could pay medical bills and buy a car. Without the stream of monthly income, he plunged deeply into debt.

Another potential problem is that insurers paying out the structured settlement are refusing to send checks to addresses known to belong to factoring companies. If that happens, you could find yourself caught in the middle of a sticky legal battle between the two companies.

For their part, factoring companies say their discount rates are reasonable and that many satisfied consumers walk away with cash they can use immediately for whatever purpose they choose. Regulations in this industry vary from state to state and may not necessarily protect your interests or prevent abuses. If you are considering using a factoring company, do so only if you have a pressing need for the cash and only after you've consulted an outside advisor, such as a financial planner or accountant, about the proposal.

Selling Your Life Insurance Policy

Viatical settlements are a growing business and an increasingly common windfall source. Under this approach, a viatical company buys a life insurance policy for 50 to 80 percent of its face value. If a policy has a death benefit of \$300,000, the company will buy it for anywhere from \$150,000 to \$240,000. The amount depends on the insured's age, health, death benefit, and number of years the policy has been in force.

Usually, people who sell their life insurance in this manner are terminally ill, although an increasing number of senior citizens who don't feel they need their policies any longer are doing it as well. Obviously, viatical companies aren't too interested in buying policies from the young and healthy, since there's a slim chance of collecting in the near future.

Unlike winning the lottery, getting a windfall by selling a life insurance policy is a far from a happy event. By buying the policy, the viatical company is betting that you'll die within a reasonably short time. Selling your policy may be truly necessary if you have a terminal illness accompanied by mounting medical bills. If you are considering selling your life insurance policy, first take the following steps:

- ❖ Talk to an attorney, accountant, or financial planner to get a second opinion and to find out how a viatical settlement might affect your estate plan.

- ❖ Find out how your state treats the proceeds from a viatical settlement. Some states allow you to receive proceeds tax free while others don't. For federal income tax purposes, the Health Insurance Portability and Accountability Act states that viaticals related to terminal illnesses are not subject to income taxes, while settlements involving people who are in good health or with a mild illness are taxed as capital gains.

- ❖ Compare offers from at least three viatical companies to see which is most competitive. Determining someone's longevity isn't an exact science; one company may offer you 60 percent of the death benefit while another may offer 80 percent.

- ❖ Talk to your life insurance beneficiaries, since they are the ones who will feel the impact of your decision directly.

- ❖ As an alternative, check to see whether your policy has an accelerated death benefit that lets you cash out early for a fee. You may prefer this to dealing with a viatical company you're not familiar with.

❖ Be on the lookout for viatical scam operators who urge you to sell your life insurance policy without explaining the potential drawbacks. Some of these companies even target people who have chronic, but not debilitating, illnesses and whose policies have generous death benefits. Hang up on any viatical company salesperson who cold calls you.

The Common Denominator

Windfalls, obviously, aren't all the same. Some, such as those coming from an inheritance, a divorce, or an insurance settlement, are the result of unfortunate events. Others, such as stock option gains, certainly qualify as cause for celebration. They may be expected, like a 401(k) plan distribution at retirement. Or like lottery winnings, they may come out of the blue. Regardless of how their fortune came about, all windfall recipients share one goal in common: To preserve and grow their wealth, they need to plot a course for the future.

CHAPTER 9

Do You Need a Financial Advisor?

Many people who receive a windfall feel comfortable investing the money on their own. Others dread the thought or at least think they could use a little help. For this group, a financial advisor may be in order.

The Wakeup Call

Receiving a windfall is one of the most common reasons people commit to getting their financial lives in order, even if they never gave it much thought before. Let's be honest—most of us haven't given it much thought at all. A casual hunt-and-peck approach to financial planning and investing is more usual than a deliberate well thought-out game plan.

Sure, we all know that's wrong. Ideally, you should have a structured program for college savings, debt reduction, or retirement, regardless of income or net worth. But more pressing matters like work, carting the kids to soccer practice, or just getting dinner ready in 15 minutes with the new puppy underfoot crowd out long-range planning.

A windfall suddenly changes everything. You become painfully aware of just how disorganized you are. It's not that taking a structured, serious approach to financial planning and investing is more important after getting the money than it was before—it's the sobering realization that there is much more to gain and much more to lose.

"For me, receiving an inheritance was a kind of financial wake-up call," recalls Maureen, a 42-year-old marketing executive who received over $300,000 in bonds and money market securities when her mother passed away several years ago. "It brought into focus the fact that while I'd been investing my 401(k) money for well over a decade and made some pretty decent decisions, I'd never gotten around to setting up a structured investment program that sets a solid financial direction. That's the main reason I started considering getting some outside help from a financial advisor."

People react differently to the notion of handling large amounts of money themselves. Some have a great deal of confidence in their abilities and are ready to meet the challenge of investing on their own. Others, like Maureen, may have mixed emotions—not the least of which is a feeling of being overwhelmed by new financial responsibilities.

Ted and Ellen, a couple in their early 30s, heard the siren call to get on track after they amassed a large sum of money through exercising stock options from their former jobs. Ted, a software designer, and Ellen, a graphics artist, were busy professionals with thriving careers. When it came to investing the inheritance, however, they admit they were close to clueless.

"Even though we're financially successful professionals, we've found that the ability to make money does not always translate into the desire to invest it," Ellen told me. "So the proceeds from exercising our stock options sat in a low-interest bank account gathering dust for months. We're both busy professionals, and we don't have time to research our investments the way we'd like to. We knew we needed someone else to do it."

Faced with the many decisions that come with handling a large lump sum, many people like Maureen, Ted, and Ellen opt to seek the assistance of a financial advisor.

Your Investment Temperament

Getting a handle on your investment temperament and confidence in your investment abilities has a lot to do with whether you decide to seek investment and financial planning advice and how you use it. When it comes to managing and investing money, you probably fall into one of three basic categories:

* **Do-it-yourselfers** have no desire to seek investment advice and relish being in control. They would not go to a financial planner if he or she paid *them*.

* **Delegators** are people who want help managing their portfolios and are happy and willing to give someone else complete discretionary control.

* **Validators** fall somewhere in-between do-it-yourselfers and delegators. When it comes to investing, these in-betweeners have confidence in their abilities, but feel they could use some outside help, perhaps in the form of a one-time financial planning consultation.

Maureen identifies herself as a validator. While she feels comfortable managing most of her own investments, she is also aware of her tendency to be too conservative an investor. She tends to shies away from mutual funds that invest for maximum growth because of their volatility. She admits she probably keeps more than she should in safe, secure money market funds.

To address both sides of her investing personality, Maureen decided to use a financial advisor to handle the aggressive side of her portfolio, while keeping most of the money she handles in more conservative investments like bonds and index funds. That way, she only pays someone to tackle the side of her portfolio she doesn't feel comfortable making decisions about.

Using a financial advisor need not be an all-encompassing or even permanent arrangement. If you're a validator, you might want to hire someone to consult with you for a few hours to make sure you're on the right track in handling your newfound wealth. Or, you might decide to hand over part of your money, as Maureen did.

People often shift between these categories at different phases in their lives. Some people are delegators soon after they receive a windfall but evolve into do-it-yourself-hood as soon as they feel more comfortable and knowledgeable about managing their money. One investment advisor told me that some people hand over a portion of their assets for him to manage and then replicate his investment moves in their own accounts. That way, they get both the benefit of his investment advice and save on investment management fees, since his charge is based on assets under management.

On the other hand, if you're a delegator, you probably don't want to have much to do with the financial side of your life. As long as you find the right people to handle things, monitor their progress periodically, and feel comfortable with the reasoning behind their decisions, there is nothing wrong with letting someone else handle your finances.

Do-It-Yourselfer, Validator, or Delegator?

Do-it-yourselfers want to make all their own financial planning and investment decisions. Validators like to do some of their own financial planning and investing but may seek occasional guidance from professionals.

You're a do-it-yourselfer if …

❏ You have the discipline to define a strategy, set a goal, and stick to a plan.

❏ You have the time and desire to research your investments (for most people, that means at least one hour a week).

❏ When it comes to investing (and maybe a lot of other matters), you trust your own judgment more than anyone else's.

❏ You like the idea of being in total control of your investment destiny.

You're a validater if …

❏ You have confidence in your investment abilities but value a second opinion.

❏ You have some time to research your investments but not as much as you need.

❑ You want someone to take at least part of the job of handling your assets off your hands.

You're a delegater if …

❑ The thought of handling large amounts of money frightens you or makes you uneasy.

❑ You've tried managing your own money in the past, and it hasn't worked out too well.

❑ You've never really done any financial planning or investing on your own and have no desire to learn how to start.

❑ You don't have the time or desire to research investments on your own.

Identifying yourself as a delegator, validator, or do-it-yourselfer will help you determine which advisor matches your investment personality, or if you even need an investment advisor. If you're an independent sort who likes to call the shots but wants a little advice now and then, a financial advisor who prefers total discretionary control over client portfolios probably won't be the best candidate for a good working relationship. On the other hand, a classic delegator may find such an individual an ideal choice.

Shining Stars, Rotten Apples

If you've decided that a financial advisor may have a place in your plans, the next step is picking the right one. While there are many worthy financial professionals out there, those who decide to seek professional assistance should expect to encounter an industry environment that, while it has generally changed for the better over the last few years, still bears the markings of a professional Wild West.

A buoyant bull market for most of the last decade has helped swell the ranks of financial service professionals. People who used to call themselves stock brokers, insurance agents, lawyers, accountants, and even used car salesmen now call themselves financial planners. Depending on whom you ask, somewhere between 100,000 and 200,000 people wear the label proudly. Just 10 years ago, the term "financial advisor" brought to mind a commissioned salesperson charged with meeting sales quotas set by a large brokerage firm. While that animal is still on the prowl, the industry has made genuine attempts over the last few years to shed its reputation for product pushing and to move toward a planning relationship with clients.

Today, going to a financial advisor means more than handing over your money and watching passively as someone invests it. You'll probably be asked about your personal financial life, including details such as income, cash flow, taxes, and retirement savings. After viewing your full financial picture, the advisor will recommend specific mutual funds or other investments. This broad-based approach can help capable financial advisors create an effective, tailor-made investment program for clients. For other advisors, however, a written financial plan can serve as little more than a starting point for a sales pitch.

As with any other profession, competence, honesty, and integrity vary widely among financial planners. Some are excellent, while others are outright crooks. And a good number have their own self-interest, rather than your financial future, at heart.

David, a professor, and his wife, Jean, a principal with an environmental consulting firm, found that out when they decided to seek professional advice at the local office of a major national brokerage firm a few years ago after receiving an inheritance from David's father.

"We were hoping to meet someone who would listen with intelligence and active interest," says David. "What we found was a commission hound who managed to spend an hour with us without trying to learn anything about our financial needs. He seemed excited about the amount of money that we might be able to invest and spent a lot of time talking about the no-brainers that he could steer us toward. Frankly, we were capable of figuring out the no-brainers on our own."

The couple continued their search, with disappointing results. "The challenge was to find a first-rate professional who views their work as a calling rather than a job," says David. "That was very difficult, especially in a relatively small urban area." Disillusioned, they decided to take charge of their investments themselves.

Don't become discouraged if your first few interviews don't click. It sometimes takes a lot of legwork to settle on someone with whom you feel comfortable divulging your most intimate financial secrets and entrusting your financial future.

Avoid giving in to the temptation to seek easy answers or formula solutions. Every year, a well-known magazine publishes a list of 250 of the country's "best" financial advisors. In my opinion, that's about as absurd as printing a list of 250 of the best mothers, doctors, dogcatchers, or ice cream vendors. Beyond examining the obvious—credentials, experience, and possible professional sanctions—choosing a planner is a highly subjective and personal matter. What makes one advisor the best to one person may be someone else's worst nightmare. A widow who wants very little to do with her finances, for example, may find someone who swoops in and takes total control appealing. A validator who just wants a second opinion every now and then might find the same professional impossible to work with.

The key to finding the right financial advisor goes well beyond claims about who has made the most money for clients. You have to decide whose style fits your own temperament and risk profile. Discuss how you would like to work with your advisor. Some financial advisors routinely call clients before they make trades in an account. Others prefer to work with people who don't want to be bothered with the details and give their advisor complete control.

Look for someone who is compatible with your objectives, tolerance for risk, time horizon, and tax situation. Some advisors swing for the fences when they invest, while others hit a lot of singles. Some trade actively, while others don't.

There are no magic formulas to define what a good financial advisor is, but here are four main C's to consider: cost, competence, compatibility, and comfort.

Cost

Financial advisors today work under a confusing array of compensation arrangements.

Commissioned or Fee-Based Advisors

A *commissioned advisor* is paid by the companies whose products he or she sells. In the case of advisors who work with individual stocks, compensation may be determined based on the number of trades in an account. To avoid the negative connotation of the word "commission," most advisors have expunged the term from their business cards. Instead, they may refer to themselves as "fee-based," which means they earn their living through a combination of fees and commissions. Typically, a fee-based advisor charges a few hundred dollars for a written financial plan, then implements that plan with mutual funds and other products carrying a sales charge.

Analyze Your Advisor's Motivation

Be careful if an advisor who works on commission seems to strongly favor high-commission products like annuities. Another red flag is when someone favors his or her own firm's investment products over other alternatives, since the compensation brokers receive for in-house products is generally higher than for other investments. Ask whether the advisor makes more money selling one product over another or if he or she is participating in a sales contest.

Advisors working under a fee-based arrangement usually earn the lion's share of their living from sales commissions. In many cases, fee-based advisors use the financial planning fee to get potential clients to commit to the planning process. Some waive it if you later decide to implement the plan by investing through them.

Fee-Only Advisors

A *fee-only advisor* is paid by his or her client, which means that compensation is not contingent on the sale of a product. Most fee-only advisors calculate compensation based on a percentage of assets under management, usually ranging from 0.5 percent to 2 percent. A minority charge according to the time they spend working with you, at a rate usually ranging from $90 to $200 an hour.

Negotiate the Fee

If you're using a fee-only planner, there's more room for negotiation than you may think. Unlike commissions, which are usually fixed by the investment company, fees are set by the advisors themselves. Some may be willing to lower their standard fee if your account is very large if your financial picture is relatively simple or if there's an opportunity for more business down the road.

Salary and Bonus Advisors

Some advisors work through a *salary and bonus* paid by the employer. Financial advisors who work for banks, credit unions, or other organizations offering financial planning are usually paid a salary. You will probably pay a fee or commission to the employing institution.

Which to Choose?

There is no easy answer as to which arrangement is best. Proponents of fee-only planning believe the arrangement creates the least conflict of interest, since compensation does not depend on the amount or type of product sold. Thus there is less incentive to push high-ticket products such as annuities—a big plus if you're concerned that an advisor may be motivated mainly by money and not working in your best interest. Drawbacks tend to be underplayed by the press, which seems enamored with the fee-only crowd because of their more "objective" compensation structure.

For one thing, the vast majority of fee-only advisors base their compensation on assets under management rather than an hourly rate. That kind of logic assumes that it takes 10 times more effort to manage a $1 million account than a $100,000 account, though financial planners themselves privately admit that often is not the case.

While there has been some talk among industry professionals about adjusting fees to account for such discrepancies—perhaps by using some kind of fee and hourly rate arrangement—many planners still use assets under management as the major determinant of how much they charge.

The commission side of the advisor fence, on the other hand, has the very serious issue of objectivity to tackle. No matter how you slice it, a higher commission is a powerful lure for recommending a particular investment product. It takes an honest forthright person not to take the bait.

A growing number of financial advisors let their clients choose the compensation arrangement they feel most comfortable with. If you work with someone with that flexibility, ask for a comparison of fee versus commission charges to see which works best for you. Whatever compensation arrangement you settle on, a financial advisor should be willing to clearly disclose all fees and commissions up front, before you invest.

What it really comes down to, in the end, is trust. There are plenty of honest financial advisors who are compensated through fees, just as there are many excellent ones who earn a living from commissions. Both camps have their share of shining stars and rotten apples.

Competence

As with other types of professions, longevity is a definite plus when it comes to gauging competence. Advisors who have been through at least one prolonged stock market downturn, such as the October 1987 market crash, certainly deserve a second look.

One of the first questions you're most likely to ask a financial advisor is how well his or her investments have performed. It's also one of the most difficult ones to answer. Unlike money managers who work for pension funds or other institutional investors, financial advisors for individuals rarely have audited performance numbers. A common trick is to highlight the performance of their most successful accounts, while keeping the clinkers hidden in a drawer.

Some advisors use software that allows them to present their track records based on the aggregate performance of all accounts they manage and thus cannot highlight the best ones. If those figures are not available, ask to see performance numbers from an account of someone in a financial and lifestyle situation similar to your own (hiding the actual name of the client, of course).

Keep your expectations reasonable. If a financial advisor says it's realistic to expect returns of 10 percent a year, on average, and you're determined to shoot for 15 to 20 percent, you're probably not going to work together very well. A good financial advisor will steer clients toward a balanced diversified portfolio, which tends to moderate the ups and downs.

On the other hand, going with an advisor based solely on claims he or she can grow your account by 25 percent every year is a bad move. For one thing, investment track records are nearly impossible for individual investors to verify. Inflated claims are easy to make and difficult to prove.

One way to track the performance of financial advisors who work with individuals is to consult Hulbert's Financial Digest, a firm that tracks and ranks the performance of advisors who publish their recommendations in newsletters. Since only a fraction of financial professionals are included in the Hulbert ranking, however, don't eliminate someone from consideration just because he or she is not listed there.

Alphabet Soup

Professional designations and credentials will give you some insight about an advisor's training. They may also provide clues on the type of products or solutions someone is likely to come up with. Someone with a professional designation that focuses on insurance, for example, may lean toward insurance-based products and solutions. Someone with an accounting background, on the other hand, may place more emphasis on taxes. Here is a translation of what all these letters mean:

* ❖ **CFP: Certified Financial Planner.** This is perhaps the most common credential financial planners obtain and is considered

by many to be a minimum industry standard. To be a CFP, a planner must have at least three years of experience counseling clients on financial matters, fulfill certain educational requirements, pass a 10-hour examination, and pledge to abide by a code of ethics.

❖ **CFA: Chartered Financial Analyst.** A prestigious designation in financial planning, a CFA is earned primarily by securities analysts, money managers, and investment advisors who focus mainly on analyzing investments and securities. It is awarded by the Association for Investment Management and Research to experienced financial analysts who pass a rigorous test.

❖ **CLU: Chartered Life Underwriter.** Held mainly by insurance agents who have expanded into financial planning, this designation is issued by the American College. CLUs must have three years of related work experience and pass 10 college-level courses. The designation is often coupled with ChFC (Chartered Financial Consultant), also awarded by the American College.

❖ **CPA: Certified Public Accountant.** CPAs are tax specialists who have passed an extensive, rigorous exam and satisfied the work experience and statutory and licensing requirements of the state or states they practice in. A growing number of CPAs have moved into financial planning to help smooth out the seasonal ups and downs of their business.

❖ **PFS:** An accountant with experience in personal finance who has passed an exam offered by the American Institute of Certified Public Accountants (AICPA).

❖ **RIA: Registered Investment Advisor.** Individuals who give investment advice and offer investment products such as mutual funds must submit a form to the Securities and Exchange Commission to become an RIA. This is a legal requirement rather than a professional credential.

Today, there are about 33,000 CFP practitioners and thousands more with some other type of financial planning designation. While having some letters after a name certainly does not ensure capability, it does indicate that the person whose name precedes them has taken the time to go the extra yard in his or her profession.

If you're seriously considering a financial advisor, ask to see a document called Form ADV, which has two parts. Part I highlights an advisor's education, business, and any problems with regulators or clients. Part II outlines an advisor's services, fees, and strategies. Before you hire an advisor, insist on seeing *both* parts of Form ADV. If an advisor won't give you that information, don't do business with him or her.

Don't assume you're safe if a broker works for a large, well-known firm. Someone who has had numerous arbitration hearing and sanctions can still perform as a broker.

If you really want to do some digging, consider using a privately owned resource called the National Fraud Exchange in Reston, Virginia. For $39, consumers access the firm's broad database, which contains disciplinary information from the National Association of Securities Dealers (NASD), federal and state regulatory agencies, and securities industry organizations such as the New York Stock Exchange.

Ask the Right Questions

A reputable broker or investment advisor will welcome your questions. As you conduct your search, don't feel intimidated about asking them. It's your money at stake.

* Have you worked with people in my circumstances before?
* What is your business philosophy?
* Do you specialize in a particular area?
* Do you work with other professionals, such as accountants or attorneys? Can you provide references?
* Where did you go to school? What is your employment history?
* Have you ever been the subject of a disciplinary action by a government regulator for improper or unethical conduct?
* Have you ever been sued by a client who was unhappy with the work you did?

* How often will you contact me after our initial meeting?
* What is the process you use to prepare a plan, and how comprehensive is it?
* Do you research the products you recommend?
* How are you compensated for your services? Are there any incentives or bonuses tied to the products you sell?
* For registered investment advisors: Will you send me a copy of both parts of your Form ADV?

As your relationship with an advisor progresses, take stock of how things are going. Monitor the progress of your relationship and investments, and make sure you feel comfortable with the answers to these questions:

* Does my advisor keep in touch regularly? Does she sound responsive when I call, or do I feel like I'm getting a brush-off?
* How often do I receive statements? Do I understand them?
* Are my investment returns meeting my expectations? Am I being exposed to a level of risk I feel comfortable with?
* Are any commissions or fees in line with what I expected?
* Have my goals or life situation changed? How has my advisor responded to those changes?

Compatibility and Comfort

Once you've looked at the standard litmus tests of experience, track record, compensation practices, and credentials, it's time to focus on that fuzzy thing called chemistry.

Bad chemistry prompted Ted and Ellen to rule out half a dozen financial planners before they settled on someone compatible. "One of them had his secretary send me a profile form that required me to disclose highly personal information, and I hadn't even spoken with the guy over the phone," says Ellen. "Another was an older gentleman who was off playing golf while his son made what I considered an overly slick presentation."

The couple finally settled on Jeff, a planner who was "low key, down-to-earth, and about our age." After several years, they consider the relationship a success. Aside from being pleased with his investment approach and results, they also like the fact that Jeff helps them with decisions that do not involve extra compensation, such as whether to buy or lease a car or how to invest Ted's 401(k).

If Problems Arise

Chances are, you'll have a good sense fairly quickly about whether or not your financial advisor is the right person for you. If problems do arise, it is important that you act promptly. The Securities and Exchange Commission suggests following these steps:

❖ Talk to your financial advisor and explain the problem. Where is the fault? Were communications clear? Refer to notes you have taken during conversations, if any.

❖ If your broker can't resolve your problem, then talk to the broker's branch manager.

❖ If the problem is still not resolved, write to the compliance department of the firm's main office. Explain your problem clearly and how you want it to be resolved. Ask the compliance office to respond to you within 30 days.

❖ If you are still not satisfied, send a copy of your letter to your state securities administrator or to the Office of Investor Education at the SEC.

The SEC will research your complaint, contact the firm or person in question, and ask for a response. Sometimes such intervention yields a satisfactory result. If it does not, you may need to take legal action on your own.

Keep in mind that losing money from investments that an advisor recommends does not, by itself, constitute grounds for legal action. If it did, brokerage firms would be out of business. Trusting your financial advisor does not, however, mean nodding agreeably at everything he or she says. The best way to avoid conflicts down the road is to fully understand your advisor's investment recommendations as well as the level of risk they carry.

If You Decide to Go It Alone

Ultimately, the search for a financial advisor might lead back to your own doorstep, as it did for David and Linda.

"In the end, we felt our finances, and our future, were too important to be left to someone else," says David. "After talking with friends about their experiences with financial advisors, we decided we could do as well on our own."

David admits he sometimes misses the hand-holding a good financial professional can provide. "We'd all like to have that big brother or sister who is there with sage advice. Given that I didn't find any advisor competent to fill that role, I think I'll ask Linda to hold my hand instead."

The good news for do-it-yourselfers like David and Linda is that when it comes to financial planning and investing, it's easier than ever to go it alone. Bookstore shelves groan under the increasingly heavy weight of personal finance books and magazines, while the Internet serves up a lush bounty of investment and financial planning information.

The product marketplace also offers ample opportunity for financial self-reliance. No-load mutual funds and other packaged products like annuities marketed directly to the public make it possible for investors to do just fine, thank you, without the aid of a broker. For those who prefer stocks, discount brokerage firms such as Charles Schwab, E*Trade, and TD Waterhouse execute stock trades at anywhere from $8 to $20 a pop.

The question is no longer whether or not it's possible to be your own financial advisor. It's really whether you want to. Handling your own finances offers the obvious advantage of cost savings because you don't have to pay fees or commissions to someone else. You also have complete control over your financial destiny—for better or worse.

Those preferring the go-it-alone route have numerous resources available. *Mutual Funds Magazine*, *Kiplinger's Personal Finance*, and *Money*

Magazine are just a few fine print publications offering a smorgasbord of fresh investment ideas. Many personal finance publications augment their print offerings with online information that's worth checking out.

Aside from getting ideas about specific funds or stocks, the Internet offers a variety of financial planning tools. Some of the larger fund companies, most notably Fidelity (www.fidelity.com) and Vanguard (www.vanguard.com) have a useful array of sophisticated and powerful financial planning tools such as college cost and retirement planning calculators and tax planning tools. Financial Engines (www.financialengines.com), a financial planning Web site founded by William Sharpe, the Nobel Prize–winning economist, is also worth a look for its useful asset allocation advice.

If you decide to take matters into your own hands, remember that financial planning is an ongoing process. Once you get your financial house in order, you'll need to review and update your plan and investments on a regular basis.

Resources

If you need financial advisor referrals, consider these resources:

Financial Planning Association
1-800-282-PLAN
www.fpanet.org.

This trade association for financial planners provides professional referrals for consumers.

National Association of Personal Financial Advisors (NAPFA)
1-888-FEE-ONLY
www.napfa.org

Referrals to financial planners who work exclusively through fees.

American Institute of Certified Public Accountants Investment Advisory Division
1-800-862-4272

Referrals to members, who are accounting professionals such as CPAs who specialize in personal financial planning.

Some discount brokers refer individuals to financial planners and investment advisors who execute trades through them. Charles Schwab & Co.'s referral program is available to individuals with $100,000 or more to invest. TD Waterhouse refers individuals to professionals it works with through its branch network of offices. Both services are free of charge to consumers.

The Securities and Exchange Commission (www.sec.gov; 1-800-732-0330) does not have a referral service but does offer advice on selecting a financial advisor.

For Background Checks

National Association of Securities Dealers Regulation
1-800-289-9999
www.nasdr.com

Provides access to disciplinary history on all registered representatives and NASD member firms.

National Fraud Exchange
1-800-822-0416
www.mari-inc.org

For $39, this organization does a comprehensive background check on financial professionals.

Investors Protection Trust
www.investorprotection.org

This Web site has information on selecting an advisor and links to federal and state regulatory agencies.

CHAPTER 10

Interest-Bearing Investments: The Beauty of Boring

Certificates of deposit, money market funds, bonds, and other investments that generate income—called fixed-income securities—might look pretty boring when the bull market in stocks is roaring. After all, there's a lot more brag appeal in talking about that great tech stock that tripled in value in just three months versus that trusty Treasury note that's paying a steady 7 percent interest rate. Many windfall recipients, however, would do well to roll out the welcome mat for these securities.

The Interest in Interest

Windfall recipients invest in interest-bearing securities for two main reasons:

* **They produce income.** If you have come into a large windfall, you may have the option of paying all or part of your living expenses with the income generated from fixed-income securities. If you have retired, that income can supplement a pension and social security.

* **They provide a balance for your portfolio.** Although history shows that stocks produce the greatest returns over the long term, interest-bearing investments provide ballast by controlling overall portfolio volatility. And, over certain short-term time

periods, they have actually done better than stocks. This is most likely to happen when the stock market isn't doing too well and people migrate to safer, more secure investments.

The benefits of balancing a portfolio with bonds crystallized in 2000. During that year, when many stocks fell in value, Treasury bills provided investors with a total return of 6.1 percent. The Lehman Brothers Government Bond Index, a widely used barometer of bonds issued by the U.S. government and government agencies, posted a tasty return of 13.2 percent. By contrast, the Standard & Poor's 500 Index, a well-known stock market indicator, fell 9 percent for the year.

Consider this: Even though stock prices have fallen dramatically since early 2000, stocks are still expensive by most measures. For most of the last 20 years, stock prices in general have risen much more rapidly than the corresponding growth in corporate earnings. As a result, the price-earnings ratio of the average stock—a commonly used figure that measures the relationship between corporate earnings and stock price—was recently about twice its historic mean.

Putting it simply, stocks are still really expensive by most historical measures. No one can tell whether that means their returns will be lower going forward than they have been over the last 20 years, but it does make the market more vulnerable to a correction, perhaps a prolonged one.

This doesn't mean you should stop investing in stocks. Most people need to invest in equities for portfolio growth. But it does point to the benefit of diversifying into money market securities and bonds, particularly when the stock market is hitting a rough patch as it has recently. Whether you're in your 20s or your 70s, money market securities and bonds should be part of your portfolio if you have recently come into a windfall.

Bonds: Risks and Rewards

Despite their steady-Eddie reputation, bonds come with some element of uncertainty. When comparing different types of fixed-income investments, you need to pay attention to certain types of risk.

Interest Rate Risk

I can't tell you how many times I've heard the following lament from bond investors who don't understand the fundamental relationship between interest rates and bond prices:

> I bought some high-quality bonds from a reputable dealer. A couple of years later, I needed to sell them before they reached maturity due to a financial emergency. I was surprised to find that I would get back less than I paid for them. I don't understand what happened.

What happened, in all likelihood, is that in the time between the purchase and sale of the bonds, new bonds of a similar quality and maturity started paying more interest. Consequently, the older bonds had to come down in price to lure investors—kind of the bond world's equivalent of a red tag sale.

The interest rate-price relationship in bonds works like a seesaw. When interest rates rise, bond prices fall. And when interest rates fall, the price of existing bonds goes up. The longer the time remaining for a security to mature, the greater the price fluctuation will be.

Here's why: Let's assume you buy a newly issued bond at a par value of $1,000 with a 7 percent coupon, the annual interest rate assigned to a bond when it is issued and usually paid semi-annually. This means that each $1,000 bond produces $70 a year in interest income. A couple of years later, coupons on new bonds of similar quality and maturity are up to 9 percent for a payout of $90 a year.

At that point, no one would want to spend as much for your bond, which pays $70 a year, as they would for a similar bond that churns out $90 a year. Therefore your older bond would have to drop in value to compensate for its now-measly coupon. When that happens, the bond is *selling at a discount.*

The opposite occurs when interest rates fall, and older outstanding bonds with higher coupons are paying more interest than new issues. To adjust for the difference, those bonds rise in price. When their prices rise above par value, they are selling at a "premium."

The longer the maturity, the greater the price fluctuation will be both up and down, reflecting the risks and rewards of locking in a specified rate of interest for a longer period of time. To compensate for the added risk, long-term bonds usually yield more than short-term bonds. Most investors classify bond maturities as follows:

- ❖ **Short-term:** One to five years
- ❖ **Intermediate-term:** Five to 10 years (Fixed-income securities that mature in 10 years or less are sometimes called *notes.*)
- ❖ **Long-term:** Over 10 years

Bonds with short maturities fluctuate in price much less than those with long maturities. Using the example of a bond with a par value of $1,000 and a 7 percent coupon, a rise in interest rates of 2 percent would cause a bond that matures in two years to inch down to $964—a loss, but a relatively painless one. However, if the bond matured in 20 years, the price would tumble to $816.

On the other hand, if interest rates fell by 2 percent, the longer-term bond would shoot to $1,251, while the short-term bond with two years left to maturity would inch up just a tad, to $1,038.

Keep in mind that price fluctuation from changes in interest rates won't affect you if you hold the bond to maturity. Assuming the issuer hasn't defaulted, you'll get your principal back no matter what interest rates have done during the time you owned the bond. But it's a different story for a bond fund because bond fund shares never mature. We'll talk more about that later.

Also remember that price fluctuation from changes in interest rates occurs with all kinds of issuers, from the U.S. Treasury to the dicey bonds of fledgling dot-coms.

Credit Risk

When you apply for a loan or credit card, a bank determines how good a credit risk you are by investigating whether you have repaid previous loans in a timely manner and whether or not you are likely to do so in the future. If you've got a clean credit record, you'll probably have to pay a lower rate of interest than someone who has defaulted on a loan in the past or declared bankruptcy. The same basic principle holds true for bond issuers.

To attract investors, issuers who are deemed a high credit risk must pay a higher rate of interest to borrow money in the bond market than those with better credit ratings. For corporate and municipal bonds, most investors turn to Moody's and Standard & Poor's, the two major bond rating services.

Bond Credit Ratings

Moody's and Standard & Poor's are two major bond rating agencies that determine an issuer's creditworthiness. They assign the credit ratings outlined in the following table.

Moody's	Standard & Poor's	Definition
High Grade		
Aaa	AAA	The highest credit quality with the lowest degree of risk.
Aa	AA	High quality, but somewhat below a triple-A rating because of the issuer's slightly less predictable long-term payment ability.
Medium Grade		
A	A	Upper-medium-grade bonds of financially sound issuers, though not as strong as double-A or triple-A credits.
Baa	BBB	Lowest investment grade. Interest payment and security of principal are considered adequate, although not as secure as upper-grade credits over the long-term.
Speculative		
Ba	BB	Below investment grade. Payment of principal and interest is highly sensitive to financial or economic conditions.
B	B	Regular interest payments and repayment of principal cannot be assured.
Caa	CCC	Poor quality with high risk of default, particularly if unfavorable economic conditions prevail.
Ca	CC	Highly speculative.
C	C	Lowest grade.
D	D	In default.

Treasury securities, Series EE Bonds, and other U.S. government issues are at the highest end of the quality spectrum because they are backed by the full faith and credit of the Treasury. Barring some unforeseen economic Armageddon, that's about as rock solid a guarantee as you'll get on any investment.

Other Bond Risks

Most bonds will always pay the same amount of interest, no matter what. Over the years, inflation will erode the purchasing power of those income payments, creating *inflation risk*. Assume, for example, you've used some of your windfall to invest in bonds and they are producing an annual income stream of $30,000. That might seem like a nice addition to your salary or pension right now. Or, if you lead a frugal lifestyle, it can pay for a good chunk of your living expenses. If inflation averages 4 percent over the next 15 years, it will take $54,000 to buy what $30,000 buys today. To adjust, you will either have to buy less or earn more. That's why it's a good idea to invest a portion of your money in investments geared for growth, such as stocks.

There's also the *risk of a credit downgrade*, which happens if an issuer's financial condition deteriorates while you're holding the bond. Although the issuer may continue making regular interest payments, the fact that the bond is viewed less favorably by rating agencies could affect its value. *Default risk* is the risk that the issuer will fail to repay principal and pay interest. Default risk is virtually nonexistent for some securities such as U.S. Treasury bonds. For others, such as bonds of newer or smaller companies, the risk can be quite high. Bonds with the highest risk of default are called junk bonds, and we'll talk more about those later. Finally, *currency risk* is the risk that a fluctuating dollar will have a negative impact on the value of foreign bonds, which are denominated in foreign currencies. If the U.S. dollar strengthens against foreign currencies, the dollar value of their principal and interest payments will decline. A weaker dollar produces the opposite effect.

Types of Bonds

Bonds come in a variety of flavors, including corporate bonds, junk bonds, municipal bonds, and convertible bonds.

Corporate Bonds

Companies use fixed-income securities to fund a variety of projects, such as building new facilities or purchasing new equipment. By investing in these bonds, you are, in effect, lending the company your money. The interest the company pays to you is fully taxable at the federal, state, and local level. Because their interest is fully taxable and because investors consider these bonds riskier than those issued by the federal government and its agencies, corporate bonds usually have higher yields than other types of fixed-income securities. Investment grade bonds are those rated at Baa or higher by Moody's, and BBB or higher by Standard & Poor's.

Junk Bonds

Bonds with ratings below investment grade levels are called *high yield bonds* or, less ceremoniously, *junk bonds.* While these bonds offer the highest degree of credit risk, they also have the highest yields. Their default rate depends largely on economic conditions and has recently ranged from a high of 9.33 percent of outstanding issues in 1991 to a low of less than one-half percent in 1994.

Many professional investors view junk bonds as an equity alternative, rather than a died-in-the-wool member of the fixed-income group. Changes in interest rates often don't affect junk bonds as much as other types of bonds since investors focus on their credit characteristics.

Junk bonds tend to perform better than other types of bonds when the economy and stock market are strong. During such times, investors view the risk of default as minimal and are willing to take on the added degree of credit risk in exchange for higher returns. In some years, junk bond returns have even resembled those of stocks. In 1995, a strong year for the stock market and a time of declining interest rates, the average junk bond mutual fund had a total return of 17.7 percent.

But junk bonds can also underperform their better-quality bond brethren when the economy weakens, interest rates drop, and defaults rise. During those periods, investors prefer the safety of higher-quality issuers to the less certain prospects of junk bonds. That happened in 2000, when the average junk bond fund was off 7.1 percent for the year, while most other types of better-quality bond funds rose in value.

Bottom line: When it comes to investment planning, look at junk bonds as an equity alternative rather than a steady source of income.

Municipal Bonds

Also called tax-exempt securities, municipal bonds are debt securities issued by cities, states, counties, school districts, and other authorities created by state governments and municipalities. Interest payments from municipal bonds are generally exempt from federal income tax, which makes them particularly attractive to higher-income investors. Interest from bonds issued in the state where you live are usually exempt from state and local taxes as well. For this reason, a number of single state bond funds are available for residents of states that tax interest and dividend income, such as Massachusetts, California, and New York.

Municipal bonds (munis) come with credit ratings similar to corporate bonds, which affects their yield. Some bonds are insured, which means a private insurance company has agreed to guarantee payment of principal and interest even if the issuer defaults. These bonds automatically receive a triple-A rating because of that backup.

There are two major categories of munis: revenue bonds and general obligation bonds. Revenue bonds are issued to raise funds for a particular project, such as a toll road or a hospital that is projected to generate enough income to pay interest and repay principal to bondholders. General obligation bonds are backed by the unlimited taxing power of an issuer such as city, state, or county and are thus considered less risky than revenue bonds.

Because of their tax advantage, municipal bonds and the funds that invest in them have lower yields than corporate bonds and bond funds. However, if your tax bracket is high enough, a lower-yielding municipal bond fund can actually leave you with more money after taxes than a higher-yielding corporate fund.

When comparing municipal bond yields with yields on taxable securities, you need to find out which yields more after taxes. The higher your tax bracket, the more valuable a municipal bond's tax-free yield will be for you.

Use this quick formula to calculate what a taxable bond would need to yield in order to equal the tax-free yield on an out-of-state municipal issue, called the *taxable equivalent yield:* Divide the tax-free yield by 1 minus your tax bracket. For example, assume you are in the 35 percent federal tax bracket in 2002 and want to buy a tax-exempt bond yielding 4 percent. Here, the formula would be 4 divided by 1 minus 0.35, or 4 divided by 0.65. That gives you a taxable equivalent yield of 6.15 percent. Putting it another way, a taxable bond would need to yield at least 6.15 percent to match the 4 percent yield of a tax-free municipal bond.

The table shows what a taxable bond needs to yield to equal the tax-exempt yield on a municipal bond.

Tax Bracket	27%	30%	35%	38.6%
Tax-Exempt Yield (%)	Federal Taxable Equivalent Yield (%)			
2.0	2.7	2.8	3.0	3.3
3.0	4.1	4.3	4.6	4.9
4.0	5.5	5.7	6.1	6.5
5.0	6.8	7.1	7.7	8.2
6.0	8.2	8.6	9.2	9.8
7.0	9.7	10.0	10.8	11.5
8.0	11.0	11.4	12.3	13.0

If you live in a state that levies a high tax on investment income, consider investing in municipal bonds from your own state, since the interest income is usually tax-free at both the state and federal level.

If you're comparing municipal bond yields against yields from taxable bonds to see which is the better deal for you, check out the yield comparison calculator at a Web site called investinginbonds.com. Presented by the Bond Marketing Association, a trade group for the bond industry, the site also offers useful articles and tips on buying bonds.

Additional Tax Pointers on Munis

Not all of a municipal bond's return is tax-free. When you sell a municipal bond or bond fund at a price higher than what you paid, the gain is subject to capital gains tax. (A few states do not tax gains from the sale of bonds issued in that state.)

You do not need to report a capital gain on an individual municipal security unless you sell it. If you own shares in a municipal bond fund, you can receive capital gains distributions even if you do not sell your shares because the fund must distribute to shareholders any net capital gains it realizes on the sale of its holdings.

Sometimes, bonds will decline in value after they are issued because of an increase in interest rates or a credit downgrade. If you buy a bond at a discount to its par value and sell it for more than that, a portion of the gain is taxed as ordinary income.

Interest on municipal bonds or bond funds may affect the tax treatment of Social Security benefits.

Don't Put a Tax Shelter in a Tax Shelter

Never buy municipal bonds for a tax-deferred retirement account. Their yields are lower, and you'll be wasting a valuable tax break by keeping a tax-advantaged investment inside a tax-sheltered account.

Convertible Bonds

Convertibles are corporate bonds that can be converted, at the option of the investor, into a specified number of shares of the issuer's stock at a predetermined price. The amount by which the price of the convertible exceeds the current market value of the stock into which it may be converted is called the *premium*.

Since each bond represents a specific number of common stock shares, a rise in the price of the stock has a direct impact on the price of the convertible. As the conversion premium narrows, that impact becomes greater and, in a bull market, the value of the bond may even move in step with the value of the underlying stock. In a bear market, however, when the bond is worth significantly more than the stock it represents, convertibles may resemble traditional bonds by responding more to changes in interest rates and less to stock price movement.

Usually, if the underlying stock's price moves higher, the bond will appreciate to a lesser degree. If the underlying stock price falls, so does the value of the convertible bond, though usually less than the stock itself. The downside cushion comes from the convertible's income potential and its principal value at maturity.

Treasury Securities

Backed by "the full faith and credit" pledge of the U.S. government, Treasury bills, notes, and bonds offer the ultimate guarantee of credit-worthiness. I happen to be partial to these old standbys and use them personally for several reasons:

- ❖ **They're easy to buy and sell.** Individual investors must often pay higher fees when buying municipal or taxable bonds because the market for bite-sized blocks of securities is limited. The Treasury arena is so huge that an investor with $10,000 is on the same footing as someone with $10 million.

- ❖ **They can't be retired early.** Many investors who think they've locked in high yields for decades often get the rug pulled out from under them when a municipal or corporate issuer redeems its bonds after a few years and replaces them with new ones at the prevailing lower interest rate. The feature that allows the issuer to do this, the *call provision*, is absent from Treasury issues.

- ❖ **Liberation from state and local income taxes.** As I live in a state that's sometimes referred to as "Taxachusetts," this feature really appeals to me. Investors in other high-tax states like California or New York might feel the same way.

- ❖ **No sales commission.** You can buy Treasuries directly from the federal government through the TreasuryDirect program, or you can buy savings bonds from your local bank.

Types of Treasury Securities

The menu at Uncle Sam's includes Treasury bills, Treasure notes and bonds, Treasury Inflation-Protected Securities (TIPS), savings bonds, and STRIPS or zero-coupon Treasuries.

Treasury Bills

Treasury bills are short-term debt that matures in one year or less from the issue date. You buy them for a price of less than their par value. When they mature, the government pays their par value. For example, if you buy a $10,000, 26-week Treasury bill for $9,750 and hold it until maturity, your interest is $250.

Treasury Notes and Bonds

Treasure notes and bonds are securities that pay a fixed rate of interest every six months until maturity. Treasury notes mature in more than a year but not more than 10 years from their issue date. Treasury bonds mature in more than 10 years from their issue date.

Treasury Inflation-Protected Securities (TIPS)

Introduced in 1997, these inflation-adjusted Treasury notes are designed as a hedge against inflation. Like regular treasury notes, they pay interest twice a year. Unlike traditional notes, their principal value adjusts twice a year to reflect inflation, as measured by the Consumer Price Index. For example, if an inflation-adjusted Treasury note has a face value of $1,000 and inflation rises 2 percent for the year, the bond's value will rise to $1,020.

The main downside with TIPS is that the increase in the face value is federally taxable as income in the year it accrues, even though you don't actually receive it until the bond matures. This makes them better-suited for tax-deferred retirement accounts. And their interest is somewhat lower than comparable Treasury notes because of the built-in inflation protection.

Savings Bonds

Series EE bonds are issued at half the bond's face value of anywhere from $50 to $10,000. The difference between the original price and the redemption value is interest, compounded semiannually. For bonds purchased May 1997 and after, the semiannual adjustment is 90 percent of the average of five-year Treasury yields for the preceding six months. Although the increase in the bond's value can be reported annually for tax purposes, most people choose to pay income taxes when they cash their bonds. Introduced in 1998, the *I Bond* is a savings bond for investors seeking protection against inflation. Like the better-known Series EE bonds, interest on I Bonds is added to the value of the bond and does not have to be reported for tax purposes until maturity. However, the interest calculation is based on a fixed rate of return and a semiannual inflation rate.

STRIPs, or Zero-Coupon Treasuries

These Treasury securities don't make periodic interest payments. Instead, they are sold at a deep discount and redeemed upon maturity at face value.

Although Treasury issues form the building blocks for STRIPs, these securities are actually assembled by brokers and other financial institutions that separate the interest and principal component of a Treasury note or bond. For example, a 10-year Treasury note makes a total of 20 interest payments—two payments a year over the course of 10 years—and a principal payment at maturity. By "stripping" the security, the financial institution creates separate securities from the principal and interest, which can be held and transferred separately. You can only buy STRIPs through a broker or financial institution.

Many people find STRIPs useful for funding a specific expense that will come up in the future, such as a child or grandchild's college tuition. You can buy the bonds when the child is very young for a fraction of their face value, and know exactly how much you'll be getting when they mature. If you're considering STRIPs, remember these features:

❖ You need to pay income taxes on the STRIPs' increase in value (which represents your interest) every year, unless the bonds are held in a tax-deferred retirement account. If income taxes are a concern, some brokers offer tax-free municipal zero coupon bonds that work similarly to STRIPs.

❖ Zero-coupon securities are more sensitive to interest rate fluctuations—and often more volatile—than just about any other type of bond. With most bonds, investors receive periodic interest payments that they may need to reinvest at rates that are lower, or higher, than when they bought the bond. With zeros, the interest is locked in from the date of purchase, producing a kind of interest rate bet on steroids. The effect of locking in a rate of return is particularly sharp for longer-term zero-coupon bonds.

The Easy Way to Buy U.S. Bonds

Buying Treasury securities through a discount broker costs around $40 to $50 in commissions regardless of the size of the purchase. That's a pretty good deal compared to the commissions on other types of bonds. But with the government's TreasuryDirect program, you can do even better.

TreasuryDirect provides a way to bypass the middleman and save the commission. It's a fairly simple process: Once the Treasury announces an auction, investors are invited to submit bids. With a noncompetitive bid—the kind most individual investors use—the buyer agrees to accept the rate determined at the auction.

Treasurydirect.gov, the Internet gateway to TreasuryDirect, walks users through every aspect of purchasing Treasury securities directly from the government. It includes a basic explanation of the different kinds of Treasury securities available and how they work, a calendar of auction dates, and instructions on how to submit a bid. Investors submitting a noncompetitive bid can conduct a transaction online or use a toll-free telephone number.

TreasuryDirect does have a couple of drawbacks, though. You have to wait until the auction date to make a purchase and remember to submit a bid as that date nears. With a discount broker, on the other hand, you can buy when the urge strikes as the firm can pull a bond out of its secondary market inventory that matches a specified maturity. That convenience may be worth the commission, particularly on a sizable purchase.

If You've Inherited Savings Bonds

Savingsbonds.gov, another government site, is worth a look if you have savings bonds from a gift or inheritance that are accumulating dust in a safe deposit box or nightstand drawer. That happened to me a few years ago, when I had to organize several dozen old savings bonds my parents, like many careful savers of the World War II generation, had purchased on a monthly basis during the 1960s. Each of these bonds had different interest rates, payment dates, current values, and expiration dates. At the time, finding out what those bonds were worth involved a trip to a bank or time-consuming digging into government bond tables. Today it's a lot easier.

An online savings bond calculator, available at savingsbonds.gov, lets you know what your savings bonds are worth on the spot. It also shows the current rate of interest, next interest accrual date, final maturity, and year-to-date accumulated interest. A new feature saves information to a file so you can update bond values periodically. The site also has instructions for buying bonds online.

Another great source of information on savings bonds is The Savings Bond Informer of Detroit, Michigan (1-800-927-1901). Founded by Daniel Pederson, a former supervisor of the Savings Bond Division of the Federal Reserve Bank, the service provides current information on the value of savings bonds you own, as well as tips on how to minimize taxes when you cash them in.

Mortgage-Backed Securities

Ginnie Mae (GNMA) is not the name of a spinster aunt from the deep South. It's a kind of popular debt security called a *pass through* certificate that is secured by a pool of VA- and FHA- insured residential mortgages.

Ginnie Maes are issued by private lenders who assemble groups or "pools" of mortgages with similar interest rates, maturities, and other characteristics. The certificates are endorsed by the Government National Mortgage Association and guaranteed by the full faith and credit of the U.S. government. Other popular mortgage-backed securities include Fannie Maes (FNMAs) and Freddie Macs. These certificates represent pools of conventional mortgages and are backed by the government agencies that issue them.

Although U.S. government agency mortgage-backed securities are considered second only to Treasury securities when it comes to credit risk, they have another risk you should know about: prepayment risk. Anyone who has a mortgage knows that their monthly payment consists of both principal and interest. Similarly, monthly payments from mortgage pass-throughs consist of both principal and interest as well. This is especially important to remember if you own these securities individually. If you spend the entire payment each month, you'll be eating into your principal as well as living off your investment income.

Prepayment risk enters the picture when interest rates fall and homeowners refinance their mortgages. This could mean you'll get your principal back sooner than you might have expected, and you'll need to invest it at lower rates. Prepayment is also a risk for mutual funds that invest in mortgage pass-throughs.

Usually the mutual fund distributes interest to shareholders and reinvests the principal portion of the payment. That's nice if you don't want to worry about spending your principal. But if interest rates are falling and homeowners are refinancing in droves, the fund manager will be forced to reinvest the principal at lower rates. That means shareholders get lower rates, too.

Foreign Bonds

Foreign governments and companies issue bonds for many of the same reasons that their U.S. counterparts do. And, as in the United States, the riskier the issuer, the higher the rate of interest a bond will pay.

Few individual investors buy foreign bonds individually because they are a very specialized area of the market that only professionals with experience in this niche should attempt to navigate. However, a number of international bond funds offer investors the opportunity to diversify into international fixed-income markets. These funds add the element of currency risk into the picture as the bonds are denominated in foreign currencies. Some fund managers use currency hedging to minimize the impact of currency fluctuation on returns.

Bonds or Bond Funds?

You can buy any kind of bond as an individual security. Or you can buy a small piece of a large portfolio of bonds through a bond mutual fund. Both options have advantages and drawbacks.

Advantages of Bond Funds

Bond funds are a convenient form of ownership because they offer ...

- ❖ **Diversification:** When you buy shares in a bond mutual fund, you're buying a small piece of a big portfolio of dozens, or even hundreds, of bonds. When you buy a bond, you're buying the debt of one issuer. If that issuer defaults or fails to make timely interest payments, you're left holding the bag. A bond fund minimizes the impact of one or two bad apples by spreading its bets over many different bonds.

- ❖ **Professional management and research:** Investment pros analyze the bonds and pick the ones they think will out-perform over the long term.

- ❖ **Liquidity:** It's easy to buy and sell mutual fund shares and follow their price every day in the newspaper or on the Internet. If you invest in a no-load bond fund (one without a sales charge), there are no transaction costs. Individual bonds may be more difficult and costly to buy and sell, particularly if an issue is thinly traded.

❖ **Income distributions:** Bond funds typically pay income monthly while individual bonds usually pay interest every six months. You can also reinvest bond fund income automatically.

Disadvantages of Bond Funds

A number of disadvantages offset some of the convenience of bond funds:

❖ **No specific maturity:** At the end of a specified period, an individual bond matures, and you get your principal back. Although its price may fluctuate while you're holding the bond, you'll recoup your investment at maturity unless the issuer defaults.

However, because the composition of a bond fund is constantly changing, bond fund shares never mature. Thus there is no guarantee you'll get your principal back. An investor selling mutual fund shares may get more or less than he paid for them. The price will depend on a number of factors, the most important being whether interest rates are higher or lower than when the shares were purchased.

❖ **Costs:** Some bond funds have sales charges of 4 percent or more that can really eat into your returns. All bond funds, even those without sales charges, have annual management fees and other expenses that usually range from .30 to 1.0 percent. Some kinds of bond funds, particularly those that invest in junk bonds or foreign bonds, have annual expenses of over one percent because of the higher transaction and research costs associated with these securities.

❖ **Variable income:** Interest payments on bond funds vary from month to month, depending on changes in interest rates, trades and sales in the portfolio, and other factors. The interest payment assigned to a bond, its coupon, usually remains fixed until maturity.

❖ **Unanticipated taxable distributions:** When a fund realizes taxable gains on the sale of its holdings, it distributes those gains to shareholders. With individual bonds, you don't pay any tax on capital gains until you sell them.

Treasuries: Go It Alone

Using the tips outlined in this chapter, most people won't have much trouble buying and selling Treasury notes and bonds on their own. Diversification (other than buying different maturities to control interest rate risk) isn't really a big issue here because the Treasury is about as solid a credit risk as you're going to find. There's little reason to pay a mutual fund one percent of your assets a year to manage a portfolio of Treasury notes when it's so easy and inexpensive to buy them yourself.

When Bond Funds Are Better

Beyond Treasuries, the benefits of individual bonds become somewhat murkier because …

❖ You need to own bonds from at least 5 to 10 different issuers for adequate diversification. Many individuals, and even many financial advisors, don't have time to adequately research all those bonds. Even if they did, credit research on bonds is much less available than stock research.

❖ A bond dealer usually builds a markup into the price of a bond when you buy or sell, which can eat into your returns.

❖ Bond prices are harder to follow because they are not generally listed in the newspaper. There are just too many outstanding issues floating around for that kind of coverage. By contrast, the value of bond mutual fund shares appears in newspapers every day.

❖ Bonds can be called, or retired, by the issuer when interest rates rise. If that happens, you'll have to figure out where to invest your money. Although bonds in a bond fund can be called, too, you don't have to decide how to invest the money. That's the fund manager's job.

Despite these drawbacks, buying individual bonds can make sense if you ...

- ❖ Plan to stick with high-quality municipal and government bonds, since credit research on corporate bonds and foreign issues is hard to find. When it comes to corporate bonds, most people are better off with bond funds as diversification protects against the higher credit risk of corporate securities.
- ❖ Have at least $50,000 to invest in bonds. According to a recent study by the Schwab Center for Investment Research, that was the level at which the cost of a portfolio of individual bonds equaled or fell below the expense of an intermediate-term bond fund.
- ❖ Plan on holding the bond until maturity. Some municipal bonds are thinly traded, so you may have trouble getting a good price for your bonds. If you hold the bond until it matures, you don't have to worry about that. You will only have to pay a transaction fee going in, so it will be less expensive than a two-sided transaction.
- ❖ Want a regular, reliable source of income. The coupon payments on bonds don't change, while bond fund income can fluctuate.

On the other hand, a bond fund may be better if you ...

- ❖ Have less than $50,000 to allocate toward bonds.
- ❖ Don't think you'll be holding a bond until its maturity date. It's much easier to sell shares in a bond mutual fund than to try to find a buyer for a small block of bonds.
- ❖ Want to invest in the corporate or foreign fixed-income markets.
- ❖ Don't want to be bothered assembling and monitoring a portfolio of bonds.

Chuck the Checks

Don't write checks against a bond fund because you may inadvertently selling shares and eating into principal. Use a money market fund for check writing instead.

What to Look for in a Bond Fund

If you decide to put all or part of your fixed-income money into a bond fund, consider the following features.

Total Return

Don't base your selection solely on which one has the highest yield. For the full picture, look at the fund's total return. This is a more accurate measure of its performance because it includes price changes, dividend distributions, and capital gains.

Be warned: Just as the fund with the highest yield isn't always the best choice, the one with the highest total return isn't necessarily where your money should go. Total return only reflects what has happened in the past, not what will happen in the future. The market conditions that made a fund a winner over the last five years won't necessarily repeat themselves.

Credit Quality

Not all bond funds that bill themselves as "investment grade" carry the highest-quality bonds. Some concentrate their holdings on the lower end of the investment grade spectrum—bonds rated Baa/BBB by Moody's and Standard & Poor's—because they have higher yields than bonds with higher credit ratings. If you only want bonds of the highest credit quality, make sure that's what you're getting.

Expenses

Some people are willing to pay a 4 or 5 percent sales commission to buy a stock mutual fund, so they can have access to the investment prowess of a specific portfolio manager.

However, bond fund performance is usually much less variable. There just aren't many star bond fund managers out there because the bond market is much more efficient than the stock market. Putting it simply, bonds of similar quality and maturity don't perform all that differently from each other. When a bond fund seems to be doing better than its competitors over the long term, there are usually two main reasons: a) the manager is taking more credit or interest rate risk, or b) annual management and operating expenses are lower than the competition.

Since low expenses are the most predictable and reliable way to boost a bond fund's total return, why not gravitate to funds with the lowest expenses? A good hunting ground for low-expense bond funds are no-load mutual fund families such as Vanguard, TIAA-CREF, and T. Rowe Price.

Duration

This is the most accurate measure of a bond fund's volatility due to changing interest rates because it takes into account a bond's cash flow from current interest payments. If a fund has a lot of high coupon bonds, or bonds that are callable, those features will shorten the length of time it takes to get your principal and interest back. Therefore, the fund's duration will be shorter. The shorter the fund's duration, the less volatile it is.

The formula for duration is pretty simple: Multiply a fund's duration by a change in interest rates to get its potential for price movement. If a fund has a duration of four, its value will move up or down by 4 percent for every 1 percent change in interest rates. If interest rates change by 2 percent, fund shares will fluctuate by 8 percent, up or down.

Don't assume that all funds with similar maturity labels have similar durations. They don't. One manager of a long-term bond fund who thinks interest rates are set to fall may manage the portfolio to lengthen a fund's duration and possibly boost returns. Another long-term bond fund manager who is concerned about rising rates will shorten the fund's duration to protect against a downturn in price.

Read Before You Invest

Much of the information you'll need in order to evaluate a bond fund can be found in the prospectus—the booklet containing information required by the Securities and Exchange Commission—including fund expenses, fund holdings, and investment objectives and policies. Newspapers and financial Web sites will provide performance information updated daily.

Plotting Your Interest Rate Strategy

If interest rates are low and you expect them to rise, or if you think you'll need the money within a year or two ...

❖ Look for bonds or bond funds with very short maturities or simply stick with money market funds or CDs. These investments are also a good bet if you think you might need the money in less than a couple of years for a major purchase, such as buying a house or a car, and you wish to minimize or avoid the risk of losing principal as interest rates fluctuate.

If interest rates are high and look likely to fall, or if you have a somewhat longer time frame ...

❖ You stand to gain the most in a falling interest rate environment when you put your money in longer-term bonds or bond funds that invest in them or zero-coupon bonds or bond funds. In times of falling interest rates, such as 1994 and 2000, some of these funds have delivered annual returns of 15 percent or more.

Avoid these securities if you think you might need the money in less than five to ten years as they can experience a dramatic decrease in value if interest rates go up.

If you're looking for a risk-reward middle ground …

- ❖ Assuming you have a time horizon of five years or more, consider intermediate-term notes or mutual funds that invest in them. They won't rise as much as long-term bonds if interest rates fall, but you'll still get more bang for your buck than you would with money market funds or CDs. But they won't go down to the same degree as longer-term bonds if interest rates go up.

If you can't decide which way interest rates are headed or if you just don't want to make any bets, consider these alternatives:

- ❖ *Laddering* is a popular technique that involves using different maturities of the same investment. For example, you could buy certificates of deposit that come due at different dates. If rates go up, you can reinvest your principal at higher rates as your short-term certificates mature. If rates go down, the longer-term CDs will continue to produce a higher level of income for several years.
- ❖ Place half of the money you are allocating toward fixed-income investment into a money market fund and half into an intermediate-term bond fund. By using this combination, you can benefit if interest rates rise because half the money is in a money market fund. If rates fall, you can still come out ahead because the intermediate-term bond fund should rise in value.
- ❖ Use variable rate securities that adjust to changes in interest rates, such as variable rate CDs or Series EE bonds.

Parking Your Cash

Just because you want to earn income from your investments doesn't mean you necessarily have to jump right into a bond or bond fund. As we mentioned in the first chapter, one of the first things you might want to do when you receive a windfall is to park it in a safe, income-producing account that won't fluctuate in value. This gives you time to take a breath, decide what to do next, and at the same time, earn a competitive rate of return.

Good places to park your cash include the following:

* ❖ **Money market mutual funds,** first established in 1972, are a type of mutual fund that invests in short-term debt instruments. Each money market fund maintains a constant price of $1 per share, so your principal does not fluctuate as it does with a bond mutual fund. The typical money market fund holds one or more of the following kinds of debt:

* ❖ **U.S. Treasury bills** (discussed earlier in this chapter).

* ❖ **Repurchase agreements,** which represent overnight loans to a bank or securities dealer that are collateralized by U.S. Treasury securities

* ❖ **U.S. government agency securities,** including those backed by the Small Business Administration, the Federal Home Loan Bank, and the Government National Mortgage Association.

* ❖ **Short-term loans to large corporations,** called commercial paper.

* ❖ **Bankers' acceptances,** or short-term notes issued by commercial banks and sold to international companies to finance exports.

* ❖ **Certificates of deposit** offered by banks in the United States or foreign branches of U.S. banks. Another type of certificate of deposit, called a Yankee Dollar CD, is issued by large foreign banks with offices in the United States.

Many tax-free money market mutual funds invest in short-term municipal debt. These funds typically pay interest free of federal taxes. Some fund companies also offer residents of states such as Arizona, California, Connecticut, Florida, Massachusetts, New York, and New Jersey single-state, tax-free money market funds that are free of state income tax as well.

Yields on all tax-free money market funds are typically lower than on taxable money market funds. Use the calculation described in the section on municipal bond funds to figure out which will leave you with a higher after-tax yield.

Yet another money market fund twist are those that invest exclusively in U.S. Treasury bills. These funds are taxable at the federal level but are exempt from state income taxes in most states. If you live in a state with high taxes on interest and dividend income, these types of funds will often outperform fully taxable money market funds on an after-tax basis. Some funds also focus mainly on U.S. government agency obligations. Dividend yields from these funds are often exempt from state income taxes as well.

Get the Highest Yields from Money Market Funds

Look for low expenses. Money market funds in the same investment category (for example, diversified, tax-exempt, or Treasury-only) do not differ that much in their investment strategies or holdings. When it comes to money market funds, lower expenses are the main factor that translates into higher yields. The average retail money market fund has annual expenses of 0.74 percent, according to iMoneynet.com, a Web site that tracks money market mutual funds. Focus on a money market fund with expenses at that level or lower.

Caution

Some of the highest-yielding money market funds waive expenses when they are first offered to attract investors. Then, later on, the fund will impose fees and hope investors will stay put.

Invest a large amount. Some funds with the highest yields require minimum investments of $25,000 or more.

Shopping at the Bank

Money market mutual funds are considered quite safe. Although some of the funds have held debt issues that went into default, the fund companies ponied up cash so their shareholders wouldn't lose any money. Plus, the SEC prohibits taxable money funds from investing over 5 percent of their assets in any one issuer, with the exception of the U.S. government. To date, no one has lost money by investing in a money market fund.

Still, the fact remains that money market mutual funds are not insured by the Federal Deposit Insurance Corporation, or FDIC. Only bank deposits get that backup. Banks offer a money market-type account called a money market deposit account (MMDA), but their yields are usually substantially lower than money market funds. In early May 2001, for example, the average bank money market deposit account yielded 2.55 percent while the average money market mutual fund's yield was nearly 2 percent higher. That's a steep price to pay for FDIC insurance. In addition, the insurance protection is limited to amounts of $100,000 or less per person.

Certificates of deposit, or CDs, are another bank option to consider that usually carry more competitive yields than bank money market deposit accounts. When you buy a CD, you invest a fixed sum of money for a specified period of time usually ranging from six months to five years. When you cash in or redeem the CD, you receive your original investment plus accrued interest. In many cases, the yield on a six-month CD is equal to, or greater than, the yield from a money market mutual fund. Money market funds are more liquid, however, since many banks charge a penalty if you try to redeem your CD before it matures.

Years ago, most CDs paid a fixed rate of interest for six months or a year. Now, many of them have variable rates and longer terms that extend a decade or more. Others, particularly those with longer maturities, have *call features* that allow the bank to retire your CD and replace it with one that yields less if interest rates drop. Be sure to ask about call features on long-term CDs.

Shop Nationally

Although most people buy CDs through local banks, many brokerage firms now offer them, too. These sometimes have higher yields than bank CDs because the firm is able to negotiate with banks for a better rate on a volume purchase.

If you're willing to shop nationally, bankrate.com has information on which banks are offering the best CD rates nationwide.

Take Your Pick

Despite their simple and innocent exterior, fixed-income securities vary enormously in their risk and potential rewards. From ultra-low-risk Treasury bills to higher yielding but riskier junk bonds, you should choose a fixed-income flavor that matches your investment goals, income needs, tax bracket, time frame, and tolerance for risk.

CHAPTER 11

Stocks: Pumping Up Performance

Almost everyone knows it's a good idea to put a portion of your windfall into stocks to achieve investment growth and protect against inflation. Beyond that, there are literally hundreds of ways to slice and dice stock investment strategies.

Time to Get Real

A survey of 1,500 investors polled in a Securities Industry Association/Yankelovich survey in early 2000 indicated that, on average, they expected to see a 33 percent total return on their investments. Yet in all of history, that only happened one year, when the S&P 500 Index soared 33.4 percent in 1997. Judging from that response, stock market investors have gotten really, really spoiled. It's no wonder, considering the bullish tenor of the market over the last 20 years and, in particular, over the past decade.

The Stock Market's Fabulous Run

Year	Russell 2000 (Percent)	S&P 500 (Percent)
1991	46	30.5
1992	18.4	7.7
1993	18.9	10.1
1994	(1.8)	1.3
1995	28.5	37.5
1996	16.5	23.0
1997	22.4	33.4
1998	(2.6)	28.6
1999	21.3	21.0
2000	(3.0)	(9.2)

The S&P 500 Index measures the performance of the stock market in general. The Russell 2000 measures the performance of small and mid-sized companies.

From 1995 through 1999, the S&P 500 Index gained between 21 and 37 percent every calendar year. As the market reached new highs in the late 1990s, even the most speculative investments flourished. In 1998 and 1999, at the height of the bubble, stocks of Internet companies with fuzzy business plans, short operating histories, and distant prospects for earnings saw tenfold increases in their share price in a matter of weeks.

Then suddenly, investors got scared. The technology stocks that had propelled the stock market to new heights started to tumble in early 2000 and other stocks quickly followed suit. By March 2001, the NASDAQ—the exchange where many technology and smaller company stocks are traded—had tumbled over 60 percent from its high just one year earlier. Even the broader-based S&P 500 Index lost nearly one quarter of its value over the same period. Yet despite the carnage, equities remained expensive by most traditional yardsticks, including the most widely used one, the price/earnings ratios, or P/Es.

If you're under age 45 or so, chances are you probably don't remember a prolonged bear market. After all, for the 17 years ending in 1999, the S&P 500 Index had an 18.2 percent annualized rate of return and the Dow Jones Industrial Average appreciated tenfold. But look further back and you will see that the stock market does not always play nice, even if you are a patient investor. In 1982, the Dow Jones Industrial

Average stood at 1,000, about where it was in 1965. The S&P 500 Index had gained just 5.5 percent over the same period. From 1969 to 1981, the S&P 500's annual return averaged 1.28 percent. You'd have been better off putting your money into Treasury bills.

Going forward, it's unrealistic to expect that stocks will continue to deliver the kinds of returns they did in the 1990s. Evan Simonoff, editor of *Financial Advisor Magazine,* gives this advice to the investment advisors who read his publication: "It's a wise idea to lower projected returns for equities to the 7 percent to 8 percent range." He goes on to point out that since 1926, the long-term rate of return on equities has been about 11 percent, far from the 20 percent plus returns witnessed for most of the past decade. Individuals who are intending to invest their windfall in the stock market should take heed.

Stocks or Stock Funds?

Aside from unusually high returns on stocks, another funny thing happened during the 1990s: Many people started thinking they could pick stocks and manage a portfolio just as well as, or better than, professional money managers. This belief was fueled by a buoyant stock market that made picking a stock that would go down infinitely more challenging than picking one that would go up.

Online trading firms opened millions of brokerage accounts to accommodate the influx of do-it-yourself investors. Internet sites with scads of stock research tools, each claiming to give investors an edge, sprouted like dandelions. Investors crowed when they picked a high-flyer that rose tenfold in a matter of weeks. Maybe you heard one of them—or maybe you were one of them yourself.

As the new era of self-sufficient investing flourished, stock mutual funds became less popular. Between 1989 and 1997, equity funds saw new cash inflows increase at an annual rate of 44 percent a year. Since then, however, a combination of declining markets and migration toward individual stock investing has put the brakes on inflows into stock funds. Some magazines and newspapers have even predicted the eventual demise of the mutual fund.

I don't think that's going to happen. Sure, there are some good amateur investors out there with the time to research stocks and the talent to pick winners. If you join an investment club and share ideas, investing can turn into a social activity. If you have some kind of inside knowledge—perhaps because you work in a specialized field and have some insight into a company that others may not have—picking stocks yourself can be a fruitful endeavor.

But there's a big difference between inside knowledge and the kind of market information most of us get. By the time we see the latest scoop about a stock on the Internet, television, or in the newspaper, chances are the rest of the world has seen it, too. Sheldon Jacobs, a veteran mutual fund observer and editor of the *No-Load Fund Investor*, puts it this way: "Too many investors don't understand the distinction between information and knowledge. To invest successfully, an overload of information has to be filtered, so that useful information is separated from the hype. For many, their immersion in investing arcana provides only an illusion of control."

Individual investors are at an inherent disadvantage when it comes to picking stocks. One of the biggest is the fact that the analysts who produce stock reports and recommendations have their paychecks signed by the very same brokerage firms that underwrite and sell those stocks. It's no surprise, and no secret, that analysts issue so many buy recommendations and so few recommendations to sell. Consequently, investors following buy signals from sources that stand to profit from such recommendations are never told the other important side of the equation—when to sell. They just go down with the ship.

When it comes to initial public offerings, or IPOs, most individuals can forget about playing on any kind of level field. Underwriters typically dole out shares of sought-after IPOs to their biggest, most valuable clients, or to close friends and family members. The rest of us can't get in on a stock until it begins trading in the aftermarket. By that time, the price has shot up to dangerously high levels. Today, there are literally dozens of lawsuits filed by individuals who got burned by what they consider the unfair trading practices of brokerage firms that work to the disadvantage of the typical investor.

The picture does not improve when you work with most brokers. At best, they have access to the same research that you do. At worst, they tout the stocks that their firms are pushing without really knowing much beyond what their internally distributed materials tell them. If they are typical, they spend more time building and maintaining a client base than wading through the murky innards of corporate reports.

Occasional dabbling in stocks when you think you have a good idea is one thing. Building a portfolio of stocks and monitoring it consistently is another. It takes lots of time and patience, and you really need to keep on top of things. If a stock tanks rapidly because of a bad earnings report and you are on vacation or just absorbed in daily living matters and not paying attention, you could be out a lot of money. Sure, a mutual fund can fall in value, too. But because a fund is usually more diversified than most individuals' portfolios, there's greater built-in downside protection.

I guess you can tell I am not a big fan of trying to pick stocks on your own. I truly believe that for the bulk of their money most people are better off with mutual funds although they are not the perfect investment (I'll explain why later in this chapter). For my money, I'd rather let someone else who has devoted a career to understanding stocks do the investment work for me.

Picking the Right Mutual Fund

Although mutual funds are a more manageable investment for most people than a portfolio of stocks, picking the best ones requires some homework. At the very least, you should understand what a mutual fund invests in, its level of risk compared to other funds, the expenses associated with it, and how it fits into your overall investment strategy.

A mutual fund is an investment that pools money from many individuals into one portfolio that is managed by one or more portfolio managers. When you invest in a mutual fund, you own shares that represent partial ownership of the fund's securities. You participate in any gains, losses, income, or expenses that portfolio incurs. The value of a mutual fund's shares is called the *net asset value*. That figure represents the current value of all securities in the fund, minus expenses, then divided by the number of outstanding shares. The performance of mutual fund shares relates directly to the performance of the underlying securities. Its net asset value changes daily and is listed in many newspapers and investment sites on the Internet.

The kinds of securities mutual funds invest in run the gamut from safe, secure Treasury bills to high-flying Internet stocks to everything in between. Usually, the securities in a mutual fund have similar characteristics and are grouped together in a manner that conforms with a stated investment objective.

For example, a mutual fund with the word "growth" in its name might focus on securities of companies with rapidly growing earnings or cash flow. A fund that looks for stock market bargains might use the word "value" in its name. Its manager would typically seek out out-of-favor companies whose stocks are selling at what he considers inexpensive levels. A fund may also invest in stocks of foreign markets or in specific sectors such as technology, energy, or health care.

Advantages of Mutual Funds

On the plus side, mutual funds offer:

❖ **Diversification.** A typical diversified stock mutual fund invests in anywhere from 80 to 150 securities. This helps minimize risk because if one stock does poorly, the loss may be offset by gains of other stocks in the portfolio. Usually, the manager will keep no more than 5 percent of the portfolio's assets in one stock, which serves to mitigate the impact of a loss in any one security. Some mutual funds, often called *focus funds*, have a charter that allows the manager to invest in only 25 or 30 stocks. Here, the manager may have a greater concentration of assets in each stock. This concentration amplifies the fund's potential risks as well as rewards.

❖ **Liquidity.** Mutual funds constantly buy back or redeem shares. Redeeming shareholders receive the current value of the shares at the close of the day they sell them. (This assumes the fund does not have a back-end sales charge or redemption fee.) You can buy and sell shares over the phone, or, if the fund families allow it, on the Internet.

❖ **Professional investment management.** A portfolio manager researches, selects, and monitors stocks in the portfolio.

❖ **Low investment minimum.** This may not be a big consideration if you've come into a windfall, but it's nice to know that you can buy into a mutual fund without breaking the bank. The minimum investment is usually around $2,500, although some fund companies allow you to open an IRA with as little as $500.

❖ **Convenience.** Mutual funds offer services such as account statements and check writing. Mutual fund supermarkets, which allow investors to buy funds from different mutual fund firms in one place, are available through discount brokerage firms such as Charles Schwab or TD Waterhouse. All the information about the mutual funds you own is consolidated on one statement, which reduces your paperwork.

Disadvantages of Mutual Funds

Here is the minus side of mutual funds. There are a number of different expenses associated with a mutual fund. All mutual funds have annual expenses associated with their investment management, as well as costs of operation such as paying telephone representatives and sending out account statements. Usually, a stock fund's total annual expenses range from 0.5 to 2 percent. Additionally, funds sold through brokerage firms or financial advisors compensated with commissions have loads, or sales charges. These commissions can take one of several forms:

❖ **Front-end loads.** Mutual funds with front-end loads deduct a percentage of the initial investment right off the top. For example, if you invest $10,000 in a mutual fund with a front-end load of 5 percent, you end up with a net investment of $9,500. Sometimes the fund company will reduce the front-end sales charge for larger investments. Fund shares with front-end loads, which can range from 3 percent to as high as 8.5 percent of your investment, are labeled A shares.

❖ **Back-end loads.** Funds sold as B shares come with a contingent deferred sales charge, or in mutual fund shorthand, a CDSC. If you sell before a specified period of time, this charge is deducted from the redemption proceeds. Typically, the load starts at around 6 percent for shares you redeem before the first anniversary of your original investment, gradually decreases, then disappears after five or six years. Larger investors don't get a break here, as they do with A shares.

❖ **Level loads.** Under a C share arrangement, investors pay a charge of one percent a year for as long as they own the fund. If you plan on holding your shares for a number of years, this is the most expensive way to buy a fund. Some funds also have D shares. Under this arrangement, the one percent level load disappears after a certain number of years and the fund shares convert to A shares. As with B shares, larger investors in C and D shares don't get a pricing break.

There are thousands of mutual funds available without sales charges, called no-load funds. If you buy these on your own, you will not pay a sales charge. If a financial advisor purchases a no-load fund for your account, you will not incur a sales charge. However, as we discussed in Chapter 9, "Do You Need a Financial Advisor?" the financial advisor will probably charge a fee for managing your account. Here are two good sources of information on no-load and low mutual funds:

The American Association of Individual Investors publishes an annual directory of no-load and low-load mutual funds, called *The Individual Investor's Guide to Low-Load Mutual Funds* ($24.95 for nonmembers, $19.95 for members; 1-800-428-2244; www.aaii.com).

The Handbook for No-Load Fund Investors covers nearly 3,000 no-load mutual funds ($45; 1-800-252-2042; www.sheldonjacobs.com).

From the Answer Desk

Is closing a fund to new investors a good thing?

Q. I am invested in a fund that has done very well and now the fund is closing to new investors. I know this is a good thing but I am not sure I understand why. Could you explain this to me?

—Ann

A. Some fund companies feel that as the size of the fund grows, it makes it harder to manage effectively and/or that their ability to add value through stock selection is diminished. There are several reasons why this might occur:

1. Market impact: Larger purchases may actually move the price of the stock, especially in small companies or some foreign markets. This wouldn't happen in the S&P 500 size stocks, but many parts of the market are not as liquid.

2. Purchase restrictions: Funds are restricted as to what percent of a company they may own. As a result, larger funds cannot buy enough of a stock to make an impact on their performance. For instance, a very large company may find that if they buy 5 percent of the total stock of a company, it may only be .005 percent of the fund portfolio, not enough to impact performance even if the company stock goes up by 100 percent.

3. Diversification can reliably add value.

Whether you agree with the above points or not, you have to give management high marks for ethical behavior. They have nothing to gain by closing the fund except the satisfaction of doing what they think is right for investors.

—Frank Armstrong, CFP

The Low-Down on Loads

There's no such thing as a no-load load fund. Level load, or C shares, are sometimes promoted as no-load funds by salespeople just because they don't have a visible sales charge. That may be part of the reason that this share class makes up about one third of load fund sales, up from just 8 percent in 1995. Over the long run, however, C shares can actually end up being more expensive than A shares because the charge is based on assets in the account, not on the initial investment. As your account grows, so does the sales charge. And, like the Energizer Bunny, a level load just keeps going, and going, and going, no matter how long you own the fund. If you're a long-term investor, say, five years or more, you're better off just paying the sales charge up front or going with a back-end load.

- ❖ **Remember your purchase date.** Many contingent deferred sales charges are reduced or disappear after a certain number of months or years from the date of purchase. Make sure to check your purchase date when you redeem shares. It may pay to wait a few weeks if doing so reduces or eliminates your CDSC.

- ❖ **Ask questions.** Ask your financial advisor why he's recommending a specific share class, and make sure he explains the pros and cons of one share class over another. If a broker recommends a mutual fund of the firm he works for, or any fund for that matter, find out whether or not the compensation associated with selling that particular fund is higher than for others.

- ❖ **Reinvest distributions.** If you receive your dividend distributions in cash and later use the money to buy more shares, you'll end up paying a sales charge on those purchases. Instead, have the fund reinvest those distributions in additional shares, which will usually be load-free.

Mutual Fund Caution

Beginning in April 2000, new mutual funds are prohibited from levying a sales charge on reinvested dividends. However, a few older funds still adhere to what I consider the egregious practice of charging a load on reinvested dividends. You can tell if your fund does this by looking at the prospectuses or by asking your broker. If you own such a fund, you should consider selling it, particularly if it produces high dividends (and high ongoing sales charges for re-investing them). If you don't own one, avoid those that work under such an arrangement.

Other Mutual Fund Expenses

Aside from sales charges, you need to watch for some other kinds of less obvious expenses.

Redemption Fees

Some funds charge a redemption fee when you sell your shares before a specified period of time, usually anywhere from six months to a year. Redemption fees differ from back-end loads because they are not used to compensate a sales force. Instead, the fee is paid into the fund to cover costs, other than sales costs, involved with a redemption. Most funds use redemption fees to discourage short-term trading, which adds to the fund's expenses.

12b-1 Fees

These additional charges pay for promotion, distribution costs, sales commissions, and advertising, and are limited to a maximum of 1 percent per year. Some funds use 12b-1 fees to mask sales charges. Since these fees increase with the size of an account, a fund with a high 12b-1 fee can actually end up being more expensive over the long run than one with an up-front sales charge.

Exchange Fee

This fee may be charged when an investor transfers money from one fund to another within the same fund family.

Management Fee

This is the fee charged by a fund's investment advisor for managing the fund's portfolio of securities and providing related services.

Total Annual Fund Operating Expenses

This figure, also called the *expense ratio*, represents the sum of all a fund's annual operating costs, expressed as a percentage of average net assets.

If you're unsure about which fees a fund charges, the fund's prospectus—a booklet that all mutual funds are required to furnish investors with—will outline these charges clearly. The prospectus will also include other important information such as who manages the fund, its recent holdings, and how to buy or redeem shares.

Lack of Transparency

Although funds have a stated investment objective they are supposed to stick to over the long-term, it's hard to know exactly which specific securities a mutual fund is holding in its portfolio at any given point in time. Funds are only required by the SEC to update full portfolio holding information for investors every six months in their semiannual reports, and few go beyond that requirement.

Some consumer groups criticize the lag, contending that investors have a right to fresher information on the funds they own. For their part, the fund companies say that they are just protecting the interest of shareholders. Fidelity's full portfolios are updated in its annual and semiannual reports, which can be downloaded from the company's Web site or obtained by mail. The firm also updates top 10 holdings quarterly and sector weightings monthly. This schedule, says a spokeswoman, "helps ensure that the proprietary research we do remains for the benefits of our shareholders. Our managers buy and sell securities over a period of weeks or months, so this kind of disclosure reduces the possibility of speculators affecting the price we pay or receive."

Maybe you don't care to know what your fund owns every day, as long as it's doing well. But if you do care, this lack of fund transparency may be frustrating for you.

Unpredictable Taxes

Windfall recipients are more likely than most people to have money in taxable accounts. Retirement plan contributions come from earned income. When you get a windfall (unless it's from a 401[k] plan or other tax-deferred account that's eligible for an IRA rollover), you cannot put the money into a retirement plan because it is not earned income. Consequently, many windfalls sit in taxable accounts, making any earnings they generate subject to income and capital gains taxes.

At the end of 1999, 36 percent of all mutual fund assets were held in tax-deferred accounts such as IRAs and 401(k) plans. Because earnings in those accounts accumulate tax-deferred, investors with mutual funds in such plans don't have to worry about taxes until they take their money out. But if you invest in mutual funds outside of a tax-deferred retirement plan, however, you need to pay strict attention to the sometimes quirky nature of mutual fund taxes.

Here's what's so strange about them: When you buy a stock, you won't incur a short- or long-term capital gains tax until you sell it (although you may incur income taxes on any dividends the shares produce). Not so with mutual funds, which have what are called capital gains distributions. If you have money outside a tax-deferred retirement plan, you can be hit with a capital gains distribution even if you don't sell your mutual fund shares.

That's because the fund's manager is busily buying and selling securities in the portfolio. If stocks have appreciated in value since the manager bought them, the fund has realized a profit on the sale. If the fund held the security for less than a year, it's a short-term capital gain that is distributed to shareholders as a dividend and taxed at rates of up to 38.6 percent in 2001. If the security was in the portfolio for more than one year, it is taxed at the more favorable long-term capital gains rate, which maxes out at 20 percent. Federal regulations require that mutual funds distribute these gains to shareholders in the calendar year they are realized.

The Double Whammy

You may think it's unfair to have to pay capital gains taxes while you're still holding on to your mutual fund shares. It's even more unfair when those taxes come in a year when the fund has actually lost money for shareholders; this is what the mutual fund industry calls the "double whammy."

This dreaded event happened in 2000, when a downturn in the stock market prompted many stock fund shareholders to bail out. The exodus that forced many mutual fund managers to sell stock to meet shareholder redemptions. Because many of those stocks had seen significant gains since they were purchased, the funds had to distribute those gains to shareholders.

Of the more than 6,000 stock funds available at the end of the year, a total of 2,841 had negative returns for 2000, according to Weisenberger/Thomson Financial. Of those, 2,311 funds made capital gains distributions during the year.

Aside from capital gains distributions, mutual funds also distribute dividends. In a mutual fund, dividends consist of income from bond interest as well as stock dividends, after expenses. And, of course, you have to pay taxes on fund shares you sell at a profit, just as you would with a stock.

Tips for Successful Mutual Fund Investing

Don't chase last year's winners. As the editor of fundsinteractive.com, a Web site on mutual funds, I can't tell you how many times people have written me a note that goes something like this:

> I bought a technology fund last year that had triple-digit
> returns. I thought it was a good bet because I saw the manager

on the cover of a personal finance magazine, and it's done so well lately. Now it's down about 40 percent. Should I sell or hang on?

Many people think that the way to make money in stock funds is to buy the fund that's run by the guy who just appeared on the cover of a personal finance magazine. Or, they choose one based on a recent thumbs-up by a fund rating service.

The problem with these approaches is that by the time a fund manager has appeared on a magazine cover, there's a good chance his fund has shot up fairly quickly or has had a long stretch of exceptional performance. After some strong publicity, fund assets may balloon quickly, making it difficult for a manager to invest the money efficiently. All of these factors could lead to making the fund ripe for a correction.

As for fund rating services, they're useful for evaluating a fund's investment style, performance, volatility, and other characteristics. What they're not good for is picking next year's winners, something you would not know when you read some mutual fund ads that hype the number of stars they received. Ratings only tell you what has gone on in the past, not what will happen in the future. Instead of chasing last year's winners, assemble a solid, balanced portfolio of funds with a variety of different investment styles and objectives.

All this does not mean you shouldn't seek out funds with strong long-term performance. Just don't make that your sole criterion, as the market conditions that made a fund a winner in previous years may not persist over the next few years. You should always compare a fund's performance against similar funds or indexes, rather than with the hot fund *du jour* or a sector that is on a roll. By gauging relative performance, or performance against similar investments, you are making a true apples-to-apples comparison.

Consider fund expenses before you buy. Although a fund's future performance is about as certain as the path of a tornado, fund expenses are much more predictable. Even though mutual funds can change their expenses, a fund that has a history of low or average expenses will usually continue along that path. Over time, high fund expenses can be a real drag on performance.

The following table illustrates the difference between a fund with a front-end sales charge versus a no-load fund. Assume that both have an annual rate of return of 10 percent.

Sales Charge	Amount Invested	Value After Ten Years	Value After Twenty Years
None	$10,000	$25,930	$67,300
$500	$9,500	$24,605	$63,935

After 20 years, the fund without the up-front sales charge is worth $3,365 more than the fund that has one.

Higher annual expenses, such as a level load or 12b-1 charge, come directly out of your returns and can have an even greater impact on the amount you save over time than the front-end sales charge. For example, if two funds have the same gross returns, but one charges 1 percent more in expenses, here's what happens after 20 years:

Amount Invested	Net Return	Value in Ten Years	Value in Twenty Years
Low-Expense Fund			
$10,000	10 percent	$25,930	$67,300
High-Expense Fund			
$10,000	9 percent	$23,670	$56,040

After 20 years, the lower-expense fund is worth $67,300—over $11,000 more than the high-expense fund.

Pay attention to the impact of taxes. According to the Securities and Exchange Commission, taxes are one of the most significant costs of investing in mutual funds. Recent estimates suggest that more than 2.5 percentage points of the average stock fund's total return are lost each year to taxes. Despite the money at stake, many investors don't understand the impact of taxes on their mutual fund investments. In a recent survey, 85 percent of fund investors said that taxes play an important role in investment decisions, but only 18 percent could identify the maximum tax rate for long-term capital gains.

The tax bite varies widely from fund to fund. One study shows that the annual impact of taxes on stock fund performance ranges from 0 for the most tax efficient to 5.6 percentage points for the least tax-efficient.

The size of the tax bite depends on several factors, including the level of portfolio trading, the amount of gains realized on the trades, and the degree to which the manager uses portfolio losses to offset realized gains. A few kinds of funds tend to be more tax-efficient than others and are thus particularly suited to individuals with a windfall sitting in a taxable account. These include index funds, tax-managed funds, and funds that are naturally tax-efficient.

Index Funds

An index fund is a mutual fund that closely tracks the performance of a stock market index by essentially replicating the group of stocks that comprise that index. Some indexes, such as the S&P 500, measure the performance of large companies, while others, such as the Russell 2000, zero in on small companies. Others seek to replicate indixes of foreign securities, bonds, emerging markets, and others.

The only time the composition of an index fund changes is when a company is removed from the index or investors request their money back. Because so little buying and selling goes on in an index fund, taxes are kept to a bare minimum during your holding period. This makes their tax efficiency comparable to that of individual stocks.

Aside from their teeny tax bite, index funds offer solid performance compared to actively managed funds. The S&P 500 Index has beaten about 65 to 80 percent of actively managed mutual funds over the long term, depending on the time period measured. Part of that comes from the fact that actively managed mutual funds usually have higher expenses than index funds, which is a constant drag on performance. One Web site, indexfunds.com, is a good source of information on how to select and manage a portfolio of index funds.

Tax-Managed Funds

The 59 funds with the words *tax managed* in their names minimize the impact of capital gains taxes by limiting trades or offsetting gains with losses.

Naturally Tax-Efficient Funds

Although they may not have the words "tax managed" in their names, some types of stock funds are better from a tax standpoint than others. Many of these funds have low portfolio turnover, which means they tend to hold on to stocks rather than trade them. Portfolio turnover is expressed as a percentage of the total assets. For example, a portfolio turnover rate of 50 percent annually means that half the dollar value of a portfolio's holdings were changed in a year. The average stock fund has a portfolio turnover rate of about 100 percent a year, meaning that the entire dollar value of the portfolio's holdings changed during the year.

Usually, a fund with a higher-than-average portfolio turnover has higher-than-average taxes. Occasionally, however, funds with a higher than average portfolio turnover ratio can be very tax efficient if the manager offsets investment gains with losses.

New SEC Rule Requires Disclosure of After-Tax Returns

It used to be hard to figure out a fund's after-tax return. Not any more. A new SEC disclosure requirement that went into effect in April 2001 will make it much easier for investors to figure out just how much they are losing, or not losing, to taxes when they invest in a mutual fund.

The rules require a fund to include after-tax returns for 1-, 5-, and 10-year periods in its prospectus. The returns must be presented for investors who have held their shares in those time frames and those who have sold them. New advertisements must also reflect after-tax performance.

Investors should welcome these new changes. In the past, some of the hottest top-performing funds were able to tout their returns without disclosing the big bite that taxes took out. That won't happen anymore. As mutual fund investors begin paying more attention to taxes, so should the fund managers who handle their money.

More Mutual Fund Tips

Keep track of your statements. When you sell mutual fund shares, you need to know how much you paid for them to figure out your taxes. If you have been re-investing your distributions in additional shares, as many fund investors do, you need to include the cost of such purchases in your calculations. Otherwise, you could end up under-figuring your cost, and overpaying in taxes.

Don't be afraid to use the KISS (Keep It Simple, Stupid) approach. If you don't want to spend a lot of time on your investments, it's perfectly okay to use the KISS approach to mutual fund investing. You don't need to have a dozen different mutual funds to diversify a portfolio. You don't even need half that many.

Some funds have such broad investment charter that you only need a few of them to build a solid well-rounded portfolio of funds. For example, Vanguard's Total Stock Market Index Fund and the Schwab Total Stock Market Index Fund are designed to replicate the performance of the entire U.S. stock market, as measured by the Wilshire 5000. This index is the broadest stock index in the United States and consists of all stocks traded on the New York and American Stock Exchanges, as well as the NASDAQ over-the-counter market. For the considerable number of people who do not want to spend more than a couple of hours a month monitoring their investments, these funds are an easy, quick way to get a broad-based comprehensive representation of small-, mid-, and large-sized U.S. companies.

Another KISS approach is to use a balanced fund. A balanced fund invests in a mix of equity securities and bonds. These funds often maintain a target percentage in each assets class and will typically have about a 60/40 mix of stocks to bonds and money-market securities. Flexible portfolio funds also invest in all those types of securities, but may change their weighting in each asset class depending on the manager's view of market conditions.

Growth vs. Value

Many people prefer to take a more active role in mutual fund investing. As you shop for a fund, you're likely to come across two basic philosophies of stock market investing: growth versus value. Many funds use the words "growth" and "value" in their names, so it's easy to tell them apart. Sometimes, however, you need to take a look at the stocks they own to figure it out.

Growth: Going for the Brass Ring

A growth stock strategy focuses on companies that are exhibiting potential for long-term, above-average revenue and/or earnings growth. Because growth stocks are issued by companies that plow back a large portion of their sales or earnings into future expansion, they generally have low or no dividends. Some growth stocks are large, well-established names with a proven history of sales and earnings. Others may be smaller companies with a little more under their belts than a glimmer in a CEO's eye. These are often called *aggressive growth* stocks.

Growth stocks and aggressive growth stocks often have higher price-earnings ratios compared to the rest of the stock market because investors are willing to pay a higher price for the faster earnings growth potential these companies have compared to others. That earnings growth, they believe, will serve to propel the stock price even higher in the future.

Growth at-a-Reasonable Price: The Middle Ground

Growth investors don't always follow the same philosophies and investment styles. Within the classification are some fairly broad variations on the theme.

Some growth investors are willing to pay extraordinarily high price-earnings multiples if they are optimistic that a company can fulfill its growth potential or think a bull market can keep the wind at their backs. The most aggressive corner of the growth group will even buy stocks of companies that have not yet shown earnings. These managers usually focus on hot initial public offerings or stocks of very small companies. In the late 1990s, technology and Internet companies dominated the growth-at-any-price category.

Another group, the growth-at-a-reasonable price (GARP) crowd, takes a somewhat more conservative approach. They want above-average earnings growth, but they also pay attention to how high a stock's P/E is. They're willing to pay a price-earnings multiple that's higher than the market average for a stock that looks promising. But they won't "shoot the moon," as a more aggressive growth investor might. They're more likely to look for larger companies with a solid earnings history as opposed to a high-flying small company technology stock.

Value Investors: Playing It Safe

If you're a bargain hunter who migrates to the markdowns in a department store, a fund with a value orientation may be for you. Value investors look for signs that a stock is selling for less than what they believe it is really worth. Such a sign may be a low P/E relative to the rest of the market, which indicates that a company's strong earnings or earnings potential is not reflected in the price of the stock.

Another commonly used value yardstick is book value, which represents a company's assets minus its liabilities. When a company's book value is high compared with its stock's price, it has a low price to book value, considered to be another characteristic of a value stock. Value stocks also tend to have above-average dividend yields and are often preferred by investors looking for a combination of long-term growth and current income. They are often found in low-growth or mature industries, in stock groups that have fallen out of favor, or in established blue-chip companies with stable earnings and regular dividends.

Value stocks sometimes fall into a category called *cyclicals*. Unlike growth companies that have a history of relatively smooth earnings and sales, cyclical stocks ride the crests and troughs of the economy and are driven by consumer demand. During an economic recovery, earnings of cyclical companies tend to get a sharp boost. During a recession, they can be abysmal because people do not want to spend money. Automobile companies, retailers, paper manufacturers, newspaper publishers, and companies that produce building materials are often classified as cyclical. These stocks tend to do best when the economy is just starting to turn around.

Other stocks that fall into the value category are those that, for one reason or another, have been depressed for an extended period of time. The tobacco group is an excellent recent example of this. During the late 1990s, the stocks in the group foundered because of slower sales in the United States and investor concerns over tobacco litigation. In 1999 alone, Philip Morris, considered by many the bellwether of the group, fell 54 percent. As a stock it was statistically one of the cheapest around, with a price-earnings ratio of just seven. The following year, Philip Morris and other tobacco stocks saw triple-digit returns as investors decided that the market had overreacted to those problems and they were just too cheap to pass up.

Value or Growth: Which Is Better?

Generally, funds that focus on value stocks are less volatile than growth funds. They won't rise as much in bull markets as growth funds, but they won't fall as much in bear markets either. On the other hand, growth funds tend to have more pronounced upturns and downturns and tend to do best in strong bull markets.

Often, the two strategies work in opposite directions. When growth stocks are doing well, many value stocks lag. That was the case for much of the late 1990s, when technology and other growth sectors led the market. On the other hand, value stocks may hold up better in bearish markets, such as 2000, because they don't have as far to fall as growth stocks. With expectations low, value stocks do not have to deliver rapidly growing earnings, quarter after quarter, to do well. They can just grow slowly and steadily. For that reason, some investors view them as a defensive play.

Taxes are another consideration when weighing value stocks against growth stocks. Growth stocks tend to reap more of their total return from appreciation than value stocks because fast-growing companies pay little or no dividends. Dividends are taxed at ordinary income rates as high as 38.6 percent, while long-term capital gains are subject to a top tax rate of 20 percent. Because of this tax consideration, some investors prefer to invest the bulk of their taxable account monies in growth investments and keep income-producing investments such as dividend-paying value stocks in retirement plans.

Value is not necessarily better than growth, and growth is not necessarily a better way to go than value. They are just different animals. For most people, it's a good idea to own both types of funds for portfolio diversification and balance.

Keep in mind that classifying actively managed funds is an inexact science because many are susceptible to what is known as *style drift*. For example, a fund manager might use an aggressive growth strategy in strong bull markets, when stocks of small, growing companies are leading the pack. But he may make a subtle shift to a less aggressive growth-at-a-reasonable price philosophy when the market cools down.

Style drift has come under considerable criticism from style purists, who think mutual fund managers should stick to their knitting. Others believe there is nothing inherently wrong with style drift, if you view part of a fund manager's job as tailoring the fund's investments to prevailing market conditions. If the manager's right, such moves will benefit shareholders. But if he is wrong, they could work against you. Index funds avoid the issue of style drift because there is no manager to make those kinds of decisions.

Mutual Fund Classifications

All stock mutual funds follow some variation of value, growth-at-a-reasonable price, aggressive growth, and growth themes. The Investment Company Institute, a trade industry association for the mutual fund industry, provides a further breakdown of stock fund classifications. These can be useful when you are comparing funds with similar objectives:

❖ *Capital appreciation funds* seek capital appreciation; dividends are not a primary consideration. These are most likely to follow a growth-investing strategy.

❖ *Aggressive growth funds* invest primarily in common stocks of small growth companies.

- *Growth funds* invest primarily in common stocks of well-established companies.

- *Sector funds* invest primarily in companies in related fields, such as health care or technology.

- *Total return funds* seek a combination of current income and capital appreciation. These are most likely to follow a value-investing strategy.

- *Growth and income funds* invest primarily in common stocks of established companies with the potential for growth and a consistent record of dividend payments.

- *Income-equity funds* invest primarily in equity securities of companies with a consistent record of dividend payments. They seek income more than capital appreciation.

- *World equity funds* invest primarily in stock of foreign companies. These funds may adhere to either a value or growth strategy.

- *Emerging market funds* invest primarily in companies based in developing regions of the world.

- *Global equity funds* invest primarily in equity securities traded worldwide, including those of U.S. companies.

- *International equity funds* must invest in equity securities of companies located outside the United States and cannot invest in U.S. company stocks.

- *Regional equity funds* invest in companies based in a specific part of the world.

As you shop around for an equity mutual fund, you're likely to come across these common terms:

- Market capitalization (or market cap): The market value of a company's outstanding stock, derived by multiplying its share price by the number of outstanding shares. Definitions of what constitutes a small-, mid- and large-cap stock vary but generally break down something like this: small-cap is anything under $2 billion; mid-cap is between $2 billion and $10 billion; and large-cap is anything over $10 billion. Many mutual funds focus specifically on small, mid- or large-cap stocks, while others place no limits on the size of companies they invest in.

❖ A price-earnings (P/E) ratio reflects how much an investor is willing to pay for every dollar of a company's earnings, and is simply the price of the stock divided by its current (or projected) earnings. For instance, a stock selling for $35 per share with earnings per share of $1 has a P/E of 35. A stock selling for $100 a share with earnings of $5 a share has a P/E of 20.

Normally, stocks of small companies have the highest P/Es because investors anticipate that these companies will grow more rapidly. But in bullish markets, even larger companies can have astronomically high P/Es. At the height of the technology boom in 1998, Dell Computer had a price-earnings ratio of 114.4. By mid-2001, the stock had fallen so much that the stock sold at just 31 times earnings, just a tad above the average P/E ratio of 25.2 for all the stocks in the S&P 500 Index.

Sometimes, newer or smaller companies will not have a price-earnings ratio assigned to them because they are not yet profitable. Instead, investors track their progress by revenue growth or other measures. Companies without earnings are the riskiest breed of stock market investments.

❖ A price-to-book ratio compares the market price of a company's common stocks with the stock's book value (assets minus liabilities) per share. Basically, it compares what investors believe a firm is worth to what the company's accountants say it is worth.

Many mutual funds measure their performance against market indixes that are comparable to the composition of their portfolios. These indixes include:

❖ **The Standard & Poor's 500 (S&P 500):** Widely regarded as the benchmark for measuring large-company U.S. stocks, the S&P 500 includes 500 companies weighted by market capitalization. It consists of 400 industrial companies, 20 transportation, 40 public utilities, and 40 financials.

* **Russell 2000 Index:** The most common small-cap indicator, the Russell 2000 Index measures the performance of 2000 companies representing about 11 percent of investable U.S. stocks. Its average market capitalization is about $592 million.

* **NASDAQ:** The NASDAQ consists of the 5,000 stocks that trade through the National Association of Securities Dealers Automated Quotations system. As this indicator is weighted by market value, the biggest companies have the most pronounced impact on performance.

* **Morgan Stanley Europe, Australasia, and Far East (EAFE):** This international index combines 20 established stock markets outside North America. Japan has a substantial presence in the index.

* **Dow Jones Industrial Average (DJIA):** This may be the index you hear about most, but it really doesn't represent many stocks in the U.S. market. The Dow is comprised of 30 actively traded blue-chip stocks that together represent only 15 percent of the value of the U.S. stock market.

Keep Your Windfall Growing

Historically, stocks and stock funds have offered better opportunities for long-term growth than fixed income investments. By diversifying across different types of stocks and resisting the temptation to chase the hottest sectors or latest market fads, you can use stocks and stock funds to help keep your windfall growing long after you get it.

CHAPTER 12

The Investment Menu

*Beyond plain vanilla bonds, stocks, and stock funds, there are a
number of other new or newly popular investments you are likely
to come across as you decide how to invest your windfall.*

All About Annuities

Windfall recipients seeking some tax relief are prime targets for a variable annuity sales pitch. The reason? Unlike an IRA or 401(k) plan, an
annuity investment is not subject to any dollar limitations. As well, it
need not come from earned income. Savings, an inheritance, or payment
from a severance plan can all be used to buy a variable annuity.

Annuities as an investment vehicle have become popular among
windfall recipients and others. According to the Variable Annuity
Research Data Service (VARDS) in Atlanta, sales of variable annuities
rose from $12 billion in 1990 to $123 billion in 1999. High costs and
other factors, however, make variable annuities unsuitable for many
people.

Annuity Basics

If you've been approached about buying an annuity, it's important to
understand how these complicated investment-insurance hybrids work.
Before you make a decision, learn about their potential advantages and
disadvantages.

An annuity is an insurance company contract in which a customer
invests a specified amount of money, either with a lump sum or in

smaller amounts over time. With a fixed annuity, investors receive a pre-determined rate of interest, which the insurer may adjust periodically. In a variable annuity, you allocate your investment among several mutual fund-type sub-accounts. Many variable annuities offer a guaranteed rate option that, like a fixed annuity, credits a fixed rate of interest to your account for a specified period of time.

Whichever annuity investment option you choose, earnings on your investment accumulate tax deferred until withdrawal. The accumulated value of a variable annuity depends on a number of factors, including the performance of the investments you select, the amount you pay into the contract, and any withdrawals you make. If you withdraw annuity assets before age $59^{1}/_{2}$, the IRS imposes a 10 percent penalty on the earnings portion of the withdrawal, which will also be subject to income taxes. At retirement, monies accumulated in the annuity may be withdrawn in a lump sum or taken gradually as needed. The owner may also choose to annuitize, or receive guaranteed payments over his or her lifetime or over another specified period.

The Pros of Annuities

Expect a salesperson to highlight these annuity benefits:

❖ **Tax deferral:** Although contributions are not tax deductible, earnings accumulate tax deferred until withdrawal.

❖ **Death benefit guarantee:** What makes a variable annuity an insurance-based product is its death benefit guarantee. At a minimum, this ensures that heirs will receive a death benefit at least equal to what the investor put into the account, less any withdrawals. This feature has taken on added appeal after recent market turbulence.

❖ **Unlimited contributions:** Unlike a 401(k) or IRA, a variable annuity investment is not subject to any dollar limitations. And it need not come from earned income. Savings, an inheritance, or proceeds from the sale of a home may be sheltered in a variable annuity.

The Cons of Annuities

Variable annuities carry a number of disadvantages:

- **High expenses:** The main drawback of variable annuities is the added annual expense for the death benefit guarantee insurance, which averages from around 0.8 percent to 1.4 percent of assets a year. That does not include the surrender charges many of them have, which can eat up as much as 9 percent of the account value if you take the money out in the first year or two. Surrender charges decrease gradually over time but may take seven years or more to disappear.

- **Turning capital gains into income:** Another concern is the fact that although profits accumulate in an annuity tax deferred, they are taxed at ordinary income rates as high as 38.6 percent at withdrawal. This is significantly higher than the maximum long-term capital gains tax rate of 20 percent in a taxable account. That favorable rate is slated to become even lower in the future. Securities purchased in 2001 or after and held for five years or more will qualify for a maximum long-term capital gains tax rate of 18 percent. For this reason, variable annuities make more sense for those who will not be in the highest tax bracket at retirement as the downside of losing favorable capital gains treatment is bigger for them.

- **The stepped-up value of the investment for heirs:** Let's say someone buys a mutual fund at $10 a share, and the value rises to $20 by the time he or she dies. If the investment were a taxable mutual fund and the heirs decided to sell, their cost basis would be the value at the time of the inheritance—in this case $20 a share. If the fund were held in a variable annuity, however, the gain would be figured based on the investor's purchase price of $10 a share.

When Variable Annuities Make the Most Sense

Because of high costs and other disadvantages, most people are better off using other tax-favored savings plans, such as retirement accounts or tax-efficient mutual funds. However, under certain circumstances, annuities can be useful.

Investing a Windfall

Let's say you have money that is not eligible for retirement plan contributions. That money can come from an inheritance, a divorce settlement, winning the lottery, or some other windfall. I once spoke with a 58-year-old divorced father of two who had moved to Hawaii after taking early retirement from his job as a computer consultant for a Dallas-based retailer. Before pulling up roots he needed to get his finances in order, a task that included figuring out what to do with his severance pay.

As he had other resources available, he didn't need the severance check for living expenses. Since it was too much money to put into an IRA, his only choices were to pay taxes every year on his investment earnings in a taxable account or to invest through a tax-deferred variable annuity. He chose the latter option.

Over the last four years, he has also put a portion of his monthly pension payments into the annuity. "I can't contribute the money to an IRA because a pension isn't earned income," he explained. "So a variable annuity is the next best thing for me if I want to defer taxes."

Annuity No-No

One thing you should not do is buy a variable annuity with money in a qualified retirement plan. By doing that, you're paying to get a tax benefit you already have.

Are Your Retirement Plans Fully Funded?

Let's say you've maxed out on your retirement plan contributions. IRAs and 401(k) plans offer the benefit of tax deferral and sometimes, an immediate tax deduction or employer matching contribution, all without the added insurance expense of an annuity. Consequently you should contribute to these first. High-income individuals or families, or pre-retirees playing catch up on their retirement savings, may already be contributing the maximum allowable amount to qualified plans and may find a variable annuity useful.

Conservative to Aggressive Investing

You can use annuities for very conservative or very aggressive investing. From a tax standpoint, putting income-producing investments like bonds or bond funds in a variable annuity makes sense. Because such investments are likely to derive much of their returns from interest income, you don't feel the pinch of losing long-term capital gains rates as much as you would in a stock fund.

Aggressive traders who don't hold on to their mutual funds long enough to take advantage of lower long-term capital gains may also find annuities attractive, since they don't have to pay short-term capital gains taxes on trading profits. No matter how active an investor you are, exchanges among sub-accounts in a variable annuity are always tax deferred (although some plans may impose extra fees for short-term trading).

Annuitizing Your Annuity

Let's say you plan to annuitize, or take money out gradually. Many annuity owners take their money out in a lump sum and pay taxes on it all at once. However, you may be better off taking the money out from an annuity gradually, or annuitizing, says Glenn Daily, a New York City insurance consultant.

That's because the money left in the annuity has time to continue growing tax-deferred during retirement, which is not the case if it is sitting in a taxable account. Although relatively few people choose to draw a lifetime income through annuitizing, that may change in the future as aging baby boomers begin to place greater weight on the security of having a regular, guaranteed income.

Exchange Your Insurance Policy

Perhaps you want to get rid of a high-cost insurance policy. Daily says that variable annuities are a good way to ease the pain of a high-cost insurance investment. "Let's say someone has paid $50,000 in premiums into a universal life insurance policy, and the cash value is now $20,000 because of commissions and insurance charges," he explains. "If you exchanged it for a variable annuity, using what's called a Section 1035 exchange, you calculate the cost basis using the $50,000 in premiums you paid into the original policy, not the $20,000 cash value. So essentially, the first $30,000 in gains within the variable annuity is tax-free when you take the money out."

Shopping Around

Variable annuities are a complicated and sophisticated planning tool. If you think they might be what you're looking for, look for a broad range of attractive investment options you can be happy with years down the road. Focus on low-expense variable annuities with total expenses of under one percent. You're most likely to find these at no-load mutual fund groups and discount brokers, such as TIAA-CREF, Charles Schwab, and Vanguard, which sell annuities directly to the public. When it comes to variable annuities, low expenses can make the difference between an investment that makes sense and one that doesn't.

Variable Annuity Sales Growth	
Year	($ in Billions)
1990	12
1991	17.3
1992	28.5
1993	46.6
1994	50.2
1995	51.3
1996	74.3
1997	88.2
1998	99.8
1999	122.7
2000	105.9*

*As of September 30, 2000; source: Variable Annuity Research Data Services (VARDS)

Exchange-Traded Funds

Exchange-traded funds (ETFs) are a new breed of investment that looks like a mutual fund but trades like a stock. Each exchange-traded fund share represents ownership of an underlying portfolio of securities. Like a traditional index mutual fund, most are passively managed and seek to replicate an index or asset class. You can buy any one of the 114 available ETFs on the market today, including those that replicate the S&P 500 Index, the Dow Jones Industrial Average, or the tech-heavy NASDAQ 100. Although most trading activity centers around the larger, best-known indexes, the newer ETFs are based on sector plays ranging from Internet infrastructure to emerging foreign markets.

ETFs differ from traditional mutual funds because they trade on an exchange just like a stock. While index funds are re-priced at the end of the day at their net asset value, exchange-traded funds are priced throughout the day and can be bought or sold almost instantly at the market price. You can sell ETFs short or buy them on margin.

While those kinds of advantages probably lure more traders and speculators than long-term investors, exchange-traded funds have two main characteristics that make them appealing to the buy-and-hold crowd. Because of their unique operating structure, they offer greater potential for tax efficiency than a mutual fund. In addition, they often have lower operating expenses. Promoters say an exchange-traded fund is the perfect marriage of two investment vehicles because you get the trading flexibility and low cost of a stock with the built-in diversification of a mutual fund.

Investors have apparently warmed up to the advantages of exchange-traded products. From 1998 to 2000, assets under management in ETFs more than tripled and now account for over $75 billion. Due to the popularity of ETFs, some press reports have declared the eventual demise of the traditional open-end mutual fund.

A Small Bandwagon

While ETFs are good for some people, they are not the best alternative for everyone. Traditional index mutual funds are often a better choice.

Some financial advisors who work with traditional index mutual funds are not stepping up to the ETF plate just yet, or are dabbling with them in a tentative, experimental way until they know more about the product.

If you feel as if you have been left out of the ETF party, you shouldn't. While exchange-traded funds have grown rapidly over the last few years, that growth has been concentrated among a relative handful of shares and among institutional investors rather than among individuals or financial advisors. At $26 billion, the SPDR 500 (Standard & Poor's Depositary Receipt, nicknamed "Spider") is the largest exchange-traded fund in terms of assets, according to Wiesenberger, Thomson Financial. Clocking in second is the NASDAQ 100 Tracking Stock with over $24 billion. Together, the two exchange-traded funds account for over 75 percent of total ETF assets, and institutional investors account for 70 percent of the money invested in these stocks.

The Five Largest Exchange-Traded Funds

Fund	Ticker	Assets ($ in Billions)
SPDR (Spider) 500	SPY	30.03
NASDAQ 100 Trust Series I	QQQ	24.23
S&P Midcap (S&P 400)	MDY	4.19
Diamond Series Trust I	DIA	2.70
iShares S&P 500	IVV	2.60

Source: American Stock Exchange (AMEX), as of June 30, 2001

How ETFs Work

Like mutual funds, ETFs give the investor the ability to diversify among many securities with a single investment. Beyond that, the two don't have much in common. The most important elements to consider in making a comparison include structure, cost, and tax advantage.

Structure

Unlike a mutual fund, which sells its shares to investors for cash, ETFs continuously swap their shares in large blocks called *creation units* with institutional investors for portfolios of securities that make up the underlying index. Once a creation unit is issued, the investor may hold on to the shares or sell them in the secondary market. To redeem them, the investor swaps the creation unit for a basket of its underlying securities, plus a balancing amount of cash.

When the value of the underlying securities exceeds the ETF price, arbitrageurs—investors who profit from trading on short-term pricing discrepancies—will quickly step in to redeem their lower-priced creation units for the higher-priced individual securities. If the price of the creation unit exceeds the value of the individual securities, arbitrageurs will trade their securities in for more valuable creation units.

This constant behind-the-scenes swapping largely excludes the individual investor, who is too small to participate in the game. But it does help ensure that the price at which the ETF trades varies little, if at all, from the value of the securities in its portfolio.

This arbitrage mechanism works best for ETFs that track larger indices, says Eric Kobren, editor, *Fidelity Insight* newsletter. "The more narrowly focused ETFs are less efficient," he notes. "You need to pay attention to any premium or discount, which has recently been as large as 1.5 percent. Unfortunately, right now, this information is hard, if not impossible, for individual investors to come by."

A number of variations have developed around the basic ETF theme. Investors can only buy Merrill Lynch's HOLDRs (Holding Company Depository Receipts) in 100-share increments, and they can exchange them for the underlying stock at any time. For sophisticated investors, this creates arbitrage opportunities when the HOLDR trades at a discount or premium to the net asset value of the underlying portfolio. The large investment required to buy the minimum lot puts them out of reach for most individuals.

The NASDAQ 100 Tracking Stock, also known as Cube because of its QQQ ticker symbol, is by far the most actively traded ETF. Unlike a traditional ETF, which is structured like an open-end mutual fund, a Cube is more like a unit investment trust because it has a fixed portfolio of securities. SPDRs are also structured as unit investment trusts. ETFs using this structure differ from open-end funds because they can't reinvest dividends immediately and may not lend out their securities. While most ETFs are based on indices, some new entrants incorporate elements of active management, which may make them less tax-efficient.

Cost

Like mutual funds, exchange-traded funds have an annual expense ratio that is expressed as a percentage of daily net assets. Sometimes it is lower than a comparable mutual fund. For example, the annual expense ratio for Barclays iShares 500 Index is 0.0945 percent, or about half that of the Vanguard 500 Index Fund.

But ETFs are not always cheaper. Three other Vanguard funds— The Mid-Cap Index Fund, the Small-Cap Index Fund, and the Tax-Managed Capital Appreciation Fund—have higher expense ratios than comparable iShares, a type of exchange-traded fund. Two others have expense ratios equal to those of the comparable iShares, and expense ratios for six comparable Vanguard funds are lower.

Aside from annual expenses, there are other cost-related issues. While the no-load Vanguard funds do not carry a sales charge, you must pay a brokerage commission to buy an exchange-traded fund. That barrier can be formidable and expensive for investors who dollar cost average with regular monthly purchases. On the other hand, for someone with a larger lump sum of at least several thousand dollars, a $15 discount brokerage commission is probably not a major consideration.

But Vanguard does not always come out ahead, so you need to compare costs based on your own investment pattern and amounts. If you invest in Vanguard funds through a discount broker's mutual fund supermarket, which tacks on a fixed charge to buy the funds, the commission may exceed the cost of buying a comparable dollar amount of iShares.

Tax Advantages

Both traditional mutual funds and ETFs distribute realized capital gains and dividends. Mutual funds distribute these gains to shareholders.

Because an ETF satisfies redemptions through transferring underlying securities to large institutional investors, its sponsor can identify which securities are most advantageous to transfer from a tax standpoint. This mechanism allows it to effectively eliminate any unrealized tax liability.

So far, at least for the larger indices, the system seems to accomplish its goal. Standard & Poor's Depository Receipts, the oldest ETFs, have had just one capital gains distribution of 0.16 percent since they were introduced in 1993.

Not all ETFs have managed to avoid capital gains distributions. Some of those that track mid-cap and foreign benchmarks have, in fact, realized some fairly sizable distributions over time. Keep in mind that any tax advantages ETFs have are only relevant for taxable accounts.

Are ETFs a Good Investment?

While Wall Street has warmed up to ETFs, they're still largely unexplored territory for most of Main Street. That does not mean you should not invest in them, especially if the idea of having "first on the block" status sounds appealing. At this point, the popular exchange-traded funds like the NASDAQ 100 Tracking Stock or SPDRs look like an attractive alternative to index funds. But for the dozens of less widely traded, newer entrants into the marketplace where pricing and tax inefficiencies are more common, it's probably best to tread cautiously.

From the Answer Desk

What are the relative merits of buying an index mutual fund versus a Spider or a DIAMOND?

Q: For anyone interested in investing in an index, there are now numerous mutual funds available and also various vehicles that can be traded directly on the exchanges. Other than comparing operating expenses vs. commission costs, is there any advantage or disadvantage in buying a mutual fund instead of, say, a Spider or a DIAMOND?

—Earl

A: Our firm commonly uses the S&P 500 SPDRs (or Standard & Poor's Depository Receipts) and Dow DIAMONDS to which you have made reference. However, both mutual funds and SPDRs and DIAMONDs have management fees. Usually fees for index funds are lower.

The S&P 500 SPDR is generally a unit investment trust that owns all the stocks in the S&P 500 Index, just like an S&P 500 index fund. However, the SPDR trades over the course of the day on the American Stock Exchange, just like a stock.

The S&P 500 SPDRs usually do not have a lower expense ratio and, therefore, cost a little more than most index funds. For that reason, they may provide a slightly lower return over the index funds. Because the SPDR trades like a stock, there are also transaction/commission charges resulting from trades. If you are dollar cost averaging into SDPRs, the ongoing purchases may become expensive.

SPDRs and DIAMONDs provide flexibility as you can buy or sell options on them, sell them short, and also lock in a price by specifying the price using limit orders. This flexibility is not available with index funds. There are also no minimum purchases using SPDRs and DIAMONDs or other similar depository receipts. Index funds usually have a minimum purchase amount.

—Richard Chiozzi, CFP

Hedge Funds

Hedge funds are the rich person's answer to the mutual fund. Like mutual funds, hedge funds pool together money from investors, which is invested by one or more professionals. But that's about where the similarities end.

Investment Minimums

Mutual funds are open to anyone who can pony up the minimum investment, typically between $1,000 and $2,500. Required minimums for

IRAs are even lower. The SEC requires hedge fund investors to have a net worth of at least $1 million or two consecutive years of household income of at least $300,000.

Hedge fund minimum investments may be as low as $100,000 for some of the programs sponsored by Merrill Lynch and other brokerage firms to $500,000 or more at independent hedge fund advisory firms. Because of their high investment requirements, institutional investors such as pension funds make up about one quarter of the hedge fund market, with high net worth individuals comprising the rest.

Regulation of Hedge Funds

Unlike mutual funds, which are subject to heavy reporting requirements and regulations regarding investment restrictions, hedge fund managers have no such oversight. They are unregistered, private investment pools governed by a contract that investors sign with the sponsor. With the exception of antifraud standards, hedge fund managers are exempt from regulation by the SEC under federal securities law.

Hedge Fund Fees

The average stock mutual fund has an annual expense ratio of 1.4 percent. Typically, hedge fund managers will charge between 1 and 2 percent of net assets, plus 20 percent of the annual return. Some peg their charges to investment performance.

Pricing and Liquidity

Mutual funds value their portfolios and price their securities daily. You can find out what your shares are worth each day simply by picking up a newspaper or logging on to financial sites on the Internet. Hedge fund pricing is less structured, and it may be difficult to determine the day-to-day changes in the value of your investment.

Hedge Fund Risk

Some mutual funds may use risky techniques to pump up profits, but the regulations governing them limit the extent to which they may do so.

Such techniques may include using leverage or borrowing money against the value of the securities in the portfolio as well as strategies involving the use of options, short selling, and futures contracts. Hedge funds also use these techniques with fewer restrictions, amplifying their potential risks and rewards.

Some Hedge Fund Lingo

Anyone considering a hedge fund should be familiar with some of the investment tools and techniques their managers use.

- ❖ **Short selling** (also called selling short): Selling securities, commodities, or foreign currency not actually owned by the seller. When selling short, the seller hopes to cover, or buy back, sold items at a lower price and earn a profit.

- ❖ **Leverage:** Borrowing money against the value of the securities in a portfolio.

- ❖ **Futures contract:** An agreement to buy or sell a specific amount of a commodity or security at a particular price on a stipulated future date.

- ❖ **Option:** The right to buy or sell shares of a stock at an agreed-upon price by a specified date. If the owner does not exercise that right, the option expires and is worthless.

The lure for potential investors in hedge funds is the potential for higher returns than mutual funds can provide. The cache of investing in a patrician hedge fund rather than a plebian mutual fund cousin no doubt adds to the draw.

Because hedge funds are exempt from most reporting requirements, it's hard to tell if they actually perform better than mutual funds. According to the CSFB/Tremont Hedge Fund Index, which tracks 2,600 hedge funds, they have returned an average of 14 percent a year over the last five years, compared with 11 percent for the average stock fund. Nonetheless, many investment advisors and individuals remain wary of hedge funds, since several of them have failed or come close to failing in recent years. If you're considering a hedge fund, be sure to speak with some clients before you invest. And don't put in more than you can afford to lose.

Section 529 Plans

A few years ago, Joe Hurley, a Pittsford, New York, CPA, discovered a way to make the ordeal of saving for college a little less painful: Section 529 plans. He first became aware of these little-known but increasingly popular state-sponsored, tax-favored savings plans in 1997, when his home state of New York adopted them.

Since then, Hurley has become what some consider the foremost Section 529 expert in the country. He wrote a book on the subject called *The Best Way to Save for College* (Bonacom Publications, 1998), and his Web site on the topic, SavingForCollege.com, gets an estimated 60,000 visitors every month.

Yet he admits that most people have not yet tuned in to his message. "Families are inundated with articles and admonitions about how to save for college, so it's kind of hard for them to absorb everything that's out there," he admits.

Until recently, most people had never heard of Section 529 plans. As fund companies marketed them directly to the public, financial advisors had no monetary incentive to sell them. But that is changing quickly as an increasing number of fund families begin offering these plans through advisors as well. You can bet that as more people sell them, more people will be buying them.

Given the attractive tax features of these plans, that may not be a bad idea. A Section 529 is a tax-favored investment plan set up and operated by a state to help save for college costs. So far, 48 states have them.

While different states have different rules and different investment options, the plans have several features in common:

❖ **A tax break:** Your investment grows tax-free as long as the money stays in the plan. Beginning in 2002, when you take a withdrawal to pay for the beneficiary's qualified educational expenses, the earnings portion is exempt from federal taxes. Individual states may offer other incentives such as an upfront deduction for contributions, or an exemption from income on withdrawals.

* **Control:** The donor maintains control of the account. The beneficiary can't get at the funds—a big advantage over the better-known custodial accounts set up under the Uniform Transfers to Minors Act (UTMA) where the child has the final say once he or she reaches the age of majority.

* **Eligibility:** Everyone can use a 529 plan and the amounts you can put in are substantial (over $100,000 per beneficiary). As there is often no residency requirement, you can set up plans in more than one state. Hurley has 529 accounts in 18 states, although for practical purposes, he says most people "would be just fine with one or two."

Despite these advantages, there are some drawbacks. People who like to take control of their investments are likely to be disappointed because the fund company that serves as program manager controls the ongoing investment of your account. You don't even get a Form 1099 to report income until the year you make withdrawals. The money must be used for education expenses or the state will assess a 10 percent penalty on the earnings portion of the withdrawals. Prepaid tuition plans, which fall under the umbrella of section 529 plans, may also affect eligibility for financial aid.

As programs can vary widely from state to state, it's important to examine the rules and investment options of each. The better ones offer a state tax deduction for contributions, a state tax exemption for earnings used for college, exclusion of 529 account from consideration in state-funded financial aid programs, and extra perks such as matching grants. On the investment side, Hurley says to look for plans that have well-designed investment strategies and highly rated investment products.

Web Folios

Folios promote themselves as an investment that offers diversification, lower cost, and greater control over taxes than a mutual fund, with lower costs for many investors than trading individual stocks.

FOLIOfn.com, launched in early 2000, is perhaps the best known of the web folio companies. Using this service, investors can assemble their own folio, or basket of up to 50 stocks. They can choose the stocks themselves or buy a group of pre-assembled portfolios with different investment objectives, as shown by the following examples.

* **Major market folios:** Folio 50, a folio of the largest 50 stocks from the S&P 500 by market capitalization; Folio OTC, a folio of the largest 50 stocks in the NASDAQ 100.

* **Risk tailored folios:** Aggressive, a folio of stocks that have been more risky than the market overall; Conservative, a folio of stocks that have been less risky than the market overall.

* **Sector folios:** Banks, a folio of bank stocks; Health, a folio of stocks related to the medical sector, including banks, insurance, and brokerage

* **Social issues folios:** Labor Friendly, a folio of companies that are not on the AFL-CIO Boycott list and more than 50 percent of the workers are represented by a labor union; SRI Large-Cap, a folio of large companies that do not derive any revenue from the manufacturing of tobacco, firearms, military weapons, or from alcohol or the operation of gambling establishments.

A flat annual fee of $295, or $29.95 per month, lets you invest in three of the prepackaged portfolios or assemble three baskets yourself. Each additional basket costs $95 a year. The all-inclusive fee allows you to place an unlimited number of trades up to 50 stocks a shot. There is no minimum trade amount. Any dividends over $1 are automatically reinvested.

To keep costs down, Foliofn executes all its trades twice a day, at 10:15 A.M. and 2:45 P.M. You can place a trade before or after those times, but it won't be executed outside those windows. The trade is only executed at the market price, not a price that you specify. For immediate execution, you'll need to pay an extra $14.95.

Folio investors have more control over taxes in the account because they choose when to buy and sell their shares. With a mutual fund, shareholders must pay taxes on any net gains when the manager sells securities that have appreciated in value since he bought them.

Web folios offer obvious advantages to active stock traders as long as they don't mind twice daily rather than immediate execution of their orders. If your commission costs at a discount broker are likely to exceed the $295 annual fee, web folios can be a great deal for you.

The advantages get a little fuzzier when you compare folios to mutual funds. Most of the articles I've seen on the subject focus on their costs and tax consequences versus mutual funds. If an actively managed no-load stock mutual fund has a fairly typical expense ratio of 1.25 percent, a $25,000 account will cost $312.50 a year, slightly above the $295 annual folio fee. On a $100,000 account, the actively managed fund's annual cost zooms to $1,250 while the folio fee remains the same.

Cost isn't the only consideration here. Professionals manage actively managed mutual funds, and you pay for that management. Investors assemble and manage folios themselves, so it makes sense that they're cheaper. Comparing the two as if they are the same animal really isn't appropriate. Lower costs probably won't hold much appeal if you don't want the responsibility of overseeing a portfolio of securities in the first place. A more fair comparison, I think, is to look at how an unmanaged, pre-assembled folio compares to an unmanaged, no-load index fund.

Annual Expenses for a $100,000 Account

Index fund with a 0.3 percent expense ratio	$300
Foliofn annual charge	$295

Here the charges run about neck-and-neck. Above the $100,000 level, folios become the clear winner. Below that, index funds are. If you have a lot of money to invest, folios can end up being less expensive than even a cheap index fund.

There are a couple of other issues to consider beyond costs and taxes. The Investment Company Institute, the mutual fund industry trade group, thinks that folio companies should be subject to many of the same regulations that mutual funds are, a notion these companies strongly resist. According to the ICI Web site, "There is little to prevent financial dot-coms and other firms from adopting the methods embedded in the program, repackaging them, and promoting them as their own." In other words, the barriers to entry are much lower than they are with mutual funds, which could encourage the proliferation of questionable players.

Aside from being largely unregulated territory, a growing number of pre-assembled folios are being formed around themes. At Foliofn, for example, you can buy a Stockcar Champs folio, which consists of companies that have been primary sponsors of the winning NASCAR Winston Cup driver for 2000. In the Media Favorites category, you can choose from several offerings including the Forbes 40, a folio of the top 40 United States–based companies that contribute the most to the annual fortunes of some of the richest people.

Call me old-fashioned, but I think building a portfolio around a sport or magazine list is not sound investing. It's trendy. In my book, companies should leave affinity marketing to credit card companies and put together a portfolio based on sound investment practice, not gimmicky themes.

Brave (and Confusing) New World

With all the ways companies now package plain vanilla securities, investors can choose to buy stocks and bonds through vehicles that match their investment style, trading habits, tax picture, and tolerance for risk. Along with this, however, there is confusion about how to handle these new investment products and who they may be suitable for. Understand them thoroughly before you invest.

CHAPTER 13

Putting It All Together: Your Game Plan

When most people think about what to do with a windfall, the first thing that comes to mind (after buying a dream car or taking a great vacation) is how to invest the money. Before you make those decisions, you need to take some financial planning steps that, in the long run, are just as important as crafting an investment plan.

Step One: Trim Your Debt

Here is one rule that applies to everyone, including windfall recipients: Pay off your credit card bills. The sooner, the better.

As simple and logical as this may sound, you're not likely to get this advice from many financial advisors. As I explained in the chapter on financial advisors, most get paid according to how much you invest—the more you invest, the more they get paid. By telling you to pay off your credit cards instead of buying investments through them, they're taking money out of their own pockets.

It takes a professional who is really looking out for your interests to make that kind of sacrifice. When you ask a financial advisor about what to do with your windfall, don't be surprised if the subject of paying off debts never comes up.

Bottom line: Shed excess debt, especially credit card debt that usually carries nondeductible interest of 16 to 19 percent. This is the quickest way to beef up your budget and save over the long term.

Janet has just received a $50,000 inheritance from her grandmother that she's thinking about investing in mutual funds. She has total balances of $10,000 on credit cards with an 18 percent annual percentage rate. If she stretches out her payments over eight years by paying an average of $197 a month, she will pay nearly $9,000 in interest charges. If she uses the windfall to increase those monthly payments to a little under $1,000 a month, she'll have the card paid off in just 11 months and her interest charges will drop to a more manageable $923. Better yet, she could save even more in interest by dedicating $10,000 of the inheritance to paying off the credit cards right away and investing the other $40,000.

The question of whether to invest or pay off credit cards with astronomical interest is really a no-brainer. If you think you can make more than the 18 percent credit card companies charge by investing, you are either (a) an investment superstar, (b) overestimating your investment abilities, or betting on getting big returns from high-risk investments that may not pan out.

Beyond credit card debt and high-interest loans, the question of whether or not to pay off a loan or to invest becomes more of a toss-up. To decide what to do, compare the after-tax return on your investment to the after-tax cost of borrowing.

Credit Card Habits

Forty percent of credit card users pay off their balances every month. For those who carry their balances, the average credit card balance is $5,610.

Source: Bankrate.com; The Credit Research Center at Georgetown University and TransUnion.

Let's say that you have a 30-year mortgage with a 7 percent interest rate. For someone in the 27 percent federal tax bracket, the net cost of the loan is actually a little over 5 percent because of the deduction for mortgage interest on your federal tax return. If you think you can get an after-tax return that's higher than that, you may want to consider investing, rather than paying off or paying down the mortgage.

Psychologically, many people who receive a windfall like the idea of using it to either reduce or eliminate their monthly mortgage payments. Knowing that the roof over their heads comes with a lower monthly price tag brings them peace of mind. This may be particularly true if they are struggling to keep up with housing expenses or want to have the option of working part-time or taking a lower-paying but more rewarding job.

Using a windfall to beef up your home equity and pare down your mortgage can drive down monthly costs dramatically. Say you decided to use your windfall to buy a new house and you are trying to decide on the amount of the down payment. Monthly payments on a $300,000, 30-year mortgage come to $1,996. Use a windfall to chop the mortgage in half, and those monthly payments plummet to $998. To get the most out of those savings, allocate the money you save every month to invest for goals such as college or retirement.

On the other hand, maybe you're perfectly happy in your current home and your income is high enough so that you are comfortably meeting your mortgage expenses. Plus, you've made some pretty good investment decisions in the past and think you can come out better in the long run by investing for growth. In that case, you may opt to keep your mortgage at its current level and invest the windfall in stocks or stock mutual funds geared for growth.

Staying on Track

If you have credit card debt, a car loan, student loans, and a mortgage, use your windfall to reduce or pay off the loans in this order:

1. High interest, nondeductible debt such as credit cards
2. Lower-interest nondeductible debt such as auto loans
3. Tax-deductible, lower-interest debt such as a mortgage

Once you've gotten your debt load down, continue practicing good credit habits. Most experts recommend that you keep debt payments, including credit card and car payments, to no more than 10 to 20 percent of income.

Step Two: Draw Up a Budget

Next on the list of nitty-gritty financial planning steps is budgeting. Yes, budgeting. Don't bail out here, please. Even people who have received a big chunk of change need to know where their money is going and how spending compares to income. It's a blueprint we can all use.

Without some kind of spending game plan, many people who receive a windfall discover how easy it is to fall into the trap of buying lots of luxury items without thinking about the impact on long-term savings goals. Stories about once-famous actors or lottery winners who are now deeply in debt point to the fact that even the wealthy can spend themselves into a hole.

With some financial flexibility created by your windfall, you may not have to stick to a budget with as much diligence as in the past. Splurging on cars and vacations may be a more viable option. Still, it's a good idea to get a handle on where your money is going. Below is a budgeting worksheet you can use to help you re-tool your post-windfall spending and saving habits.

Budgeting Worksheet

Net Income

Salary: _____ Monthly _____ Annually

_____ Yours

_____ Spouse's

Self-Employment Income

_____ Yours

_____ Spouse's

_____ Interest

_____ Dividends

_____ Capital gains

Pension

_____ Yours

_____ Spouse's

Social Security

_____ Yours

_____ Spouse's

_____ Alimony

_____ Child support

_____ Other income

_____ **Total**

Expenses

Housing

_____ Mortgage/rent

_____ Home equity loan

_____ Property taxes

_____ Condo fees

_____ Parking fees

_____ Garbage collection

_____ Grounds/lawn maintenance

_____ Snow removal

_____ Other

Utilities

_____ Heat (oil/gasoline)

_____ Electricity

_____ Telephone

_____ Water

_____ Sewer

_____ Other

Household

_____ Groceries/cleaning supplies

_____ Cleaning service

_____ Other

Automobile

_____ Gasoline

_____ Loan payment(s)

_____ Repairs/maintenance

_____ Property tax

_____ License/registration

_____ Other

_____ Other transportation

_____ Public transportation

continues

Budgeting Worksheet   *continued*

Automobile

_____ Parking

_____ Tolls

_____ Other

Child Care

_____ Day care

_____ Live-in help

_____ Babysitting

_____ Summer camp

_____ Lessons

_____ Other

Personal

_____ Clothes

_____ Dry cleaning

_____ Uniforms

_____ Haircuts

_____ Other

Health Care

_____ Prescriptions

_____ Medications

_____ Dentist

_____ Orthodontist

_____ Other

Insurance

_____ Automobile

_____ Homeowners

_____ Umbrella

_____ Health

_____ Disability

_____ Life

_____ Other

Savings

_____ 401(k) or other employer savings plan

_____ IRA/pension plan

_____ Personal savings

_____ College savings

_____ Other

Miscellaneous

_____ Alimony
_____ Child support
_____ Tuition
_____ Other education expenses
_____ Pets
_____ Union dues
_____ Credit cards
_____ Discretionary
_____ Meals out
_____ Entertainment
_____ Club memberships
_____ Vacations
_____ Charitable contributions
_____ Subscriptions
_____ Gifts
_____ Cable TV
_____ Hobbies
_____ Other
_____ Tobacco products
_____ Internet access fees
_____ **Total expenses**

Subtract from total income:

_____ Surplus (deficit)

How much should you be spending every month on various expenses? Although that depends on personal circumstance, the Consumer Credit Counseling Service offers these guidelines:

Budgeting Guidelines

Type of Expense	Percentage
Housing	38
Food	12
Automobile	15
Miscellaneous	5
Medical	5

continues

	Budgeting Guidelines *continued*
Type of Expense	Percentage
Savings	5
Clothing	5
Recreation	5
Insurance	5
Debt	5

Source: Consumer Credit Counseling Service

Step Three: Define and Quantify Your Goals

Developing a long-term game plan involves the following steps:

- ❖ Defining your goals
- ❖ Determining how much they will cost and timeline for meeting them
- ❖ Developing an asset allocation and investment strategy based on those factors, along with your personal willingness to accept risk

Buying a Home

A windfall can bring the goal of buying a primary residence or second vacation home much closer very quickly by enabling you to beef up your down payment. Dividends and interest from a bigger investment pot may also boost your income level, which will raise the amount of house you can afford.

Generally, lenders like to see no more than 28 percent to 33 percent of monthly income devoted to regular monthly payments, which include a mortgage (including principal and interest), property taxes, and homeowners' insurance. If your total household income is $100,000, your monthly payments as suggested by this guideline would be no more than $2,333 ($100,000 ÷ [12 × 28%]) to $2,750 ($100,000 ÷ [12 × 33%]).

The following table will let you figure out how much monthly mortgage payments will be for every $100,000 you borrow. Add the cost of property taxes and insurance to determine your total monthly housing expenses.

Monthly Payments for Every $100,000 Borrowed		
Rate (Percent)	Thirty-Year Mortgage	Fifteen-Year Mortgage
6	$599.55	$843.86
6.5	$632.07	$871.11
7	$665	$3,089
7.5	$699.21	$927.01
8	$733	$7,695
8.5	$768.91	$984.74
9	$804.62	$1,014.27

You can use multiples of $100,000 to figure out the monthly payment on various amounts borrowed.

Example: A $200,000, 30-year mortgage at 7 percent would cost $1,330.60 a month ($665.30 × 2).

A $350,000, 15-year mortgage at 6.5 percent would cost $3,048.89 a month ($871.11 × 3.5)

Home Sweet Second Home

If you are considering using a windfall for a second home, be aware that lenders often have tougher qualification requirements than they do for primary residences. They know that in times of financial difficulty, borrowers are more likely to let payments on the mortgage for a vacation home fall behind or lapse than they are for their mortgage on a primary residence. To help cover this risk, lenders may have higher interest rates for second homes or require larger down payments. You may get more favorable terms with seller financing, so it pays to ask the owner about that possibility.

Before you commit to buying a vacation home:

❖ Spend a few weeks in the area you are considering to get a feel for whether or not it offers the kinds of activities you enjoy. Better yet, rent a condo or house for a season to see how often you're able to go there. Between soccer games, work, and other personal obligations, you may find that you don't rack up enough time at a vacation home to make purchasing worthwhile. Even though renting may not be as fulfilling as ownership, it may make more financial sense.

* Shop around. Many of the rules that apply to shopping for a primary residence apply to a vacation home. Examine pricing trends, proximity to amenities such as parks, beaches, or golf courses, and consider appreciation potential.

* Look at the tax angles. If you rent a property for 15 days or more, it becomes an investment property governed by a complex set of tax rules. You can rent the property for 14 days or less each calendar year without having to report the income or pay taxes on it.

There are other tax rules governing second homes that are fairly complex, so be sure to consult a tax professional before you buy.

Saving for College

Wouldn't it be nice if your kids could attend the college of their choice without carrying a big debt load along with a sheepskin? With some good planning and enough time, even a relatively modest windfall can make that happen.

First, you need to get over the sticker shock of what four years of college will cost. According to the College Board, the average annual cost of tuition, fees, room, board, and personal expenses in 2000 was $22,533 for a private four-year college, and $10,458 for an in-state public college. Assuming that these costs increase at a rate of 4 percent annually (that's a reasonable estimate based on recent increases), here's what you can expect to pay over the next 20 years:

	Annual Costs	
Year	Private College	Public College
2000	$22,533	$10,458
2001	$23,434	$10,876
2002	$24,336	$11,295
2003	$25,237	$11,713
2004	$26,364	$12,236

Year	Private College	Public College
2005	$27,490	$12,759
2006	$28,617	$13,282
2007	$29,744	$13,805
2008	$30,870	$14,327
2009	$31,997	$14,850
2010	$33,349	$15,478
2011	$34,701	$16,105
2012	$36,053	$16,733
2013	$37,630	$17,465
2014	$38,982	$18,092
2015	$40,559	$18,824
2016	$42,137	$19,556
2017	$43,939	$20,393
2018	$45,742	$21,230
2019	$47,545	$22,066
2020	$49,347	$22,903

You can find out the total cost of a four-year college education by adding the four years you anticipate your child will be in college. For example, if your child will be entering college in 2010, the cost of a private education would total $141,733.

Once you get a fix on how much college is going to cost, you can use the chart below to help determine how much of your windfall to set aside to reach that goal.

This chart shows how much $1 will grow over a given amount of time at different rates of return, compounded annually. It's also a handy-dandy reference for a number of calculations.

Windfall Growth

Years	5%	7%	10%	12%	15%
1	1.05	1.07	1.10	1.12	1.15
2	1.10	1.14	1.21	1.25	1.32
3	1.16	1.23	1.33	1.40	1.52
4	1.22	1.31	1.46	1.57	1.75
5	1.28	1.40	1.61	1.76	2.01

continues

	Windfall Growth	*continued*			
Years	5%	7%	10%	12%	15%
6	1.34	1.50	1.77	1.97	2.31
7	1.41	1.61	1.95	2.21	2.66
8	1.48	1.72	2.14	2.48	3.06
9	1.55	1.84	2.36	2.77	3.52
10	1.63	1.97	2.59	3.11	4.05
11	1.71	2.10	2.85	3.48	4.65
12	1.80	2.25	3.14	3.90	5.35
13	1.89	2.41	3.45	4.36	6.15
14	1.98	2.58	3.80	4.89	7.08
15	2.08	2.76	4.18	5.47	8.14
16	2.18	2.95	4.59	6.13	9.36
17	2.29	3.16	5.05	6.87	10.76
18	2.41	3.38	5.56	7.69	12.38
19	2.53	3.62	6.12	8.61	14.23
20	2.65	3.87	6.73	9.65	16.37
21	2.79	4.14	7.40	10.80	18.82
22	2.93	4.43	8.14	12.10	21.64
23	3.07	4.74	8.95	13.55	24.89
24	3.23	5.07	9.85	15.17	28.63
25	3.39	5.43	10.83	17.00	32.91
26	3.56	5.80	11.92	19.04	37.86
27	3.73	6.21	13.11	21.32	43.54
28	3.92	6.65	14.42	23.88	50.07
29	4.12	7.11	15.86	26.75	57.58
30	4.32	7.61	17.45	29.96	66.21

You can use the preceding chart to determine the amount of an initial deposit needed to reach a goal:

Example: You would like to have $50,000 for a child's college education in 10 years. If your investments earn 10 percent a year, you will need to make an initial deposit of $19,305 to reach your goal ($50,000 ÷ 2.59). If growth averages 5 percent, your initial investment would need to be $30,675 ($50,000 ÷ 1.63).

You can find out how much a given amount will grow over time.

Example: You would like to earmark $50,000 of a recent inheritance toward retirement, which you anticipate in 25 years. If the money grows by 10 percent a year, you will have accumulated $541,500 at retirement (10.83 × $50,000). If growth averages 5 percent a year, the accumulation amount will be $169,500 (3.39 × $50,000).

Use the chart to determine the impact of inflation on savings.

Example: Your goal is to have your investments produce $2,000 a month in today's dollars when you retire in 20 years. Assuming a 5 percent rate of inflation, you will need $5,300 ($2,000 × 2.65) by the time you retire to replicate what $2,000 a month buys today.

Retirement

For some people, a windfall can make the once-distant dream of early retirement a reality. But before you collect your gold watch, be reasonably sure you will have enough money to get you through your golden years. Experts say you need 60 to 80 percent of your pre-retirement income in order to live comfortably in retirement. However, that can vary depending on personal circumstances.

To figure out how much of your windfall to set aside for retirement, you need to have an idea of what you can expect to receive from other sources such as a pension or Social Security. That can be hard to predict if you are more than, say, 10 years away from retirement. The amount of savings you are able to accumulate in qualified retirement plans, such as a 401(k), will depend largely on how the market is treating your investments.

Even people who are closing in on retirement may not have a firm idea of what they will have to work with a year or two down the road. Many employees contemplating retirement in early 2000, for example, decided to put those plans on the back burner a year later, after the stock market decimated the value of their retirement accounts.

Many pensions are based on how much you make just before you leave a job, which you obviously can't predict. A promotion or substantial raise could boost that figure substantially, while an unanticipated job loss would deliver a devastating blow to your bottom line. Even if you have an idea of how much your pension will be, keep in mind that most pensions are not indexed to inflation. You may need to beef up savings to offset the loss of purchasing power of a fixed payment.

Consider new developments on the ever-changing Social Security front. Starting in 2000, the age at which full benefits are paid was raised for anyone born after 1937. Anyone born in 1960 or after will have to wait until age 67 to receive full benefits. Those born between 1943 and 1954 will have to wait until age 66. Early retirement benefits will still be available at age 62, but they will be reduced by 30 percent rather than the 20 percent for previous early retirees.

Many people who are a decade or more from being eligible for early retirement benefits at retirement have ample reason to be concerned about whether Social Security will be there when they need it. This is a pay-as-you go system, which means that current taxes are used to support current benefits. Currently, there are just over three workers paying taxes for each retiree who receives benefits. As baby boomers retire, there will be fewer workers to pay for their benefits.

Finally, longer life expectancies because of improvements in health care make it possible for the average person retiring at age 60 to live another 25 years. When people live longer, they need to have more in savings to carry them through their retirement years.

Bottom line: You may need more from outside sources, including a windfall, than you think to maintain a comfortable standard of living in retirement. Despite the obstacles, a windfall can put you in a position to leave the rat race before many of your co-workers.

There are several sources of information to figure out how much you will need to save for retirement and whether or not early retirement is a viable option for you. One of the best I've found is called Ballpark E$timate, which you can find at the Web site for the American Savings Education Council at www.asec.org.

How Long $100,000 Will Last	
Years	Withdrawal in First Year
10	$11,700
15	$8,300
20	$6,700
25	$5,700
30	$5,000
35	$4,200

Assume withdrawals increase at a rate of 4 percent a year for inflation, and an after-tax return of 7 percent.

Example: You have a $100,000 account that you want to last 15 years. You may withdraw $8,300 in the first year, $8,632 in the second year, and so on, until the account is depleted in 15 years.

You can multiply these numbers by the applicable multiple to determine the withdrawal rate for a personal account.

Example: For a $350,000 account that you want to last for 20 years, you can withdraw $23,450 in the first year ($6,700 × 3.5).

Investing and Asset Allocation Strategies

Once you have an idea of what your goals are and how much they will cost, the next step is to arrive at an asset allocation and investment strategy to help you meet them.

Deciding how to allocate and invest your assets will depend largely on how much risk you need to take to reach your investment goal and, just as important, how much risk you feel comfortable taking. Stocks and stock funds, while volatile in the short-term, have historically provided the best opportunity for long-term growth over most time periods. Retirees should have some money in them to help prevent inflation from eroding the value of their savings.

However, not everyone feels comfortable about investing heavily in the stock market. One widely used rule of thumb to determine how much to invest in stocks is to subtract your age from 100. So if you're 30 years old, this guideline suggests you should have about 70 percent of your money in the stock market. But that's just a starting point, not the last word. If you're a 30-year old whose stomach turns at the thought of losing money in the stock market, the fact that traditional wisdom suggests you put 70 percent of your money into stocks won't make you feel more comfortable about doing so. At the same time, a 60-year old with a generous pension and other assets might feel restricted by having just 40 percent of his money in stocks, since he can afford to take more risk.

While there are no hard-and-fast rules about how to allocate assets, here are some of the considerations that go into making that determination.

Your Time Frame

If you have received a windfall and buying a house is a near-term goal—say, something you want to do in the next two or three years—investing the money in anything other than money market funds, Treasury bills, or other short-term security that won't fluctuate in value probably is not a good idea. The stock market could fall, leaving you with less than you need for the house you want. And because your time frame is so short, you won't have the flexibility to wait out the market's bad times.

On the other hand, you don't want to play it too safe if you have a longer time horizon—say, five years or more. The most important thing to keep in mind is that the longer your time horizon, the more risk you can afford to take.

One way to afford risk is to have a long time frame to offset short-term market fluctuation. Another is to have more money and assets than you need. If you have substantial wealth and a high income, losing money in the stock market probably won't affect your lifestyle. On the other hand, wealth also has a conservative flip side. If you already have enough money to meet your goals and maintain a comfortable lifestyle, you may feel little motivation to take on investment risk. Someone in those circumstances might opt for a more conservative strategy, even though his or her time frame and available assets would point to a higher-risk, aggressive growth approach.

Your Total Financial Picture

Many people make two common mistakes when they decide how much to allocate to stocks, bonds, and money market securities. First, they view each account as a separate entity rather than seeing their entire portfolio as a whole.

> Tom has just received an inheritance of $300,000. He already has several investment accounts, including a 401(k) plan at work, a rollover IRA from a previous job, and two UTMA accounts for his son and daughter. Before deciding how to allocate the inheritance, he needs to consider how the other accounts are invested. His 401(k) plan is heavily loaded with employer stock, so he wants to diversify into other industries to avoid putting all his investment eggs in one sector. Plus, since the long bull market has tilted the accounts more heavily toward stocks than he is comfortable with, he will probably allocate a substantial portion of the new money toward more conservative investments such as bonds or bond funds.

Another common mistake is not factoring a home, employee stock options, or one's profession into the picture. These are sometimes called *inherent assets*, and while they are not securities like stocks or bonds, they still have a strong influence on your total net worth and financial picture.

Let's say you work as a software engineer. Given your professional background, you might be tempted to invest more heavily in technology stocks than most investors. But what would happen if the technology sector tanked? You could be laid off, or have any stock options from your employer rendered worthless. In addition, your tech-centric investment portfolio would be in shambles. Instead of aligning your investment portfolio with your inherent assets, it's probably better to diversify away from them to provide more of a balance in your life.

Your Risk Tolerance Level

This is also called the *sleep test*. It reflects the level of risk you can take without lapsing into a round of all-night pillow thumping. Could you absorb the impact of losing 15 percent or more of your portfolio in a few months without turning to sleeping aids? How about 25 percent? That's what you'd have to endure in a bear market. Even if you have the luxuries of a long time frame and lots of capital, the emotional inability to withstand a stock market downturn may make it necessary to take your investment risk level down a notch or two.

Your Employment Situation

If you feel relatively secure in your job or are a couple with two steady incomes and little debt, you'll probably want to allocate somewhere in the neighborhood of three to six months of living expenses toward liquid investments that you could tap in an emergency, such as certificates of deposit or money market funds. On the other hand, if you have just started your own business and are not sure it will fly, or if you may be losing an income because of the birth of a child, keeping a year's worth of living expenses in readily available securities that are easy to tap into is a good idea.

When it comes to investing, risk and reward are always a tradeoff. The more risk you take, the more reward you're likely to reap over the long term. There's just no way around it. The key to successful investing is balancing the level of risk you can prudently take to reach your goals with the emotional tug of losing money from time to time.

Model Asset Allocations

Conservative

Stocks	40 percent
Bonds	30 percent
Cash	30 percent

Best for: Someone who wants income from their investments, low volatility, and some exposure to growth.

Moderate

Stocks	60 percent
Bonds	30 percent
Cash	10 percent

Best for: Someone who wants moderate growth and volatility along with some income. Considered a middle-of-the-road asset allocation strategy.

Aggressive

Stocks	80 percent
Bonds	15 percent
Cash	5 percent

Best for: A growth-oriented investor who can afford to take significant investment risk and is willing to ride out short-term volatility. Individual should have a long-time horizon of 10 years or more or sufficient assets and/or income to offset potential portfolio losses.

Invest at Once or Gradually?

People who received a windfall often wonder if they should invest all their money at once or do it gradually and regularly over a period of months or years. The latter approach is called dollar cost averaging. While this strategy is usually associated with regular monthly savings arrangements, such as a 401(k), you can also use it with a windfall if you are wary about the stock market and don't want to jump in all at once.

Not everyone agrees with the premise of dollar cost averaging. Some investors believe that because the stock market generally heads in an upward direction, you should put all your money into the market in one fell swoop if you have a lump sum and are investing for the long-term.

But how would you feel if you had done that in March 2000, just before the stock market turned south? A year later, many stocks and mutual funds had fallen 20 percent or more. That would have left someone with a $300,000 lump sum sitting with a loss of at least $60,000. Although chances are good that a patient investor would be rewarded over the long term, it could take years to recover from that kind of loss.

That's where dollar cost averaging comes in. Stock market investment decisions have two basic components: what to buy and when to buy it. There's no way to get around the "what" part, but it is possible to eliminate some of the uncertainty of "when" by using dollar cost averaging—putting the same amount of money into an investment on a regular schedule regardless of what is happening to the price.

Whether you use it for stocks or mutual funds, dollar cost averaging serves to lower your average cost per share because it assures that you buy more shares when prices are low and fewer when they are high.

Here's a hypothetical example that shows how dollar cost averaging works.

Example: Alan has just received a $200,000 insurance settlement that he plans to invest. He's a little wary of the stock market right now because it has been so volatile, so he is not sure he is ready to commit the entire amount all at once. Instead, he decides to invest half the money now in a mutual fund that invests in growth stocks and gradually invest the other half over a period of several years. Here is what happens in the first year to the portion he has allocated toward dollar cost averaging:

Monthly	Price per Investment	Number of Share	Shares Purchased
January	$2,000	$10	200.00
February	$2,000	$11	181.81
March	$2,000	$10	200.00
April	$2,000	$9	222.22
May	$2,000	$12	166.66
June	$2,000	$10	200.00
July	$2,000	$9	222.22
August	$2,000	$5	400.00
September	$2,000	$8	250.00
October	$2,000	$6	330.33
November	$2,000	$8	250.00
December	$2,000	$10	200.00

Total invested: $24,000

Total shares purchased: 2,823

Average cost per share: $24,000 ÷ 2,823 = $8.50

Year-end account value: $28,230 (2,823 × 10)

In this example, Alan came out ahead with dollar cost averaging because the price dipped during the purchase period and rose later in the year. Of course, he could have done even better by investing the entire amount in August when the stock bottomed. But that's not human nature. As most people tend to buy when prices are rising, and sell when they're falling, they end up buying fewer shares at higher prices. Consistent dollar cost averagers buy more shares when prices are low and fewer when they are high.

"Consistent" is the key word here. You can't decide to bail out when the market turns down and start over again when it gets better. That's timing the market, tough for professional money managers to do with any success, let alone the average investor.

Sticking with the program does not guarantee profits either. If a stock or mutual fund keeps going down, you are going to lose money. It's small comfort to know that early losses are minimized by subsequent purchases at lower prices. Even if you manage to sell at a price that is higher than the starting price of your dollar cost averaging program, your gains can be nonexistent if the market is flat or rising for longer periods than it was declining. The reason is that you will be buying stocks at close to the same price each time or at an increasingly higher price.

The strategy works best on more volatile kinds of investments, such as aggressive growth stock funds, because they have the steeper dips that allow you to accumulate shares at sharply lower prices. You also need at least three years of consistent investing to even out the ups and downs, so don't use money you think you may need before that. Otherwise, you could be forced to sell in a falling market.

Different Goals, Different Strategies

Everyone's optimal game plan for handling a windfall will be different. For some, the most sensible action will be to pay off debts to free up more money for investing. For others, it might be firming up an asset allocation strategy or getting started on a savings plan to meet long-term goals.

CHAPTER 14

Tackling Taxes

A windfall will introduce a new smorgasbord of tax issues you may not have had to consider before.

Estimated Taxes

When you work for someone else, your employer withholds money from your paycheck to help cover your tax bill. However, many other kinds of taxable income are not subject to withholding. People who receive income from such sources often need to figure out how much tax they owe and pay those amounts on their own through estimated taxes.

Windfall recipients should pay particular attention to estimated taxes because they often receive taxable money that is not subject to withholding. For example, when you exercise stock options, your employer is not responsible for withholding taxes from any profit you make. It's your job to figure out how much you owe and to pay it.

Commonly, estimated tax payments also kick in when a windfall generates a significant amount of investment income or capital gains. Unless the money is sitting in a tax-deferred account such as an IRA or comes from income attributable to a nontaxable source such as municipal bonds, you'll need to pay taxes on that income for the year in which you receive it.

To estimate whether or not you need to pay tax on income not subject to withholding, or on other income from which an insufficient amount of tax has been withheld, calculate whether the total tax you will owe on your annual tax return will be covered by the amount of tax you have already had either ...

❖ Withheld from wages and other payments, or

❖ Paid in earlier estimated payments for the year, or

❖ Credited to your account from adjustments or overpayments to previously filed returns

Generally, you should make estimated tax payments if you expect to owe tax of $1,000 or more, after credits and withholding, and the total amount of tax withheld and your credits will be less than the smaller of …

❖ 90 percent of the tax to be shown on your tax return, or

❖ 100 percent of the total tax you paid the previous year

If your previous year's adjusted gross income was more than $150,000 ($75,000 if you're married but filing separately), you need to use a higher percentage of the prior year's tax than everyone else. In 2001, you will need to pay 110 percent of the amount shown on your 2000 return, instead of 100 percent, to avoid an estimated tax penalty. The percentage usually changes from year to year. If you don't pay enough taxes from withholding and estimated payments to comply with one of the two rules, you'll be hit with an underpayment penalty.

Using the second of the two calculation methods provides a safe harbor. As long as you pay 100 percent of what you owed last year (or the higher percentage that applies for high incomes), you will not be penalized. This holds true even if you have received a large windfall that boosted your income dramatically over the previous year.

Example: Assume that you exercised some stock options and reported income of $100,000 from the sale of the stock. As long as your withholding and any estimated taxes you pay at least equals the amount of the tax shown on your previous year's return, you won't have to worry about any underpayment penalties, even though your income may have ballooned.

In certain situations, though, it makes more sense to try to estimate your current year's tax and pay 90 percent of that amount for the year. For example, if your income is much lower this year than it was last year—say because you worked for a dot-com that went belly-up and you lost your job—your tax bill is also much lower. It would not make sense to figure out what you owe based on last year's return, because you would probably end up paying much more than you have to. Form 1040-ES comes with a worksheet that can help you figure out how much tax you will owe for the current year.

If you determine that you owe estimated tax, there are five ways to go about paying it:

- **Crediting an overpayment.** When you file your tax return and have overpaid your taxes for that year (i.e., you are getting a refund), you can apply all or part of that overpayment to your estimated tax for the following year. You may use all of the over-payment for your first quarterly tax installment, or spread it among all or some of your payments through the year. Your refund will be reduced by the amount you apply toward your estimated taxes.

- **Using payment vouchers.** You can send in your payment with a payment voucher from IRS Form 1040-ES. If you made esti-mated payments last year, you should receive preprinted vouch-ers with your name, address, and Social Security number in the mail. Using the preprinted vouchers will reduce the chance of error and speed processing.

- **Paying electronically using the Electronic Federal Tax Payment System, or EFTPS.** For more information on how to use the system, call 1-800-945-8400.

- **Direct debit.** If you file your taxes electronically, you can authorize a direct debit payment from your checking or savings account to the IRS.

- **Credit card.** You can use your American Express card, Discover card, or MasterCard to make estimated tax payments. Call the Official Payments Corporation at 1-800-2PAY-TAX (1-800-272-9829), or visit the Web site at www.officialpayments.com. You will be charged a "convenience fee" based on the amount you are paying.

When to Pay Estimated Taxes

The year is divided into four payment periods:

For the Period	Tax Due Date
January 1 through March 31	April 15
April 1 through May 31	June 15
June 1 through August 31	September 15
September 1 through December 31	January 15 of the following year

Usually, taxpayers like to spread payments over four quarters. If you're flush with cash, however, and want to put those payments behind you for the year, the IRS won't object if you pay your estimated taxes for the year in the first quarter.

Avoiding the Alternative Minimum Tax

Years ago, wealthy individuals could effectively wipe the tax slate clean through liberal use of tax torpedoes such as credits, tax shelters, deductions, and exclusions. To close those loopholes, Congress introduced something called the alternative minimum tax (AMT). It's supposed to hit the rich where it hurts by making them figure out their taxes twice—first using the regular way and then a second time at a lower rate, but without many of the deductions and exemptions otherwise available. They pay according to whichever of the two methods results in the highest tax.

The AMT kicks in most often among those who use lots of deductions and credits to lower their tax bills. Because it is one of the most mind-numbing and difficult kinds of taxes to explain (yes, even in the world of taxes there are degrees of pain), it's best to consult a tax professional who will give you an idea of how much you may owe and take steps to minimize your tax liability. Those most likely to fall into the AMT's clutches include individuals who ...

❖ Have exercised incentive stock options. AMT rules require you to pay a tax based on the difference between the price at which you exercised the options and the market value at the time of exercise. For example, if you exercise an option to buy 100 shares of stock at $5 a share when the market value of the stock is $15 a share, the AMT will be based on the $10 per share spread between the two prices.

There is really no way to figure out the precise amount of any AMT tax when you exercise incentive stock options or even if you will owe any tax at all. Your liability will depend, among other things, on the size of your profit, whether you own stock you have from exercising the option or have sold it, and income and other elements of your regular tax return.

Plan Before You Exercise Options

Depending on your circumstances, and with the help of good tax planning, you may not owe any alternative minimum tax when you exercise incentive stock options. That's why you should consult a tax professional before, not after, you exercise stock options to help minimize or eliminate your tax bill.

❖ Live in states with high state and local taxes. If you itemize your deductions, as about one third of Americans do, you probably take a deduction for state and local taxes. These deductions, which typically include state income and property taxes, are deductible from income but are not considered in AMT calculations. If you live in high-tax states like Massachusetts, California, Connecticut, New Jersey, Maryland, and New York, the AMT may unexpectedly kick in.

❖ Have a second mortgage. You may deduct interest from a second mortgage from any AMT liability if the money is used to improve your principal residence. However, if you borrow against your home for nonhousing-related reasons, you can't deduct the interest from your AMT (although it is still deductible from regular income).

❖ Have a large amount of long-term capital gains. Adding a large long-term capital gain to your other income may also trigger the

AMT. This can happen, for example, if you sell a large amount of stock or mutual funds that have been gifted to you.

❖ Have large families. Personal exemptions, such as those you claim for children, a spouse, or other dependents, are not allowed under the AMT.

❖ Have bonds that generate ample tax-exempt interest. While interest income from municipal bonds is usually tax-free income, it may still be subject to the AMT. Some bonds are specifically exempt from the alternative minimum tax, so be sure to ask your broker about these if you think the AMT may be a concern for you.

❖ Have lots of miscellaneous deductions. Tax preparation fees, investment fees, and other miscellaneous expenses that can be deducted from income are not deductible for purposes of figuring the AMT. So if you have large amounts of itemized deductions, you may be subject to the tax. Itemized deductions for medical expenses on your income tax return may also be disallowed for purposes of figuring the AMT.

No AMT Relief in Sight

Rather than provide some relief, the 2001 tax cut promises to make even more taxpayers subject to the alternative minimum tax. Why? According to Chicago-area tax attorney Kaye Thomas, "The amount of alternative minimum tax you pay depends on how much regular income tax you pay. When your regular income tax goes down, your AMT goes up. Overall, you don't pay more tax. Instead, you're simply exchanging one kind of tax for another."

Even though the AMT was created to make the wealthy pay their fair share of taxes, flaws in its design make it a Damocles sword to middle- and upper-income individuals and families as well. Enacted over 30 years ago, the rules governing the tax have been revised only sporadically and do not account for inflation and changes in regular income tax rates. In 2001, an estimated 1.5 million taxpayers, most of them with incomes between $72,000 and $627,000, will be hit with this tax.

The recent legislation provides only a smidgeon of AMT relief by raising the limit on deductions that are exempt from the tax—also called the AMT exemption amount—by $4,000 for married couples filing jointly and $2,000 for singles. However, the increase, which takes effect in 2001, disappears in 2005. Once that happens, experts estimate that as many as 35 million people will have to pay the tax. "For millions of people," says Thomas, "the AMT will take away some or all of the advantage of the tax cuts in the new law."

People most affected by the AMT live in states with high state and local taxes. Coincidentally, President Bush did not carry the majority vote in most of these states in the 2000 election. Makes 'ya wonder.

Your New Tax Bracket

You have probably heard people talking about which tax bracket they are in. And you probably realize that now that you have more money, you might be in a higher tax bracket. But what, exactly, does that mean? And why should you care?

When people talk about their tax bracket, they often think of it as the tax rate on their last dollar of earned income. But it's a little more complicated than that.

For example, suppose you are single and your taxable income puts you in the 30 percent tax bracket in 2002. Remember, your taxable income is not the same as your gross income from employment, investments, or other sources. It's your income after deductions (such as mortgage interest and charitable contributions) and exemptions (such as the dependency exemption). This is your taxable income, or the income on which your tax is based. Once you know your taxable income, you look at the tax rate schedules that come with the instructions to Form 1040 to determine the income tax rate that applies to you. Voilà! You know your tax bracket.

Now, let's say your taxable income puts you near the ceiling for which the 30 percent tax rate applies. Suddenly, you receive a large windfall and are wondering about the best way to invest it. If you put the money into securities that produce taxable interest, most of it won't be taxed at the 30 percent rate. Instead, you'll pay income tax at the next highest rate because the additional income thrusts you into a higher tax bracket.

A common misconception many people have is that their entire tax is based on their highest level of taxable income. Actually, there are five federal tax brackets for income and short-term capital gains, currently ranging from 10 percent to 38.6 percent. If your taxable income puts you in the top tax rate of 38.6 percent, your tax is actually based on a blended rate of all five tax brackets, not just the 38.6 percent rate.

It's important to know your tax bracket for a number of reasons, including the ability to determine the following:

- ❖ The value of tax deductions. A tax deduction is worth more to you when you pay a higher income tax rate. For example, the after-tax cost of a $1,000 donation for someone in the 27 percent federal tax bracket is $730. For someone who pays the highest tax rate of 38.6 percent, the after-tax cost is $614.

- ❖ The benefits of tax-exempt income. Should you invest in tax-free municipal bonds or higher-yielding but taxable corporate bonds? To a large extent, the answer depends on how much income you have left after taxes. Obviously, tax-exempt income is more valuable to those who pay higher taxes.

- ❖ Whether you should start a gifting program that shifts income from investments such as stocks, bonds, or mutual funds to children or grandchildren, who pay lower taxes.

- ❖ Whether you should try to shift income to another year, when you will be in a lower tax bracket.

Lower Tax Brackets

The tax legislation passed in 2001, officially titled The Economic Growth and Tax Relief Reconciliation Act of 2001, created several changes that will impact your tax rate.

Beginning July 1, 2001, regular income tax rates were reduced:

Year		Old Tax Rates		
2000	28%	31%	36%	39.6%
		New Tax Rates		
2001 to 2003	27%	30%	35%	38.6%
2004 to 2005	26%	29%	34%	37.6%
2006 and after	25%	28%	33%	35%

You can find your tax bracket for 2001 (the latest information available as of this writing) in the following table. Although the applicable income level will change from year to year, you can use it to get an idea of what your federal tax bracket will be in future years under the new law.

Federal Tax Bracket	Applicable Income Level	
	Single	Married Filing Jointly
15% taxable income up to:	$27,050	$45,200
27.5% taxable income between:	$27,050 to $65,550	$45,200 to $109,250
30.5% taxable income between:	$65,550 to $136,750	$109,250 to $166,500
35.5% taxable income between:	$136,750 to $297,350	$166,500 to $297,350
39.1% taxable income over:	$297,350	$297,350

Accelerate Tax-Deductible Expenditures

If you're thinking of making a large charitable donation, you may want to consider doing it sooner rather than later. The tax deduction for a charitable gift of $100,000 in 2002 for someone who pays the top tax rate would be $38,600, compared to $35,000 in 2006.

The legislation creates a new 10 percent regular income tax bracket for a portion of taxable income that was taxed at 15 percent, effective for taxable years beginning after December 31, 2000. The 10 percent rate bracket applies to the first $6,000 of taxable income for single individuals ($7,000 for 2008 and after), and $12,000 for married couples filing jointly ($14,000 for 2008 and after).

Keep Up with New Tax-Saving Opportunities

Increased wealth creates a greater need for tax-favored saving and investing opportunities. The recent tax legislation presents such opportunities by increasing the dollar limit on contributions to retirement savings plans.

Contributions to Traditional IRAs and Roth IRAs

Beginning in 2002, the dollar limit for contributions to these plans will increase to $3,000, up from the $2,000 a year level that has been around since 1981. From 2005 to 2007 the limit will rise again to $4,000 and increase to $5,000 in 2008.

Individuals over age 50 can contribute $500 more than those amounts beginning in 2002, and $1,000 more beginning in 2006.

New Maximum Contributions to IRAs and Roth IRAs		
	New Limit	Over Fifty Limit
2002 to 2004	$3,000	$3,500
2005	$4,000	$4,500
2006 to 2007	$4,000	$5,000
2008	$5,000	$6,000

New Contribution Limits for 401(k), 403(b), and 457 Plans

Contribution limits to 401(k) plans, 403(b)plans for nonprofit workers, and 457 plans for government employees, which ranged from $8,500 to $10,500, will become identical and increase to $11,000 in 2002. The limit will increase in incremental $1,000 steps every year until 2006, when it will reach $15,000. Increases after that date will be pegged to inflation.

Anyone aged 50 years and older can make "catch-up" contributions to these plans. The extra contribution amounts start at $1,000 in 2002 and rise in increments of $1,000 until 2006.

Contribution limits for SIMPLE plans (Savings Incentive Match Plan for Employees), which are used in companies with 100 or fewer workers, will also increase from $7,000 in 2002 to $10,000 in 2005, and will be indexed to inflation thereafter. Individuals aged 50 or older can make catch-up contributions to these plans as well. The additional amount starts at $500 in 2002 and increases in $500 increments until 2006.

Roth 401(k)

Currently, high-income individuals do not qualify for a Roth IRA. In 2001, married couples with income of at least $160,000 and singles with income of at least $110,000 are included in that high-income group.

Beginning in 2006, a provision permitting nondeductible contributions to a 401(k) plan regardless of income will take effect. This new savings opportunity is called a Roth 401(k).

With traditional 401(k) plan, employees can currently save up to $10,500 annually in pre-tax income. The earnings in the plan accumulate tax-deferred until withdrawal, when both contributions and investment gains are taxed at regular income rates. Some plans also permit after-tax contributions to a 401(k), but earnings attributable to them are taxed as income at withdrawal.

With the new Roth IRA arrangement, workers can make nondeductible contributions to a 401(k). Earnings accumulate in the account tax-free, and no taxes are due on either contributions or earnings at withdrawal. The combined maximum contribution levels for the traditional and Roth 401(k) plans will be $15,000 a year ($20,000 for those aged 50 and older).

Expanded Education IRAs

Using an Education IRA, you can make after-tax contributions each year on behalf of a child under age 18. While contributions are not tax-deductible, earnings in the account grow tax-free and are tax-free at withdrawal if the money is used to pay for educational expenses.

Under the old law, a $500 maximum annual contribution limited the amount you could save in these plans. The new law makes the Education IRA more attractive by expanding the annual contribution limit to $2,000 beginning in 2002.

This makes it possible to put a real dent in tuition bills and to pay them on a tax-favored basis. If someone opens an Education IRA for a five-year-old and contributes the maximum amount every year, the account will grow to $46,430 by the time the child reaches age 18, assuming an 8 percent return. Because none of the money is taxed, all of it can go toward paying tuition.

You can use the money from an Education IRA to pay for a broad range of education expenses, including elementary and secondary school expenses, as well as higher education expenses. Previously, tax-free withdrawals were permitted only for higher education expenses.

There are income limitations for those making Education IRA contributions. Beginning in 2002, a married couple filing jointly with annual adjusted gross income over $220,000 is not eligible. The income ceiling is half that amount ($110,000) for single taxpayers.

Other IRA Flavors

There are a few other choices that will allow your windfall to grow tax-deferred: the rollover IRA and the IRA triplets—deductible IRA, nondeductible IRA, and the Roth IRA.

You can open a rollover IRA to receive distributions from a 401(k), 403(b), or other type of qualified retirement plan when you change jobs or retire. For more details on how and when to use them, see Chapter 7, "401(k) Plans."

There are also IRAs you contribute to directly, rather than transfer amounts from other sources. These include the deductible IRA, the nondeductible IRA, and the Roth IRA.

For many years, the contribution limit for all of them was $2,000. Starting in 2002, the maximum annual contribution rises to $3,000 for those under age 50, and goes up to $5,000 in 2008 (see the "New Maximum Contributions to IRAs and Roth IRAs" table earlier in this chapter for more detail on the new contribution limits). All of them allow for tax-deferred growth of investment earnings as long as the money remains in the retirement account. Beyond that, there are some significant differences in tax deductibility for contributions and how withdrawals are treated.

Deductible IRA

As the name implies, a deductible IRA allows you to take a tax deduction up front on your contribution. If you are in the 27 percent tax bracket in 2002, for example, each $1,000 contribution shaves $270 from your tax bill.

The tax break comes with a price, though, because withdrawals are taxed at ordinary income tax rates. If you are under age $59\frac{1}{2}$, you may also be hit with a 10 percent penalty. This penalty is waived when the money is used for medical bills that exceed 7.5 percent of your gross income, a first-time home purchase, or higher-education expenses. It is also waived if you die or become permanently disabled. Even if you qualify for these exceptions, you will still need to pay applicable income taxes on the entire amount of the withdrawal.

If you are not covered by a retirement plan at work, either because your employer does not offer one or you are not eligible to participate, your contributions are deductible. However, if you or your spouse participate in an employer-sponsored retirement plan, you can't deduct any of your IRA contribution if your income exceeds $44,000 in 2002 ($64,000 for a married couple filing jointly). This obviously limits the appeal of deductible IRAs for those with incomes above those thresholds.

Nondeductible IRA

Contributions to a nondeductible IRA are, as the name implies, not deductible from taxes. When you take the money out at retirement, only the earnings in the account are subject to taxes since contributions are made with after-tax dollars. Withdrawals prior to age 59½ may be subject to a 10 percent penalty, unless they qualify for one of the exceptions noted above.

Nondeductible IRAs come with the restrictions of deductible IRAs, but without the benefit of that nice up-front tax deduction. They are not very popular and lost even more appeal with the 1998 introduction of the Roth IRA.

Roth IRA

First, the bad news: You make contributions to a Roth IRA with after-tax dollars, so you lose a tax deduction up front. But the beauty of a Roth IRA is that when you take the money out at retirement, none of the withdrawals—neither contributions nor their earnings—will be subject to income taxes. To qualify for this treatment, you must be at least age 59½ and have held the Roth IRA for at least five years.

Even if you are younger than that, it is still possible to access your money without penalties or taxes as long as you limit your withdrawals to the amount of your original contributions. That's right. Regardless of your age or the reason you are taking out the money, you can withdraw contributions to your Roth IRA at any time without paying a cent to Uncle Sam. But you can't touch the earnings, because you could be hit with income taxes and a 10 percent penalty on those amounts.

Withdrawals from a Roth IRA are done on a principal first basis. Unless you take out more than you've contributed, you won't have to worry about taxes or penalties.

This flexibility does not mean you should dip into your Roth IRA for discretionary expenses or luxuries. First and foremost, it's a retirement account. But it is nice to know that if you ever need the money, it's accessible.

You can have a Roth IRA if you are an active participant in a pension plan, but you become ineligible if your adjusted gross income is more than $110,000 ($160,000 for married couples filing jointly). If your

AGI is between $95,000 and $110,000 ($150,000 and $160,000 for married couples filing jointly), you can make a partial contribution.

Converting to a Roth IRA

You can convert a traditional IRA or a rollover IRA into a Roth IRA. To do this, you will need to pay taxes on any amounts you convert that have not been subject to taxes, including pre-tax contributions and investment earnings. In a sizable account, that tax bill can be substantial.

Example: You have a rollover IRA with a balance of $300,000, all from pre-tax contributions and earnings. If you want to convert to a Roth IRA and you are in the 30 percent federal tax bracket, you'll have to pony up $90,000 for the privilege.

You could pay taxes out of the rollover IRA, but that has some disadvantages. For one thing, you won't have as much money growing tax-deferred in the account. The amount you withdraw would be subject to income taxes and, if you're under age $59\frac{1}{2}$, a 10 percent penalty. Still, converting to a Roth IRA might make sense if you ...

- ❖ Can pay the taxes from sources other than the IRA you are converting. This allows the entire account balance to continue growing tax-deferred.

- ❖ Are relatively young. The younger you are, the more time you have to recover from the tax hit. You may also be in a lower tax bracket than someone in his or her peak earning years.

- ❖ Think your income will be higher in retirement than it is now. Although that's usually not the case, converting now and paying the tax bill when you are in a lower tax bracket could save you some money.

- ❖ Are concerned about taxes for heirs. With a traditional IRA, heirs pay income taxes on withdrawals. With a Roth IRA, withdrawals are completely tax free. Also, with a regular IRA, you must begin taking the minimum required distributions at age $70\frac{1}{2}$ and pay income taxes on them. With a Roth IRA, there is no minimum distribution requirement, so all the money can go to heirs.

On the other hand, converting may not be an attractive option if ...

* You don't have outside money to foot the conversion tax bill.
* You plan to use all or most of your IRA for living expenses in retirement, which would minimize the impact of income taxes for heirs without needing to convert.
* You will be in a lower tax bracket in retirement. This makes it less attractive to convert now, when the tax bite is more severe.

Your Estate Plan

With a windfall, your estate may now be in the taxable range, even if it wasn't before. For more guidance on estate taxes and estate planning, see Chapter 3, "Estate Planning: The Next Step."

Softening the Blow

If a windfall is sizable, it can have a significant impact on your tax situation, both when you receive it and on an ongoing basis for years to come. Taking advantage of newly expanded tax-favored saving options can help soften the tax blow considerably, and by doing so, leave more money available for saving and investing.

CHAPTER 15

The Greater Good

"Make all you can, save all you can, give all you can."
—*John Wesley*

"Money, like dung, does no good till 'tis spread."
—*Thomas Fuller*

Getting Involved with Philanthropy and Socially Responsible Investing

The word "philanthropy" is derived from the Greek words meaning "to love mankind." For windfall recipients and others, the benefits of charitable giving go well beyond the obvious ways that money can enhance worthy causes. Philanthropic endeavors have many personal rewards, including the following:

- ❖ The ability to help support and raise awareness of the values and causes you consider most important by contributing to organizations that promote them.

- ❖ The honor of creating a legacy. If your wealth is inherited, contributions in the deceased's name help keep his or her memory alive. Regardless of your windfall source, legacies can begin with you through a private foundation or generous contributions to worthy causes.

- ❖ Letting people know you're rich. Sure, you can do that by buying expensive cars or a mansion. But nothing shouts "I've got money" in a more subtle and agreeable way than a generous charitable contribution. And you will get lots of positive feedback and thank yous from the organizations you donate to. (Be warned that this recognition may lose some of its appeal as friends and charitable organizations learn you have money to donate and start bombarding you with solicitations.)

❖ The satisfaction of being able to make a difference. This is the best reason of all.

How Much Should You Give?

The easy answer is "as much as you feel comfortable with." That amount varies from person to person. If you grew up in modest surroundings and your family needed to budget carefully to get by, chances are your first thought when you receive a windfall won't be how quickly you can give it away. On the other hand, if you have lived comfortably for most of your life and are already satisfied with your standard of living, you may feel more inclined to spread the wealth.

The fact that you have received a windfall does not necessarily mean you will feel more generous than you did before. Statistics show that the amount people donate to charities doesn't keep pace with increases in assets or income. People in lower income groups donate more of their wealth, on a percentage basis, than people with a higher level of income and assets.

According to NewTithing Group of San Francisco, a philanthropic research organization, U.S. tax filers could have comfortably afforded to give to charity at least double the estimated $150 billion that they donated. The group's research, extrapolated from the IRS data on tax returns filed for 2000, suggests that individuals could have given a total of $320 billion to charity.

Virtually all the $170 billion shortfall, the group says, could have come from the three wealthiest tax brackets. People with adjusted gross incomes of $1 million or more could have given over 10 times what they donated.

When the Wealthy Fall Short

It is in the area of charitable giving that the wealthy fall short:

Adjusted Gross Income	Salary	Investment Assets	Actual Donations	Affordable Donations*
$25,000 to $49,999	$29,586	$60,838	$661	$661
$50,000 to $74,999	$49,166	$114,252	$1,268	$1,268
$75,000 to $99,999	$67,522	$193,772	$1,909	$1,909
$100,000 to $199,999	$93,975	$462,275	$3,156	$4,500
$200,000 to $499,999	$166,068	$1,458,420	$7,558	$21,000
$500,000 to $999,999	$323,629	$4,104,121	$18,260	$87,000
$1,000,000 or more	$924,495	$18,125,000	$122,940	$1,031,000

*Comfortably affordable donations to charity based on annual surplus income and the market value, after debt, of investment assets. Source: NewTithing Group, San Francisco. Reprinted with permission.

The group's Web site, newtithing.org, has a PrudentPal calculator that helps determine an "optimal" level of giving, depending on your income and assets. Use it as a guideline, but don't feel wracked with guilt if your giving level comes up short. Unless you are already wealthy, you may need to use a windfall to catch up on personal goals such as paying down debt or funding a college education for your children. Many people find that as they come closer to reaching their goals and achieving a lifestyle they are happy with, charitable giving ascends their priority list.

A Giving Nation

Charitable contributions in the United States totaled over $203 billion in 2000, an increase of 3.2 percent from 1999 and double the giving level of a decade earlier.

Deciding Where to Give

The decision about where to donate will depend on a host of personal factors, including the following:

❖ **The values and causes you support.** Your love of the outdoors may lead you to hook up with environmental groups. A strong religious background might guide your choice to a local house of worship or religious organization.

❖ **Your life experiences.** Someone with a close relative who has had a life-threatening illness, or anyone who has had such an illness, may donate to causes dedicated to related research.

❖ **Your desire to be close to a cause.** Some people like the idea of giving to a large, well-known organization. Others prefer to donate to a smaller, local group with fewer bureaucratic layers such as a homeless shelter or a local town library. At a smaller facility, a large donation can make a real and visible difference and allow the donor to actually see where the money is going.

❖ **How efficiently an organization uses its resources.** Does the organization you want to contribute to spend most of its money on fundraising and administration or on the programs that actually help the cause you are interested in? While support services are necessary in any philanthropic endeavor, spending too much on them detracts from the overall mission.

The Better Business Bureau's Philanthropic Advisory Service breaks a charitable organization's expenses into three categories: program services, management and general costs, and fund raising. Program services, the heart of an organization, might cover research grants, food supplies to feed starving children, or salaries for medical personnel on overseas missions. Management and general costs cover expenses such as accountants' or attorneys' fees, rent, salaries for administrative personnel, and other general expenses. Fundraising costs include creating and printing brochures, paying fees to professional fundraisers, and advertising.

Percentage of Income That Goes Toward Programs for
Some Charitable Organizations

Organization	Percentage Toward Programs
American Red Cross	83
Christian Children's Fund	79
Easter Seals	76

Organization	Percentage Toward Programs
Habitat for Humanity	67
Make-A-Wish Foundation	77
March of Dimes Birth Defects Foundation	72
National Wildlife Federation	87
Planned Parenthood Federation of America	66
Special Olympics	61
World Wildlife Fund	72

Source: Better Business Bureau Philanthropic Advisory Service (bbb.org)

In general, the Council of Better Business Bureau standards call for (1) at least half of the charity's total income to be spent on programs, (2) at least half of public contributions to be spent on the programs described in appeals, (3) no more than 35 percent of contributions to be spent on fund raising, and (4) no more than half of the charity's total income to be spent on administrative and fund-raising costs.

If you are considering contributing a substantial amount to a charity, ask to see a copy of its latest annual report and financial statements along with a list of its board of directors. These documents will help you get a clear picture of who runs the programs and how the organization raises and spends its money. Beginning donors who are unsure about where to give can start by donating smaller amounts to a number of organizations rather than large amounts to one or two. As donors begin learning more about the organizations they choose, they can decide which ones they feel most comfortable entrusting their donations to and refocus their efforts accordingly.

The Do's and Don'ts of Charitable Giving

Do check the background of any charity to which you are considering donating a substantial amount.

Do use checks made payable to the charity, not to the individual who made the solicitation.

Do keep good records of amounts donated. If you volunteer your time, any costs such as automobile expenses or materials are tax-deductible.

Do ask about deductible amounts if a contribution is associated with some type of benefit such as membership in an organization or a gift. You may only be permitted to deduct any amounts above the fair market value of such items.

Do ask for identification from door-to-door solicitors. When speaking on the phone or in person to a solicitor, do not yield to pressure to make an immediate donation. Ask to receive some background material on the organization first.

Don't give cash.

Don't confuse tax-exempt with tax-deductible. While some organizations do not have to pay taxes, contributions you make to them are not necessarily deductible from your income. Most of the organizations that qualify for tax-deductible contribution treatment have received what's called Section 501(3) status from the Internal Revenue Service. If you are unsure whether or not your contribution is tax-deductible, ask to see a copy of the IRS determination letter that verifies Section 501(3) status. Examples of organizations where contributions are typically deductible from income include the following:

* Churches, temples, synagogues, mosques, and other religious organizations
* Most nonprofit charitable organizations such as the Red Cross and the United Way
* Most nonprofit educational organizations including the Boy Scouts and Girl Scouts of America, museums, and colleges
* Nonprofit hospitals and medical research organizations
* Utility company emergency energy programs, if the utility is an agent for a charitable organization that assists individuals with emergency energy needs
* Nonprofit volunteer fire companies
* Recreation facilities and public parks
* Civil defense organizations

Write a Check

When it comes to charitable giving, most people think "check." The appeal here is that these contributions to qualified charities are deductible from income, a benefit that increases with your tax bracket.

Federal Tax Rate	Cost of Donation Contribution	Tax Savings	After Taxes
27.0%	$50,000	$13,500	$36,500
30.0%	$50,000	$15,000	$35,000
35.0%	$50,000	$17,500	$32,500
38.6%	$50,000	$19,300	$30,700

Donate Appreciated Securities

Consider donating appreciated stock or mutual fund shares, an option many people ignore. By using this approach, you get to deduct the full market value of the shares (subject to adjusted growth income limitations). You do not have to pay any capital gains taxes on the sale of the donated shares.

Let's say you want to donate $10,000 to a favorite charity, using stock you own to fund the donation. Assume the shares cost you $3,000 and all the $7,000 gain is taxed at the maximum long-term capital gains rate of 20 percent. Here's what happens under two possible scenarios:

Donation	Sell Shares and Donate Cash	Donate Shares
Value of securities	$10,000	$10,000
Capital gains tax	$1,400	$0
Value of donation	$8,600	$10,000
Value of income tax deduction		
(30 percent tax bracket)	$2,580	$3,000
Cost of donation after taxes	$7,334	$7,000

By donating shares directly, the charity would receive $10,000 instead of $8,600. And your after-tax cost is $334 less than a cash donation.

Donor-Advised Funds: The Easy Way to Donate Securities

Donating securities can have some drawbacks. While many larger charitable organizations can handle securities donations, smaller local groups often lack the accounting and record-keeping know-how to do it properly. Even in large, well-established organizations, more paperwork is usually involved than with a cash donation. This can be time-consuming if you are thinking of using this strategy for more than one organization.

To make securities donations less cumbersome, several firms, including Fidelity Investments, T. Rowe Price, Vanguard Group, and Charles Schwab, have set up *donor-advised funds*. Under these arrangements, you make an irrevocable donation of stock or other securities to anywhere from one to three or four portfolios of your choice with different investment objectives. Donation assets are pooled together for investment purposes but are tracked separately. The minimum initial donation at Fidelity, T. Rowe Price, and Schwab is $10,000; at Vanguard, it's $25,000. Incremental donations range from $1,000 to $5,000. Your donations have the opportunity to grow in the investment pools, potentially increasing the amount you are able to contribute.

Once you set up your account, you can begin making grants to charities of your choice (the firms sponsoring the accounts check to make sure contributions are tax-deductible before they approve them). Alternatively, you can leave the choosing up to the firm's panel of experts. Minimum grant amounts are as little as $250 and grants can be made any time of the year. The donor-advised funds handle all the paperwork, including quarterly summaries of account activity and performance information, confirmations of each grant and contribution, and a single form for tax filing purposes.

Windfall recipients might find donor-advised funds especially useful as they are an easy way to reduce an impending tax bite quickly. Let's say you own stock from exercising company stock options. Because the stock has appreciated substantially, you're faced with a huge tax bill. Instead of contributing cash to a charity to reduce your taxes, you could instead donate the stock to a donor-advised fund and use it for future charitable gifts over many years.

Donating Other Kinds of Property

Many people donate other kinds of property to charity, including artwork, jewelry, rare books, or stamp collections. The kind of tangible assets you can touch and feel are much more difficult to value than cash or securities. Before you donate them, you need to get a fix on how much they are worth, or their fair market value. A professional appraisal is not necessary for items for which you claim a deduction of $5,000 or less. If the deduction is over that amount, support it with a written appraisal from a qualified and reputable source.

Jewelry and Gems

A written appraisal from a specialized jewelry appraiser should include the gem's setting and cut, the style of the jewelry, the stone's brilliance, weight, coloring, and any flaws it may have.

Art and Antiques

The popular PBS program *Antiques Roadshow* has fired the imagination of art and antique buffs around the country. If you think a piece of artwork or an antique may have value and are thinking about donating it to a charity, your local antique store may not be the best place to get an appraisal. The IRS will usually give more weight to appraisals prepared by someone specializing in a particular niche, such as old masters, Revolutionary War–era antiques, or nineteenth-century art. Such individuals will be able to provide information on recent sales of objects similar to yours to support their opinions.

You can check with a local museum or college to find an appraiser specializing in a particular niche. Auction houses that specialize in valuable art and antiques, such as Sotheby's or Skinner's, may also be able to refer you to someone.

Among other things, the art and antique appraisers will examine the physical condition and extent of restoration of a particular item. Because these factors weigh so heavily in determining a piece's value, they will need to be reported in the appraisal. A damaged antique, or one that has been refinished or restored in some way, will be worth much less than a similar piece in close to its original condition.

If the items you claim as a deduction are valued at $20,000 or more, you must attach a complete copy of the signed appraisal to your return. For individual objects valued at $20,000 or more, the IRS may request a clear color photograph or color transparency of the item.

Collectibles

Collectibles include items such as books, autographed documents or photographs, stamps, coins, guns, and natural history items. As a starting point, consult publications such as catalogues or specialized hobby periodicals, which often contain pricing guidelines for various types of collectibles. These figures aren't always the last word. There could be pricing discrepancies if, for example, a value reflected in a catalogue came from an aberrant auction bidding war for a particular collection. If you think the collection has some value, consult an appraiser as well as published reference guides.

Books

An appraiser specializing in books will consider condition, including the presence of missing pages, stained pages, or a loose binding. Books that are old or rare may not be very valuable if they are in poor condition. First editions are usually the most prized by collectors.

Coins

Coin catalogues, available at many dealers, will list coin values based on age, condition, demand, and rarity. These catalogues usually categorize coins based on their condition—mint or uncirculated, extremely fine, very fine, very good, good, fair, or poor—with a different value assigned for each category. A reputable coin dealer should be able to determine which of these categories a coin falls into.

Stamps

Libraries and collectible stamp dealers usually have books reporting the publishers' estimates of value. Each stamp usually has two different price levels for postmarked and nonpostmarked stamps. A professional stamp dealer can prepare an acceptable appraisal for a valuable collection.

Handwritten Works

Written works include manuscripts, autographs, signatures, and diaries. Handwritten items by famous people are in high demand and usually carry substantial value. Writings of relatively unknown people may also be valuable if they have some literary or historic significance.

Cars, Boats, and Aircraft

Some firms and trade organizations publish regular pricing guides for these items. Perhaps the most famous is the *Blue Book*, the well-known pricing guide for cars. These sources, while not considered as reliable as a professional appraisal, will give you a good idea of what similar items are selling for. As with any kind of tangible asset, you need to take condition into account. A car with a nasty, unrepaired fender-bender will be worth significantly less than an undamaged vehicle of the same age and model.

Real Estate

Many homeowners are familiar with real estate appraisal reports from their experiences with purchasing or refinancing a home. A real estate appraiser usually arrives at a value by comparing the donated property with several similar properties in the area that have been sold recently. Adjustments may be made for a property's condition, location, size, zoning restrictions, and other features that can affect its value. Some appraisals may also factor in replacement costs or whatever it would cost to reconstruct a building. This figure takes into account factors such as materials, size, and quality of workmanship and makes adjustments for physical deterioration of the property.

Interest in a Business

The fair market value of any interest in a business is defined by the IRS as "what a willing buyer would pay for the interest to a willing seller after consideration of all relevant factors." These factors typically include assets, past and current earnings, and the value of goodwill. Copies of reports from accountants, engineers, or technical experts made on or close to the valuation date will be necessary to verify the valuation.

Sophisticated Planning Techniques

More sophisticated giving techniques may be appropriate for those able to donate several hundred thousand dollars or more.

Private Foundations

Affluent individuals with a philanthropic bent might want to consider a private foundation as a way for themselves and other family members to fund worthy causes, while maintaining maximum control over how the money is invested and which organizations receive grants. Unlike a donor-advised fund, which pools contributions from many investors, contributions to a private foundation are invested and managed separately. Most private foundations enlist trust companies to invest the money as well as handle administration and tax-reporting requirements. Some also hire outsiders to decide how and where to allocate grants.

According to the latest figures from the nonprofit Council on Foundations, there are some 47,000 foundations in the United States with endowments totaling $385 billion. Many of these are private or family foundations set up by wealthy individuals and their families. These private foundations, ranging in size from a few hundred thousand dollars to $1 billion or more, have cumulative assets of over $150 billion and make grants of approximately $7 billion a year. Many are run by family members who serve as trustees or directors on a voluntary basis.

Family foundations have enriched our lives in ways that affect us every day. Consider just three examples of programs that these foundations made possible:

- ❖ *Sesame Street.* Each day, millions of preschool children learn the alphabet, numbers, and new words from a cast of now-familiar puppets, as well as their human companions, on *Sesame Street.* It is the most widely viewed children's series in the world, attracting some 16 million viewers every week.

  Although *Sesame Street* is self-supporting today, it got its start with funding from foundations. The first one, made in 1966 by The Carnegie Corporation of New York, was used to underwrite a feasibility study on using television for preschool education. The foundation later gave the Children's Television Workshop a two-year grant to launch *Sesame Street.* Grants from other foundations, including the John R. and Mary Markle Foundations, soon followed.

- ❖ **The 911 Emergency System.** The first telephone number that many people teach their children did not even exist less than 30 years ago. In the early 1970s, the Robert Wood Johnson Foundation provided 44 grants in 32 states to help develop regional emergency medical services. After these grants solidified the concept of regionalized, systematic emergency response, the federal government stepped in to fund a nationwide 911 system.

- ❖ **White highway lines.** In the early 1950s, inventor-engineer Dr. John V. N. Dorr noticed that drivers hugged the white line in the middle of the highway when they could not see well because of snow or fog. He believed this created many accidents and convinced highway engineers in the New York area to paint white lines along the outside shoulders of roads as well. There was a dramatic decrease in accidents, and Dorr used money from his own foundation, the Dorr Foundation of New York, to publicize the results of these test. Today, state funds pay for those life-saving outside shoulder white lines.

Although these stories sound inspiring, a private family foundation is only for the very wealthy. Because they are fairly complicated to set up and expensive to administer, only consider starting one if you have at least several hundred thousand dollars to donate.

Philanthropic Resources

The Council on Foundations Web site (www.cof.org) has information and resources on how to start a private foundation.

The Association of Small Foundations (www.smallfoundations.org) is geared for those with small fortunes but big hearts.

JustGive (www.justgive.org) is an online giving resource with a large database of charities. Check out the celebrities section to see where entertainment industry luminaries donate.

CharityWave (www.charitywave.com) is another giving resource that facilitates online donations.

More Than Money (www.morethanmoney.org) offers a list of philanthropic consultants who specialize in administering foundations.

Charitable Remainder Trusts

Charitable remainder trusts (CRTs) are useful for people who want to make a charitable contribution, but who do not want to part with the property or the income it produces right away. Using a CRT, an individual donates assets to a charity through a trust and receives a tax deduction in the year of donation. The trust can provide an income stream provided by its investments to the donor (or the donor and his or her spouse) for a specified number of years, or for their entire lives. After the specified period the amount that's left in the trust—the *remainder*—goes to the designated charity or charities. As these amounts go to charities, they are effectively removed from the estate, which can result in significant tax savings.

A CRT can also help avoid immediate capital gains taxes when the donor transfers ownership of appreciated stock to the trust. This will probably produce a higher level of income than selling the stock, paying capital gains taxes, and investing what is left.

Charitable remainder trusts have a couple of drawbacks. First, they are irrevocable. Once you have set one up, you can't change your mind and take the money out later on. And the amount of the deduction for charitable contributions is lower than for an outright charitable gift because it is based on a complex IRS formula that takes into account the present value of the income you will be getting. For these reasons, CRTs should only be used by those who are sure they will not need the money later on, who want their investments to provide an income stream while they are alive, and who want to dedicate all or part of their estate to charitable causes.

Charitable Lead Trusts

A charitable lead trust is the mirror image of a charitable remainder trust: The charity receives income from the trust for a specified period of time. After that, the property in the trust is transferred to designated beneficiaries such as children or grandchildren. This technique is designed for individuals who:

- Do not need the current income from trust property.
- Wish to have a charity receive the benefit of that income for a designated period of time.
- Want the property to pass to their beneficiaries.

Naming a Charity as Beneficiary of an IRA

As I've already noted, beneficiaries confront significant tax consequences when they inherit an IRA. Assuming the entire balance came from tax-deductible contributions and their earnings, the entire amount may be subject to federal income tax and, possibly, estate taxes as well.

Example: Assume that you leave a $1 million IRA to a child who is in the highest federal income tax bracket (38.6 percent in 2002) and who will pay an estate tax of 50 percent. After deducting $500,000 for the federal estate tax and $193,000 for the federal income tax, the child would be left with $307,000, or just a fraction of the IRA's original value.

If you left the IRA to a charity instead, the entire $1 million would remain intact because charities are not subject to estate or income taxes. Of course, your child would not receive over one quarter of a million dollars. Even after taxes, however, that's a fairly significant sum.

If you're considering leaving an IRA to a charity, you need to weigh the tax benefits of such a strategy against your family's need for the money. Someone who has significant assets outside an IRA and whose family can do without the money, might consider such a move. On the other hand, it may not be a great idea if an IRA constitutes a significant part of your estate and your family may need the money.

Socially Responsible Investing

Aligning his conscience with his wallet was a notion that always made sense to Alex, a 35-year-old program development director for a Washington, D.C.–based nonprofit organization. In the early 1990s, when his employer offered the option to invest his retirement money in a mutual fund that screens out stocks of alcohol, tobacco, and other companies whose businesses do not adhere to certain ethical or moral practices, Alex decided to take the plunge into socially responsible investing.

"If I don't support the actions of a company intellectually, then I am certainly not going to support them with my money," he says. "Over the long run, I believe that a company that tries to do good will perform better than one that doesn't pay attention to the ethical concerns of its stakeholders."

The Parnassus Fund was the first socially responsible mutual fund Levin invested in. Since that investment, he has also put money into the Citizens' Core Growth Fund, Citizens' Emerging Growth Fund, and Calvert Index Fund, three other socially screened mutual funds.

As Alex's story shows, windfall recipients certainly are not the only ones interested in socially responsible investing. As with philanthropic endeavors, however, the wealthy, including the suddenly wealthy, are a driving force.

Thanks in part to America's growing ranks of windfall recipients, the practice of socially responsible investing has grown from a fringe subsector with a flower child reputation into a mainstream strategy among pension funds and, increasingly, individuals. According to the nonprofit trade group Social Investment Forum, more than $2 trillion is invested today in the United States in a socially responsible manner, up a strong 82 percent from 1997 levels. That's nearly twice the rate of asset growth of all assets under management in the United States.

Much of that growth has come from mutual funds. The number of screened mutual funds increased to 175 in 1999 from 139 in 1997 and just 55 in 1995. The introduction of two socially responsible mutual funds in 2000 by industry giants Vanguard and TIAA-CREF signals to some observers the true coming of age of socially responsible investing.

Says Social Investment Forum President Steve Schueth, "The clear message is that socially responsible investing is now firmly on a path of steady growth, thanks to the nearly universal acceptance of social investment as a viable and value-added approach to asset management."

While some investors view socially responsible investing as a moral or ethical choice, the strong long-term performance by several of the largest, most visible socially responsible funds has added to their appeal and popularity. Two of the most well-known funds, the Domini Social Equity Fund and the Citizens' Core Growth Fund, have outperformed their benchmark S&P 500 Index over much of the last 10 years. They have done so, in part, both by avoiding the litigation woes of tobacco and oil companies and gravitating toward technology stocks and other "growthy" sectors the market favored for most of the past decade.

Moral Compasses with Different Directions

Broadly defined, socially responsible investing is the practice of integrating values-based criteria into the investment process. But the notion of what represents "values" spans the rainbow of individual moral compasses and varies enormously from fund to fund. Before you take the plunge into socially responsible investing, it's important to determine whether a mutual fund's values align with your own as well as whether its investment strategy makes sense for you.

Socially responsible mutual funds are broadly divisible into religious or secular funds. The latter group, considered to constitute the mainstream of socially responsible investing, includes some of the largest and best-known names, such as the Domini Social Equity Fund,

Parnassus Fund, and the Citizens' Funds. At a minimum, they usually avoid companies involved in tobacco, alcohol, nuclear power, and weapons production. Depending on the fund's charter, other screens might include animal testing, gambling, labor relations, or community investment.

Secular funds may have anywhere from one or two screens to ten or more. The Bridgeway Fund falls loosely into the socially responsible category by sidestepping companies involved in the tobacco or defense industries. (Many mutual funds that are not labeled socially responsible have no presence in those sectors anyway because their managers do not view them as good investments, although avoiding them is not an official policy.) At the more stringent end of the scale are families like the Citizens' Funds, which include alcohol, tobacco, gambling, defense, animal testing, the environment, human rights, labor relations, employment equality, and community relations in their screens.

A number of funds zero in on specific social concerns. The Women's Equity Fund invests in companies that have exhibited fair treatment of women and minorities in their hiring and promotion practices and the way they portray them in advertising. Green Century Balanced Fund emphasizes companies that promote a healthy environment. New Alternatives Fund invests mainly in companies concentrating in the solar power and alternative energy industries. And Meyers Pride Value Fund scouts out companies with progressive policies toward the gay and lesbian community.

Social criteria vary among religious funds as well, and not all funds apply the same screens. Some of the companies they include, or exclude, may surprise you.

Noah Fund, one of the top-performing large company funds over the last three years, does not invest in companies involved in alcohol, tobacco, and gambling. It also avoids those with a record of involvement in pornography and abortion.

The fund's list of no-buys contains some surprising names, including Walt Disney. Fund founder William Van Alen, a former attorney and a born-again Christian, does not like some of the sexually explicit material produced by the company's film division. At the same time, Noah includes many companies that provide domestic partner benefits for unmarried couples because it takes into consideration only what companies do to make profits, not what they do with those profits afterward. That allowance has made it possible for the fund to invest in large, growth-oriented companies that often provide such benefits and that have outperformed the market over the last few years.

By contrast, the Timothy Plan, another Conservative Christian fund offering, avoids companies that promote "nontraditional married lifestyles" by providing domestic partner benefits. With its emphasis on small-company value stocks, which have been out of favor for most of the last few years, investors taking this fund's moral high road have had to suffer through some lengthy periods of low returns.

Other religious funds focus on concerns of specific denominations. The MMA Praxis funds, for example, caters to Mennonite investors while Amana funds serve Islamic investors.

A good place to get a handle on what kinds of issues the universe of the socially responsible funds focus on is the Social Investment Forum Web site at socialinvest.org. The site also has information on how to find financial advisors who specialize in this area of investing. Christian investors looking for religious fund alternatives can consult Crosswalk.com.

Performance Varies

Investment performance among socially responsible funds varies as widely as their social screens. Their investment strategies may focus on value, growth, large companies, small companies, indexing, or any other genre you would find in the broader mutual fund universe.

Some of the largest, best-known socially responsible funds use the S&P 500 Index as a benchmark, but screen out stocks that do not meet their social criteria. These include the Domini Social Equity Fund, the Citizens' Core Growth Fund, The Calvert Social Index Fund, the Vanguard Calvert Social Index Fund (based on the index devised by The Calvert Fund group), and the TIAA-CREF Social Choice Equity Fund.

Established in 1991, The Domini Social Equity Fund is the oldest, followed by the Citizens Core Growth Fund (formerly the Citizens Index Fund), founded in 1995. The Calvert, Vanguard, and TIAA-CREF offerings are all less than a year old.

All of them are no-load funds except for The Calvert Social Index Fund, which carries a maximum front-end sales charge of 4.75 percent. The Vanguard and TIAA-CREF funds have low expense ratios of 0.25 percent of assets and 0.27 percent, respectively. The Domini Social Equity Fund's expense ratio is noticeably higher at 0.95 percent, while the Citizens' Core Growth Fund expense ratio stands at 1.58 percent.

Even though all these funds are based on a broad market benchmark, they don't own all of the same stocks. Each fund uses its own set of screens, which creates portfolios that are somewhat different from each other. That means that even though two funds may be based on the same index, their performance can differ substantially from one another.

The Domini offering, for example, contains about 400 stocks, only half of which are in the S&P 500. The rest are winnowed out because of various social and ethical concerns and replaced with 150 stocks allocated in line with the sector weightings of the S&P 500. The Calvert Social Index Fund and the Vanguard Calvert Social Index Fund screen from among the 1,000 largest companies in the United States and contain 464 names. Of the 300 companies in the Citizens' Core Growth Fund, 200 are in the S&P 500 Index.

Because these funds screen out many value stocks in the industrial and energy sectors, they tend to be underweight relative to their benchmarks in those areas and overweight in technology and other growth sectors. Depending on which direction the market winds are blowing, they can underperform or outperform their benchmark by a substantial margin from year to year, a phenomenon professionals call *tracking error.*

The Domini 400 Social Index, a widely used benchmark of the performance of large-company socially screened stocks, provides some insight into the performance pattern of some of the bigger index-based socially responsible funds. For the 10-year period ending December 31,

2000, the average annual return of the DSI 400 was 19.01 percent, compared to 17.48 percent for the S&P 500. However, the DSI 400 lost 14.32 percent for the calendar year 2000, compared to the S&P's loss of 9.01 percent for the same period. The DSI's underperformance relative to the S&P 500 occurred largely because of its overexposure to the computer hardware industry, which led the market downturn that year, and underexposure to the energy reserve industry, one of the few market sectors to post positive returns in 2000.

Aside from index funds, the socially responsible universe has a number of noteworthy actively managed offerings. These include Parnassus Fund, a mid-cap value offering, and Pax World Fund, a balanced fund.

Build Your Own Fund?

Even though the number of socially responsible mutual funds has mushroomed over the last five years, you may still have trouble finding one that adheres to your personal principles and performance criteria. Foliofn, the Internet service described in Chapter 12, "The Investment Menu," might be an alternative for investors who want to assemble their own socially responsible portfolios without buying individual stocks.

With mutual funds, it's kind of an all-or-nothing thing when it comes to social issues. You have to accept what's there. But a lot of people have just one or two areas of concern such as tobacco or the environment. This service is a good fit for these people.

Using Foliofn, an investor can choose from six pre-assembled stock portfolios—called folios—geared toward specific social issues. Another alternative allows the user to screen out specified companies from a basket of stocks designed to mirror the performance of an index such as the Dow Jones Industrial Average or S&P 500 Index.

The service does have some limitations. Each folio is limited to 50 stocks. And, particularly for smaller investments, a mutual fund may be more cost-effective. The Foliofn site includes a cost calculator that can help you determine the alternative that best fits both your budget and your conscience.

Giving Back

The phrase "It is better to give than to receive" takes on a new meaning when your windfall allows you to financially promote causes you deem worthy in a meaningful and significant way. You can take that concept one step further by investing in companies whose business practices align with your social conscience.

CHAPTER 16

Family, Friends, and You

In some ways, getting a windfall changes nothing. For better or worse, you're still the same person you always were. In other ways, particularly in the way people close to you perceive you and the way you react to those perceptions, it changes everything. You'll need to assess own feelings about the emotional and financial responsibilities of wealth.

Love and Marriage

A prenuptial agreement—do you need one? These days, you don't have to be famous or even rich to have a prenuptial agreement. With half of all marriages ending in divorce, agreements stipulating who gets what in the event of a breakup have become almost as ubiquitous as wedding rice.

The driving force behind most prenups is usually the individual who stands to lose more if the marriage dissolves. If you've received a windfall, that person could well be you. Here are some common situations where prenuptial agreements come into play:

* You have substantially more assets than your fiancé coming into the marriage. A prenuptial agreement will often list property that the wealthier partner wishes to separate from marital property that the couple divides according to state law in a divorce.

* You want to protect the inheritance rights of children. Without a prenuptial agreement, the current spouse and children of someone who dies will normally receive the inheritance, leaving any children from a previous marriage without a legacy. A

prenuptial agreement that specifies the inheritance rights of children from a previous marriage will help ensure that your wishes are carried out.

❖ You want to control who will run your business if you die or get divorced. For example: A husband may name a trusted advisor to take over a business, rather than his wife.

❖ You are giving up something substantial, such as a lucrative job or alimony, to get married. For example: A woman who leaves behind a substantial salary and benefits package to move to another state when she marries may stipulate additional compensation beyond what state law might normally allow if a divorce occurs.

Prenuptial agreements are tailored to meet individual needs and can include provisions regarding who will be responsible for which debts, how much alimony will be paid, the handling of property acquired during a marriage, and who will receive or waive interest in a business or retirement plan.

There are certain rights, however, that can't be governed by a prenuptial agreement. For example, you can't include binding provisions about child support for unborn children. And courts will generally not consider frivolous provisions of a nonmonetary nature, such as a requirement that a spouse keep a clean house or mow the lawn every Saturday.

On the plus side, prenuptial agreements can be very effective in protecting property rights and clarifying inheritance and ownership issues. They can also serve to reinforce the provisions of a will, which may prove particularly valuable when it is contested.

Without a prenuptial contract, assets in a divorce are divided according to state law. In community property states, property acquired during the marriage (other than an inheritance or gift) will be divided equally. Other states give courts the discretion of dividing assets equitably in a divorce.

Ginita Wall, CPA, CFP, a San Diego financial planner who specializes in the financial issues of divorce, says people with substantial wealth are well-advised to have a prenup. "When you don't have a prenuptial agreement, you're basically handing over the laws that govern the distribution of marital property to the state," she says. "And the laws can change when you move from one state to another. People draw up wills so they can distribute their assets according to their personal wishes, which often do not coincide with state law. Why shouldn't the same apply in a marriage with a prenuptial agreement?"

The biggest potential minus, of course, is that the person being asked to sign such an agreement will feel hurt and angry. Some will view the request as a sign of the marriage's impending doom or a lack of trust by a future spouse. For the less wealthy spouse, a prenuptial agreement also carries with it the possibility of receiving less in a divorce settlement than the state would allow.

"There's a right way and a wrong way to approach someone about signing a prenuptial agreement," says Wall. "The wrong way is to shove a pen at someone and say 'Sign here' as the wedding march is playing. The right way is to bring up the issue as early as you know you're getting married by saying something like 'we need to figure out how we're going to work our finances in a way that's fair to both of us.'"

Sometimes the very notion of signing a prenuptial agreement is so abhorrent that the person being asked to sign will become incensed and refuse. "There's no question that some people will become extremely emotional about it and threaten to walk away," says Wall. "But if the wealthier partner gives in and gets married without a prenup, the money issues aren't simply going to melt away."

Making It Stick

Drafting a prenuptial agreement improperly can cost big money. Director Steve Spielberg hand-wrote a prenuptial agreement without advice from an attorney. Even though both he and bride-to-be Amy Irving signed it, the court ruled against Spielberg and awarded Irving a rumored $100 million because neither party had had legal representation.

While courts will often uphold prenuptial agreements that are drafted properly, there are ways to help ensure that it will stick in the event of a divorce:

- ❖ **Have lawyers on both sides review the document.** Some courts have upheld the validity of a prenuptial agreement, even though it wasn't reviewed by separate attorneys representing each party. Still, it's much easier to argue that both you and your spouse knew what you were getting into if you each had legal representation. If you insist on drafting a contract yourself, at least be sure to have an attorney review it.

- ❖ **Get witnesses.** The signing of the document should be witnessed by two disinterested parties (other than those individuals addressed in the agreement) and notarized.

- ❖ **Be honest about what you have.** Drastically understating the value of your property can give your spouse's attorneys fodder for accusations of fraud and misrepresentation in a divorce. It is probably a good idea to attach financial statements to the contract as an exhibit, as well as a signed statement that says each spouse is aware of the other's financial status.

- ❖ **Don't wait until the last minute.** This is a bad thing to do from a legal as well as personal standpoint. Thrusting a prenuptial agreement in front of your fiancé an hour before the wedding ceremony and threatening to call the whole thing off unless he or she signs might be viewed by some courts as evidence of coercion, making it unenforceable. (These last-minute ploys are sometimes called "Wagner Agreements" after the wedding march that plays as the contract is signed.)

- ❖ **Be prepared for a last-minute signing.** Even if you try to get a prenuptial contract out of the way soon after you know you're getting married, it may still work out to be a last-minute endeavor. Often, says Wall, the partner being asked to sign becomes so emotional about the issue that it gets tabled for months. Then, as the wedding date draws closer, the partner who proposed a prenup brings the issue up again. "That's the reason that so many prenuptial agreements are signed just days before the wedding," says Wall. "But it's not the best of circumstances because in the event of a divorce, a court could interpret that as meaning that the agreement was signed under duress."

❖ **Be reasonable.** Some states require that prenuptial agreements be fair and reasonable, while other set a lower standard that the agreement should not be unconscionable. An unconscionable agreement might be one that stipulates that the wealthy partner does not have to pay any alimony to an ex-spouse who has minimal or no means of support.

Both parties affected by a prenuptial agreement should have legal representation and sufficient time to review the document. But even if that doesn't happen, the court may still uphold it.

The California Supreme Court ruled in August 2000 that the prenuptial agreement that Barry and Sun Bonds had signed the day before their 1988 Las Vegas wedding was valid, even though she did not have her attorney review it. At that time, Bonds, a baseball player for the Pittsburgh Pirates, had an annual salary of $106,000. By the time the couple divorced six years later, his annual earnings from the San Francisco Giants had zoomed to $8 million. But Sun would not share in the major league bounty because the agreement stipulated that future earnings would be kept separately and prohibited community property claims upon divorce.

In 1997, Marla Maples learned about the lasting impact of her decision to sign a prenuptial agreement that she says her husband of 12 years Donald Trump had presented to her just days before their marriage. She signed the document, she says, without even reading it. Despite her contention that Trump had made verbal commitments to pay more than the prenup stipulated, she eventually settled for the $2 million granted under the terms of the agreement.

Laws vary from state to state, but in many cases, having a prenuptial agreement declared invalid is very difficult unless there is evidence that the document was signed under coercion (for example, if you threatened to post embarrassing photos on the Internet), or that one party withheld substantial information about property he or she owned. Even in cases of domestic violence or adultery, courts usually honor prenuptial agreements.

If You Are Already Married

A postnuptial agreement works similarly to a prenuptial agreement, except that it is between individuals who are already married. You might use it, for example, if you receive an inheritance and want to clarify that those assets as well as the income they produce are separate property.

According to Wall, postnuptial agreements are much less common than prenups. "Usually, I see them when the marriage has hit some kind of money crisis," she says.

The Title Trap

When couples acquire property during a marriage and take title in joint tenancy, it is usually viewed as marital property, even if some provisions of a prenuptial agreement state otherwise. To help avoid conflict, be sure to title assets according to the provisions of the agreement.

Heading Off Spousal Money Fights

Money is one of the most common causes of disagreement among couples. A windfall often brings this issue to the forefront. Following are some tips from experts in the field of money management to help resolve some common financial differences:

❖ Don't try to prove that the other person is "wrong." Everyone has his or her own money style. Some people are high rollers who enjoy the power and recognition money brings but, at the same time, find it difficult to be content with what they have. Other people are chronic savers who can't seem to break out of overly frugal habits, no matter how much money they accumulate. And there are all sorts of styles in between. Respect your partner's attitude toward money and try to come to a solution that works for both of you.

❖ Set up regular family meetings to discuss budgeting and other financial priorities. Don't try to resolve money conflicts through heated arguments.

❖ Both partners should be in the loop about money matters. Share financial responsibilities such as investing and paying bills. When it comes to money, ignorance is never bliss.

❖ Talk about what money meant to you when you were growing up and what it represents to you now. This will help your partner understand why you feel the way you do about money.

❖ Formulate mutual goals such as funding a college education or an early retirement. Discuss how you plan to meet them.

Money arguments among couples, whether they are wealthy or not, are hard to avoid. Understanding your partner's attitudes about money and the reasons behind them is a good first step toward arriving at workable solutions you can both live with.

Developing Money Values in Children

Wealthy or even well-off parents need to strike a delicate balance in teaching their children how to handle and view money. On the one hand, they probably want to provide their children with luxuries they may not have had when they were kids. At the same time, they also want them to grow up with a sense of money values, good money sense, and a decent work ethic.

Setting an Example

The best way to teach a child about financial responsibility is to set a good example yourself. After all, you can hardly expect a child to know how to handle money responsibly when you and your spouse are constantly coming up on the budgetary short end of the stick, despite a six-figure household income.

When it comes to conveying good money sense, parents are like Davids working against a world of media Goliaths. Television, radio, and Internet advertising bombard children with "spend money" mantras. If advertisers spent half as much time and money promoting fiscal responsibility and the satisfaction of nonfinancial rewards as they do telling kids what they should buy next, the consumer engine that drives the under-21 economy might come to a grinding halt.

Nonetheless, there is at least one counterbalancing force—you. As a parent, it's your job to help your children figure out how to spend money wisely, master the basics of investing, and recognize the benefits of charitable giving. This applies to parents of modest means as well as those with substantial windfall wealth. Following are steps you can take:

* **Differentiate between needs and wants.** Long before children learn about saving and investing, they should appreciate the distinction between wanting and needing. Without the ability to draw a clear line between luxuries and necessities, children may find themselves without the tools they need to control spending as adults. Help young children list several things they own and decide which are necessities and which are luxuries. You can clarify and emphasize the gap between the two by talking about the consequence of taking away one versus the other.

* **Take advantage of money examples all around you.** A three-year old can begin learning about money by counting out coins and bills. When you go to the store, talk about which items provide the greatest value for your money. Have a child count out the change you need to make a purchase. Ask your children what they hear about money in school or on television.

* **Start a bank account.** Opening a bank account for a child can be a learning experience. This isn't terribly difficult to do, since many banks that tack on fees for smaller accounts waive those fees in the case of minors. If the child is old enough, show her how to fill out a deposit slip and let her bring it to the teller window so that she can understand the mechanics of making deposits and withdrawals.

❖ **Explain that when you open a bank account, you are essentially lending the bank your money.** The bank pays depositors a certain rate of interest and charges people borrowing money a higher rate for the privilege, which is how they make money.

❖ **Introduce older children to investing.** Talk about recent financial news, such as how the stock market is doing, or about specific stocks or mutual funds. Relating these discussions to actual investments a child may have in the stock market for college education and other goals (or money you have invested on his or her behalf) will bring the seemingly distant world of the financial markets a little closer to home.

❖ **Let allowances teach a lesson.** Once children reach age six or so, they understand the basic concepts behind money and can start handling it on a limited basis. Many families begin giving an allowance at that age.

Some parents give a fixed allowance that's based on the acceptable performance of household chores. For younger children, this can start with things like keeping a bedroom clean or hanging up bathroom towels. As kids get older, you can raise their allowance or pay them on a task-by-task basis as they take on greater responsibilities like mowing the lawn or babysitting. Pay them the going rate for these responsibilities, in amounts similar to what you would pay an outsider, so that they feel fairly rewarded for their efforts.

❖ **Require children to spend part of their allowance on discretionary items, such as clothes or toys.** This will help reinforce their sense of independence and teach good spending habits. Give children more discretion about their spending as they get older, and don't be tempted to bail them out when they spend too much and run out of money. This will reinforce the message that they, and not you, are responsible for knowing where to draw the spending line.

❖ **Talk about where your money came from.** Keeping family wealth shrouded in mystery can lead to unpleasant surprises down the road. A child who knows he has money but isn't provided with some parental guidance about where his wealth comes from or how to manage it may grow up to be an adult who squanders the family fortune.

You don't have to go into great detail about the exact size of your bank account or how you minimized your tax bill when you exercised stock options (they probably won't care anyway). When children are younger, discuss in general terms the nature of the business or occupation that led to your wealth. Because young children tend to reveal their "personal business" to friends, emphasize that these are private, family discussions. As they get older, you can talk about things like how the money is invested, whether it is in trust funds, and estate planning issues that involve them.

❖ **Introduce philanthropy.** To introduce kids to the satisfaction of charitable giving, some families initiate a holiday tradition of allowing children to pick causes of importance to them. Then, parents select and make donations to the organizations that support these causes. As they grow older, children can donate some of their own money from an allowance or part-time job to a charitable organization of their own choosing.

❖ **Let kids make their own inroads.** Wealthy parents often have "connections" that make it easy for them to pick up the phone and make a call to get a child into a particular college or to land a great job. Although you might have the power to open doors for your children in many areas of life, it is important to step back enough to let them feel motivated by their own accomplishments and learn from disappointments.

I find it interesting that schools incorporate things like cooking, auto mechanics, and sex education into the curriculum, yet fail to teach children the important skills involved in managing and investing their money. As a parent, you will need to fill that educational gap.

Lending to Friends

Even if you don't broadcast the news, friends will probably find out through the grapevine that you have come into some money. And chances are good that at least one or two will bring up the subject of borrowing some of it.

It probably won't take the form of a simple request. More likely, you'll suddenly start hearing stories about money problems or a business that could make a mint with a little seed capital. Regardless of the form, the "I could sure use some help" message will be clear.

> Len, who recently inherited a trust fund, voices some fairly typical concerns about loaning money to friends. "On the one hand, I've heard some terrible stories about loans between friends and family members that went wrong—the loan was never repaid, or someone interpreted it as a gift. Those kinds of things can ruin relationships, which is why I'm so hesitant to lend people money. On the other hand, I feel bad about holding back money I can easily afford to lose when people I care about have a financial need or emergency."

Some people have a policy of never making loans to anyone at any time. Instead, to avoid possible complications or conflicts, they just give gifts of money with no strings attached.

Others may decide that, as long as they lay some ground rules and don't fly into a rage about late or missed payments, lending money can actually strengthen bonds between friends and family members. *More Than Money*, an Arlington, Massachusetts–based magazine that explores the "personal, political, and spiritual impact of wealth in our lives," offers these tips for making loans between friends work.

Step One: Collect Information

Spend some time talking to your friend about the loan request. Of course, the amount of time and detail you require at this stage will depend on the size of the loan. The potential downside of a $50 loan until payday is very different from one involving $50,000 to start a business.

On the potential borrower's side, find out:

* Details about what she needs the money for.
* Her financial situation and borrowing history. Check with friends she has borrowed from before, if possible.
* Plans for repayment and how the loan would be repaid if an unforeseen event, such as a job loss, crops up.
* Other possible sources of money.
* Her feelings about borrowing.

Also explore your own feelings and comfort level about making the loan. Is the repayment schedule satisfactory? How important is repayment, financially and emotionally? Has any past experience in making loans been positive or negative?

Step Two: Think It Through

After gathering information, tell your friend you will give it some thought and get back to her. Don't make a snap decision. Ask yourself if she seems committed to repaying the loan and what she would do if she could not live up to the terms of the agreement. Consult a financial advisor if it is a sizable sum or a business loan. Gather more information, if necessary.

Step Three: Negotiate

Some people inadvertently turn a loan into a gift by saying things like "pay me back when you get around to it," or not following up when the loan isn't repaid. Even if you don't feel that strongly about being repaid, your friend might feel awkward about the unmet obligation. If you have any doubts and feel generous enough, consider making a gift rather than a loan. Or just say "no" politely but firmly.

Step Four: Make an Agreement

Talk about any concerns with your friend. If you feel satisfied with the answers, draw up a detailed agreement that both of you sign. The agreement should include the amount of the loan, any interest amount, a repayment schedule, and what happens if payments are late or other difficulties arise.

Step Five: Follow Up

Realistically, expect that at some point the loan will need a follow-up because of late payments or other reasons. If that doesn't happen and things go according to your agreement, you can be pleasantly surprised.

If payment is late, follow up with your friend promptly. Although she should contact you about why the payment will be late, it's usually the lender who has to make the call. You don't have to come down hard, but be clear that you would like to arrange a suitable payment plan. If you decide to change the loan to a gift at this point, say so explicitly. And remember to thank a friend who is making good on an agreement.

What About You?

Coming to terms with your windfall and growing into your new money skin may take some time. At first, you may feel overwhelmed by your new responsibilities, the changes in the way people interact with you, and they way they perceive you. Perhaps the most important thing to remember as you become more comfortable with your windfall and the implications it has for your and your loved ones is a simple truth your mother or father probably told you when you were a kid: Money won't necessarily make you happier. It may help to know that research confirms this traditional homespun wisdom.

According to a recent study in the *Journal of Personality and Social Psychology*, achieving wealth or attaining luxury is not what makes people the happiest and, in fact, is very low on the list of psychological needs. In the study, psychologist Kennon M. Sheldon, Ph.D., of the University of Missouri-Columbia examined which of 10 basic psychological feelings humans find most fundamental. Those needs included independence, relations with friends and family members, popularity, money, feeling in control of one's life, health, self-esteem, enjoyment, and competence.

The first study asked participants to identify the single most personally satisfying event they experienced in the last month. Study number two posed the same question, but changed the time frame to the past week. The last study looked at the most satisfying and unsatisfying event of the semester. One of the studies included college students from Korea to determine cross-cultural differences.

Across all the time frames and cultures examined, independence, competence, relatedness, and self-esteem emerged as the most important psychological needs. Respondents cited a lack of those top four needs as the biggest causes for dissatisfaction. Money was near the bottom of the list of needs.

Research from the University of Michigan at Dearborn echoes the contention that money ranks well down on the list of things that contribute to one's positive well-being. According to Aaron Ahuvia, assistant professor of marketing and co-author of the study "Income, Consumption, and Subjective Well-Being," aspiring to wealth is "the most common type of hope for the future among Americans discussing what would constitute a desirable life."

However, it appears that there is a broad gap between what individuals say would make them happy and what actually does. Concludes Ahuvia:

> It is safe to say, based on what data on the mega-rich are available, that the power of money to bring happiness, even among the very rich, is far less than is popularly believed.

Researchers do note a strong correlation between money and unhappiness at the lowest end of the economic scale, where there is not enough money to make ends meet. Those who are unemployed or who are overwhelmed by large amounts of debt feel more dissatisfied than the rest of the population.

Once basic needs for living have been met, however, the correlation between happiness and money is very low. Says Ahuvia:

> Among the nondestitute, money seems to have little unique value in helping people achieve the goals they most care about.

While money is valuable to the extent that it helps people achieve their goals, individuals do not see money and material possessions as relevant to their most important goals such as self-confidence, social skills, and family support. "Money may provide people more freedom to spend their time in intrinsically rewarding activities, but it is rarely an absolute requirement for their enjoyment," he concludes. "Enjoyable leisure is available at all price points."

In a seeming contradiction to the conclusion drawn by these studies that wealthy individuals are generally no happier than anyone else, a survey by Roper Starch Worldwide found that the United States, Denmark, and Australia—countries with high levels of individual wealth compared to the rest of the world—rank as the "happiest" countries.

In a survey of 22,500 adults in 22 countries, 46 percent of citizens in the United States reported being "very happy" with their overall quality of life. Forty-nine percent of Denmark's respondents felt the same way, as did 47 percent of Australians. By contrast, 67 percent of Russians report being unhappy, as did 54 percent of those in the Ukraine.

Globally, "your relationship with family and friends" stands out as what people are happiest about (40 percent are "very happy" with their relationships). In second and third place as the aspects of life people are most happy about are "your level of self-confidence" (27 percent) and "the role of religion in your life" (23 percent).

Even though people in wealthier countries report higher levels of happiness, it is not necessarily the money that produces that frame of mind. According to Professor Ahuvia:

> Richer nations do provide a higher material standard of living for their citizens, but they also tend to be more open, free, educated, and pluralistic. Economic development increases subjective well-being by creating a cultural environment where individuals make choices to maximize their happiness rather than meet social obligations. It seems that people in individualistic countries tend, on average, to be happier than people living in collectivist societies.

In other words, doing something because your inner compass tells you to, rather than because society expects it, produces greater levels of happiness.

The Next Step

Like the individuals in Chapter 1, "Will Money Make You Happy?" your windfall may change your life substantially by allowing you to pursue a new career, quit your job, travel, or make sizable contributions to worthy causes. It opens up new lifestyle options and eases the burden of financial concerns such as saving for college, retirement, or a home. In short, it can give life to new opportunities and create new paths that were not available to you before.

At the same time, don't be surprised if you feel overwhelmed from time to time. It's natural to experience some personal conflict over what to the outside world should be an unmitigated, uncomplicated blessing.

Milwaukee therapist Jessie O'Neill suggests taking these steps to cope with the feeling of confusion that often accompanies a windfall, getting your priorities in order, and integrating money into your life in a positive way:

- ❖ Don't equate money with happiness. Your loved ones and relationships come first. Remember your priorities, and that happiness comes from within.

- ❖ Focus on your goals. If peace, balance, and joy top your list, make financial decisions based on those goals.

- ❖ Don't make snap decisions. Put your windfall in a safe interest-bearing account and get used to the change in your life.

- ❖ Build a team of professionals, which may include a financial advisor, wealth counselor, or therapist familiar with money issues, to help you make financial decisions.

- ❖ Decide how much is enough. Look beyond financial security and consider emotional safety and security. A rule of thumb is to spend one third of your income, save one third, and donate one third. Each person, however, can adjust that to fit their own comfort level.

❖ Make sure those close to you, including children, are present at discussions with the professionals involving estate planning or philanthropic donations. A good team will help ensure that this approach enhances intimacy among family members.

❖ In the case of an inheritance, feelings of "survivor's guilt" may surface. If you feel as if you don't deserve the money and that bothers you, talk to a close friend or advisor. You can "earn" good fortune after the fact through charitable giving.

❖ Remember the joy of giving, but don't be afraid to say "no" and accept the consequences.

Money is the single most transformational substance in the world. Form your own intentions for it and create a spiritual context for using it wisely.

Last, but far from least, enjoy it!

More From the Answer Desk

Throughout the book, you've seen questions and answers relevant to each chapter. As I mentioned in the Introduction, these originally appeared on my Web site, fundsinteractive.com.

Because we get so many great questions from viewers and so many helpful answers from our panel of financial advisors, I wanted to share more of them here. The panel of experts includes Frank Armstrong, CFP, Investor Solutions, Inc., Miami, Florida; Richard Ferri, CFA, Portfolio Solutions, LLC, Troy, Michigan; Greg Hilton, JD, CPA, CFP, Chicago, Illinois; Paul Pignone, CFP, CLU, ChFC, Salem, New Hampshire; Lou Stanasolovich, CFP, Legend Financial Advisors, Pittsburgh, Pennsylvania; Sidney Blum, CFP, CPA/PFS, ChFC, and Richard Chiozzi, CFP, both of Successful Financial Solutions in suburban Chicago, Illinois.

Should I Bail Out of My Stock Fund?

Q. I am losing so much in my 401(k) (from peak of $195,000 now down to below $145,000) that I am very tempted to withdraw all of it and put it in a 6 percent interest-bearing account to keep from losing more. I hate to do that because it would take so many years to make up what I have lost already. I would prefer to tough it out in hopes the market will turn around. I am 60 years old.

The fund that lost so much money was one of the options for my 401(k) at my former place of employment. In 1998 I lost out on some market gains by taking too much money out of the market, and I don't want to make the same mistake again. Should I just take my losses and get out of this stock fund before it gets any lower? Or should I wait it out?

—Panicked in Michigan

A. Unfortunately for you, it sounds like you are a prime example of someone who chased returns in the past and should have diversified instead. A 6 percent return may not look so bad when you consider that according to Morningstar's Principia Pro software, the S&P 500 from January 1, 1998, through February 28, 2001 (3 years, 2 months), has compounded at only 9.46 percent.

Your situation is a tough one. Fortunately, you probably have a long life expectancy to build your balance back up (you're only age 60). However, it may take a couple of years to get back to even assuming normal (8 to 13 percent) returns. It sounds as if your existing fund choice is heavily weighted with technology stocks. If you continue to stay the course while the fund could recover, it could just as easily go down another 25 percent from here.

My advice would be to diversify into some value funds including those that invest in small stocks. Also consider placing some monies (20 to 30 percent) in the fixed income fund that you have available. Having accomplished this, I would seek out some professional counsel and move the monies into an IRA rollover account (you are eligible since the money is at a former employer) at a discount brokerage firm where you have almost limitless investment options. I would then invest into a well-diversified portfolio of mutual funds that includes fixed income investments, large and small, growth and value domestic equities, international stocks, REITs, and perhaps a few hedge-oriented funds (a nonsimilar pattern of return to the S&P 500). This should lower your future volatility, yet provide you with normal long-term returns (9 to 12 percent).

—Lou

Should I Be Concerned About Investing Largely Within One Fund Family?

Q. When evaluating the level of diversification in my portfolio, is it valid to be concerned with the fact that the majority of one's investments are with one mutual fund company, such as Vanguard?

—Tim

A. Not since the Bernie Cornfield/Robert Vesco scandal of my childhood has there been a significant case of fraud in the mutual fund business. Mutual funds are the best regulated, best audited investment medium that exists.

Counting all the different classes of funds, there are over 11,000 funds in the Morningstar Universe. Perhaps a small company may someday have a problem. It's possible. Heck, today anything is possible. But, the chance of a large family of funds having undetected problems (such as theft, embezzlement, etc.) leading to a loss by investors seems pretty remote.

Some fund companies may not have all the different investment classes that you might like to invest in. So, you wouldn't be able to properly diversify. But that is hardly the case with Vanguard.

As long as you can execute your preferred investment strategy within a single family of funds, I see no reason that you should spread yourself out to multiple families.

—Frank

How Do I Take Money Out of My IRA for a Medical Emergency?

Q. I am 54 years old and I would need to withdraw a sum of money from my IRA account for a medical emergency. Is this subject to a penalty? Will the bank where I have my IRA charge a bank penalty? What do I need to do to apply for this emergency funding?

—Guy

A. If medical expenses exceed 7.5 percent of AGI (Adjusted Gross Income), you may withdraw funds from your IRA and not be subject to penalty. You may avoid the 10 percent penalty for early distribution from your IRA (prior to age $59^{1}/_{2}$) if the distribution from the IRA is not less than the amount that exceeds the 7.5 percent of AGI and is therefore deductible as a medical expense. This is covered under the IRS Code Section 213 and you need to complete tax Form #5329 to explain that you qualify for an exemption to the penalty for early distribution.

At the time you complete this transaction, discuss the early withdrawal with a bank representative to see if the bank will waive the penalty. This penalty is subject to bank policy for which they may be willing to exempt you in this case of medical hardship.

—Richard C.

What Is Standard Deviation All About?

Q. Please help me understand fund risk analysis. If a fund's return is 15 percent per year and risk is 10, what does that mean in terms of standard deviation?

—Ronald

A. Standard deviation is a convenient way for us to compare relative investment risks.

In your example, the annual average return is 15 percent and the standard deviation of that return is 10 percent. Which means that about two thirds of the time the return will fall within plus or minus 10 percent of the 15 percent average.

Of course, returns often fall outside of that range. A standard deviation range of two is plus or minus 20 percent (or from –5 percent to 35 percent) and returns will fall within that range about 95 percent of the time. A standard deviation range of three is between plus or minus 30 percent and accounts for about 99.5 percent of all expected returns.

—Frank

Can I Transfer My Variable Annuity Without Penalty?

Q. Can any variable annuity be transferred to another under a 1035 exchange without penalty?

—Neil

A. Under IRS Code Section 1035, you do not need to report the gain or loss from the exchange of annuity contracts if the new contract provides for regular payments beginning on a date not later than the date payments would have begun under the old contract. There may be surrender charges assessed by the original annuity company that you should research prior to making any decisions.

—Sid

Are Financial Advisors' Fees Deductible?

Q. Are fees paid for financial advisors services for both IRA and non-IRA accounts invested in funds-deductible expenses when preparing individual tax returns (Form 1040)?

—Alfred

A. Fees paid for financial advice for IRA and non-IRAs can be deducted as a miscellaneous deduction subject to the 2 percent of adjusted gross income (AGI) limitation. If deducted from IRA funds, there is no tax deduction, but the financial advisor fees will reduce the eventual taxable income that you would have received on the account balances.

—Sid

Is Interest on a 401(k) Loan Tax-Deductible?

Q. I have taken a 401(k) loan for the express purpose of using the money as a down payment on a house. Is the interest I pay on this loan tax-deductible?

—Tahn

A. The loan interest may be tax-deductible if your 401(k) plan administrators issue you a mortgage note for you to sign and if the administrator agrees to secure the plan's loan against the property. The administrator must record the mortgage with the county in which the property is located in order to secure the plan's interest. When these conditions are met, the interest can be deemed mortgage interest and therefore deductible subject to mortgage deductibility rules. Otherwise, the interest is deemed personal interest and is not deductible.

In my experience, most 401(k) plan administrators will not take the necessary steps to deem the loan interest to be mortgage interest.

—Sid

Can I Offset a Gain with a Loss from a Custodial Account?

Q. I am the custodian for my kids' two custodial accounts. Unfortunately, one of them has a loss on a stock I want to sell. But they don't have any realized gains or income to offset the loss. I, however, have some short-term gains.

If I sell my daughter's losing investment, can I use it to offset my gains? I've been holding it for months hoping her other investment will advance enough to sell them both and move on, but the loss is so big it hasn't happened.

—Jean

A. The main thing to know about custodial accounts is that a minor is considered to own (though he or she does not control) the assets of the account from the second the assets are placed into the account. These are set up as UGMA/UTMA accounts that are trusts just like any other trusts except that the terms of the trust are set in the statute instead of being drawn up in a trust document.

Your failure, as trustee, to comply with the terms of the UGMA/UTMA would expose you to the same consequences as a trustee who fails to comply with the terms of a specially drawn-up trust.

With this in mind, the answer to your question is an emphatic NO. You cannot use your kids' losses to offset your gains any more than you could use my losses. If you tried, you would be guilty of breach of fiduciary duty, income tax evasion, and an unwinding of the entire string of transactions (including the original gift to the children). Be patient, one day your daughter will be in a position to use her losses to advantage.

—Greg

Where Can I Find a Fund That Tracks the DJIA?

Q. I am looking for a mutual fund that tracks the Dow Jones Industrial Average and can't seem to find one with the major firms. Everyone seems to track the S&P or some other broader index.

—Greg

A. The Bridgeway Ultra Large 35 index is very close. They chose not to exactly track the Dow in order not to have to pay license fees to keep expenses down. It's no load and, with a 0.15 percent expense ratio, it's a great way to get large-cap U.S. exposure. (See www.bridgewayfund.com for more information.)

The Strong Funds Dow 30 Value is also no-load, invests in the Dow stocks, and boasts a 0.10 percent expense ratio. (See www.strongfunds.com or call 1-800-368-1030.) Management has the right to over- or under-weight the fund as they wish, so there will be some tracking error to the index.

—Frank

Do I Have to Pay Capital Gains Taxes on Funds That I Hold and Don't Sell During the Tax Year?

Q. Do I have to pay the capital gains tax every year on the funds that I invest in, regardless of whether I sell the funds or not? In other words, do I pay tax in the year the mutual fund realizes gains in its portfolio, or every year, even if I don't sell my fund shares?

—Ravi

A. I am assuming you are referring to funds invested in accounts outside of qualified retirement plans or IRAs. The dividends received and capital gains of the funds are distributed to the fund's shareholders at least annually and therefore are subject to taxes for that year. The fund will break out ordinary dividend and capital gains.

There is also the potential for additional capital gains when you liquidate your position depending on the amount of appreciation on holdings within the fund. Morningstar publishes information on potential capital gains exposure, but this information is constantly changing and does not include appreciation in the value of the fund shares after you have purchased (NAV).

—Richard C.

What Is a Sharpe Ratio?

Q. I just received my retirement statement with the funds' performance figures. One of the parameters included is a "Sharpe ratio." What is a Sharpe ratio? How does one arrive at the Sharpe ratio? How does it relate to fund performance?

—CT

A. The Sharpe ratio was developed by Bill Sharpe, the Nobel Laureate. It measures the risk-adjusted return of a fund. The measurement allows comparison of funds with different risk and reward histories. The higher the Sharpe ratio, the better.

For instance, a balanced fund with a 10 percent rate of return might have done better on a risk-reward basis than a growth fund with a 12 percent return. So, it would have a higher Sharpe ratio. Said another way, the balanced fund generated a higher return per unit of risk than the growth fund.

—Frank

Is a Spider the Answer to My Tax Concerns in a Bear Market?

Q. My husband and I are in our mid-40s and hope to retire in 12 years. We find it difficult to build the taxable portion of our portfolio and want to make good investments that are also tax-efficient. I am convinced that index funds are most cost-effective and are the best long-term investment.

My only concern is with redemptions in a bear market. I don't want to pay big capital gains in my taxable account because other shareholders have forced the index fund to sell stock and realize capital gains. I have read a little bit about Spiders, which would seem to solve this problem. How do I purchase SPDRs? Please discuss in detail how they work and the tradeoffs with index funds.

—Vickie

A. I'm not sure that redemptions are a very important issue. Vanguard Funds has estimated that in a severe bear market, about 30 percent of the shares would have to be liquidated before anyone would suffer the first cent of tax consequences. The question may be more marketing hype than substance.

Having said all that, exchange-traded funds may still be attractive. They look a lot like mutual funds, but trade on the open market like stocks. Because shareholders do not redeem shares as they do in funds, the question of taxes for redemptions never comes into play.

The trading mechanism—rather than redemption—resembles the old unit-investment trusts or closed-end funds. But, the older closed-end funds often traded at a premium or discount to their net asset value. The new funds hope to solve that problem by allowing larger redemptions to be in kind. If the prices get out of line with net asset value, traders can make a risk-free profit by demanding redemption of assets. In theory, this will keep prices in line. In practice, it seems to work pretty darn well.

—Frank

What's a Good Core Holding in a Large-Equity Growth Portfolio?

Q. What are your suggestions for a core holding and percentage in the holding in a large-equity growth portfolio of about $3 million? There is no need for income or need for any of the money for at least 6 to 10 years. The account is a taxable account and I am in the highest income tax bracket.

—"R"

A. Over the long haul, it is very unlikely that any active manager can add value on a pre-tax basis. It's almost delusional to believe that they might add value on a post-tax basis. In addition to market risk, actively managed funds add manager risk. That's the very high likelihood that the manager will underperform the market. Our expectation is that manager risk will cost us about 2 percent below market returns on a pre-tax basis. On an after-tax basis, every trade kills us. With turnover in active managed funds averaging over 90 percent, far too many dollars leave the investment pool to enrich the IRS. Those dollars are never, never coming back. Taxes are the largest expense investors face, and a pure dead drag on performance. In your tax bracket, it's pure suicide.

So, the lowest-cost, lowest-risk, and most tax-effective exposure to large stocks is to use an index fund like the Vanguard S&P 500. For even greater tax efficiency, you might consider the Vanguard Total Market Index. While this index holds some smaller stocks as part of the portfolio, it has even less turnover.

Another alternative to consider is an exchange-traded fund.

—Frank

Are Index Funds a Good Way to Defer Taxes?

Q. I am considering the tax advantage of index funds. Do indexes and the funds that follow them change holdings often? If not, I would think that this would be a great way to defer taxes. The tax savings, along with the performance of index funds compared to managed funds, should make a diversified holding of index funds a great approach to investing.

I am a novice investor, so please let me know if this is a correct assumption.

—Ronnie

A. For a novice investor, you have asked a very astute question. There are two ways taxes can bite into your performance.

Most investors know that when they sell or trade shares of a fund, they must pay taxes. But many do not know that when the portfolio manager buys and sells securities, the investor must pay taxes on any capital gains generated by these sales.

Portfolio turnover refers to the percentage of the portfolio that the manager buys and sells each year. A turnover of 50 percent means half the securities are exchanged each year. A rate of 200 percent means that the portfolio turned over twice. If you are concerned about your mutual funds generating taxes, look for a lower turnover ratio.

One good place to find low turnover is in an index fund. Turnover ratios are typically 1 to 3 percent. The average diversified U.S. stock fund has a 90 percent turnover! Not only are index funds tax efficient, they are also sold without load and operate with very low expense ratios. Only about 10 percent of the fund managers can overcome these advantages and outperform the index funds.

—Greg

What Are Value-Oriented Mutual Funds?

Q. I've heard about funds being referred to as "value" funds, but I'm not exactly sure what that means. Can you explain?

—Steven

A. A value stock picker attempts a rough valuation of companies by taking apart their balance sheets, looking at their various businesses, and estimating their breakup value. The best-known value investor is the oracle from Omaha, Warren Buffett.

Value investors, whether they be a fund manager or not, never buy on instinct, only on the numbers. Value investors also typically have a formula for selling a stock. When a stock reaches some predetermined measure of value, they dump it.

Compare this to growth funds or investors. Growth managers look for companies that are growing much faster than the rest of the economy. Forget the cost.

Since neither growth or value funds guarantee success, have some of both for both small and large company stocks.

—Greg

How Can I Best Invest for My Six-Year-Old?

Q. I am looking for a fund for a six-year-old. My objective is to avoid the kiddie tax and defer as much tax until after she reaches the age 14. I assume I should look for a fund with little turnover and high tax efficiency. Do you agree?

How should I go about researching those two (or other) goals? Do any specific funds come to mind?

—Steve

A. You are on the right track.

Rather than give the funds to the child—in a Uniform Gifts to Minors Act (UGMA) account—I would hold them in my own name until the child is old enough to use them responsibly. This keeps your options open and ensures that the funds are used for their intended purpose.

The use of a tax-efficient mutual fund like the Vanguard Total Market Index Fund will reduce the tax drag on performance to a tolerable minimum while you hold the fund. When the child is of age, you can gift shares to him or her. When the shares are sold, the child will pay the tax on the appreciation at the child's presumed lower capital gains rate (presently 10 percent).

—Frank

What Are the Pros and Cons of Variable Annuities Versus Wrap Accounts?

Q. What do you feel are the advantages and disadvantages of rolling qualified assets into a variable annuity instead of a wrap-fee mutual fund account IRA?

—Christopher

A. First, a word about variable annuities. The prime advantage to annuities is that, because they are insurance products, they offer tax-deferred growth. So does your IRA and other qualified assets. But remember, insurance companies don't do anything for free so you pay more (sometimes a lot more) in the form of insurance costs and transaction fees. My general rule is that variable annuities are appropriate for high income tax payers who need more tax deferral than their qualified plans can provide. Insurance salesmen are the only ones who disagree with me.

A wrap account will solve your money management problems because it places your money with an array of institutional money managers. For this you typically pay a percentage of assets—between 2.5 and 3.5 percent. A mutual fund wrap spreads your money over several funds and charges around 1.5 percent. Added to the mutual funds' money-management fees and your total cost is again around 2.5 to 3.5 percent. I hate wrap accounts because these fees amount to a bloodletting.

You have several better options for managing your IRA. Work with a fee-only financial planner who will manage your wrap for 1 percent or less. Regularly visit my Web site and read a book on fund selection and asset allocation and do it yourself. Use the free asset allocation suggestions offered by many no-load mutual fund families.

—Greg

How Do Fund Supermarkets Make Money?

Q. How do companies such as Schwab make money when they sell no-load mutual funds with no exit fees? Do they get a kickback from the mutual fund company that is not made public?

—Merilyn

A. Schwab's public relations people would probably dispute the term "kickback." But, they do receive a fee from the fund families that participate in the No Transaction Fee (NTF) Network. This fee averages about 0.35 percent of the total value of the fund per year. This fee is included in the fund's expense ratio. While disclosed somewhere deep, deep in the fund prospectus, it is certainly not publicized heavily.

There is some economic justification for the fee. Schwab must take over many of the fund family's duties. These include bookkeeping, custodian functions, distribution of prospectuses, and account statements.

Because the various Fund Supermarkets dominate the distribution systems for no-load funds, many fund families find that they cannot compete without participation in the program. They gladly pay a distribution fee for access to Schwab's and other fund supermarket customers. The fund families equate this charge to buying "shelf space."

It may strike customers that do not hold their account at Schwab as somewhat unfair to charge their account for services that they do not enjoy. But, that's the way it is. Even if they buy their funds direct from a participating fund company, they will be charged the additional expenses. So, the various NTF programs contribute to the rise in fund expenses.

As a class, NTF funds have higher expenses than funds that do not participate in these programs. These expenses are not just chump change. If you think about it, the 0.35 percent charge exceeds the entire expense ratio of many index funds. All other things being equal, always buy the fund with the lowest internal costs. Regardless of the size of your account, a 0.35 percent difference in compounding returns will add up to serious money over a long period.

One of the biggest claimed advantages of the NTF programs, being able to trade for "free," has been greatly reduced in recent years. Schwab has begun to charge a 0.75 percent redemption fee (minimum $39, maximum $299) for funds traded within 180 days for retail accounts. While I don't personally think investors should trade funds, it certainly reduces the value of the program for those who intend to trade.

Customers who think about it may prefer to avoid the NTF funds. As you know, there is no free lunch on Wall Street. At the end of the day, these distribution charges are paid by shareholders in real charges against earnings. These expenses reduce returns dollar for dollar. NTF charges go on forever, while a transaction fee happens only once. Who would want to pay $350 per year forever on a $100,000 portfolio in order to avoid a one-time token transaction fee? If you are forced to make repeat small transactions, you may find yourself considerably better off with an account directly with a fund family like Vanguard in order to avoid the transaction costs associated with the discount brokerages for funds that do not participate in the NTF program.

—Frank

Is It Better to Invest by Monthly Deposits?

Q. Is it better to deposit your money into a Roth IRA all at the same time or to do it in monthly deposits?

—Todd

A. Assuming straight-line returns, you would be best served to make a single deposit on the first day of each year that you are eligible. That way you will maximize your time value of money and should have a small but measurable increase in total performance.

Because market returns are variable, some investors believe that they spread their timing risk by making monthly deposits. However, many studies conclude that because the market is so strongly biased upward, you would be better off in the vast majority of time periods to make the deposit at the beginning of the year. So, either way you look at it, the time to invest is as early as you can.

—Frank

Should a New Retiree Purchase Annuities?

Q. I find myself suddenly retired at 60. I will need supplementary periodic payments from my existing funds. Or should I establish annuities with monthly retirement checks? I will not be entitled to Social Security payments at age 60.

—Barbara

A. Few retirees would be well advised to purchase annuities. They are aggressively marketed because of the high commission level generated for the salesman and the high profits reaped by the insurance company. Few consumers understand how they work. A close examination of annuities reveals serious flaws in both the fixed and variable models. Neither effectively solves the retirement income problem.

The first problem is common to all annuities: The insurance company confiscates any remaining capital at the death of the annuitants. Few retirees will accept that outcome in return for the mostly theoretical but minuscule increase in income that insurance companies predict. In practice, high contract expenses consume the theoretical benefits of annuity income increases as a result of mortality.

❖ Fixed annuities are generally sold and the benefits calculated based on "current" credited interest rates. However, the contract guarantees only a lower interest rate, usually in the 4 to 5 percent range. Pressure from sales and marketing to illustrate high current rates results in wildly inflated assumptions. In fact, once the investor purchases the contract, surrender charges effectively lock him or her in, and they find themselves held hostage to the tender mercy of the insurance company.

❖ The spectacular failure of this model over the last 20 years of falling interest rates is well documented. Income rates fell dramatically. Existing policyholders often found that their credited rates were below rates being promised to prospects or holders of newer contracts. Several large companies collapsed and policyholders were left with less than they had been led to expect. It wasn't pretty!

❖ Variable annuities promise an income for life, but they don't promise any particular amount. The first month's payment is calculated based on an assumed earnings amount. Thereafter, the entire payout is based on future earnings of the various separate accounts. Poor investment results will result in ever decreasing income to the retiree. There is no floor or guaranteed minimum payment included in any variable annuity contract.

To summarize, annuities fail to deliver on their promise of low-risk, low-cost, reliable income generation for retirees.

In the real world, retirees must continue to plan, invest, monitor, and revise as necessary as long as they live. You should inventory all of your liquid resources, take a look at your short- and long-term income needs, and develop a comprehensive investment and asset allocation plan tailored to your situation. You can't shortcut the process by purchasing annuities.

—Frank

Does My Gift Recipient Get Taxed If the Gift Is Within My $10K Limit?

Q. When you donate something of value, as long as it is below the $10,000 per person limit, is the recipient taxed in any way? Must the recipient claim this gift in any way on their income tax return? Does the donor get a tax deduction for the entire amount?

—John

A. You are allowed to gift $10,000 per person, without limitations, to any number of people without incurring any gift tax ramifications. A gift tax return is not required to be filed. The recipient does not have to claim this gift on their tax return nor does the donor get a tax deduction for any part of the gift.

—Sid

Can My Twelve-Year-Old Start a Roth IRA with Money He Has Earned?

Q. My 12-year-old son wants to open a Roth IRA with money earned from his paper route, lawn mowing, and allowance. None of this earned income is reported on a W-2 form.

Is he eligible to contribute to this type of account with this form of earned income? Would this be a custodial Roth IRA account until he turned 18? He keeps a record of when he mows a lawn and how much he was paid (usually cash). Is this good enough? Are those who paid him then subject to paying Social Security tax on him? He wants to have a million tax-free dollars when he retires!

—Russ

A. There's no minimum (or maximum) age to set up a Roth IRA. Some IRA providers permit you to establish an IRA for a minor child, some don't. And there is no requirement that the same dollars that were earned be used to fund the IRA. If your child earned money on a summer job and spent it on whatever kids spend money on these days, there's nothing wrong with using money provided by parents to establish the IRA.

The major impediment to IRAs (Roth or otherwise) for children, especially young children, is the earned income requirement. The income has to be compensation income, not investment income. And it has to be taxable compensation income. That doesn't mean you have to actually pay tax on the income. If the total amount of income is small enough and you don't have to pay tax, that's okay. But you have to have the kind of income that would call for a tax payment if you had a large enough amount. Fortunately, your son's lawn-mowing money is earned compensation and therefore qualifies him for a Roth IRA contribution.

—Greg

How Can I Match Funds with My Asset Allocation Plan?

Q. After using a few calculators and risk-analysis scenarios, I've decided to invest my IRA and 401(k) funds based on the following asset allocation:

> 50 percent large cap
>
> 30 percent international
>
> 20 percent mid/small cap

I'm willing to dispense with bonds and take on more risk for a better return since I can leave the money for 20 years. I prefer index funds and funds that use a buy-and-hold strategy. My money is evenly spread between Vanguard and Fidelity.

Here are my questions:

1. What is a good source for identifying funds that match these asset allocations? The tools I have found online are good at picking "hot" funds that churn a lot. Or they show funds that have a mix of asset types.

2. I want international funds that spread the risk across many regions and sectors, not funds that buy and sell a lot to pick winners. Any suggestions?

—Jim

A. You are definitely on the right track.

First, with 20 years to go before you expect to use the funds, you can comfortably invest in all equities.

Your decision to use more than one asset class will most likely provide you with both superior returns and reduced risk. I won't quibble about your asset allocation because reasonable folks could disagree on the exact weights, and we won't really know what the perfect plan is until we meet back here in 20 years. Yours is a very reasonable and defensible approach to long-term investing.

I also agree with your position on index funds. You might get lucky with an actively managed fund, but you might also lose big. It's not worth the risk that you will underperform the market. Did I say risk? Well, another way to look at the problem is to say that you are 80 percent certain to underperform the market with an actively managed fund. Why try to beat the market when you can own it?

If you use index funds, you avoid all the problems with style drift, turnover, individual stock, country and sector bets that you mentioned. The Fidelity Spartan Index Funds are very reasonably priced if you can meet their minimum account size. At Fidelity, only the Spartan International Index Fund is available to meet your international need. Of course, Vanguard is my favorite retail fund family. Either their Vanguard Developed Markets Index Fund or the Vanguard Total International Stock Index Fund (which includes the emerging markets) would be great choices for your international allocation. Vanguard also would let you tilt toward Europe, Asia, or Emerging Markets with broad-based index funds if that was your intention.

—Frank

Is a Variable Annuity Program Right for Us?

Q. My spouse made an appointment with a local financial advisor, who works with a large bank in our area. He would like us to put all of our investments in a variable annuity program he recommends. He indicates that our investments are too conservative and are losing money if inflation is considered. The advisor would like us to make the changes as soon as possible.

My spouse, who will be 65 in May, works part-time. I am 68, retired, and drawing a teacher's pension and Social Security. We have accumulated a nest egg of $700,000 through various annuities, mutual funds, and stocks during the past 20 years.

I feel a little queasy about moving this sum of money into one account. What are your thoughts on this?

—Roland

A. Your concerns are well founded. This "local financial advisor" you met sounds like an insurance agent or stockbroker who works on commission, and it is very likely that the variable annuity he or she is pushing carries a large one.

If you are drawing a teacher's pension, you are already invested in annuities, so there is no need for more. If you think an annuity makes sense, than check out www.vanguard.com for the lowest-priced annuities on the market. More than likely, sticking with high-quality stocks and low-cost mutual funds is a better option.

Although it is not possible to give specific advice, the best advice I can offer is to seek the help of a qualified financial advisor, one who has several years in the business and holds a Certified Financial Planner (CFP) designation. Look for one who will charge a flat fee or a small percentage of assets under management and avoid those who are compensated on commissions.

—Richard F.

What Are Some of the Disadvantages of Mutual Funds?

Q. Can you list or tell me the disadvantages of a mutual fund? I know the advantages, but would like to be made aware of the disadvantages.

—Grace

A. Despite their many advantages, mutual funds have several disadvantages:

1. There are annual fees to pay in a mutual fund and possibly a sales commission to buy the fund. On average, the fee for a stock fund run over 1 percent per year, and that does not include the cost for trading stocks inside the fund. Studies show that the typical total cost of mutual fund investing is about 2 percent for large funds and greater for small funds.

   For the best value in mutual funds, turn to index funds. The fees are less than one quarter of the national average.

2. The best performing funds do not persist. Since everyone wants to own a winner, the best funds fill up with money fast, handcuffing the manager. This is especially true for funds that invest in small stocks. One good question to ask before buying an "outperforming" fund is to find out how much money was under management when it outperformed. Typically there was much less money in the fund when it outperformed.

3. Picking a mutual fund creates its own problems. Overwhelmingly, the public bought what did best last year, which often sets them up for poor performance this year. This is called "chasing the hot dot" in the investment business. Remember, prior performance is NOT an accurate way to predict future returns.

4. Taxes are another issue. If you own a fund in a taxable account, prepare to receive a 1099 at the end of the year telling you to pay taxes on the realized capital gains and dividend income, *regardless of whether the fund made any money*. In April of 2001, many people were screaming that they had to pay taxes on capital gains and dividend income even though their mutual funds went down in value.

5. Mutual fund managers bounce around a lot. The manager that generated the wonderful returns displayed in the newspaper advertisement may have been gone a long time. I frequently see Peter Lynch touting Fidelity funds, even though he no longer has anything to do with the day-to-day management of the individual funds.

In the long run, the lowest-cost funds with the best tax-efficiency ratings typically end up on top. That is why I recommend index mutual funds. They are low-cost, low-tax, low-maintenance investments that no individual money manager can mess up.

—Richard F.

How Can I Avoid the Penalty for an Early Withdrawal from My Retirement Fund?

Q. I was made aware of an option to withdraw funds from a qualified plan before the age of 59½ without the 10 percent penalty. If I understood this correctly, this is different than the health or early financial hardship withdrawals. Please let me know how this works.

—Justin

A. This is one question that I am often asked and that continues to confuse investors. I will cite the exceptions to the 10 percent premature penalty tax, and you can determine if you qualify.

They are ...

* Death
* Disability
* Extraordinary medical expenses exceeding 7.5 percent of AGI

- ❖ Medical insurance premiums for specified unemployed persons
- ❖ Specified higher education expenses (post-secondary education for the IRA owner or the IRA owner's children or grandchildren)
- ❖ Substantially equal periodic payments, based on the IRA owner's life expectancy, that continue for at least five years and until after the owner attains $59\frac{1}{2}$
- ❖ A first-time home purchase

I hope that's helpful to you, Justin, and hope you don't have to withdraw any of your retirement funds.

—Paul

Is It a Good Idea to Have One Brokerage Firm Handle All of an Investor's Retirement Funds?

Q. My wife has recently retired and is thinking of moving money from several different mutual fund accounts to a brokerage firm tied into a company currently handling our 403(b) accounts. The reason given by my advisor for the company is that all accounts will be under one statement, it will be easy to switch funds, etc.

What is your feeling on this? I am fairly well read in the mutual fund area and follow and read many articles. However, I'm not too familiar with brokerages.

—"G"

A. Your advisor is right. There are many advantages to using a brokerage to hold your various funds. You will get a consolidated statement, can switch funds easily, have a single tax report for withdrawals at the end of the year, and will be better able to manage the various accounts.

But, it comes at a cost. You will have to decide on the value of the advisor, and whether or how you want to pay him. Be clear on how he gets paid and what value-added services you will receive.

Traditional brokerages or "wire houses" will only invest in load funds. You don't need to pay loads just to consolidate your accounts.

The discount brokerage houses all either charge transaction fees or receive payments from the fund companies for "shelf space" in the various no-transaction fee (NTF) services. Transaction fees can be significant, especially for smaller accounts, and the higher expense ratios of the NTF funds will be a drag on performance.

Depending on the size of your account, and your investment objectives, you might avoid these costs by transferring all the funds to a company like Vanguard or TIAA-CREF in a single IRA. That IRA could invest in any number of the company's no-load funds. This approach will provide for diversification into high-quality funds without the additional costs of loads or transaction fees, yet still give you the advantages of consolidation.

—Frank

What Are the Benefits and Drawbacks of Investing in New Mutual Funds?

Q. My financial advisor is recommending a new mutual fund for my portfolio. Can you explain the benefits and drawbacks of new funds?

—John

A. Unless a new fund represents an entirely new asset class that you would like to invest in, I'm unaware of any advantages. There are plenty of good known funds out there. Last time I looked, Morningstar tracks over 11,600 nonmoney market funds! It's really unlikely that a new fund is going to be able to find an idea that hasn't been tried before.

On the other hand, there may be potential problems. Not every fund will have any or all of the following, but why take the risk?

❖ New funds may have higher expenses because they can't spread the fixed costs as well as larger funds. Expenses come right out of your pocket.

❖ New funds may not survive. A fund liquidation could spell tax problems and result in time out of the market and reinvestment costs. If the fund is merged with another fund, you may end up in a much different type of investment than you started out with. At very best, such an event would be aggravating.

❖ New funds may take extra risk in order to get noticed. Fund managers know that a big performance early on might generate huge positive cash flows. Being number one or two in a category drives cash to funds and enriches the fund sponsors. To the extent that managers might be tempted to swing for the fences to enhance their own compensation, there may be a conflict of interest. The extra risks of concentrated portfolios and/or frantic trading are not compensated (on average) by additional return.

Unless you had a compelling reason to purchase a new fund, I would suggest that you pass.

—Frank

What's the Best Way, from a Tax Standpoint, of Purchasing a Fund for My Newborn Grandson?

Q. I would like to purchase a mutual fund for my newborn grandson. What is the best way to do that in relation to tax liability? What tips can you give me to maximize this investment? In whose name should the fund be purchased? Should I make additional purchases throughout the years? How can his parents add to the purchase?

—Jo Ann

A. Depending on your tax bracket or your child's tax bracket, you can own the assets or your child or grandchild could. I usually do not like giving money to children using the Uniform Transfer Gift to Minors Account (UTMA), as you lose control when the child reaches the age 18 or 21 depending on your state. You can set up a trust for the child if you plan to make regular gifts of $10,000 per year. Otherwise, the cost may be too high.

Taxes can be reduced by using tax-efficient investments such as an ETF (Exchange Traded Funds) or index funds to keep the taxes low. The child would have to file a tax return if income exceeds $750 and the UTMA is used; if the trust is used, a trust return will also need to be filed.

—Sid

What's a Good Investment for a Soon-to-Be College Graduate?

Q. I am a 21-year-old senior in college interested in investing. I already purchased shares of Vanguard's S&P 500 Index fund. I was told by some of my friends and colleagues to invest in a Roth IRA. I would like to know what kind of Roth I should invest in, and what other mutual funds I should look into. I inquired about stocks but was told by my financial advisor that I shouldn't invest in stocks because I would get killed on broker's fees. Also I was told to only invest in no-load funds. Why is that?

—Jason

A. If you have earned income, then you can consider a regular or Roth IRA. And it's a great idea for you to start early. The value of time and compounding earnings is enormous.

IRA investing is a long-term commitment. Having given you large tax advantages, the government doesn't want you to tap into the funds until you are ready to retire. So, with certain exceptions (death, disability, first-time home purchase, etc.) funds withdrawn before age $59^1/_2$ are subject to tax penalties.

Given the long-term nature of IRA investing, you may find that it is appropriate to have a rather aggressive investment policy. After all, fluctuations in value are not a major concern if you don't expect to use the funds for many years. All other things being equal, you should be comfortable with a "risky" portfolio. That might include small company stocks, value stocks, foreign, and emerging market stocks. Since you already have the Vanguard S&P 500 Index, why not put your IRA into one of their other excellent index funds in these categories?

I certainly agree that no-load mutual funds are the best way to go. Why pay a huge commission for a fund that is unlikely to do any better than one without a commission. It's like running a 100-yard dash from 6 yards behind the start line. You might win, but you certainly have made it a lot tougher. Fees and expenses are important to long-term results. There is a direct relationship between high costs and low returns.

Buying individual stocks will most likely cost many times as much in commissions as a fund. And you are unlikely to get sufficient diversification in your portfolio. Inadequate diversification introduces unnecessary risk into your portfolio without increasing return.

You are on the right track, and it sounds like you are being given good advice. Good luck!

—Sid

Is Now the Time to Correct Flaws in My Portfolio?

Q. I know it's panic time for a lot of people in the market and experts are advising to sit tight.

However, I began investing in no-load mutual funds via IRAs about five years ago. I have only seen a good market and I got greedy. I didn't balance my portfolio—even though I knew I should. Five of the eight mutual funds I've invested in are large growth and the top holdings of these funds greatly overlap.

I have seen the error of my ways and have spent hundreds of hours researching funds and fund advice. I know which funds I want to invest in—large-growth, large-value, mid-cap, small-cap, and world stock, and what percentage of each to invest in.

My question is whether I should roll over my current nonperforming mutual funds into the new funds I've researched and selected for my portfolio now—at a loss—or later, when the market turns back up. Five of the eight funds I hold are down below the dollars I invested.

My husband says we haven't lost anything if we don't sell—we're in it for the long term. However, these aren't the funds I want to be in for the long term—I know that now and I'd be glad to e-mail funds now versus funds desired. So, if I move the money now into a fund I want to invest in long term, is the loss worth the possible long-term gain of the new funds? I can sit and wait for my funds to improve or I can move and wait to recoup the loss—HELP!

Also, I am considering going to a fee/commission planner. I feel I've done my homework and don't really need to invest in load funds, but I'm not totally sure of myself. Does it make sense to go to a planner who invests in load funds? I'm 40 and plan to retire at 60. My husband and I have a household income of $120K+. Our IRAs and 401(k)s equal about $150K.

—Debbie

A. Relax! You've got plenty of time. You are not going to retire for another 20 years. The stock market went on vacation for a while, but it ALWAYS comes back.

This bear market is actually a GOOD thing for people like us (I am only 43). In fact, I LOVE this market! I can buy stocks today at low prices and sell them at much higher prices when I retire.

You are right about your lack of diversification, though. Many people make the mistake of buying four or five top-performing mutual funds and think they are diversified. Unfortunately, most of yesterday's top-performing fund managers owned the same 50 stocks, have the same information about those stocks, relied on the same Wall Street analysts, and all got lucky at the same time.

To avoid a lack of diversification in the future, I suggest owning one mutual fund that does it all, the Vanguard Total Stock Market Fund. It is low cost, tax efficient, and you do not have to guess which segment of the market will be up or down next year because the Total Market Fund owns the entire market. It is okay to liquidate your current holdings and invest in a TSM fund now, because you are only swapping one stock funds for another as opposed to market timing.

Finally, if you are looking for professional help, do not, I repeat, DO NOT go to someone who sells loaded mutual funds or variable annuities. These people are not "financial planners," they are "salespeople." Most commission salespeople (stockbrokers included), are under-trained, under-educated, and offer biased advice. I can say that because I used to be one. If the financial professional is properly trained and well educated, he or she would not be selling investment products on commission. Go to a fee-only investment advisor or a fee-only financial planner.

—Richard F.

Index

F

N

O